Orphan Train Series

~~ Complete Series ~~

Wendy May Andrews

ISBN - 978-1-989634-15-8

Sophie

BOOK 1

Orphan Train Series

WENDY MAY ANDREWS

Sparrow Ink
www.sparrowdeck.com

www.wendymayandrews.com

She'd happily give him her heart ... if only it wouldn't cost her the only home she's known

Sophie Brooks thought she had everything she could want in life. Friends, loved ones at the orphanage where she was raised, a job that gives her purpose, and a chance to help children every day ... what more could she need? But a chance encounter with a handsome stranger has her wondering if a life—and love—outside the orphanage might be exactly what she never knew she needed.

Renton Robert Rexford III has never wanted for anything. Until he meets Sophie. The charming, intelligent beauty draws him like no other. But, thanks to a disapproving benefactor who threatens to pull the orphanage's funding, his pursuit of her could cost Sophie everything she holds dear. She's all he wants in the world, but how can he ask her to give up so much when all she'd get in return is his heart?

It's not long before Sophie is forced to weigh her loyalty to the only home she's ever known against the needs of her heart. Can love prevail—or is the cost simply too high?

Dedication:

To all those yearning for a better life – May you find the happy ever after you're searching for.

To Mum and Dad for being excited about my orphans and heroines and helping me round out my stories.

To Marlene and Suzanne for being such great critiquers.

And last, but certainly not least, to Mr. Andrews for being the very best always.

Chapter One

New York City, spring 1854

"Sophie! Wait up!"

As she heard the familiar voice, her heart rate picked up, but so did her feet. Without turning to acknowledge his call, Sophie did her best to hurry away. Of course, hampered by her layers of skirts to ward off the chill and her much shorter legs, her effort was wasted. He quickly caught up to her.

"Good morning, Sophie. How are you this morning? I called out for you, but you must not have heard me."

"Good morning, Mr. Rexford," she acknowledged politely, not slowing her pace.

He paused in his stride but then hurried to catch up to her. "Sophie, are you trying to get away from me? What's going on with you this morning?"

She wanted to tell him that yes, she *was* trying to get away from him, but that would only raise more questions from him. She needed to be wily, she reminded herself. He mustn't find out the truth.

"Of course not, everything is just fine," she finally answered him, trying to infuse her voice with as much sincerity as possible, even though she couldn't quite meet his eye. "I'm just in a bit of a hurry. It's my turn to collect the donations from the bakery for the children today, and I'm afraid I'm going to be late."

"Well, then I'll come with you and help you carry it. That way it will be easier for you, and then we can talk as we walk."

His deep voice, obviously trying to sound reasonable, made her breath catch in her throat, and Sophie had to will the tears to remain behind her eyelids where they belonged. He could not sense her emotions or it would spoil everything. She cast him a tight smile. "That's kind of you to offer, Mr. Rexford, but I really cannot tarry. I will wish you a good day." She offered him a small nod before picking up her skirt and willing her legs to move even faster without actually breaking into a run.

Thankfully, her primness had gotten through to him sufficiently that he stopped in his tracks. She could feel his gaze on her back but managed to control herself so that she didn't turn back to glance at him or wave or in any other way indicate the turmoil churning in her chest.

Sophronia Brooks, Sophie to her friends, finally stopped to catch her breath, leaning wearily against the corner of a building and pulling her skirts in around her to prevent them from being brushed by the bustle that continued on around her. Renton, that is, Mr. Rexford, would have been useful to have with her. She would have felt safer, for one important thing. And with his much larger build, he would have been of great assistance to her in carrying what was sure to be a large gift from the bakery. But she needed to dismiss the thought, she reminded herself. Mr. Renton Robert Rexford the Third was not for her. And no matter how much she enjoyed his company or how much he seemed to enjoy hers, he was never going to be for her, and she needed to get that realization through her thick skull.

With that determination, she stepped away from the wall, straightened her shoulders, raised her chin, loosened her grip on her skirts, and strode purposefully toward her destination. Besides, she reminded herself, she didn't need a man's company in order to accomplish her task. She was out at the safest time of the day and was marching along the safest route possible. Nothing about her would proclaim her as a likely target for anyone. There was nothing for her to fear, and even though his company would have been nice, she was good enough company for herself. She didn't need Mr. Rexford, or anyone. She, Sophie Brooks, was all she needed. *And don't you forget it*, she reprimanded herself.

Before long, she arrived at her destination. She quickly glanced at her reflection in the glass of the neighboring shop. Despite the accumulated grime on the window, Sophie was able to see that her cheeks were rosy from her brisk walk and the crisp air but that her speed hadn't disrupted much of the tight knot she had twisted her unruly chestnut curls into. She looked sufficiently neat and tidy, despite the pink that tinged the tip of her nose, not to cause offense to the shopkeeper who was being so generous to the orphanage.

Stale doughnuts wouldn't be most people's idea of a treat, but the children at the orphanage would be delighted when they found them served that evening. Sophie wished she could hold her breath while she was at the bakery; smelling all that sweet deliciousness only made her wish for what could not be. But such was life. She braced her shoulders once more. She hesitated for a moment, though. Should she go to the front door or the back? She had forgotten to ask when Mrs. Parker had sent her on this errand. She glanced at her reflection once more. There was nothing terribly off putting about her appearance, so even if she ought to be at the back, she doubted it would offend the shopkeeper if she came in the front. At least she certainly hoped not. It was tricky business receiving charity.

With a polite smile pinned to her face, Sophie hoped for the best and opened the door, inhaling deeply of the sweet, doughy aroma permeating the bright shop. It just couldn't be helped. She stood still for a second, taking another deep, appreciative sniff but then stepped to the counter. She was fortunate, there was an obvious lull in the shop's business, and there was only one customer being cared for at the moment.

"Can I help you, miss?" The shopkeeper turned to her as his customer stepped away.

"Good morning, I'm Sophie from the Foundling Hospital." She kept her smile polite and her gaze unwavering even though the man's expression changed from being eager for new business to disappointment.

"Fine. Come through here. We have a sack prepared for you." He eyed her speculatively. "You going to be able to manage on your own? Should've sent a man for this."

Again, Sophie kept her smile polite and in place. She was quite used to being underestimated. And there were never enough men to help with the work that needed to be done. This was probably going to be one of the less onerous assignments she had been given, so she didn't bother replying. When she saw the sack he indicated, she worked hard to fight her dismay. She only wished it were bigger, even if it would have been harder to carry. From the looks of it, they wouldn't be able to offer each child a doughnut of their own. With a mental shrug, she decided half a doughnut would please the children almost as much.

Sophie grabbed the sack and nodded to the man. "Thank you for your generosity, sir, the children will be delighted."

The baker merely grunted in acknowledgement before frowning and demanding, "You sure you can manage? Looks to me like you'll blow away with the wind. I'm not sure I should be sending my product off with you."

Now Sophie was starting to get irritated. Part of her wanted to stamp her foot and use colorful language, but she struggled to keep her face serene. "I'm quite certain I shall be fine, sir. I appreciate your concern. Good day." Without waiting for any further doubts to be uttered by the obtuse man, she turned away and exited through the conveniently propped open back door. She could have told him the bag was only half full so it wouldn't be any trouble at all for her to manage, but she had been told a myriad of times by Mr. Brace and the directors of the Children's Aid Society that they could never look a gift horse in the mouth. She always needed to be grateful for whatever was offered to them, no matter how she might wish otherwise.

With a sigh, as soon as she was away from the shop, Sophie swung the sack up over her shoulder, making it a simple task to carry it. She understood that she looked small. It had always been the bane of her existence. Being small was forever causing people to underestimate her. Of course, that could, on occasion, work to her advantage, but it was usually a pain rather than a pleasure. But it didn't matter today. Her size wasn't much of a factor. And the size of her bundle would prevent any undue attention to be drawn toward her. She should be able to return to the orphanage without any trouble at all. As long as she didn't run into Renton again. That had been unnecessarily awkward. Sophie sighed again as she failed to suppress her memories of the first time she had met Renton.

It was the Winter Formal that Mrs. Rexford, Renton's mother, had planned in her continued efforts to raise money for the Foundling Hospital. Mrs. Rexford was one of the Children's Aid Society's biggest donors. Since the Society was such a new organization, Mr. Brace was dependent on the woman's generosity. Mr. Brace had invited Sophie to join a few of the other staff members at the event. She had been beside herself with excitement and had spent hours with some of the older girls at the orphanage planning her clothes and hair for the evening. It had been such a joy to share it with the children. Even though they couldn't attend, they had been nearly as excited as Sophie herself.

Sophie's heart clenched as she remembered how even the most sober of the girls had giggled along with her as they helped her pin up her hair in what was surely the most elegant style her curls had ever managed. It had been like a fairy tale. If only they would all get their happily ever after. Her musings continued.

Sophie arrived in the center of the cluster of staff members who would be attending. She had to exert considerable effort to keep her jaw from dropping open as she gazed about at the most beautiful room she had ever seen. Mrs. Rexford was standing ready to greet her guests as they entered. Always polite, Sophie approached her to express her appreciation.

“Everything looks so amazing, Mrs. Rexford. Thank you for including us in your evening.”

Mrs. Rexford's smile didn't quite reach her eyes, but Sophie didn't pay it much heed at the moment.

“Of course, Sophie, I'm sure you'll have an enjoyable evening.”

Sophie was a little confused as to how to reply to those words. She nodded and dipped a slight curtsy before turning away, trying not to allow a frown to form on her brow. She understood she needed to represent the orphanage well.

She was just pinning what she hoped was a gracious smile back onto her face while scanning the gathering crowd, looking for the rest of her group, when her gaze collided with that of the most handsome man she had ever seen. His blue eyes were so clear and bright, they reminded her of the Atlantic on a sunny day. His dark hair was almost black and was clipped short. It looked as though it would have a tendency to curl if he had not controlled its length. His square jaw and high cheekbones should have looked fierce, but his lips quirked up in the corners as though he had a propensity for smiling or laughing. Sophie's breath caught as she tried to take it all in and once again found herself hoping her mouth wasn't hanging open.

He strode toward her, as she was frozen in place. There wasn't much space separating them, so he was beside her in a few paces.

"Good evening, miss. I haven't had the pleasure of making your acquaintance. I just saw you talking with my mother."

Sophie blinked and almost turned to look behind her before she remembered that she had just been speaking with Mrs. Rexford. Feeling a blush stain her cheeks, Sophie tried to achieve coherent speech, but nothing intelligent came to mind so she merely offered him a slight curtsy like she had done with his mother.

"Oh no, let's not be formal, I beg of you." His words surprised a laugh out of Sophie. She was even more surprised by the embarrassment that stained his cheeks as his grin turned rueful. "Are you laughing because my mother has called this event a Formal? And now I'm begging you not to be formal?"

Sophie just smiled at him. She still didn't have any words to offer. He didn't seem to mind her silence. He caught her hand and tucked it into his elbow.

"It's getting a bit crowded in here. I could escort you to your table."

Finally, Sophie's brain became unfrozen. Even though she didn't pull her hand from his elbow, she offered a half-hearted protest. "I couldn't possibly occupy your time, Mr. Rexford. Surely you have others you need to be speaking with."

"Not at all, my mother has everything under control. All I need to do is show up to these things."

"Does your mother host parties like this regularly?" Sophie couldn't even imagine it.

"Certainly. It is her greatest" —he paused almost imperceptibly before finishing— "joy."

Sophie was fascinated by his hesitation but didn't feel brave enough to question him. She allowed her gaze to circle the room once more. "Her experience has paid off. She is certainly very skilled. Everything is beautiful, and everyone seems to be happy to be here."

"Are you happy to be here?"

"Absolutely." Sophie's reply was filled with conviction. She doubted she would have the opportunity again and was determined to wring every drop of enjoyment she could from the experience. The man at her side returned her grin.

"How rude of me, I haven't introduced myself," he said, turning the subject. "I'm Renton Rexford, of Rexford and Associates."

Sophie nodded graciously in acknowledgement. "I'm Sophie Brooks." She hesitated for a second before adding, "Of the Foundling Hospital."

His eyes widened in surprise, but his reception of her hadn't noticeably cooled, much to Sophie's surprised relief. "Are you one of the orphans? You don't look like a child, I must say."

Sophie grinned. "Thank you, kind sir. I am an orphan, or I guess you could say I was. Mr. Brace has allowed me to stay on and work there now that I am grown."

Mr. Rexford didn't ask any more questions just then. "It is a pleasure to make your acquaintance, Miss Brooks. Are you seated with the rest of Mr. Brace's group, then?"

"I would imagine so. I stopped to speak with Mrs. Rexford, and the others went ahead without me."

"That was rude of them," he observed.

Sophie giggled softly. "Not at all. They probably didn't notice I had stopped. And surely I cannot get lost in one large open room."

He patted her hand where it sat in the crook of his elbow and then left his hand covering hers. Sophie's stomach fluttered at the contact. She was torn between relief that she was wearing gloves and a desperate wish that neither of them had their hands covered so that she could get the full sensation. It was a ridiculous thought since she would not have been considered properly attired if she had not worn gloves and thus would not have been allowed entrance.

Sophie tried to stem the flow of these vivid memories. They caused such a cacophony of pleasure and pain as she thought back to that exquisite evening.

He took her the long way around the room, even though he professed to know where Mr. Brace's group had been seated. When they reached one corner of the room, Sophie allowed her gaze to scan the room and was surprised to see Mr. Brace in the direct opposite corner, the farthest away possible.

"Oh Mr. Renton, I do apologize. I believe my group is quite far away."

He grinned at her. "Why would you apologize?"

"Well, if you are truly going to escort me all the way, that is surely going to occupy your time needlessly."

"Like I told you, I know exactly where Mr. Brace has been seated."

Sophie frowned at him. "Are you perfectly sure?"

"Yes, and we will get there in due time." He must have noticed her puzzled frown because he gave her a lopsided grin that made the flutters in her tummy start up again. "I didn't think you were in a rush, and I wanted to enjoy the pleasure of your company a little while longer."

Sophie protested no further. She had no wish to hurry him on his way. She had never enjoyed such a moment of bliss as she listened to him discretely explain who the various people were as they passed them. He entertained her with amusing anecdotes about the people she had only heard tell of prior. She would have enjoyed walking on his arm even if they had walked for miles. But even though the room had seemed vast when she had first stepped foot into it, and even though he had gone the longest way around possible, long before she was ready for it to be over, they arrived at her table. She introduced him politely to her friends and colleagues. Mr. Brace had cast her a quizzical glance but didn't comment until Mr. Rexford was far enough away, after Sophie had taken her seat next to him.

"How does it happen that Renton Rexford the Third was escorting you to our table, Sophie, my dear?"

Shaking her head and shrugging lightly, she tried to answer. "I have no idea, Mr. Brace. It seemed to happen quite by accident."

He looked torn between worry for her and glee, which caused Sophie to wrinkle her nose at him. Mr. Brace laughed. "Be very careful, my dear girl, but maybe you can encourage them to open their purse strings a little bit further."

Grinning but shaking her head, Sophie turned her attention to the rest of the table. Everyone looked so nice. Nothing like their usual, serviceable clothing. Even their facial expressions looked different. Mrs. Parker, usually so prim and anxious, with about ten things too many to accomplish in any given moment, looked relaxed for the first time in Sophie's memory.

"Have you been to one of Mrs. Rexford's gatherings before?" Sophie asked, hoping to divert attention away from her arrival on Mr. Rexford's escort.

"Yes, once before. You are in for a treat, Sophie. The food will far surpass anything you have ever tasted. Definitely far better than anything we can ever produce from our kitchens."

"Maybe we could ask Mrs. Rexford to give us some tips."

Mrs. Parker laughed but shook her head at Sophie. "You are such a dreamer, my dear."

Sophie blinked in surprise, wondering why she would react in that way. Before she could question Mrs. Parker, though, someone began ringing a bell. Looking all the way down to the end of the room and seeing a man preparing to make some announcements, Sophie realized that their table was the furthest away from any action. They most likely wouldn't be able to hear much of what was about to be said. She didn't allow it to bother her though. If she couldn't hear, no one could expect her to pay attention, she thought with an impish feeling. All the better to be able to take the time to gaze about at the beautiful room.

As she thought about that first encounter, Sophie remembered that she *had* looked around at the stunning architecture and chandeliers as well as the well dressed people nearby. But again and again, her eyes were drawn to the handsome man standing beside his mother, looking serious, and delicious, and approachable. Sophie giggled at the thought, even though she knew she shouldn't even be thinking about the man. But despite who he was and how good looking he was, he really was an approachable person. It was one of the things she liked best about him.

With a shake of her head, she pushed the thoughts away. It mattered very little. There was nothing to be done about it. He would have to accept her disinterest. And if he didn't, it mattered even less, since she would be getting on the train in a little over a week and would then be gone for at least a month.

Maybe she ought to take Katie and Melanie up on their offer to stay with them in Bucklin, Missouri after they escort the shipment of orphans to their new lives. No one could argue that she didn't need a fresh start. But what little a life she had was here in New York City. She didn't know if she was brave enough to start over from scratch like those two were planning. She had already done that more than once in her short life. It had been forced upon her before. Sophie didn't think she would voluntarily choose to uproot and start over even if it held a certain appeal.

Living at the Foundling Hospital wasn't the most prosperous life available, that was for certain, but it was the life she had and knew, and well, loved. It was as though she had scores of younger siblings. And she felt as though she were making a difference in their little lives, helping them to adjust to their new circumstances, whether they were newly orphaned or just newly off the street.

She had been one of Mr. Brace's earliest achievements, he was often telling her. When he opened the Foundling Hospital, she was the first girl he had admitted. And she had stuck. Making herself as helpful as possible had ensured security for herself. Now that she was nineteen, she was trying to convince herself she didn't have to be quite so insecure about her future, but in some ways it felt less secure than ever. Mr. Brace would never turn out one of the children. But since she was no longer a child, she was fearful that he might no longer have a place for her. His suggestions of arranging an apprenticeship for her were probably well intended, and she ought to take him up on it, but she truly just wanted to stay safely tucked up in the attics of the Foundling Hospital. *Is that really too much to ask?*

Her restless musings had kept her company all the way back, and she was surprised to find herself already home. She looked up at the imposing building, attempting to be unbiased as she gazed at it. She wondered if others would think it ugly and stark. But she couldn't; she was completely biased. She loved this place with her whole heart. It was the most stable home she could remember ever having. Her mother's stories of their prestigious background were most likely fairy tales, since she couldn't remember anything before they found themselves destitute and alone on the meaner side of the city before her mother got sick. Her poor, sweet mother. Mama had never ceased promising that Papa would return for them, but when she died, all her stories went with her. Sophie didn't have time for fairy tales. She would rather accomplish something practical and have food in her belly and a warm, dry place to sleep, thank you very much.

'Stop dawdling, girl,' she could almost hear Cook bellowing at her. Sophie needed to get her prize down to the kitchen so it could be dealt with before the next meal. She hurried around to the back of the building to enter there before running up to her room to wash her face and hands.

"Were you accosted on your way back?" Cook demanded as he eyed the half full sack.

Sophie smiled at his obvious attempt to make light. "No, the bakery overestimated their generosity, I think. This was all there was when I got there."

"Humph. We should have gone last night. He probably sold off some of his stale stock as fresh to some poor, unsuspecting customer."

Sophie wanted to shrug but merely nodded in agreement.

"Well, never mind, we'll just cut them in half," Cook declared.

Sophie laughed. "That's what I figured."

"What are you doing still standing here? Go get washed up. I'm going to need you to do the slicing. You're the only one who will make sure there's no fighting."

Sophie laughed again. "Yes, I'll be sure to make the cuts even." She hurried to the door, calling over her shoulder as she went. "I'll be as quick as a bunny."

The grumpy overseer of the kitchens barely cracked a smile at her as she rushed away. Sophie didn't care. The man was her family. She had known him since she had arrived at the age of ten. She actually loved his gruff grumpiness. It never wavered. It gave her a sense of security. She never had to wonder what mood he would be in. His growl was almost comforting. It was home.

With a grin, Sophie ran up the stairs to her room. Within moments she had washed her face and hands and was back in the kitchen with an apron on, a sharp knife in her hand, and a pile of sliced doughnuts growing beside her.

Chapter Two

Renton stared at the urchin holding the door. “What do you mean she’s too busy to come to the door? Did you tell her my name?”

When the child nodded vigorously, Renton asked suspiciously, “Are you sure?”

“I’m surer than sure, sir. Mr. Renton Rexford the Third, you said, sir, and that’s what I said. But she said she can’t come to the door.” The child shrugged. “Nothing I can do about that, mister.”

There was nothing Renton could do either. It was most peculiar. This was the third day in a row that Sophie had brushed him off. The first day, he had at least seen her as she was rushing off to do some sort of errand, but for the last two days, when he had knocked at the door, she had refused to see him. He knew she was always kept busy with her work here at the orphanage, but it wasn’t like her to refuse to so much as greet him. *She’s never been this busy before*, he grumbled to himself, while he wondered if she had lost interest in him and was being too kind to tell him so. *Not that it’s really a kindness to keep me dangling on a string*, he grumbled some more. *No*, he thought, *she is far too forthright for that.* She would have the honesty to tell him if she didn't want him calling on her anymore, he was sure of it.

Standing on the sidewalk, staring up at the unimpressive, large building, Renton wrinkled his nose. Perhaps he ought to volunteer there in order to lift some of the burden from her slim shoulders. Surely if they had more help, Sophie wouldn't be too busy for him. With a nod, he set off for his parents' house. His mother would know who he needed to talk to. She was always involved in some form of fundraising for the various charities that were her pet projects. He knew the Foundling Hospital was one of them. That was how he had met Sophie in the first place.

Thus decided, his steps were lighter, and he whistled a merry tune as he turned toward his mother's house with long, purposeful strides. Glancing at his timepiece, he wagered he would be able to catch her having her tea before she left for her calls.

As he walked toward his mother's house, Renton thought about the last time he had spent time with Sophie. They had been "conveniently" running into each other at least once or twice a week ever since the fundraiser four months ago. Each time he got to spend time with her, he would make sure to ascertain what her schedule was for the upcoming days and make sure he was on the same street or attending the same event. She had been participating in some of the fundraising efforts for the orphanage so that had made it even easier to be with her. It had been just such an event, organized by his mother, at which he had seen her the week before.

She had looked stunning, as usual, as she scurried around doing his mother's bidding, finishing up the myriad last minute details that his mother always left undone. Renton had been amazed at Sophie's patience with his mother's constant dictates. When he had commented about it to Sophie, all she had done was smile serenely. "I'm willing to do just about anything for the orphanage, Renton, surely you realize that. Fetching a few things for your mother is really nothing for me to object to. She does so much good for the children. I can only be grateful to her."

Renton couldn't really argue with her reasoning but finally, halfway through the evening, he had insisted she had done enough. "My mother has actual paid staff, Sophie. They can look after things for the rest of the evening. Come dance with me. You are looking far too pretty to be wasting your time back here in the kitchens."

The way she had blushed and stammered and then spent the rest of the evening by his side had made Renton think she was just as happy in his company as he was in hers, but the way she was now avoiding him was making him wonder if he had somehow offended her. His chest felt tight at the thought. Meeting her this winter had been the best thing that ever happened to him. He had to get to the bottom of her changed behavior.

He tried to think over every detail of that last evening. They had discussed some of Wordsworth's poems as well as Alexandre Dumas' latest book.

Renton always enjoyed listening to her enthusiastic descriptions of her favorite bits when they'd both read something. He would rather hear her describe the book than read it himself. Her interesting way of elaborating on it was far better than what his own imagination could conjure. They'd also had a rather heated discussion about the Baltimore Female College that had just opened a few years ago in order to educate teachers. It was not that he didn't think she was capable of doing the studies, far from it, he just didn't want her going away for such a long time. He thought he had made that clear. But maybe after she thought about it afterward she had decided he was too wrongheaded for her to deal with.

Renton shook his head. Sophie would have the courage to tell him to his face if she thought he was wrong; he was sure of it. *But what could it be?* She had seemed so happy that night. There was no indication of anything that would lead her to severing contact with him. Maybe he was reading too much into her refusal to see him that morning. Maybe she really was just too busy to come to the door.

The walk from the orphanage to his mother's house was further than he had anticipated, but the time passed quickly as he thought more about that night. The only time he had seen Sophie's smile dim was as she had taken leave of his mother. Renton had been caught up in a conversation with a business associate so he had not accompanied Sophie as she went to speak with her hostess. He found it hard to believe his mother would have reprimanded Sophie for not continuing to run about for her all evening. Sophie had already done so much before Renton had whisked her away to the dance floor. But Renton knew his mother didn't always consider people to be her equal. She could be a little snobby at times, thinking those of less means were also of less worth. But no, his mother surely wouldn't have said anything untoward to Sophie. Sophie was such a darling, no one could have anything less than kind to say to her.

Upon arrival at his parents' home, Renton had been right in his assessment of his mother's whereabouts. He asked for her when the door was opened by one of her maids.

"She's just having her tea, sir. I'm sure she'll be glad to see you. Would you like me to take your coat?"

"Thank you," he answered, distracted by the fact that he couldn't remember her name.

She smiled politely and led him to his mother's parlour. "Your son is here to see you, ma'am."

"Renton, darling, what a wonderful surprise. Bring a fresh pot and another cup, Maisie," she called out as the maid was leaving. Maisie didn't bother answering, she just dipped a small curtsy and hurried away to do Mrs. Rexford's bidding.

"Good morning, Mother. How are you today? I'm glad I found you at home."

"I'm even better than I was now that you have arrived," his mother answered coyly and he strove not to roll his eyes.

There was an awkward silence wherein his mother must have realized she had gone a little far. She quickly asked, "To what do I owe the pleasure of having you arrive unannounced and unsummoned?"

Now Renton really did roll is eyes. But his mother was right, he pretty much never visited anymore without a summons. After his disrespectful eye roll, his face creased into a grin. It wasn't possible to remain serious with his mother.

"I need some information, and I am certain you are the best one to ask."

"Really?" Her eyes sparkled at his words. "How can I help you?"

"I want to volunteer at the Foundling Hospital. With whom should I speak in order to make the arrangements?"

He would have laughed at the shocked look on her face if he wasn't so serious about needing access to the Hospital, and therefore access to Sophie.

"I don't understand your question, my son," she began carefully. "Do you wish to make a donation?"

"No, I am certain our family donates quite enough. I would like to actually do some work there. Surely they accept volunteer help." He was becoming frustrated with her lack of understanding.

"But why? We help with donations. We don't actually go there."

Renton had always suspected this was her attitude but was surprised to hear her actually express it. "Now I have to confess that I don't understand. Why wouldn't you want to go there? Are you not always talking about how much you help the less fortunate in the city?"

"Well of course we help. We just don't do it in person. That is for others to do, Renton. Surely you are too busy and too important to go down there. It is so very dirty and vulgar."

"Mother, I am shocked by your reaction. Haven't you ever wanted to see for yourself what you're involved in with your charities?"

His mother let out a tinkling laugh that Renton had the sinking suspicion was less than sincere. "Not at all, my son. Our family has been very fortunate, so we share that with others. That doesn't mean we need to get personal about it."

Renton blinked. While he had occasionally suspected his mother was shallow in her interests, he had never realized she was so very insincere in her charitable works. "Well, I want to get personal about it," Renton insisted.

"This is about that girl, isn't it?" his mother demanded shrewdly. "She told you what I said, didn't she?"

Feeling all the hairs on the back of his neck stand on end, Renton demanded, "What girl? Sophie? What did you say to her?"

He saw a flash of discomfort cross her face. "I don't know what you're talking about," she tried to prevaricate.

Renton sighed. "You said, and I quote, 'she told you what I said, didn't she'. Was the *she* you are referring to Sophie? What did you say to her?"

"I don't care for your tone, Renton Rexford. I am your mother."

"Yes, you are my mother, but I am a grown man. You cannot control my life any longer, Mother. Now, respectfully, tell me what you said to her."

His mother narrowed her eyes at him while looking down her nose as haughtily as she could manage. "I think it is time for you to leave, Son. I have things to attend to."

Renton sighed again. Clearly, he wasn't going to get anywhere with her in this mood. But he now really knew enough. It was obvious she had said something off putting to Sophie, which was why she would no longer walk with him comfortably. He needed to get himself inside the Foundling Hospital. If he could make Sophie see him as a real companion rather than his mother's son, he had a much better chance of getting somewhere with her. Or at least he hoped so. His stomach clenched at the thought of losing her affections. He had to do something.

Chapter Three

Sophie felt her eyes widen. She didn't care if she looked like an owl blinking in shock. She could hardly believe the sight before her.

"What are you doing here?" she demanded as Mr. Rexford turned and grinned. Sophie had to bite her lip not to grin at him in return. He was draped in an apron, which looked incongruous over his neatly pressed shirt and tie — along with his shiny black shoes peeking out from the bottom. But just seeing him in her own familiar place caused a flurry of emotions to ripple through her. A part of her was excited to have him there in her home and a frisson of attraction shivered up her spine. But another part of her needed to protect her home. The Foundling Hospital was the only place of security she had ever known, and she needed to make sure that didn't change. That overrode everything. It didn't matter that the man was deliciously handsome. She didn't want him there.

But how could she get him to leave? A delicate balance needed to be struck. It would not do to offend the deep-pocketed Rexfords. She would need to make him think it was his idea, she supposed. *But how to accomplish that?* she wondered.

She started with a tentative smile to the room at large, since no one had bothered to reply to her demand as to what Mr. Rexford was doing in the orphanage's kitchen. Since he was covered in an apron, it was obvious he wasn't merely there to check on his family's donations. Or maybe he was. Maybe that wasn't so very obvious. Maybe he was just the hands on sort who wanted to see for himself how his contributions were being used. Not that she had ever heard of anyone doing that, but she supposed it was as reasonable an explanation as any as to why the handsome young man had suddenly turned up in the orphanage kitchen.

In fact, perhaps she ought to apologize for her outburst. Otherwise he might be tempted to pull the family's considerable funds. Sophie stifled a sigh. She didn't actually know what would be the best thing to do at this moment.

Sophie finally determined that the best thing, for the moment at least, would be to ignore all her uncertainties since it didn't seem as though anyone was about to offer her any answers. With another vague smile to the room at large, when she realized everyone was still gazing at her, she stepped briskly into the room. Grabbing her own large apron, Sophie covered herself from neck to ankle and made her way toward the table. Without looking at Mr. Rexford again, she set to work chopping. After a moment's hesitation, everyone else resumed their work as well, following her lead.

The morning passed with remarkably little eventuality. Sophie kept glancing toward Renton and was surprised to see how well he was doing with each task Cook assigned him. Her ears perked up as he began whistling a jaunty tune as he chopped. It was no time at all before everyone had finished their assigned tasks.

"That was much harder than I had expected."

Sophie nearly jumped out of her skin, she was so startled by the deep, low voice coming over her shoulder. She had been so aware of him all morning, she was shocked that she hadn't notice him approach her as she checked on the last-minute touches as they finished making the children's lunch.

"Sorry to have startled you."

He didn't look sorry as he grinned down at her. Sophie bit her lip in order to quell her emotions. She wasn't sure if it was irritation or attraction that fluttered uppermost in her chest, but it wouldn't do to be displaying either.

After drawing a deep breath to quell her feelings, she offered him a small smile. "So, how did you come to be working in our kitchen this morning?"

"Cassandra Morley's mother is a friend of my mother. I remembered my mother mentioning to me that Cass was volunteering here, so I called on her and she made the arrangements."

Sophie had to exert effort to keep her smile in place as she felt herself turning green with envy over the comfortable way he discussed the other young woman. Cassie was lovely and Sophie would actually say they were friends, but in that moment it was a struggle to remember that fact.

"How nice," she managed to say. Sophie was hoping to be able to scurry away, now that their task had been concluded, but she needed to avoid being overtly rude to the generous man.

Before she was able to make her escape, he prompted her with another question. "Do you always prepare so very much? Or was that for my benefit, since you had an extra pair of hands?"

Sophie had to laugh. "Actually, you weren't extra. Normally two other women are helping in the kitchen, but they were busy today, making preparations for the train ride next week."

At his quizzical look, Sophie explained. "Don't you know about Mr. Brace's new initiative to send some of the orphans on the train out to farming families in the west?"

When Renton shook his head, Sophie elaborated. "I will try not to bore you with too many details, but it is a wonderfully exciting opportunity for the children he has selected. He has already sent out two groups of children, and they were all successfully placed with families to look after them. This time we're going as far as the train tracks go. All the way to Missouri!"

"What is the purpose of this?" Renton seemed puzzled, but genuinely interested.

"Mr. Brace believes that farm families all have room for at least one more place at the table and could all use a hand with working their land. Since here in New York so many children have lost their parents to different things, he's sending them out of the city to new lives, lives where they have a chance for a new family."

"You seem pretty excited about it. Do you wish you had been sent on the train when you lost your parents?"

Sophie forced a laugh despite her discomfort. "The train didn't go anywhere when I lost my parents. But every orphan dreams of having a family."

Renton's face filled with sympathy, and Sophie had to fight so that her eyes didn't fill with tears. But then he interrupted his own thoughts with a question. "Wait, you said *we* are going as far as Missouri. What did you mean? Are you moving away?"

Sophie's laugh was much more genuine this time. "Not at all. I still love New York despite everything. No, I'm not moving, but the children cannot just be loaded on the train and left to themselves. It will take almost two weeks to get all the way to the end of the line. A few of us who work or volunteer here will be accompanying the children to their new lives."

"So how long will you be gone?" To Sophie's ears he actually sounded angry at the thought of her being away. Her heart wanted to soar with that knowledge, but she frowned to quell the impulse.

"About a month. Our return tickets haven't been arranged. It will depend on how long we remain with the children when we reach our destination. And of course, with any type of travel, despite all the wonderful innovations, you can never be completely sure if things won't go wrong." She paused when she noticed his scowl.

"Are you all right, Mr. Rexford?"

His face cleared at her question. “Yes, of course, I’m fine. I just worry a little bit about you going off on this train ride.”

Sophie could feel her eyebrows reaching toward her hairline.

He quickly added, “I’m not questioning your competence, Miss Brooks, I assure you. It is just, as you said, things can go wrong and you never know who else might be traveling in the same direction.”

Sophie laughed. “Well, I never said that last bit. But I am fully confident that Katie, Melanie, Mrs. Parker, and I shall be just fine.”

“Only women?”

Sophie laughed again, although this time it was a bit more forced. “Very competent women.”

He had the grace to flush. “Of course. I’m sure you are all highly competent. But are you not nervous about it? What if something goes wrong?”

“Things go wrong every day of the week, Mr. Rexford. I am well aware of that. And well experienced in the matter of dealing with all those misfortunes that come our way. Mrs. Parker and I have already had this experience a couple times already. This will be Katie and Melanie’s first time. And in fact, they won’t be returning to New York. That is why they aren’t here today. They have to tie up any loose ends of their lives here before heading west.”

He was quiet for a moment while he gazed at her as though he were assessing her. “Are you absolutely certain you are coming back?”

"Absolutely," Sophie repeated. Part of her wanted to demand what business it was of his, but she couldn't bear to hear the answer, whatever it might be. *He is not for you*, she reminded herself with as much fervor as she could muster, *remember what is at stake*. That finally brought her to her senses. She could feel the color draining from her face. With a tight smile, she tried to make her escape.

"Your help was certainly appreciated this morning, sir. I must be going to complete the rest of my chores."

He tried to stop her. "Can I help you?"

Sophie wanted to be elsewhere. "It would probably be best if you speak to Mrs. Parker," she said, desperate to be away, and finally turned on her heel and fled, uncaring if he thought her rude.

Renton watched as Sophie rushed away. He was more confused than ever. He knew girls could be contrary creatures, but she was worse than any he had ever met. He had thought they were attracted to one another. At the very least, he had thought they were friends. Even today, there were moments when he had been certain she was enjoying his company, and then she turned around and ran off on him. He frowned as he looked in the direction in which she had departed. Should he chase after her? It would hardly be appropriate since he rather suspected the bedrooms were located up the stairs she had climbed. It would also hardly be seemly. He could just hear his mother now. 'Rexfords do not need to pursue relationships, Renton, dear, surely you know that.'

But he *wanted* to pursue a relationship with Sophie. Despite their being from different stations in life, he found her company far more engaging than that of any other female of his acquaintance. She was well read and articulate despite not having attended finishing school or moving about within his usual social circle. Besides, he thought, this is America. His mother was always going on about how their name means Son of a King, but he rather doubted they were of legitimate birth. And very few of their friends were of noble birth. Of course, many were the sons of younger sons of the nobility back in England, but what did that matter? To his mind, being clever enough to make your own way was what mattered. Just like his father had managed to do, making his fortune from small beginnings. Even he, himself, didn't have anything to boast about. Being his father's son meant that, while he prided himself on working hard, he had a position ready made for him by his father. Sophie, on the other hand, had so many things working against her in her young life, but look at her. She managed to keep a joyful disposition and worked hard for the benefit of others. He was proud to call her his friend. Or so he had thought. He sighed and went in search of Mrs. Parker as Sophie had admonished him.

"Oh, Mr. Rexford, how has your morning been so far? I must say, I could hardly believe it when Cassie told me you wanted to help out here in a literal way. We are always open to extra hands, but today it was particularly helpful."

Renton cleared his throat, a little uncomfortable with the woman's effusive praise. "Yes, Miss Brooks mentioned that a couple women who would normally be here were tied up today."

"Yes, such dear girls. Katie and Melanie had some things to take care of today." Mrs. Parker looked disinclined to elaborate.

"I suppose you will be particularly short-staffed when you are away escorting the children on the train." Renton was well aware that he was prying, but it didn't strike him as being rude. As a donor to the orphanage, he *was* interested in its smooth operation. And he *did* actually care about the welfare of the orphans. Really, what was going to happen when four of the usual caretakers were absent?

Now Mrs. Parker had begun to look harried. "Yes, of course, but there will be far fewer children to care for as well. Mr. Brace has it well in hand." There was a pause while she appeared to struggle with how to handle him.

Renton wanted to laugh but controlled the impulse. It was obvious the poor woman wasn't used to dealing with donors on a personal level. It struck Renton as odd that his mother and her cronies had never actually stepped in to help in a literal way.

Mrs. Parker surprised him with her next inquiry. "Are you offering to make yourself available, Mr. Rexford? It would be a beneficial experience for the children, especially the boys. We appreciate any offer of assistance from whatever quarter it comes from, but it is pretty much only females who volunteer here. And even our employed staff is almost only female. In fact, I was going to suggest, if you intend to remain any longer, that you might wish to look in on some of the boys. Have you any experience with children, sir? If you knew of some games you could play with them, or if you thought you could help them with their lessons, it would be so very beneficial for them."

Renton hesitated. He had made arrangements to volunteer that day in order to gain access to Sophie, but that hadn't yet worked out the way he had hoped. And now, seeing how much help was truly needed, he wanted to do what he could, but he suddenly felt inadequate.

"I have several young cousins I've spent time with, but I'm not absolutely certain how I could be of assistance." He could hear the uncertainty in his voice and just barely managed not to cringe. He was not used to feeling incompetent. He was quickly questioning the wisdom of his visit.

"Anything you could manage would be just fine," Mrs. Parker soothed.

Again Renton had to suppress the urge to laugh. It was obvious the older woman was used to managing people. She was already coming around her desk and taking his arm, obviously enthused with the idea of his providing company to the children.

"There is still some time before lunch. Has anyone shown you around?" Without waiting for his response, she steered him out of the room and carried on talking. "Oh, the boys will be so happy to see you. Surely you must know some games they'll enjoy. It hasn't been so very long since you were a boy yourself, isn't that right, Mr. Rexford?"

Renton felt as though he were choking on his desire to laugh, but he was also torn between that and a gut-wrenching fear of facing the children all of a sudden. Before he could formulate a coherent objection, they had stepped into a large classroom. It wasn't like any classroom Renton had been in though. All the children were currently standing beside their desks, marching in place. The intruders hadn't made much, if any noise, especially not to be heard over the sound of many footsteps, but still, all heads turned in their direction, leaving Renton feeling awkward and out of place.

"Good morning, children, we have the pleasure of Mr. Rexford's company today. Who wants to tell him why you are all standing right now?"

Several hands began waving eagerly in the air.

"Tony, what can you tell us?"

"Teacher says we can learn better if we ain't, I mean, aren't having so many fidgets."

"Very good, Tony. Do you think it works?"

The child shrugged but grinned as he kept right on marching.

"Who would like to tell Mr. Rexford what you were learning this morning?"

Many more hands were now waving, much to Renton's surprise. When he had been in school, it had always seemed like no one wanted to participate. Renton was impressed. Obviously the strange methods were working.

"Ross?" Renton was now also impressed with Mrs. Parker's knowledge of the children and their names.

He was certain there were at least 200 children in residence at the orphanage. The fact that Mrs. Parker knew the names of all the children, who looked like just a sea of faces to Renton's mind, told him that she either had a remarkable mind or truly cared about the children. From the scattered appearance of her office, he would be willing to bet money on it being the latter. That thought made him grin until the child stepped forward and started to explain their lessons.

"We're learning about villeinage and feudalism in the fourteenth and fifteen centuries," came the explanation from a small lad in the front of the room. To Renton's untrained eye he looked like he couldn't be much more than seven or eight years old.

"Good heavens, why?" he blurted without thinking. He didn't expect an answer but to his surprise, the small boy provided one.

"Teacher says to understand the past leads to a better future."

Renton cleared his throat. "Sounds to me like your teacher is a wise man."

The children were obviously growing restless with their curiosity but his statement resulted in grins and quiet cheers. Mrs. Parker's gaze was shrewd.

"Perhaps Mr. Rexford could stay with the class until you break for lunch," she stated to the teacher rather than asking either of them before she swept from the room.

Renton was at a momentary loss. He felt as though she had just thrown him to the wolves. Of course, they were only children, but he hadn't expected to be left with the full focus of what felt like hundreds of children. In actuality, it was probably only thirty, but it certainly felt overwhelming as he returned their steady gazes.

Thankfully, the teacher came to his rescue.

“Very good, boys. Now, take your seats and we’ll try for a little more instruction before the bell rings for lunch.”

Renton watched, fascinated, as the teacher managed to regain the full attention of the classroom and he really did lead them in learning something more. Before he knew it, there was a loud ringing. It was time for lunch. He could hardly believe how quickly the morning had flown. Despite feeling exhausted, he was sure it had been the most enjoyable morning he had experienced in ages. And it wasn’t just the opportunity to see Sophie that had made him so happy, he realized as he spotted her across the large room when he accompanied the boys down to lunch. Their eyes met and he was surprised to feel a flutter of excitement. Of course, he knew he was attracted to her, but he hadn’t felt this type of awareness since he was a lad first discovering that girls were pretty. It made him nervous. He was torn between running toward her and running away like a coward. He was saved from ignominy by the urchin at his side.

“Hey, mister. Wanna eat lunch with me?”

The small boy couldn’t have been more than five or six. Although since he looked like he hadn’t been properly fed for most of his life, it was entirely possible he was older than he looked. But the resigned look on his face as though he expected life to throw another disappointment at him, made him look ancient. And made Renton unable to refuse.

"I would enjoy that very much, thank you for asking," he answered politely, making the boys around him laugh and giggle like the children they were. Renton's heart went out to them. It was coming home to him just how very unfair life truly was.

He looked across the room briefly and saw Sophie's intense interest. He wasn't sure what his smile might have told her. He wasn't completely sure what he was feeling himself. But her return smile was warm and encouraging.

Lunch passed in a blur. He could hardly keep up with all the chatter as each little boy tried to outdo the other as they entertained him with their stories. Renton couldn't be sure how much was truth and how much exaggeration, but if even a fraction were true, the youngsters had all led colorful, traumatic lives.

That afternoon, he joined another one of the teachers who was focusing on physical education for the children.

"We try to keep the children occupied as much as possible so they aren't tempted to return to their former lives."

"What do you mean, their former lives? Aren't their parents dead? There's no going back to their former lives." Renton was confused.

"Most of the children, the boys especially, have spent time on the streets before coming to us at the orphanage. Most of them have been forced here after running into trouble with authorities. Very few of them were happy about winding up in an orphanage. They had made communities or families for themselves out on the streets. Most are resistant to following rules after the freedom they have experienced. Or they have dealt with terrible abuse in their past and trust no one. Either way, they resist being here for the most part. Running around and being occupied helps them to focus on the merits of being here. And keeps them from causing us too much trouble."

Renton hadn't realized the children wouldn't want to be there. Of course, it would make sense that they would rather have their families back. But if their families were dead, there wasn't much that could be done about that. Being at the orphanage struck him as the lesser of evils. But the teacher's explanation made sense, and Renton looked at the children and the service being provided by the orphanage in a new light. He was all the more determined to do whatever he could to help out. He nearly ran himself ragged playing with each classroom of children as they changed throughout the afternoon.

Renton was a little embarrassed when Sophie came across him as he was gasping for air, hanging over the balustrade late that afternoon. She laughed and asked, "Have the children worn you out, Mr. Rexford?"

"Yes!" he answered simply but he returned her grin. "I fear I did not dress properly for the exertions of the day."

Sophie glanced down and winced. "I don't think your feet will appreciate what you've been doing."

"No, they don't, but it has been worth every blister I'm sure to have."

"Really, Mr. Rexford? I didn't really picture you as being the hands on type."

Renton was hurt by her words but thought that might explain her strange behavior. His feelings must have displayed themselves on his face because she suddenly started blushing.

"Is that why you have been avoiding me? You don't think I could share your interest in the orphans?" he asked.

He watched, fascinated as the color in her cheeks deepened further. "I haven't been avoiding you," she protested.

"Liar," he said to her, keeping his voice firm even though part of him wanted to tease her for her discomfort. She was so appealing. He needed to know why she was trying to distance herself from him.

Sophie's eyes darted everywhere but toward his own gaze as she clearly struggled to formulate a response. Renton felt bad for making her uncomfortable, but he held silent in the hopes that she would explain herself. When tears filled her eyes, though, it was the last reaction he had expected.

"Sophie, what is it? Surely you can tell me."

"I can't," she said, her voice wretched. Without saying anything else, she gathered her skirts and ran away.

Despite his sore feet, Renton did his best to chase after her.

Chapter Four

Sophie tried to get away from Renton, but she was choking on the tears she was trying to hold back. She almost tripped over her own feet as she hurried away. The pain in his feet didn't seem to be encumbering him over much as he quickly caught up to her. They were just outside an empty classroom when he grabbed her arm and pulled her inside.

"Sophie," he said in a soft tone. His deep voice contained only compassion and questions, making Sophie feel all the more desperate. She had so many feelings for him, but she just couldn't tell him the truth. She tried to get herself back under control. There was too much at stake for her to give in to her own weak emotions.

"Sophie, my dear, you must tell me."

She tried to brazen it out. Sophie pulled herself together and raised her chin. There was barely a wobble in her voice as she began to speak. "You really don't have any claims over me, Mr. Rexford. You have no right to tell me what I must or must not do. And I do not appreciate you calling me a liar."

His searching gaze studied her face, and Sophie fought to remain impassive. She wasn't sure if she had been successful when his puzzled frown remained compassionate instead of withdrawing as she had hoped.

"I thought we were friends," he said, remaining calm and kind.

"What made you think that, Mr. Rexford?" Sophie was hoping for a cold tone but the remaining teariness in her voice put a lie to her efforts.

He was still holding her arm, which was a relief and a torment all at once. She was so distraught she might have sunk to the floor without his support, but his warm grasp on her arm was interfering with her efforts to be stolid and firm. He smiled, apparently not put out in the least by her efforts to distance herself from him.

"What made me think we were friends?" He repeated her question after a few beats. "Perhaps it was the way my heart lifts every time you are near, or the way your face lights up when our eyes meet across a crowded room. Or maybe it's the long conversations we have whenever our paths cross, as though we're two halves of a whole. Even when we disagree our conversations are enjoyable."

As he was talking, Sophie's breath caught in the back of her throat and her heart sped up. She desperately wanted to throw herself into his arms and beg him to stay her friend. But she couldn't. She had to think of the children.

Her heart shrank within her chest and her chin wobbled as her eyes filled with tears, but she lifted her chin and looked him right in the face as she told him, “Well, Mr. Rexford, you thought wrong. We are not friends. We cannot be friends. You are a wealthy business man. I am an orphan working at the Foundling Hospital. No friendship is possible between us. And I would ask that you unhand me so that I can carry on with my day.”

Renton blinked and his face fell. For a moment, Sophie’s heart sank and she wanted to throw up, as she thought she had been successful in her attempts to end their fledgling relationship. His hand loosened on her arm and she was about to pull away from him. But then he tightened it and brought his other hand up to grasp her left arm. He wasn’t hurting her, but it was evident he would not be letting her go.

“No, Sophie. I don’t believe you. I *know* you. And this is so unlike you that I know there must be something else going on. What did my mother say to you?”

Sophie gasped as she felt all the color drain away from her face and she was suddenly light headed. “How do you know about that? Renton, please, you cannot say anything to her.”

“So there *is* something. Out with it, Sophie. You know we’re friends. And you know I won’t let this go. Tell me what is going on.”

She had tried so hard to be strong and it was all falling down around her feet. The tears she had been trying to hold back slipped silently down her cheeks. If she wasn’t so caught up in her own misery, she would have enjoyed the wretched look on his face as he despaired over her distress.

"It's bigger than us, Renton. It's the children. All of the children. I cannot. You have to try to understand. You've been here all day. You've seen the children. I cannot allow this to be taken away." Her words bolstered her own determination. Her spine got its steel back, and her tears dried. Sophie stepped away from his suddenly loosened grasp. It would have been funny to see his mouth gaping in shock if it wasn't such a deadly serious situation.

Her heart was breaking but her determination was stronger than ever. She was about to sweep from the room, running away to find somewhere private to scream and sob. But before she could leave, his hand clamped on her arm once more and he spun her to face him.

"Are you saying my mother has threatened the orphanage? How?"

"No, I'm not telling you anything. Please, Renton, let this go. Let *me* go. There's nothing for us to pursue here." She was prepared to beg if she had to. She just wanted to get away and nurse her emotional injuries.

"There's plenty for us to pursue. I wasn't mistaken. We *are* friends. Maybe we could even be more than friends. I am not prepared to just let this go."

Sophie's resolve hardened further and her chin raised to a stubborn level. "Any friend of mine would not jeopardize something that I hold so dear."

Renton's stance softened. "Sophie, my dear, you know I won't allow my mother to do anything to this place."

"How do you think you could possibly stop her? No one can force her where to put her charitable donations. The Foundling Hospital and the Children's Aid Society are completely dependent on the munificence of others." Sophie could feel her chin trembling with the force of her tumultuous emotions, but she held it at a firm angle. "This has been my home since I was ten years old. I depend on it. But I am a grown woman at this point. I could manage. But the little ones cannot. I cannot take the chance on my actions harming their future."

Renton's stare was hard, making her squirm. "Tell me what she said to you. You owe me that at least."

Sophie couldn't look him in the eye as she finally told him the truth. She knew it would be awkward for him to hear that his mother was interfering in his life in such a way. "She said if I do not cut my ties with you, she will cut her funding efforts. She said there are many charities that would be happy to cooperate with her wishes. She also told me I wasn't to tell you so you really cannot say anything to her. Please, Renton, you must swear it to me."

He continued to stare hard at her. Sophie could almost see the wheels of thought turning in his head as she finally met his gaze. Slowly a gentle, beautiful smile bloomed on his face.

"If I can find a reliable solution to the funding problem, will you stop resisting my efforts to spend time with you?"

It seemed to Sophie as though her heart stopped for a moment before it began hammering madly within her chest. She wanted to throw herself into his arms, but she had to try to see sense.

"You cannot give your own money, Renton. Your mother would stop you. Besides, she gets so many other people to donate. I've seen the ledgers. It's too much."

"First of all, Sophie, darling, my mother doesn't have any say over how I spend my money. Even without the family funds, I do quite well for myself, have no fear. But I have another idea that just might work swimmingly. So I will repeat my question. Will you, Sophie Brooks, allow me to court you with serious intention if I can solve the problem of funding for the Foundling Hospital?"

Sophie finally allowed hope to flood into her heart. She could feel her cheeks stretching from the smile that bloomed on her face. She couldn't speak around the emotion clogging her throat, so she nodded tentatively. Renton whooped, picked her up, and spun her around in a circle. He put her back on her feet and then quickly planted a quick kiss softly on her lips.

She could only stare as he grinned at her. "I will return as soon as I have it all sorted," he promised her before rushing from the room.

With trembling fingers, Sophie covered her mouth and looked at the empty doorway through which he had disappeared. *Had it all been a dream?* With a shake of her head, she tried to pull her hopes back down to earth, but she couldn't prevent her smile from remaining fixed in place as she slowly made her way down to supper.

Chapter Five

Sophie remained on tenterhooks for three days. The hours dragged by as she went about her duties. For two days she could barely eat, but by the third day she took herself to task. *You are being absolutely ridiculous*, she told her reflection as she pulled her hair back into a severe style, jabbing pins in haphazardly, trying to regain a sense of control over something in her life, even if it was merely her unruly curls. *I told you not to get your hopes up. Look what it leads to. You are moping around here as though you have lost out on something. Nothing has been lost that you didn't already have. If you do not pull yourself together, you are going to give the children the vapors. Especially the children bound for the train.*

Thus admonished, she did indeed manage to get her emotions under a semblance of control. She managed to choke down at least some of the hearty breakfast placed before her, and she was able to smile sincerely at the little girl sitting next to her at the table.

"Are you excited about leaving on the train in a few days, Annie?"

The child's eyes were huge in her face as she turned her attention from her plate. "I think so, Miss Sophie."

Sophie actually laughed, although it was soft and brief. "Why aren't you sure?"

Annie scrunched her nose as she thought. "Well, I'm afeared, for one thing. I've never been on a train before. And none of my friends are going."

Sophie's heart ached for the child. Mr. Brace was sending very few girls on this trip. "You will make lots of friends in your new home, I'm sure."

The little girl nodded vigorously. "I sure hope so."

"So what are the positive things that make you think you might be excited about it?"

"Mrs. Parker said maybe my new family will let me have a kitten." The blissful smile that accompanied this statement made Sophie react with another laugh, this one much more sincere.

"That *is* powerful incentive for leaving, I would imagine."

"And it *will* be nice to have a mommy and daddy." The child's voice was wistful but not weak. Sophie was grateful the poor little girl's hope had not been completely squashed despite the tragedies she'd endured.

Sophie nodded and clasped the child's hand. There wasn't anything she could say to that. It was every orphan's heartfelt wish to belong to a family. She, herself, was too old to be wishing for parents but as she looked around the large room, she felt this was the closest she was going to get to having a family of her own. She had two hundred little brothers and sisters. And all the staff members were like aunts and uncles for her. But she did not begrudge the children leaving on the train their opportunity to get a family of their own. Nor the opportunity to have a kitten, she thought with a wistful smile. It would have been her own dearest wish when she was younger.

"There is nothing to fear about going on the train, though. I have been a couple of times already. It is actually rather spectacular. Before my first trip, I had never been outside of the city. You will be amazed at how vast everything feels as we ride by. We will drive through fields that feel like they go on and on for miles. And forests and streams and farms. It is really beautiful. And at night. Oh, Annie, wait until nighttime! You won't believe your eyes when you see the stars."

"Really, Miss Sophie? What else will we see?"

"Cows and sheep and horses and chickens."

Annie wrinkled her nose again. "Won't they be stinky?"

Sophie giggled and so did the little girl. "Well, you won't be able to smell the animals from the train, but I do have to tell you that the train itself is a little stinky. But when we get off the train when it stops from time to time, you won't believe how sweet the air smells. It's the one thing that makes me wish I was staying behind when the train heads back to the city."

Annie looked at her seriously for a moment, making Sophie's heart clench for the world of experience she could see in the youngster's gaze despite her few years of life. She was relieved when the little girl broke into a grin. "That sure sounds nice."

"Wait until you see it for yourself. I promise, you will love it."

With a grin and a wave, the child hurried off to wash her face and get ready for her classes. Watching her go, Sophie realized her own spirits had been lifted by their conversation. She was reminded of the important work she was involved in here with the orphans. If Renton never returned, it meant the funding from Mrs. Rexford was secured. She needed to keep her focus on the children and their needs. Her own were secondary at most. Thus resolved and restored to a measure of her usual cheer, she got to her feet and set about clearing up from the children. With the help of the older children whose assignment it was to help in the cafeteria that day, it wasn't long before they had the entire room squared away.

Sophie was just on her way to her next task when Cassandra Morley, one of the wealthy young woman who volunteered at the orphanage, approached her with a wide grin.

"Sophie! I've been looking for you. There's someone down in Mrs. Parker's office looking for you."

"Good morning, Cassie! Who is it?"

Cassie just shook her head and grinned. "You'll have to go and see for yourself."

Frowning, Sophie went to the kitchen to remove her apron before hurrying to Mrs. Parker's office. When she got there, Mrs. Parker too had a wide grin on her face.

"Sophie, my dear, Mr. Rexford here has a few things to discuss with you. You may feel free to use my office for as long as you need. I shall be in the east classroom if you need me."

Sophie hadn't noticed Renton was there when she first stepped into the room, but as soon as she caught sight of him, she barely noticed as Mrs. Parker left the room. The wide smile on his face and warm twinkle in his eyes made her heart skip a beat and the butterflies take flight in her stomach. But she tried to maintain a dignified façade.

"Mr. Rexford, you wished to see me?"

"Yes, Miss Brooks, I did." He kept his tone serious, to match hers, but she could see his lips twitching with amusement.

"Are you laughing at me again, Mr. Rexford?"

"Maybe just a little," he replied as he stepped forward and grasped her hand. "I've come to make sure you uphold your end of our bargain."

Sophie's stomach dipped and danced as her hopes took flight once more. She'd had her hopes dashed so many times in her young life, but her stupid heart refused to listen as Sophie tried to tell it to stay calm. She could feel tears gathering behind her eyes, but she wasn't sure if they were of joy or despair. Her lips trembled slightly as she took in a breath. Her nerves clenched more deliciously as she noticed his focus narrow on her lips before he dragged his gaze back to her eyes. She managed to find a smile.

"What bargain are you speaking about, Mr. Rexford?" She needed him to spell it out for her. She couldn't afford any assumptions.

"You promised to allow me to court you if I could ensure that you and the children would be safe from my mother's interference."

She had to smile over the gentle way he paraphrased her fears and emphasized his request for a courtship. Her heart clenched with the depth of her feelings for the man. She couldn't do anything but nod.

"Is that a yes, that you are still amenable to my courtship?" Sophie couldn't believe that he would even need to ask.

"Of course, I am," she answered with a laugh.

With a chuckle, he stepped forward, grabbed her and twirled her around in a tight circle, mindful of her skirts in the small, crowded room. Sophie allowed her joy to bubble up into laughter, but she forced herself to remain cautious as he restored her to feet.

"So? What solution have you found to solve the issues at hand? Were you able to convince your mother?"

Renton shrugged. "I did speak with her briefly this morning before coming here, merely to tell her that if she wanted to maintain a place in my life and that of any future grandchildren, she would have to ensure that she was pleasant to whomever I chose to share my life."

Sophie blinked as her heart soared and sank all at once. It was lovely to hear a man declaring his feelings, or rather she supposed, implying them. But she couldn't find her own happiness at the sacrifice of the children. She didn't know what to say. Her wrought feelings must have been written on her face because Renton was quick to continue as he maintained his hold on her hands, squeezing them gently as though in admonition for her doubts.

“The wife of one of the business partners in our firm, I’m not sure if you’ve met her, Mrs. Fitzhugh, a delightful woman, you’ll enjoy her when you’ve become friends. Anyhow, she is in a constant rivalry with my mother. I visited her two days ago, and she was fascinated to hear about the good works being done by Mr. Brace and the Society. She will arrange a time for you to give her a tour when we go there for tea next week. I visited her again yesterday to hear all the details of the gala she has already made plans for to raise the needed funds to maintain the orphanage for the foreseeable future. Of course, I happened to mention this to my mother when I visited with her for a coffee this morning, so now she is in a tizzy of epic strategizing how she can arrange an even more successful fundraiser than Mrs. Fitzhugh. To benefit the Children’s Aid Society, of course. So you see, my darling, the orphanage and Mr. Brace’s Society will now have at least twice as much funding than it had, and it’s all thanks to you.”

Sophie broke into a fit of giggles. “Well, I rather think it is thanks to you. I will have to remember never to cross you. You are devious beyond belief but even more brilliant than I had realized.”

Renton bowed comically to her before growing serious once more. “So, once again, I will remind you, you and the children are now safe. I was happy to be of assistance to the dear orphans, and I have no intention of coercing you into a courtship with me, despite my words of a bargain. But, please, my dear Miss Sophie, do say you will allow it."

With a grin, Sophie dipped into a curtsy. "I would be honored, kind sir."

Renton grinned. "There's just one other thing, and I truly hope you don't think I am trying to take over control of your life because I promise you that I'm not. I know you are a smart, independent woman. It is actually one of the things I love about you, so I wouldn't want to take that away."

Sophie's joy led her to laugh again at his rambling. "Just say it, Renton, I promise to withhold judgment until you've explained yourself."

Renton smiled but maintained a worried mien. "It's about your trip on the train. I was so hoping you would agree to let me court you, and even that we could keep it short and sweet and soon begin our life together, you see, so I spoke to Cass Morley."

Sophie was again torn between a soaring heart and a frown over his words. "What do you mean?"

"She agreed that if you want to remain here, she would be happy to take your place with the children on the train."

"Really?" Her frown fled and Renton pulled her close again.

"Really. If you still want to go, I will try to maintain my patience. I will wait for you as long as you need, but I would ever so much rather get on with our future."

Sophie's heart fluttered and delicious shivers made their way down her spine, but she tried to keep a serious expression. "Do you have our future planned already, Mr. Rexford? I thought you promised me a courtship."

"I do promise you a courtship, my darling. One that will curl your toes with delight, I vow to you. But do not doubt that I have already made up my mind about you. The only purpose of the courtship is for you to be sure about me." He grinned sheepishly at her. "I don't want to scare you off, but you *have* met my mother. You aren't getting the very best bargain with me."

Sophie's joyful heart turned over in her chest, and she placed her palm gently on his cheek. "I beg to differ, Renton. You're the best bargain I will ever make."

With a soft whoop of joy, Renton bent his head and sealed their deal with a fervent kiss.

The End

Cassie

BOOK 2

Orphan Train Series

WENDY MAY ANDREWS

Sparrow Ink
www.sparrowdeck.com

www.wendymayandrews.com

She ran away and found home

Spring 1854

New York City debutante, Cassandra Morley has grown close to a trio of young brothers while volunteering at an orphanage. When the three boys are sent on the train to Missouri to be adopted, she accompanies them despite how displeased her high society family is likely to be.

Single rancher, Charles Ainsworth, is glad to be in a position to provide a new home for three brothers. He has no use for the citified young woman who keeps stopping by to check on them, despite how beautiful he finds her. He feels obligated to tolerate her visits to please his new sons.

Their differences cause them to fight their attraction to one another, but when one of the boys goes missing, they have to learn to trust each other in order to bring him home.

Dedication

To Marlene, Suzanne, Monique, and Alfred:

Thank you so much for the awesome critiques. Your help has been invaluable in moving this series along.

To Mum & Dad:

Thank you for being such great fans through this crazy path I'm travelling.

To Andrew:

You're the best husband, friend, travelling companion, and book formatter a girl could hope for. Thank you for being excited about my Orphan Train books. I love you to the moon and back.

Chapter One

As she stepped down from the train, Cassie quickly looked around and couldn't prevent the momentary scowl of distaste that covered her face before she smoothed out her features. It seemed the bright sun had bleached all color from the landscape, which was surprising since the train had passed enough bodies of water that everything should be perfectly lush. Every building in the small town was a dull gray. She supposed they just didn't much care about making it attractive. They had practicalities to worry about as they tried to expand and grow their enterprises. Cassie wrinkled her nose again as thoughts flitted through her mind, wondering what sort of activities kept the folks of Bucklin, Missouri busy. Clearly it wasn't painting their storefronts or planting flowers.

As she looked around, she saw the new arrivals were drawing considerable attention. It appeared even the townspeople were bleached out. There was very little color other than gray or brown wherever her gaze landed. Except for the piercing blue eyes of a disturbingly handsome man that seemed to be watching her intently.

Cassie shook her head and wrenched her eyes from the attractive face. "What have I done?" she asked herself for at least the tenth time in the past ten days. Her straw hat, which provided perfectly adequate protection in New York, was insufficient to keep her from squinting as she gazed about under the bright afternoon sun. She lifted her hand to provide a bit more shade for her eyes and a scowl marred her features once again as she saw how grubby her gloves had become.

That will teach you never to leave without a spare pair, won't it? she thought to herself with a slightly sardonic twist of her lips.

She forced her attention away from such senseless worries and back to the youngster holding tightly to her other hand. Cassie forced a cheerful smile to her lips and took a deep breath.

"Doesn't the air smell lovely here? Nothing like in New York, is it, Wally?"

Wally's worried face rearranged itself into a grin as he shook his head vigorously. "Do you think we'll like it here, Miss Cassie?"

Cassandra Marie Victoria Morley blinked at her young charge for a moment, and she swallowed the lump that had appeared suddenly in her throat. "I am quite convinced that you shall love it here, my dear boy. Now come along, all of you. We must gather our things and join the others. Let's not dawdle. The other children will be getting restless, and we don't want to keep the manager waiting. Your brand new lives await."

She was once again swept with awe and gratitude for the resilience of children. The six boys who had been entrusted to her accepted her feigned enthusiasm and quickly gathered their meager belongings. Cassie forced her eyes not to linger on the sight of her six charges and their small bundles of clothing. The anticipation and trepidation warring in their eyes caused the lump in her throat to grow and she couldn't allow them to see her distress. She covered her momentary weakness with brusque movement.

Tightening her grasp on Wally with one hand and her own bundle with the other, she admonished the other boys to stay close to her as they hurried to join the others. Unconsciously she found herself once again counting heads to make sure everyone was there. This wasn't her responsibility, of course, but she knew she would be unable to cope with the distress if they were to misplace any of the youngsters.

Finally, genuine amusement was able to make its way through the quagmire of her feelings while she watched the antics of some of the boys as they took advantage of being out in the open air after ten days cooped up on the train. It was futile for her to remind them to keep their clothes clean, but some of the other women were trying their best. Once again Cassie congratulated herself on the exercises she had made her boys do multiple times each day. She was quite certain it was the only reason the six were managing to contain themselves and remain by her side. That and the fact that her six were amongst the youngest of the large group, and they were still fearful of getting lost or separated from the familiar.

Her heart wrenched again. Cassie cleared her throat and blinked vigorously.

“Are you all right, Miss Cassie?” Wally’s little hand tugged on her.

“I am perfectly fine, my dear. I think some dust got in my eye is all.” Her explanation satisfied the small boy before their attention was snagged by the approach of a large, red-faced man.

“Welcome, welcome,” he boomed, obviously wanting to appear jolly. “I apologize that I was not here before the train’s arrival. It seems it arrived a little ahead of schedule.”

Cassie grinned as she saw Melanie check her watch and sniff skeptically. Her amusement died quickly when she remembered that her boys’ fates rested in this man’s seemingly incompetent hands. She tried to shake her negative thoughts and determined to wait and see what would unfold.

“You must be the manager.” Mrs. Parker stated the obvious, but Cassie knew it gave her a sense of control, so she tried not to allow her amusement to show. “We are more than ready to follow your lead, sir. What arrangements have been made for the children?”

“Well it is good that you arrived when you did. It will give us time to feed them all a little bit so they aren’t too rambunctious before their new families arrive. The last train load I oversaw in another town didn’t go very well because they were late and the youngsters were hungry and tired and cranky. We don't want to repeat that experience." The man's discomfort was apparent, and Cassie almost felt sympathetic for him at that moment, if not for the fact that he had yet to look at any of the boys. She wondered if he even liked children.

Mrs. Parker must have had serious doubts about the manager's competence, but there was nothing they could do at this point. She met the eyes of all the women with her as she looked around comprehensively. With a nod she took charge.

"You are Mr. McDonald, correct?" He had not introduced himself, and she was not about to follow a stranger out of the train station.

"Yes, yes, where are my manners? I do apologize. I was just so flummoxed from being late. You are Mrs. Parker, if I'm not mistaken?"

"That is correct. Very well, Mr. McDonald, lead us to whatever you have prepared for us. You are right in your assessment that the children would appreciate a meal and a chance to recover from the movement of the train before we proceed any further."

Without much more delay, they collected even the most rambunctious of the boys and made their way from the station.

By now Cassie's eyes had adjusted, for the most part, to the bright light, and she allowed herself to gaze about at the sights that confronted her. It was amazing to see how primitive it was. It felt like she had stepped back in time. One would think that by 1854 nowhere would be quite this backward. Obviously she was even more spoiled by her high life in New York than she had realized. It struck her as odd that there wasn't a single brick in sight. The strangeness of it all made her nervous, but she tried to hide her reaction from the others, ensuring that no one noticed her trepidation.

She could feel the interest their arrival had stirred in the tiny little town and was uncomfortably aware of many eyes examining her. Cassie lifted her chin, tightened her hold on the small hand in hers, and followed the others as they made their way from the station.

ꕥ

He watched the large group as they made their way from the station. Everyone in the area would easily be able to tell who they were. Most, in fact, were anticipating adding to their households with at least one of the new arrivals. He hadn't realized the children would be accompanied by ladies, not that he had given the matter much thought. Now that he was thinking on it, it made sense that the children would not be able to travel on their own. He wondered what manner of woman would accompany a bunch of orphans to their new home. The ones he had noticed seemed to be widely varying. The young-looking one had certainly caught his eye. She had actually looked slightly familiar. It was probably just her New York attitude that had been clearly stamped on her face and had almost marred her beauty.

Charles gave his head a shake. He was not in the market for a wife. Women were nothing but trouble. That was why he was interested in some of the boys who had just arrived. A man in his position needed to have sons. This was the best way to get one, or more, without cluttering up his life with a woman.

Straightening from the post he had been leaning upon, Charles shoved his hat back on his head after wiping away the perspiration that had gathered. If it was already this hot in April, it didn't bode well for what kind of summer they'd be having. There was no sense in standing around; they wouldn't be gathering the children until later that afternoon.

But despite his determination, he could not prevent his eyes from following the young woman's progress as she made her way down the sidewalk. He should have been turned off by the look of revulsion he had seen on her face as she gazed about at the town. He had no interest in high maintenance city girls. Her fancy clothes and disapproving glance told him she was far too complicated for the likes of him. But it had also been impossible to miss the tender look she had bestowed upon the boys in her care. And her physical beauty was downright arresting. Besides, he reasoned with himself, she would obviously not be staying in town for more than a couple of days; there was no harm in feasting his eyes upon her. Convinced, he relaxed back into a slouch in the shade of the overhang in front of the saloon.

His curiosity was stirred by the new arrivals. He hadn't expected so many children to be accompanied by so few adults, and only women at that. He wondered again what manner of woman would have volunteered for such a task. The one he had noticed most appeared to be quite young despite the scowl that had painted her face. Her curly, yellow hair had reflected the sun's rays in quite a fascinating manner. He couldn't quite see the color of her eyes, as they were shaded by her bonnet, but he couldn't help but note her slender build. *Such a wispy little thing wouldn't last longer than a couple days in an environment such as this*, he thought with another shake of his head.

It didn't matter much to him, he insisted to himself. No woman was going to be his responsibility, especially not out here in the wilds of Missouri. He reminded himself once more that he loved the wilds of Missouri and ignored the motivations that kept his eyes fixed to the retreating form of the beautiful young woman from the train.

"Why are so many people watching us, Miss Cassie?"

Cassie glanced down at the boy by her side and strove for a neutral expression. "There aren't very many people around, Wally, so there aren't that many watching us."

"But all of them are watching us."

She couldn't argue with the youngster's words. Everyone *was* watching them. It looked to her as though the entire population of the small town had turned out to observe their arrival.

"They probably don't get very many visitors around here, so they're curious about us. Besides, all these handsome young men to look at, they cannot help but stare." She realized her explanation was probably the truth. The further west they had travelled, the more sparsely populated the countryside had become. And they had arrived at the most western stop of the train line. She had heard the train company was planning to lay more track, but for now, this was as far as you could go by train. If you wanted to go any further west, you would have to travel by wagon. The thought of any more travel turned her stomach sour. The thought of being this isolated also made her shiver. But she didn't want Walter or his brothers to sense her discomfort, so she quickly continued talking.

"This is also the first time Mr. Brace has sent any of the orphans this far away, so it's very new for this town. It is to be expected that everyone would be curious."

"Are they going to like us, Miss Cassie?"

"They are going to love you, my dear boy. They will not be able to help themselves." She let go of his hand and pulled him closer to her side in a quick hug. Conscious of his manly pride despite being only six, she didn't prolong the contact and quickly let him go. She could see he appreciated the gesture by his bashful smile and the glance she received from him from beneath his eyelashes.

Both shaking themselves from the sentimental moment, they hurried to catch up with the others.

Chapter Two

Cassie watched Mr. McDonald closely as he wandered around the room. She could tell the man was trying to appear as though he were taking an interest in everyone, but she hadn't detected even an ounce of warmth in him as he spoke briefly to the boys who were huddling near her. Her heart constricted as she thought of the fear the youngsters were valiantly trying to hide. The round, balding man had gone to no effort to alleviate the fear that anyone with eyes could have seen written on their faces.

"Will you be heading back to New York on the next train?" Katie asked, making Cassie jump since she had not noticed her approach, so caught up was she in worrying about the incompetence of the manager.

Cassie turned to the other woman with a smile. "I don't think so."

"Your parents are going to be furious," Katie warned.

"They are going to be furious no matter what. Staying here a little longer isn't going to make any difference. In fact, it might help if it allows them time to get over their initial upset." Cassie couldn't help her negligent shrug. She really wasn't overly concerned about her parents' feelings on the matter. She had notified them of her intentions. If they didn't like it, that was their problem, not hers.

"I would have thought you would be anxious to get back to your life in the city," Katie persisted, obviously perplexed by the younger woman's decision to remain in the small town. "Is this not a rather backward place for you?"

Cassie huffed an impatient breath. "Of course it is. It's a backward place for all of us," she reminded her companion. "Are you overwhelmed with a desire to remain here for the scenery?"

It was obvious from her expression that Katie agreed, but she still argued, "I would imagine the scenery would be quite beautiful if it wasn't so dry and hot. But I always planned on staying. You never even intended to come. So I'm curious as to what could persuade you to be so long gone from your comfortable life back home."

Cassie held her breath and counted to ten, trying to swallow down the surge of anger she felt over the other woman's words. She couldn't really blame Katie for her opinion. Miss Cassandra Morley was a New York debutante, the spoiled only daughter of a wealthy landowner. This was quite decidedly not her usual milieu. And the other woman probably couldn't imagine why anyone would leave her life, even for a brief time. But volunteering at the orphanage, something she had originally done to prevent people from thinking her a complete egoist, had become the highlight of her days. She had become so attached to the children, and when she had found out some of her charges were being sent on the next orphan train, she had felt compelled to accompany them in order to ensure they found good homes.

She had begged her parents to adopt a few of the children. They had refused. Of course, Cassie was well aware the problem was too large for her parents to be able to solve it on their own, but she had been appalled by their attitude toward the poor abandoned waifs. She knew this fresh start in the Midwest was the children's best chance for a good life. Provided the incompetent manager undertook to get them placed, that is. There was no way Cassie could leave until she was sure her darlings were going to be well cared for. She would deal with the consequences of her parents' anger later.

Returning her attention to Katie's question, Cassie hoped her polite smile had not slipped. "Just as you are curious, so am I, Katie. I find I cannot bear to head back until I know for certain that the children will prosper."

There was enough truth in her answer to give it the twang of sincerity, and Cassie blew a small sigh of relief when Katie merely threw her a slightly puzzled glance before her attention was turned by a question one of the youngsters had posed. Cassie allowed her gaze to return to Mr. McDonald. She tried to keep a frown from forming on her face as she watched him talking with some of the townspeople. With another sigh, she realized she would have to write a letter to

Mr. Brace warning him of the manager's unsavory demeanor. Cassie was worried his manner would turn off sincere folks who wanted to help the children while attracting those who might exploit the defenceless orphans.

"You aren't developing a tender for Mr. McDonald, are you, my dear girl? Surely with all the gentlemen present this evening, you could find a more worthy object for your affections."

Cassie gasped over the audacious words and the impudence of the one uttering them. She tried to ignore the shiver that threatened to slither up her spine over the delicious, deep timbre of the low, male voice near her ear. She turned to confront the speaker, shocked and dismayed to find it was the handsome man she had seen across the street from the train station when they arrived.

She was repulsed by his implication, despite the veracity of his words. In her opinion, nearly any man would be more worthy than Mr. McDonald. But the stranger's impudence could not be tolerated. The man deserved a set down.

Pulling herself to her tallest height, which she couldn't help noticing was still only around his chin level, Cassie gazed down her nose in her best imitation of her mother's proud stance. "My affections are none of your concern."

To her chagrin, it did not have the desired effect. The bounder laughed, which made her feel as though her blood was about to boil. She could feel hot color flooding her cheeks, but she decided to ignore it and him. She turned on her heel and marched over to Miss Melanie Jones.

Trying to hide her discomfort over the stranger's words, Cassie asked Miss Jones for a progress report. "Do you know what the delay is, Miss Mel? I understood this meeting was set to commence at 3:30. It is now 3:40."

Cassie was instantly soothed by the other woman's calm smile. "As I understand it, things are not always as organized as we are accustomed to out here in the wilds, my dear Cassie. It would seem Mr. McDonald is expecting more people to turn up, and he doesn't want to start without them."

Cassie glanced around once more, noting the people milling around, speaking to the children. "I guess it would be best if there are more people. I'm not sure if there are enough here right now to look after our lot."

"Unless some of them are planning to take more than one."

"Do you think anyone would be willing to take more than one boy? It would be wonderful if Wally and his brothers could be placed together." Cassie hadn't wanted to give voice to her deepest concern before then.

"I pray you don't get your hopes up, my dear. Three young boys would be a lot to take on for most people."

"I know, Melly, but the thought of those boys being separated from one another nearly breaks my heart."

The other woman apparently didn't have any wisdom to offer because she merely grasped Cassie's hand in a warm clasp for a moment before they drifted away from one another to check once more on the children. The boys were getting restless and needed to be distracted in order to keep them on their best behavior while still on display in front of their potential new families.

As much as Cassie thought this was a great opportunity for the children to find new homes and a better future than the stews of New York had offered them, the experience of watching strangers examining her charges put her in mind of a retail experience, and she was beginning to find it repugnant. She was quite certain she would not be returning to repeat the experience ever again. Perhaps she would have to find a new project when she returned home, as this one was threatening to be a heart breaking one.

"Are my new parents here, Miss Cassie?" Walter asked her anxiously.

"I surely hope so, Wally," she answered with as much positivity as she could infuse into her voice.

"Which ones are they?" he asked, his eager eyes darting around the room.

"Heavens, I don't know. We'll have to wait and see what Mr. McDonald says. Oh, hush now, it looks as though he's finally going to get things under way."

Cassie watched and tried to keep the skepticism from her face as the placement agent stepped to the front of the room and cleared his throat loudly.

"Good afternoon, everyone. Thank you so much for coming. We have a roomful of youngsters here that could use your help and are looking forward to being a part of your lives."

Cassie stifled her sigh. The words he was saying were great — if only he could inject a note of sincerity into his voice, she might actually believe that he meant it. She bit her lip to prevent any tears from forming as she glanced at the boys by her side. As she was returning her gaze to the speaker, it was snagged by the handsome cowboy who had been so rude to her. He was watching her intently, so she shot a scowl at him before dragging her attention back to what Mr. McDonald was saying.

ꕥ

The young woman was so beautiful it made him uncomfortable. Charles fought his grin. She was obviously one of those females who was always changing her mind about how she felt. There weren't nearly enough women this far from the East Coast — why did such a complicated one have to turn up in his town? He had the impression she was a spoiled little rich girl, but then he saw her tenderness with the youngsters in her charge and was amazed at how the boys huddled around her. They were too young to be responding to her beauty. *They must actually like the young woman*, he marvelled, as he struggled to maintain his neutral expression after she sent that glare in his direction. She was obviously determined to keep him in his place.

It had not been well of him to be vulgar towards her earlier, but she brought out such strange reactions in him. He did not doubt it was the air of monied privilege that hung about her, despite her association with the orphans. He hadn't even had a conversation with her, but he had heard her speak. Her accent and vocabulary, besides the obvious quality of her now travel-worn clothes, all screamed privileged background. He wondered how the poor dear was managing so far from the gilded halls she had obviously grown up in. He searched his memory, trying to determine why she looked so familiar. She was far too young to have been an acquaintance of his. Perhaps he knew her parents.

Charles dragged his attention away from its infatuation with the beautiful blonde and endeavored to focus on what the manager was saying. Despite how irritating he found the other man, Charles was determined to collect a few of the children for himself. It was a worthy cause and the only way he could envision himself achieving the status of father figure. And to be sure, his spread could use some extra hands to help, even if they were little ones.

Thankfully the dull-witted agent kept his message short, merely reminding everyone of what they had agreed to in relation to the boys – namely to educate them and provide for them as though they were members of the family until they reached the age of seventeen years. Charles glanced around and observed varying degrees of agreement amongst the assembled crowd. He'd had no trouble getting members of the committee to vouch for him, but he wondered how some of those present had managed to get anyone to agree to entrust them with young lives. He made a mental note to keep an eye out for some of the others. He wished he could take the entire lot of youngsters, but he reminded himself once more that was not a liveable solution.

Now the agent was reading out the names of the new parents that had already been matched up with some of the boys. Charles looked around, anxious to know who would be joining his life. He was surprised when there was a stir around the beautiful blonde after his name was read followed by the names of three boys.

"Did you hear that, Miss Cassie? We get to stay together."

She quickly hushed him, but Charles could see that she was not unaffected by the news. Her smile had begun to wobble, and he could see the tears welling in her eyes that she quickly blinked away. Charles did not want to find her any more appealing than he already did. Seeing her as a warm, compassionate woman did not help him. He gritted his teeth and determined to ignore her.

That was far easier said than done. When Mr. McDonald stopped talking, Charles had to go meet the boys who would be coming home with him. Unfortunately, they were still clinging to the beautiful blonde. He forced himself to approach her once more as he fought the urge to apologize for his previous behavior.

"Hello," he began, after clearing his throat to alleviate his unexpected nervousness.

He could see that she was trying to ignore him, but the boys by her side did not do so.

"Are you going to be our father?"

Charles looked down into the earnest young faces and felt his hardened heart crack just a little bit. “I sure hope so — if you'll have me,” he answered. “What's your name?”

“I'm Anton, but you can call me Tony,” came the reply. “These two are Walter and Ross. They're twins. They're six. I just turned ten.”

“It's a pleasure to meet the three of you, Tony. Are you ready to go?”

This question brought a quiet sound of distress from the one member of the group he had not yet acknowledged, forcing his eyes to search her face. He could see that she was trying to hide her reaction, but she obviously had not expected them to be leaving her side so soon. It was also apparent that she was embarrassed to have revealed her feelings. Charles was amused to see her efforts to place a glare back onto her face despite her wet eyes.

“Where is your wife?” she asked, her tone accusing.

“I don't have one.”

His reply made her blink. “How do you intend to care for these boys on your own?”

“Well, they strike me as fine young men that shan't require a mother, since they're clearly big enough to be house broken.”

He had to bite his tongue to control his laughter as hot color rose in her neck and cheeks. He could tell she wanted to smack him but was too polite to do so. It was fascinating to watch her try to draw her composure around herself.

"Are you quite sure you are prepared to take three youngsters into your home all at once? Perhaps there was some sort of mistake with Mr. McDonald." Her feelings were clearly torn on the subject. Charles guessed that she wouldn't want the boys to be taken away from each other, but she doubted his ability to care for them.

"No mistake, ma'am," he replied politely, keeping a straight face before he took pity on her and explained. "I had originally signed up for two boys, but when I heard about these three brothers, I figured there wouldn't be very many who'd be in a position to add three to their household, and it would be terrible for them to be broken up. So I said I'd be happy to have them."

Her face now grew even more suspicious. "What does a single man want with three boys?"

Charles was becoming tired of her issues. "Not that it's any of your business, ma'am, but I have a large spread that I could use some sons to help me with. Seeing as I don't have a wife, this is the best way for me to gain some."

Seeing her expression soften once more only served to irritate Charles, so he turned his shoulder to her and crouched down in front of the younger two boys. "Do you have all of your stuff with you, or do we need to go somewhere to pick it up? I would just as rather get going so we can get you nicely settled before it gets dark."

"We have our stuff with us, mister. We didn't have very much to bring," Ross answered while Walter turned his face into the blonde's skirt.

She quickly kneeled down in front of the boy. "Oh, Wally, don't you worry. This nice man is going to take you and your brothers home with him. I bet he has some lovely horses he'll let you help him with. Isn't that right, mister?" She broke off as their eyes met. Charles let the silence drag for a moment as he almost got lost in her bottomless gaze.

That silence was broken as the youngster still clinging to her asked, his voice plaintive, "But aren't you going to come with us, Miss Cassie?"

Chapter Three

Cassie felt as though her heart was being wrung right out of her chest with Walter's question. The silence stretched for an uncomfortable moment before she kneeled down in front of the boy.

"My dear, you do realize that you're going to stay with Mister—" there was a pause while she digested the fact that she didn't even know the man's name. She quickly carried on. "You're going to go stay with this nice man. I bet he's actually a real, live cowboy. You are going to love it at his house." She bit her lip, willing her tears to stay away, praying that she was not lying to the little boy.

"But I want you to come, too," the little boy insisted, his tone starting to become a bit querulous.

The only thing Cassie could do was pull him into her arms and give him a tight hug. "I know, my darling, but I can't come to stay with you."

When he pulled back from her arms and looked at her with tears welling in his eyes, Cassie's heart cracked, and she looked at the cowboy in desperation. She didn't know what to do about the fact that he merely gazed back at her, showing no reaction to her plight or the child's distress. Now Cassie had another thing to worry about. *Will these dear boys be in good hands with this man? I never should have volunteered at the orphanage,* she thought in despair, but it was far too late for that, she already cared too deeply for the children. She would have to stay in town long enough to ensure they were well cared for. While she had grown closest to Walter and his brothers, Cassie was concerned for all the children they had brought with them.

With that determination, Cassie stood and turned to the taciturn man watching her. A part of her wanted to turn on her heel and sweep from the building without ever giving the man a second thought, but if he was going to have the care of the boys, she would have to swallow her pride and make peace with him.

She tried for a conciliatory smile and put her hand out to shake his. After a brief hesitation, he engulfed her small hand in his warm one. The sensation was distracting, but Cassie ignored it. "My name is Cassandra Morley. I fear I was so caught up with the children that I failed to introduce myself."

Cassie was surprised to see that the man looked as though he wished to ignore her introduction, but he must've been raised properly and his inborn manners won out. "I'm Charles Ainsworth." He kept his response as brief as possible.

Swallowing back her ire, Cassie was sure her smile was slipping and did her best not to grimace at the uncommunicative cowboy. "Would it be acceptable with you, Mr. Ainsworth, if I were to visit the boys a time or two before I leave town? It might help them adjust to their new surroundings" —she paused for a moment before admitting in a rush— "and I've grown rather fond of them and find I cannot yet bear to say goodbye."

She was surprised to see him appear to soften toward her but then thought it had been all in her imagination as he began to frown. She thought he was going to refuse her request and was preparing to argue when he again surprised her by agreeing. "There shouldn't be any harm in you stopping by. Anyone in town will be able to give you directions."

She dipped her head in acknowledgement, not bothering to say anything as the man was obviously not overly fond of words. Instead she kneeled down next to Walter once more.

"See now, Wally my dear, it is settled. You go with your brothers with Mr. Ainsworth, and I will come and see you. You will have so much to tell me and show me when I come to visit you. Won't that be lovely?"

Walter didn't look completely convinced, but he finally let go of her and followed his brothers as they were being ushered out by their new guardian. Cassie had to turn away so she wouldn't give way to tears. She didn't know how she would be able to enforce it, but that man had better treat her boys well or she would figure out a way to make him pay, she thought with a fierce protectiveness she had never felt before.

Struggling to maintain her composure, Cassie turned away, not able to watch as the boys left with their new guardian. She was grateful to see Mrs.

Parker approach. Hopefully she had an assignment for her. She could use the distraction.

Charles breathed a sigh of relief as soon as they were away from the lovely blonde. It had been obvious to him that she was distressed about saying goodbye to the children, but she had been valiantly trying to hide her feelings. He did not want to find her attractive and had to fight the urge to comfort her. Maybe he should have allowed the boys longer to say their goodbyes to her, but he doubted drawing it out would have made it any less painful. And he had been correct about why she had looked familiar to him. He was fairly certain he had met her father. It wasn't likely there were too many rich Morleys in New York City.

"So do you have horses, Mr. Charles?" the little guy asked him. What was his name? Oh yes, Walter.

"I have lots of them, Walter," he answered, startled when he felt a small hand slipping into his. He didn't think he had ever held a child's hand before. It made the strangest sensation spread in his chest. Instinctively, he wanted to let go but knew that would hurt the boy's feelings and damage their chances of developing a relationship. Charles rather thought the boy was a little old for wanting to hold hands. Even his twin brother was hurrying along, trying to swagger like the older boy. On further consideration, though, Charles thought that the loss of his parents might have made him more emotionally fragile. He was going to have to think about how to help the youngsters deal with their loss and settle into life here on the prairies. Maybe he should have talked with the young woman a little longer. She was probably more in touch with feelings than he was.

But she was also a beautiful, young woman from the city, and she would have no idea how to ease these boys into life on his spread. He was on his own with this challenge. He reminded himself that he was an intelligent, competent, successful man. He could manage these three youngsters just fine on his own. And he wouldn't be truly on his own, anyway. There were all his hired hands that helped on his spread. Surely they would be of assistance. The boys would love them as much as he did, he was sure.

He realized the boy was still gazing at him expectantly, and he thought back to their conversation. They had been talking about horses.

"Have you ever ridden on a horse?"

The vigorous shaking of the boy's head lead Charles to wonder if he would be afraid of horses.

"Have you ever seen a horse up close?"

"No," was the response, accompanied by more head shaking.

"Do you want to?"

Finally there was some nodding of his head. Charles felt relief spread through him. "Well now you'll get your chance. We'll have to ride in my wagon to get home, and it's pulled by two horses."

"Will they like me?"

Charles stifled a sigh. His misgivings were correct. The youngster had all sorts of negative feelings that would have to be sorted out, poor little mite. “I’m sure they will. They’re fairly reasonable nags. If you were to offer them a carrot or an apple, they’d probably be your friend for life.”

“But I don’t have any carrots or apples,” Walter worried.

“I’ve got plenty at home, don’t worry. Now come along, your brothers are going to get away on us.” Charles was relieved to note that this worked magically on the boy to hurry him along. Within moments, they joined Ross and Tony and reached the Smithy where he had left his wagon.

All three boys were pretty excited about the horses, making Charles glad he had brought that particular pair. He had other, more excitable horses that would have found the attention a bit much. But the two mature mares took it all in stride, almost as though they recognized how young the boys were and thus their inexperience was tolerable.

Before long they were all loaded up and rattling their way along the rutted road toward his property. The boundary of his property wasn’t too terribly far from the town, but it would take them a little while to get to the house. The laughter from the boys as they bounced around in the back of the wagon reminded him that he ought to do something about how rough the road was. He mentally added one more item to the long list of things he needed to do.

He was content with his decision to add the youngsters to his household, no matter how much work they might be. He was tired of being alone out here on the prairies. He did not regret his decision to leave his old life behind and usually enjoyed the solitude this vast land offered, but he was glad that he would now have others to share his life with. And a man ought to have heirs to leave the fruitage of his hard work to, whether they were of his own blood or not. His parents would never agree with such a sentiment, but he couldn't be bothered to care about their thoughts on the matter. He shook himself from the maudlin train of thought and tried to engage the boys in conversation.

"Tell me about yourselves, boys," he began. The silence that followed reminded him that this was too broad of a conversation starter, especially when dealing with youngsters. He glanced back to see how they were reacting.

Charles had to stifle the urge to chuckle over their wide-eyed confusion as they nudged one another, urging the oldest to say something. He spoke up, focusing the conversation.

"Have the three of you been in school?"

Now Tony spoke for all of them. "Yes," he answered briefly at first, but when Charles remained silent, the boy elaborated. "When I was little, our mother taught me, but then when we were on the street, after our parents died, none of us could go to school. We learned lots on the street, but it's not what most would consider proper. Then Mr. Brace, the man who arranged for us to come on the train, is really big on schooling. He doesn't have much care for anyone who doesn't want to learn. He says learning's the only way we're going to get ourselves anywhere in life."

"He sounds like a wise man," Charles commented. He thought he ought to comment on the loss of their parents but wasn't sure what to say. While he was still debating with himself, the boy continued.

"But look how far we've come, and I don't see how it has anything to do with learning."

Charles again had to stifle his amusement over the boy's reasoning.

"Mr. Brace sounds like he must be a well-educated man. You came all this way because of his success. But you're still youngsters. If you want to have your own success when you're grown up, you'll need an education for that."

"Miss Cassie says the same thing. She was pretty nice about it, but she still insisted we had to do our studies, even on the train. Even during the first couple days when Ross' tummy felt poorly, Miss Cassie made us read to him. She said it was probably just the movement of the train making him sick and it was just his tummy, not his brain, so he could still learn."

Now Charles couldn't hold back his laughter. The boy sounded so aggrieved by this strange adult behavior. But Charles wanted to learn more about the boys so he pressed on.

"What have you been learning? Do you enjoy any of it?"

Walter spoke up then. "I loved all of it when Miss Cassie was the one teaching." This brought another chuckle from Charles, but he waited for the other boys to chime in.

Tony went into more detail. “All three of us know how to read fairly well. The twins are still learning the bigger words, but they do pretty good. The numbers is where we have a bit more difficulty. We don’t really see why we need to know that stuff.”

Ross finally made himself heard. “Miss Cassie said there’s any number of reasons why we’ll need to know how to add and subtract.”

Charles responded, “I will have to agree with Miss Cassie. I need to know how to deal with numbers all the time. Mostly to make sure I’m not getting cheated by anyone.”

Tony stared at him with an attentive gaze.

Charles continued, “I’ll show you the next time we go to the store.” This produced three identical grins from the youngsters behind him. Charles laughed again. He hadn’t felt this positive in ages. He realized he was grinning back at the boys and tried to return to a more serious mien.

After clearing his throat, Charles commented, “I’m glad to hear you aren’t completely averse to going to school. You’re all going to need at least a few more years of school.”

This did not meet with any enthusiasm but Charles was glad he didn’t get much resistance from them either. But then Anton wrinkled his nose. “Didn’t you tell Miss Cassie that you needed help on your land? How are we going to help you if we’re off at school?”

“Well school isn’t every single day, and it’s not all year round, so there will be plenty of time for you to lend a hand.”

There was silence for a moment while the boys pondered his words. Then Walter piped up with another question.

"How come you don't got a wife, Mister Charles?"

"Have," Charles automatically corrected, shocking himself by it instinctively coming out of his mouth.

"Hunh?" Walter didn't understand.

"You should have asked, how come you don't have a wife," Charles repeated, wondering why he had bothered. This wasn't really the time for a grammar lesson. "Never mind. I don't have a wife because there aren't too many women out here in the wilds of Missouri, and I haven't yet met one that I would consider spending all my days with."

"Miss Cassie isn't married. She'd probably be a good wife," the little boy persisted.

"I think Miss Cassie would be too much work. Besides, she's going back to New York. I don't think she'll stick around these parts much longer than it takes to book a ticket on the next train headed east."

After glancing at the troubled expressions on the boys' faces, Charles realized he should not have said anything less than positive about the youngsters' friend, so he quickly changed the subject.

"We're just about home, boys. You'll have to figure out which bedrooms you'll want to use. We'll get you settled and have our supper. I think a tour of the place will have to wait until tomorrow." This certainly did the job of distracting them. It became apparent they were undecided about the thought of having separate bedrooms.

After exchanging uneasy glances with his brothers, Anton spoke up. "Your house is so big that you have extra rooms?" he asked with surprise.

"Out here there's plenty of space. There's no need to be crammed together like you're probably used to from the city."

"Are you rich?" The boy sounded suspicious.

Charles laughed. "Having a house with more than one bedroom does not necessarily mean a man is rich, Tony."

The boy, despite his rough background, had the grace to realize his question was probably not a polite one, and color could be seen flooding his cheeks. Charles laughed again. "Don't let it trouble you. We're going to be family. I want you to be comfortable to ask me whatever you want."

Tony ducked his head in an awkward nod before getting to the crux of the issue. "We've never slept anywhere but together pretty much since my brothers were born. They probably won't be able to sleep if I'm not with them. And there's only one of me, so maybe it would be better if we still share."

Charles managed to keep from laughing at the boy's serious tone. Of course, he would never admit that he might not be able to bear the separation either. But to spare all of their feelings, Charles merely nodded. "I never thought about how much you'll have to get used to out here since nearly everything will be different than you're used to. Why don't we start out with the three of you sharing the room next to mine, that way I'll be able to hear you if there are any problems in the night. Then, if you change your mind, we can always change it around later."

All he got was solemn silence after his words, so he was glad when, at that moment, they rounded the bend in the road and his homestead could be seen through an opening in the trees. Quiet gasps came from the boys. Charles was a little nervous about their reactions after the conversation they had just had, but when he turned to look at them all he could see was their wide grins.

"I think we're going to like living with you, mister," Ross quietly said as the three brothers stared around with wide eyes, trying to take everything in, even as the light was beginning to fade.

Charles pulled his pair of horses to a standstill near the barn. "We just have to look after these ladies before we head in to get ourselves settled. There's no time like the present for you three to start learning how to look after our animals."

Chapter Four

Cassie tried to keep a smile pinned to her face while Katie hovered over her. It wasn't that hard to do, actually, when one considered how funny it must look for the tiny little widow to be trying to hover over her when Cassie was at least half a head taller than Katie. But she appreciated the sentiment behind the actions, so she refrained from laughing.

Gazing at her friend, Cassie shook her head in wonder. "How could you bear to do this trip more than once? I can't believe this is your third time to escort a train full of children away from the city."

Katie's eyes softened as she took in her friend's distress. "I know it's hard to say good bye to the children, but I am absolutely convinced that they will have a far better life out here than they would as gutter snipes in New York. What future would there be for Wally if he had stayed in the city?"

"Oh, I believe you — that's not the issue. I know the boys have a far better chance here than they ever did back home. But how could you bear to part with them?" To her dismay, a tear slid down her cheek as she said those words. She hated to admit to such feelings. Her mother would be aghast at such a display of emotion. But she would have to be made of stone to feel nothing over parting with the dear boys.

"Oh my poor dear," Katie crooned as she pulled Cassie into a warm hug.

Cassie chuckled through her tears. "You can barely reach me and yet you're going to comfort me?"

Katie joined her in laughter and shrugged lightly. "Just because I can barely reach your towering height doesn't mean I can't still offer you a shoulder to cry on."

Cassie laughed again but then pulled herself together. "Morleys don't cry." She offered her friend a soft smile to take the sting out of her rejection of the comfort Katie was offering.

Much to Cassie's regret, Katie looked embarrassed. She quickly rallied and smiled kindly at Cassie. "Morleys may not cry, but I know for a fact that you have a huge heart, and it is perfectly all right to have feelings, you know." There was a slight pause before the older girl continued. "To answer your question, it was far from easy to make any of these trips. And I don't think I can do it anymore. I am actually planning to stay here in Bucklin. There is nothing for me in New York. I need a fresh start. I was working at the orphanage to try to get over the loss I had faced. But as you pointed out, it carries the pain of continual loss, and I don't want to face any more."

Cassie was fascinated with the other woman's decision. "What will you do here?"

"In a town like this, there will be no shortage of opportunities. With an influx of children like this, they will probably need at least one new teacher. The town could probably use a seamstress. The doctor might need an assistant. I doubt I will have trouble finding something to occupy me."

"I have noticed that the male population far outnumbers that of the female. You would have no trouble finding another husband," Cassie pointed out.

"I will never remarry."

Cassie was surprised at the vehemence in Katie's declaration and regretted her statement. She had only been teasing. From what she could see, all the men were much too rough for her taste, so she couldn't blame her friend for not wanting any of them. But she couldn't help her concern and had to point it out to the other woman.

"Don't you think this is a little bit rough of an environment for a woman on her own? Won't you be a little nervous staying here?"

"Cassie, my dear, New York is just as dangerous, perhaps even more so, for a woman on her own. Most of us don't have rich, protective fathers to provide for us."

Cassie felt hot color creeping up her cheeks at her friend's words, no matter how kindly her tone had been. She could no longer meet Katie's gaze. Katie must have regretted what she said as she quickly changed the subject.

"Never mind about me, I have no idea yet what I'm going to do. What about you? Are you going to catch the next train back to New York? I'm pretty sure there's supposed to be another train the day after tomorrow."

With a sigh, Cassie shook her head. She couldn't prevent her frown as she allowed her gaze to sweep over what she could see of the town. "No, despite my discomfort here, I cannot leave yet. The man who was placed in charge of the orphans here does not inspire me with confidence. I have to stay and make sure the children are going to be all right. I know they haven't all yet been placed with families. And I mean to check on all of the ones that have been." When she saw Katie's puzzled expression, she quickly continued, "I feel responsible for them, Katie. I never should have started spending time at the orphanage, but now that I have, I have grown quite fond of the children. And since I made the impulsive choice to come as an escort with the children here to Missouri when one of the others who was supposed to go got sick, I have to make sure they will be well cared for. My conscience would never let me rest if I found out later that they were placed in a bad situation and no one had done anything about it."

"Since I'm staying here, you could leave it with me."

Cassie squeezed her friend's hand. "I know, my dear, but I feel like I need to see with my own eyes that each one is fine. Then I will get myself safely back to my own life. And as soon as I get back to New York, I will find something else to do with my time. I have absolutely no intention of spending any more time with orphans. My weak heart cannot bear it."

"I've always meant to ask you, what ever prompted you to volunteer at the orphanage in the first place? I must say, when you turned up, no one expected you to last longer than the first day."

There was so much truth to the statement that Cassie could not take offense. "The whys and wherefores are a much too long story. We need to be seeing about getting some food for ourselves. I have a sneaky suspicion that tomorrow is going to be a long day."

ꕥ

Cassie squinted against the bright sun filling her room. She had slept deeply, her first night in almost two weeks not spent on a train. She hadn't realized quite how tired she had been. But now, feeling fully restored, she regretted not asking to be awakened at an earlier hour. If she wasn't careful, she would allow the day to pass her by with nothing to show for it. She mustn't tarry in this town; it would be hard enough to convince her parents to forgive her as it was. Overstaying in Missouri would surely anger them further.

With that thought, Cassie resolved to visit the telegraph office in order to inform her family that she had arrived safely in Missouri and would be returning shortly. She needn't tell them how long shortly might be. She could see her own wry smile on her face as she glanced in the mirror while she arranged her hair. Getting back to civilization would certainly have its perks, she reminded herself as she lamented her poor skills at styling her hair and wished for her mother's maid to have accompanied her.

She couldn't help chuckling over that thought. Her parents might be upset with her for leaving New York on impulse, but her mother would never have forgiven the breach of taking her maid from her. Cassie's critical eye surveyed her appearance. She was sufficiently satisfied with the efforts the hotel's staff had gone to in order to tidy up her clothes. The worst of the travel wear had been removed, so she was adequately presentable. And she doubted anyone would be able to find fault with her hairstyle. This was far from New York, and no one here knew her or her family. All she really needed was to be clean and tidy. And she could easily manage that without the help of a maid.

Cassie was determined not to be the spoiled rich girl others thought she was. Out here in Missouri, no one knew who the Morleys were, and she rather liked it. Others would judge her for herself, not any preconceived notions. Even if she was only going to be here for a few days, she was determined to make the most of them.

With one last pat to her blonde curls, now under firm control with a multitude of pins, Cassie frowned at her reflection before pinning a neutral smile to her face and sweeping from the small room. First on her agenda would need to be food, she realized as her stomach began to grumble when she caught the smell of baking bread wafting up the stairs. She went down one flight into the saloon. She had been put to the blush the previous night when she had realized that the only accommodation available was over the saloon. Fortunately the owner had appeared to be reasonably respectable. Cassie comforted herself with the realization that no one in New York need ever know where she had slept while away. As long as she was kept safe and warm, she would accept what was on offer. It wouldn't be for too long, she reminded herself once more.

Refusing to dilly dally like a widgeon, Cassie hurried to seat herself at a table. The bartender had promised that there would be food available, and Cassie was starving. Before long she was served. She quickly disposed of the meal and then hurried from the room. Despite it being empty, Cassie could not be comfortable spending any time in what she suspected would be a disreputable place at night.

She was glad that Katie was sharing her room but hadn't heard her leave that morning since she had slept so deeply. Now she realized they would both be pursuing their own interests while here in the town, and she shouldn't feel dismayed that her friend had not waited for her. And were they really friends, anyway? More like acquaintances, Cassie reminded herself with a sniff. All this ridiculous self reflection was going to turn her into a watering pot, she acknowledged to herself with disgust.

Cassie walked briskly, trying to escape the discomfort of her own thoughts. She was hoping to catch the placement manager before he got busy with his day. Cassie wondered how busy the man could possibly be if he hadn't managed to arrange for all the children to have homes organized before they arrived. She reminded herself that she couldn't give in to her indignation. One caught far more flies with honey than with vinegar. In her experience, men were far more likely to accommodate her wishes if she smiled at them than if she frowned. She determined to hold onto her temper no matter the provocation.

She found Mr. McDonald sitting at a dingy desk at the back of the train station. He was leaning back in his chair and had his feet propped up on the edge of his desk, staring off into the middle distance. He didn't seem to notice her approach. Cassie held her breath and counted to ten before she rapped on the door and straightened her smile.

"Good morning, Mr. McDonald," she called as pleasantly as she could manage. His startled reaction made it easier to maintain her smile as genuine amusement flooded her for a moment. And then she once again remembered the children and had to fight to keep her smile in place.

"Miss Morley, what a pleasure to see you this morning." His ingratiating tone lacerated her nerves, but she made an effort to ignore it. "To what do I owe the pleasure of your company?"

"That is kind of you to say, Mr. McDonald. I was just stopping in to see if you had made any progress in placing the last few children." She could see that he was not happy about her question so she batted her eyelashes a little bit, being careful not to roll her eyes, and explained her feelings to him. "It just worries my poor mind and heart what will become of the children if we don't find them a good home."

She must have been convincing because the belligerent look on his face was replaced with a rather smarmy grin. Cassie suppressed her shudder of revulsion and blinked a little more.

"Now you shouldn't be worrying your pretty little head about anything, but I can assure you that I am making every effort to get those boys situated as quickly as possible." He chuckled and winked at her. "You can be sure I don't want them on my hands for any longer than necessary."

"No, of course you don't." She tried to keep her distaste out of her voice. He would at least be motivated now that the children were here since he would be responsible for them until he could find them somewhere to live. Cassie sighed but then managed to turn to him with a smile. "If you need any help, you be sure to let me know."

"But of course, my dear."

Cassie was glad that he seemed to be accepting her interest in the children as natural, so she persisted. "Would it be possible for me to visit with the children while I'm still in town? I'm sure they're feeling a little left out since the other children have already gone to their new homes."

"Well, isn't that sweet of you to be thinking that those orphans have feelings."

She held onto her temper with the last shreds of her self control. "Of course, they have feelings, Mr. McDonald. Just because their parents have died doesn't mean they aren't normal children."

Now it was his turn to blink at her as though he had never even thought such a thing were possible. Cassie wanted to smack the obtuse man but managed to keep a smile pinned to her lips and she batted her eyelashes a little more. She started to wonder if she might perhaps be starting to look like a cow with all the vacuous blinking, but since it was working, she couldn't stop now.

Mr. McDonald looked at her as though he couldn't fathom why she was still there.

Trying not to sigh over how dimwitted he seemed to be, Cassie reminded him gently. "What do you think, Mr. McDonald? If you wouldn't mind, I would like to visit the boys this afternoon, just to try to bolster their spirits, you know?"

"Yes, yes, but of course. You're probably right. Of course they would like to see you. I don't see it to be a problem. I won't be able to be there, seeing as I have to keep working on trying to find them homes, you know?"

"Of course, it is such an important job you have, Mr. McDonald. You must sleep better at night knowing what a service you are performing for these poor children."

The flattery was working like a charm on the incompetent man, and once again, Cassie had to fight not to burst into laughter. Cassie watched in amazement as the man puffed up his chest like a little rooster. Her flattery clearly put him in mind of his duties. Cassie wondered if perhaps he was not as bad as she had thought. Mayhap all the man needed was a little appreciation. She regretted for a moment that she had been insincere in her words until she remembered that incompetence was inexcusable when the children's future was at stake. She maintained her smile, though, hoping that the man's new motivation would hold and he would manage to find homes for all the children before many days had passed. It would have to be disheartening to the ones left behind!

Cassie renewed her determination to visit the youngsters. "Thank you, Mr. McDonald. I know how busy you must be, so I will not keep any more of your time. If you could just point me in the right direction, I will be on my way to see the children."

Within another moment or two she was on her way. Of course, the boys were all happy to see her. Ten of them were squeezed into the inadequate accommodations along with Mrs. Parker and Miss Jones. The two ladies were delighted for additional help in keeping the youngsters occupied. Before long, Cassie had persuaded them all to accompany her out of doors where they wore off some of the boys' excessive energy with a vigorous game of tag.

By the time she took her leave of the group, Cassie was very much in need of tidying and wondered if she should postpone the idea of visiting Walter and his brothers. But those three might be in even more need of her visit than the group had, since they were in unknown surroundings without any adult they were familiar with. After combing some neatness into her curls and washing her face during a brief stop at the hotel above the saloon, Cassie made her way to the smithy to arrange for transportation and directions to Mr. Ainsworth's house.

Cassie wondered if the man could tell she was an excellent horsewoman or if he was trying to get her killed when he walked out of the barn with a huge horse that was tossing his head restlessly. It didn't really matter because she *was* a skilled rider, but it didn't fill her with confidence in the man's reliability. She would have to trust his directions, but she determined to pay attention to her surroundings so she could find her way back to town, just in case she couldn't find Ainsworth's spread.

"You'll be on to his land before you know it, miss. I'm fair to certain he'll be glad for a visit from you." The wiggling of the man's eyebrows did nothing to add to her confidence.

"I am going to check on his children," she replied firmly.

With a shrug, the smithy spat what she could only assume was chewing tobacco, toward a pail not far from her feet. It didn't quite reach the pail but luckily missed her boots. Cassie had to repress a shiver of revulsion. "Anyways once you reach his land you'll still have a good fifteen or twenty minutes of riding before you reach the house. The man bought half the state or thereabouts."

Cassie was surprised at the note of jealousy she heard in the man's voice. She tried to tell herself she didn't care what the man thought of Ainsworth. It only mattered how it might affect the boys, she insisted to herself then decided to ignore the matter all together.

"Thank you for the directions," she replied politely as she stood on the mounting block and climbed onto the huge horse. She allowed her joy at being on horseback to momentarily shake away her concerns as she gave the horse its head and hurried away from the smithy.

Chapter Five

Charles had been momentarily confused when he awoke to the sound of young laughter that morning. Thinking about it as he worked was enough to make him smile. It was definitely something he was looking forward to getting used to. His smile remained in place as he watched the three boys playing in the field. He had been given the impression that they hadn't had very much clean air and open space in their young lives. They hadn't yet talked about it, but he knew there was a great deal of tragedy in their past. There must be; they were orphans after all. But at least they had each other and they were with him now, making a fresh start. He determined once again that he would do his very best to make a good life for them.

His thoughts strayed to Miss Morley, or Miss Cassie, as the boys liked to call her. It had been obvious that she doubted his ability or sincerity in taking on the task of raising the boys without the assistance of a wife. He allowed her doubts to trouble him for a moment. *What if she was right and I won't be able to provide everything the youngsters will need.* He pushed the ridiculous thoughts from his mind. *She was probably concerned about their feelings,* he scoffed, but *if they are to grow into confident men, they needn't concern themselves overmuch about such distractions as feelings, so a woman won't be necessary.* He could provide everything they would need.

Had he conjured her with his thoughts? he wondered almost fancifully before he shook his head for even more foolishness as he watched her approach. It was obvious to Charles that she had a great deal of skill, as he watched her controlling the nearly wild animal the smithy had chosen to lend her. What the man had been thinking to send the young woman off alone with such an ill trained beast, he couldn't imagine, but Miss Morley seemed well able to handle him. She had a wide grin splitting her face, so she obviously didn't mind the effort it had taken to find his property.

Walter and his brothers spotted the lady, and they ran yelling toward her. Their noisy approach upset the horse, and he began to rear. Charles felt his heart lodge in his throat as he took off after the boys, intending to avert disaster.

Miss Morley must have foreseen the trouble. She slid gracefully out of the saddle and had the horse under control before any harm was done, but Charles could not control the rage that rose in him and caused him to lash out at everyone before him.

"How could you be so foolish as to ride this wild animal where there would be children in harm's way?"

he demanded of her, his harsh tone ringing louder than usual. "And you boys should never run toward a horse like that! Have you any idea how much damage a large animal like this could do to you?"

All four faces were staring at him with almost identically rounded eyes, shock and dismay displayed equally on each face. Some of the farm hands approached to see what the ruckus was about. Embarrassment piled onto his fright and Charles glared at everyone in equal measure. He couldn't help notice that the young woman was continuing to pat the horse soothingly to prevent him from shying away from his own loud anger.

Feeling his face flush now with embarrassment rather than anger, Charles could not look the young woman in the face. But he felt obligated to apologize to the children. Crouching down on one knee to better reach their level, he put out a beseeching hand. Walter, always the more demonstrative of the three, leaned into him despite the perplexed expression on his face.

"I'm so sorry. I shouldn't have yelled like that. I was doing the exact thing that I was yelling at you for doing. It was not well done of me, and I will try not to let it happen again." He could see that his apology was going a long way to soothing their feelings, but he still had to explain himself. "You have to be careful around any large animal. That horse has not been well trained, but even a well trained horse can be dangerous if it is frightened. He couldn't be sure if you were friendly or not, and the three of you running toward him could have felt like an attack."

"But we were just so excited to see Miss Cassie," Walter pointed out.

"I know, and no doubt she's happy to see you, but you still have to be careful."

The three hung their heads as though they were ashamed of themselves even if they didn't really know what he was talking about. He couldn't bear to think that he had crushed their exuberance and tried to recover from his blunder. "But now you'll know for next time, and there's really no harm done. Nobody got hurt, and Miss Cassie has the beast under control."

He finally made himself look over to where she had taken her mount. Charles was surprised to see that the huge horse appeared docile enough as he drank from the trough and stood beside her quite calmly. Miss Cassie, on the other hand, looked far from calm if you looked her in the eye, but she was doing her best to hide that fact from the children and the horse. She tied the horse's reins in a shady spot and approached the children.

"Now that Hector is under control, I will be very happy to receive the hugs you have ready for me," she told them with a genuine smile on her face. He realized when her focus wasn't on him, she was able to completely hide her displeasure. It was obvious she truly cared about the boys. He tried to amend his first impression of her, but he couldn't manage it. Despite her skill on horseback and her affection for the children, she was a rich, spoiled woman from the city, and she had no business being in Missouri. Knowing who her father was did nothing toward improving his opinion of her. If anything, it made it all the harder for him to tolerate her presence. But despite that, he couldn't help but feel a warm flutter in his midsection whenever he looked at her.

Charles valiantly ignored his feelings of attraction towards the beautiful young Miss Cassie. Despite her appeal, he refused to accept that it was more than skin deep. He would not allow the children's attachment to her to sway his own opinion.

"Where did you get such a huge horse?"

"I didn't know you knew how to ride."

"Did you change your mind and come to stay with us?"

The boys pelted her with questions. Her laughter made his gut clench in a pleasurable fashion, but the last question made his stomach plummet uncomfortably.

He watched as she crouched beside Walter, obviously the one who asked the last question. Cassie kneeled down, seemingly heedless of the dirt to her skirts. It surprised him, but he supposed she could afford to be heedless of her clothes. Since her father was a wealthy cit, he would no doubt just buy her new gowns when she returned home.

But one could not argue that she did not have affection for the boys. Even he was not so cynical as to suppose that her attention to them was feigned. He could not force his gaze away as she drew the small boy into her arms to comfort him.

"No, my dear boy, I am not here to stay. I am here to see where you live. You must show me all the best things about your new home."

Ross and Anton were eager to tell her all about the place.

"And there are ten horses and more cows than we can count and Mr. Charles says we are to each have our own room when we are ready and we're going to go to school just like you said we should."

ꕥ

Cassie couldn't prevent a trill of laughter from escaping her despite the glowering stare of Mr. Charles watching her, like a hawk awaiting its next morsel. The boys really were so dear when they filled her ears with their tales. She tightened her grip on little Wally before releasing him and regaining her feet.

"Now you must show me everything before I have to head back to town. We mustn't tarry, as I do not want to be caught out after dark."

Her words prompted the boys to action. Ross and Walter each grabbed one of her hands, and Anton lead the way. Cassie was uncomfortably conscious of Mr. Ainsworth bringing up the rear without uttering a word.

"Isn't it amazing how much space there is around here, Miss Cassie?" Anton asked her.

"What do you like about that, Tony?" Cassie had wondered if the city dwelling children would be able to adjust to the isolation of Missouri.

"We can't hear the neighbors or smell what they're having to eat. There are birds out here, Miss Cassie."

Ross interrupted with excitement. “And the birds make the prettiest sounds.”

“And we saw baby cats, Miss Cassie. Mr. Charles says they’re called kittens. He said we can hold them when they get a little bit bigger, but the mama cat won’t like it if we touch them now.”

They were talking over each other in their eagerness, and Cassie had to bite her lip to prevent tears from forming in her eyes. The poor dears had missed some of the simplest pleasures in life due to their life of poverty. She had known this was a good move for them, but she was even more convinced than ever. Despite how dour Mr. Ainsworth was, she could not suppress the smile of appreciation she cast over her shoulder toward him. The sour man just glowered back at her. She returned her attention to the boys and determined to ignore their new guardian.

“We will be very careful not to disturb the mama, but I would dearly love getting a glimpse of the baby cats, or yes, you are quite correct Walter, kittens. And yes, Tony, I do agree with you, all the birds are lovely, but I cannot decide if I prefer the blue ones or the yellow ones. Which are your favorite?”

“The blue ones, Miss. Although I can see why you would like the yellow ones.”

“Are they not the most cheerful color?” she asked.

“They are, but I think the blue ones sound nicer.”

They shared a grin.

“You will have to see if you can tame them so that they will come and sit on your finger.”

That got all three boys' attention. "Is that even possible?" Ross asked, his eyes wide with eagerness.

She had to shrug. "I would imagine with enough patience and perhaps a bit of bribery with bread crumbs, it would be possible."

Walter and Ross laughed. "We would never have enough patience to sit around and wait for a bird to land on us."

Cassie laughed with them. "No, but Tony might." The boy's eyes lit up at her assessment.

They reached the barn where the cat had nested with her babies.

"Mr. Charles said we have to be very quiet." Wally's whisper was the loudest she had ever heard, but Cassie managed not to giggle as they tiptoed through the large building, past the empty stalls to the last one, where it was dark, warm, and quiet. A mound of hay was piled up in front of the stall door, all the better for the youngsters to be able to peer over its edge. Cassie found she could not detest the dour man, who had still not said anything. If he was so thoughtful toward her boys, she would not judge him for seeming so stern. It was obvious he must have a kind heart despite his severe exterior. Or perhaps he did not like women. She chose to ignore his gruffness and think well of him. All thoughts of the grouchy man were pushed to the back of her mind as she joined the children in their delighted examination of the mother cat with her babies.

The boys couldn't stand still watching for very long. When she realized they were beginning to fidget and would soon make the cat anxious, she drew them away with a tap on their shoulders and a beckoning gesture.

"There are too many other things to see before I leave," she reminded them when they were a little away from the last stall.

"You'll come back again, though, right, Miss Cassie?" Walter worried.

"Of course, my dear. You will soon grow weary of my visits."

"Never," he declared with determined loyalty.

Cassie laughed, taking his hand again and following Tony and Ross as they continued their tour of the property.

"We haven't seen everything yet. Mr. Charles says we have to learn to ride before he can show us all over the place."

"Oh, have I interrupted your opportunity for riding lessons?" she asked with dismay. "But I would love to watch. Do not, I pray you, allow my presence to prevent you." She turned toward Ainsworth as she spoke.

"But you still haven't been in to see the boys' rooms." Ainsworth finally spoke. Cassie wasn't sure if he didn't want to give the boys' their lesson while she was there or if he was trying to prevent the necessity of her returning. She ignored either possibility.

"That can wait until next time, I'm sure. Perhaps I could be of assistance with the riding lessons so that the boys needn't take turns. They could learn all the faster that way."

She had thought she was being reasonable, but he merely looked annoyed. She ignored his reaction and turned back to the boys.

"You are going to love riding! It is the best feeling."

"But are you not afraid being so far off the ground?" Walter asked, his nerves evident.

"Not if your saddle has been adjusted properly and you have firm control of your mount. And I am most certain that Mr. Ainsworth will be very careful in his selection of which horses he shares with you. You can be sure they will be gentle and dependable. There will be nothing to fear."

"I'm not afraid," Tony boasted while Ross chimed in. "Me neither."

Walter looked up at her with pleading eyes. Cassie squeezed his hand reassuringly but said nothing else. It was a skill the boy would require living out here on such a large property and so far from town. He could only walk so far on his little legs. She was delighted she would be there to share the treat of helping her young friends learn.

An hour or two later, she had lost all track of time, she was exhausted from all the laughter she and the boys had shared. Mr. Ainsworth had barely thawed toward her and so had not shared in most of their laughter, but Cassie was relieved to see that he was not so stern with the boys despite the scowl that creased his face continually.

Despite the fact that the boys had barely even seen horses in their young lives, Cassie was heartened to see they had an aptitude for riding and it would soon seem as though they had been born in the saddle.

Even Walter was beginning to enjoy the activity, she was relieved to see. Glancing at the location of the sun, she bit back a gasp of alarm.

"Oh dear, I really must be off or I will lose myself in the dark on the way back to town. I had no intention of staying this long."

There was a chorus of protests from the boys, but she hugged them all in a hurry and promised to return as soon as she could manage. She hadn't felt particularly welcomed by their new guardian so she didn't want to promise to return the very next day. She would have to give the matter a little more thought before she braved his presence again.

She was gazing at the stirrup in dismay, wondering if there was a mounting block handy when Ainsworth actually laughed. The sound startled her into glancing in his direction for the first time in at least an hour. She had been ignoring him as steadfastly as she could manage. The man discomfited her. But when he laughed she felt a flutter in the region she was pretty sure housed her heart, which made her frown. He really was distractingly handsome even when he scowled. But when he smiled, his appeal was almost overwhelming. She couldn't help smiling in return.

Without saying a word, he cupped his hands, silently offering to hoist her up onto her horse. She was uncomfortable placing herself so close to him, but admonished herself not to be a ninny. There was very little other choice, and she really needed to be on her way. Taking a deep breath, she drew close to him, placed one foot in his hands and clambered up onto the horse with as much grace and dignity as she could muster, quickly settling her skirts and hoping she did not appear anywhere near as flustered as she felt.

"It really was much easier to give them their first riding lesson with you here. Maybe you could come back tomorrow and we could try again." His low voice sent a shiver up her spine, while his words nearly robbed her of speech.

The stern man was inviting her back? Wonders would never cease it would seem. She hoped her face was not flaming as she felt a myriad of feelings assailing her.

Without answering him, she called out to the boys a goodbye and wheeled her horse around. "I really must be off. Farewell," she said as she goaded her horse into a trot. She left the yard in a small cloud of dust. She realized that was probably quite rude of her. She wasn't used to the dirt like there was around here; in the city everything was cobbled or at least oiled. But as her horse progressed to a cantor and then a gallop, she allowed the wind whipping by her to blow away her concerns, at least for a few minutes.

Chapter Six

When she pried her eyes open the next morning, Cassie was dismayed to see she had again slept later than she had planned. She was being far more active than she was used to, and it was making her need more sleep. She hurried to ready herself and set out for more visits with the children. She intended to return to Ainsworth's property to see Walter and his brothers after she made stops with some of the other children who had been placed. While the three brothers held a bigger piece of her heart, she felt compelled to check on all of them before she returned home to New York.

The prospect of getting back on the train held no appeal for her at the moment, so she shoved the thought away and concentrated on the instructions the smithy was giving her on how to arrive at her first destination. He gave her a vague warning about being careful out on her own, but since all the places she was going were reasonably close to town, she chose to ignore him. He made her slightly uncomfortable. She couldn't decide if the smithy was being helpful or suggestive.

She crisscrossed the remote scenery, vaguely admiring the rugged beauty, but her attention was focused on ensuring she didn't get lost, while her thoughts were occupied with the children she left behind at each stop and the ones she would see at the next. More and more convinced that she could no longer volunteer with orphans, Cassie wondered what she was going to do with her life after this venture was concluded.

With a sigh of relief, she saw Mr. Ainsworth's house come into view. She had saved the best for last, she thought with a frisson of misgiving as she remembered the cold reception she had received from Ainsworth the day before. She shoved that thought from her mind as she concentrated on her joy at seeing her favorite boys again.

Cassie was dismayed at how quiet the property seemed when she approached the house. She wasn't really surprised by the depth of her disappointment. She knew she would have to leave Missouri sooner rather than later and wanted to spend as much time as possible with her favorite trio before she returned to New York.

She had never realized she would get so attached to the children when she had signed up to volunteer at the orphanage. She didn't know how she was going to live without them when she left, but she knew for a fact that she couldn't handle going back to the orphanage. Her heart couldn't take the losses.

Feeling melancholy, she sat atop her rented horse, gazing about at the beautiful prospect, reflecting how different it was from the city, when she was startled by an exuberant shout from behind her. Within minutes, she was off her mount and surrounded by the three youngsters who were again all talking over each other, each wanting to tell her everything that had happened since the previous afternoon.

"Mr. Charles has arranged for us to have all the clothes we could possibly need."

"We're going to start going to school in a couple days."

"He says if we don't start soon we'll be too far behind."

"There was so much food, Miss Cassie, we couldn't even finish it all."

Cassie had to laugh. This last statement was said with such reverence, and then all three boys grew silent as though this was too overwhelming to even contemplate. It wasn't really a laughing matter that the poor boys had experienced hunger, but the alternative was to cry and they wouldn't have appreciated that.

"It certainly sounds like you are being well provided for," she observed as she made herself meet Mr. Ainsworth's gaze. "Thank you for that, sir."

He offered her a half shrug and a lopsided grin, as though he were uncomfortable with her weak praise. It heartened Cassie to see his reaction. It seemed obvious to her that he had not taken on the boys in an attempt to curry favor with someone. Unlike the socialites of New York. Including her. Cassie was ashamed of her early attitude and was very conscious of others' motivations. Despite his off-putting demeanor, Cassie was determined to try to think better of Mr. Ainsworth. She offered him a brilliant smile but then had to fight not to laugh when suspicion crossed his face.

"Are you going to help us with our riding lessons again today, Miss Cassie? We waited, hoping you would come."

"Mr. Charles didn't think you would and said we ought to go ahead without you, but we knew you would be here."

Cassie's feelings of appreciation for Mr. Charles slipped slightly when she heard these words, but she forced herself to remain polite even though she could no longer look at him.

She squeezed Walter's hand. "I'm glad you had confidence in me, dear boy. Of course, I'm here for your riding lesson. We had such fun yesterday, I couldn't bear to miss out today. Thank you for waiting for me. I'm sure it wasn't easy for you."

As she was talking, they began to walk toward the barn.

"Why did you look sad when you were waiting for us, Miss Cassie?"

Cassie was surprised by Tony's question. The children had rarely expressed any notice of the feelings of the adults around them.

"I thought I had missed you. It seemed so quiet when I rode into the yard, so I was sad that I wasn't going to get to see you today. Then you came running out to greet me and I was happy again."

“I wish we could see you every day for always.” This from Walter, and Cassie had to blink to keep the tears from her eyes.

“I know, but we’ll always be friends. Once you know how to write really well you could write letters to me, and I will be happy to stay in touch with you.”

The boys didn’t look convinced. “But that won’t be the same as seeing you.”

“No, but it’s better than nothing,” she answered as briskly as she could manage. “Let’s not think about it now. I’m going to stay around for a little while longer. Let’s make the most of the time we have.”

Walter still lacked a little enthusiasm, but the three boys ran ahead of her to get the horses ready for their lesson.

Charles came up beside her. Cassie was uncomfortable around him but tried not to show it. She offered him a tentative smile.

“They’re such sweet boys,” she began before she had to clear her throat because of the wobble in her voice. “They sure have become captivated with what you’re doing for them here. I’m glad to see how quickly they’re adapting. They’re going to have a great life here with you.”

She could feel tears forming in her eyes and was quick to blink them away. She didn’t figure the grumpy man would appreciate her softer side.

ꕥ

Charles watched as she nervously licked her lips and blinked back the tears that had formed on her eyelashes. He wondered if she was trying to gain his sympathy. It was a tactic he had seen girls try before, but he had no interest in hard-hearted women who were into manipulation. He knew what girls like her were like, and he wanted none of it.

But he knew the boys were fond of her, so he would tolerate her presence for as long as she stayed in town in order to provide them with a sense of continuity. Even though he wasn't inclined to like her, he had to admit she had handled the youngsters' concerns quite well. Even though he expected the New York socialite to be a flighty little thing, he grudgingly admitted that he could learn a thing or two from her about dealing with the boys.

"Was this your family's land, Mr. Ainsworth? Have you lived here all your life?"

He never appreciated anyone asking him questions about his past. "No," he answered her simply, trying to keep the anger out of his voice as he said it. He must not have been completely successful, he realized, when she turned her startled gaze up to meet his eyes.

"I apologize, Mr. Ainsworth, if my questions were impertinent, I was merely curious. But my mother has, on occasion, informed me that curiosity is vulgar. It would seem she was correct." She offered him a tight smile that he did not return. He did not want to be friends with her. She deftly changed the subject. "What will we be teaching the children today?"

Once again, the afternoon passed quickly. Charles was surprised by how much he enjoyed teaching the boys. They were so receptive and eager. And he had to admit that Miss Morley was of great assistance. Now all the youngsters needed was practice, to reinforce what they had learned.

“Will you come back very soon, Miss Cassie, and go for a ride with us?” Ross asked.

“Yes, please come.” Walter added his plea.

“Mr. Charles said he would show us more of his spread once we knew how to ride. You would probably like to see it too, wouldn’t you?” Tony asked. His shy smile revealed how much he hoped the young woman would join them.

Charles couldn’t resist the boys’ wishes. He added his invitation to theirs. “It would probably be good if you came too, Miss Morley. I think they need one more day of practice, and then we can plan for a longer ride. It would make it easier for me to lead the way if I knew you were bringing up the rear, keeping an eye on the boys’ riding progress. Then I would only need one hand to come along to watch for any dangers.”

He shouldn’t have added that last bit, as he was met with four pairs of rounded eyes. “What kind of dangers?” Cassie asked for all of them while obviously trying not to look too scared.

“There are any number of things we need to be concerned about. I won’t go into too much detail at the moment. You needn’t worry. My men and I will keep you safe.”

He could tell she didn’t appreciate not being told what she wanted to know. He found her good looking whatever she was doing, but when she was irritated and trying to hide that fact, he found it particularly endearing. It was unlikely she would appreciate his thoughts. He ignored the pull of attraction. She was too pretty and soft for the life he was living here. It didn't matter if he thought she was the most beautiful woman he had ever laid eyes on, she was not for him, and it would be well for him to remember that.

Charles watched as Walter grabbed Miss Morley's hand. "You'll still come, though, right, Miss Cassie? Mr. Charles said you don't need to be scared."

He watched as she blinked at the boy and then smiled widely at him. Crouching down beside him, she looked the boy in the eyes. "Of course, we needn't be afraid. I am quite certain Mr. Ainsworth is capable of keeping us safe. I wouldn't miss it for anything."

Charles was pretty sure she had to force herself to look at him. "You are planning for the day after tomorrow, right? That works well for me as I have a few things I ought to take care of in the meantime. What time would you like me to arrive for our ride, Mr. Ainsworth?" Her tone was polite and cool. The perfect voice for a New York socialite, he thought in derision, ignoring the pull in his belly at the sound of it.

"If you could come at eleven, that will leave us enough daylight to go for a nice long ride and you would still have time to make it back to town before dusk. Perhaps we could even eat our lunch at the back of the property by the river."

She nodded briskly and turned back to the boys. "Then I will see you all at eleven o'clock, day after tomorrow. Make sure you don't leave without me."

The three boys clamored to hug her goodbye while insisting they would never leave her behind. Charles gritted his teeth, ignoring his jealousy over their attachment to the young woman. He had always thought children were good judges of character, but now he wasn't so sure. He wouldn't trust this woman farther than he could throw her, but the children would give their lives for her, he was sure. He was glad she would soon be returning to New York. Since the boys loved her, he couldn't deny her access to them, but he didn't want her around any longer than necessary. He would ask her tomorrow which train she planned to take.

Charles almost smiled as he watched Walter, Ross, and Anton talking over each other and Cassie gamely trying to keep track of what each of them was saying while they walked toward her horse. They came to stand with him as she rode away. Walter's hand made its way into his grasp. Charles was still a little uncomfortable with such displays but didn't want to hurt his feelings so allowed it for a moment. His heart went out to the little boy. Charles knew he was going to love being a father.

"Why do you s'pose Miss Cassie doesn't want to stay here with us, Mr. Charles? Maybe you could adopt her, too." Ross' six-year-old logic left a little to be desired, Charles thought as he wondered how to answer him. Thankfully Ross' big brother stepped in.

"Don't be stupid, Ross. She still has her parents, so she can't be adopted."

"But I don't want her to go away." Ross' voice trembled, and Charles' heart clenched in sympathy.

"What do you like about Miss Cassie, Ross?" Charles asked. "Maybe there are some ladies around here you could be friends with."

The boy shook his head. "It wouldn't be the same, Mr. Charles. Miss Cassie knew us before. It's different, you know."

Charles didn't know, but he couldn't argue with the boy.

"I like that she always listens," Walter piped up.

"And remembers," Ross added. Charles' confusion must have been evident because Ross elaborated. "Grownups often pretend to listen to what you say but don't remember what you told them. Miss Cassie always listens *and* remembers."

"And then she asks you about it, like to check on you," Anton chimed in. "Like if you had a loose tooth or had been planning to play a game, she would ask you how did it go."

Charles was surprised by their words. "I can see why you would appreciate qualities like that."

Walter summed up how all the boys felt. "The other ladies that were at the orphanage, and especially the ones who came on the train with us, are nice, but Miss Cassie is the best."

"I'm sure she would appreciate knowing you feel that way," was all Charles could say before he changed the subject. "Now, who would like some dinner? I don't know about you three, but I sure did work up an appetite today."

"Me!" "Me!" "I do, too." They were easily distracted, and the evening drifted to a comfortable close.

Chapter Seven

Cassie was less than comfortable sitting in the saloon eating her supper. If her parents could see her, they would lock her up and throw away the key, she thought with reluctant amusement. They were going to be less than pleased with her for going on this trip in the first place, even if they never found out what her accommodations were like.

She tried not to draw any attention to herself and ate as quickly as possible. It was still early, so the bar wasn't crowded, but Cassie was well aware that the men of the town were unused to having a proper woman in their presence while they were drinking. But she had been far too hungry after leaving her mount at the smithy and couldn't wait to eat until morning. She would have no strength for her ride tomorrow if she skipped supper tonight.

It was one more reason why she needed to make up her mind to buy a ticket back to New York. She knew Kate and Melanie, two of the other women who had accompanied the orphans on the train, were planning to stay in town and had already arranged for a place to live. Katie had only shared her room in the hotel that first night. She and Mel had quickly found a more permanent accommodation. Perhaps she could see if they had a little bit of room for her to stay with them for a couple more days. She just couldn't tear herself away from the children. She doubted it was going to get any easier as the time went on, but she just had to be sure all the children from the train were looked after. Maybe she would buy the ticket once Mr. McDonald had finished placing them all. She knew she wouldn't be able to have a clear conscience until that was looked after.

As soon as she finished her last bite, she signalled to the bartender and hurried up the stairs to her room. She was sure to get indigestion from how quickly she had eaten, but she couldn't be comfortable with all the attention focused on her.

Once she got to her room, she contemplated her plans for the next day. She resolved to visit Mr. McDonald again to see if he had made any progress. She would speak with Kate and Melanie as well, to see if they would mind her staying with them. Cassie would happily pay them what the hotel was charging her. She knew they were both needing to take on work as soon as possible, so they must not have very much money. And it was only fair that she contribute. She would just be glad to be away from the saloon.

She managed to drift off to sleep despite the rising volume from the men in the bar. All the riding and fresh air were certainly making for deep sleep, she thought vaguely as her exhaustion finally swallowed her. She thought of nothing else until the sun streaming through her window woke her early the next morning. She was glad to see that she had managed to be up at an early enough hour this time. She could not spend another night above the saloon!

After quickly dressing and gathering together her few things, she made her way downstairs. The saloon was empty except for the ever present bartender. Cassie wondered if the poor man ever slept. He offered to make her breakfast, for which she was grateful. Before the large clock struck the hour she was on her way.

Deciding first to speak with Mr. McDonald just in case the man was going to leave his office that day, Cassie headed toward the train station, as his office was next door.

"Miss Morley, what a pleasure to see you this morning." The fat man's friendly greeting was surprising.

Cassie smiled. "Thank you, Mr. McDonald. How are you on this fine day?"

"I am well, my dear, I am well." His exuberance was making her nervous for a reason she couldn't quite define. "You will be happy to hear that I have now found a place for all but two of the orphans you brought with you. And I am fairly certain that the last ones should be placed before the week is out. I just have to make one more visit to confirm with someone who had expressed an interest previously."

"That is wonderful news. Are you confident the children will be happy where you've placed them, sir?"

Cassie winced when she saw how the man reacted to her question and quickly tried to disarm him. "I apologize, sir, I have no intention of questioning your abilities. I just find that I am so worried about the poor children. You know how it is, don't you?" It wasn't hard to make tears gather in her eyes. She truly was worried for them, especially with their fates being left in the incompetent hands of this uncaring lout.

Her words had the desired effect. No longer looking mulish, Mr. McDonald patted her awkwardly on her shoulder. "Of course I understand. Don't get yourself in a taking, young lady. I have every confidence that I am finding good homes for each and every one of those orphans. Anywhere out here is going to be a far cry better than where they come from, wouldn't you agree, Miss Morley?"

No, I do not agree, she thought with fierce anger that she made every effort to hide. What she said out loud was far different. "I am certain they are all happy to be getting settled into families once again. Would you be so kind as to give me the direction of the children that have now found a good home? I wouldn't want to leave town without saying goodbye."

"Of course, of course." He was back to being jovial, no doubt relieved that she wasn't going to give in to a fit of the vapors and glad to have a reason to send her off.

Within moments she had the paper with all the names clutched in her hand and she was on her way from his office heading away from the train station toward the small house Kate and Melanie were renting.

"Cassie! What a pleasure to see you! What has been keeping you so busy that we haven't laid eyes on you in the last couple of days?" Kate's welcome was warm but censorious.

"You look as though you have settled in already. It has only been a couple days, but I'm sorry if you were expecting me earlier. I have been junketing about the area checking on the children. I don't trust that Mr. McDonald was particularly interested in the welfare of the children when he made the arrangements. I could not leave here with a clear conscience if I did not see with my own eyes that the children were content with their new homes."

Kate nodded in sympathy. "Oh, you poor thing. You haven't managed this experience very well, have you? Of course, I understand. That's one more reason I'm glad that I'll be staying here. I will be able to lend a hand if any of the boys find themselves in need of a little assistance." Kate smiled warmly and turned the subject. "Please say you can stay for a little visit. I have just put the kettle on. Say you'll have a cup of tea with me."

"That would be lovely, thank you. I just left Mr. McDonald and could use a cup of tea to put a better taste in my mouth."

The two young women shared a chuckle. Cassie glanced around the small but comfortable space.

"This is a lovely home you have, Kate. I can see that you're already happy here."

"Yes. Having a fresh start is wonderful. I'm sure there will be a few things that I will miss from the city, but I never would have been able to have a home like this there. It was all I could manage to afford a small room in an ugly tenement."

Cassie, being from far different circumstances, became a little uncomfortable, but happy for her friend. She turned the subject. "Is Melanie home?"

"No, she is out considering her options. Since I have already been promised the position of schoolteacher, she is looking about to see what her employment prospects are. She is highly skilled with a needle, so she is thinking she might be able to be a seamstress. There is already a tailor in town, so she has gone to speak with him. Perhaps he can refer her to some clients, or she could assist him."

"I do hope it works out for her," Cassie answered as she nodded her thanks for the piping hot cup of tea Katie placed before her.

"How long do you expect to stick around, Cassie? I thought you would have caught the train back to New York that went through this morning."

Cassie shook her head. "I know my family will no doubt be furious. I didn't even get a letter ready to send on the train to them. Do you know if there is a telegraph office? I hadn't thought to check yet. I have just been so occupied with worry over the boys."

Soft-hearted Katie grasped her friend's hand. "What are you going to do, Cassie? You have become far too attached to these children. There is very little you can do for them."

Cassie appreciated her friend's concern but she refused to accept her words. "Perhaps little, but not nothing." She softened her hard words with a smile. "The good news is, so far, the children that I have visited in their new homes are happy with their new arrangements. For the most part, the families who have taken them in are kind and delighted to expand their families. From what I can see, it's a tough, lonely life out on these large spreads, and the couples who have taken in some of the boys are happy to have more people at their table."

"Have you seen Walter and his brothers?" Kate asked with a hesitant tone.

Cassie nodded. "While I found Mr. Ainsworth to be a grumpy, even cold, man, the boys have quite taken to him. I worry that he won't understand their struggles as they deal with all that they've lost in their young lives, but he certainly seems to have the ability to provide for them well in a material way. His house is quite large and he has many animals and extensive gardens. The boys were commenting how much food there has been at each meal." Cassie's laugh was a little strained as she and Kate shared a glance.

"It will be better for them here, you know that," Kate reminded her.

"I do know that, as long as they are with kind people. That's all I ask. I could not bear it if any of the children were placed with someone who will mistreat them, Katie." She paused for a moment and Kate merely waited for her to continue. "I saw Mr. McDonald this morning. He kept calling them orphans. I know that's what the children are, since they have lost both parents, but the way he said it was as though that made them lesser creatures. It was all I could do to remain civil with the man, but I had to because I fear he will be even more incompetent if I upset him in some way."

They both sighed before Katie spoke up. “It is a cruel and unjust world. Mr. Brace’s idea is a sound one, but in reality, it’s only as good as those implementing it. But as you observed, most people are good and decent and will provide a satisfactory home for the children, which is far better than they had living on the streets of New York.”

Cassie’s smile was fraying, but she tried to hold onto her composure as she met her friend’s eyes. “I know. In reality, I never should have volunteered at the orphanage in the first place. I don’t think it will do the children any good to see me going to pieces over saying goodbye to them. But I cannot leave town until I am convinced that they will all be well. I know I don’t have much power, but I have a little, and I will use it in whatever way I can to ensure that they will be well after I leave.”

“You have a good heart, my friend,” Katie said.

“No, I don’t,” Cassie countered, amused when she saw how surprised Kate was over her words. “My motives have never been completely pure in connection with the orphanage. And now, I am not fully convinced that my concern for the boys is purely for their sake or for my own. I don’t want to have to live with a guilty conscience over them.”

Katie let out a peel of laughter. “Well, even if your motivation is merely to keep your conscience clear, the fact that it would bother your conscience says something good about you.”

Cassie joined her in chuckling before she got to the point of her visit. “Either way, I find that I cannot yet leave this town, but the hotel is unacceptable.” She glanced around the small space. “I know it would be an imposition, but do you think I could possibly stay...”

Kate did not allow her to finish asking. “Of course you must stay here! I am so sorry that I didn’t think of it myself. I thought you might be more comfortable at the hotel and that you would only be a night or two anyway.”

“It is certainly not your fault, my dear Kate. But no, the hotel is not a fit place for me to stay, and since I can’t leave for at least a couple more days, I need to make other arrangements.”

“Well, just bring your things over here. We don’t have much, but you are welcome to it anyhow.”

“Thank you so much. It’s kind of you to say. I know I’ll be imposing and I will try not to stay too long.”

Kate interrupted again. “It’s never an imposition to make room for a friend. You are welcome to stay as long as you need.” She gestured around. “This might not be much space compared to what you’re used to, but for me and Melanie it’s grand, so we won’t mind sharing and you can have a room to yourself. You’ll have to excuse the simplicity. The place came furnished, thankfully, but it has been empty for a while and in need of a little attention.”

“That’s generous of you, Katie. After living on the train for almost two weeks, I too am thinking that any space bigger than a train car is grand, so I don’t mind sharing either. But since you have said yes, I will gratefully take whatever you offer.” With a grin she got to her feet. “Now, I will hurry back to the hotel and get my things. I have promised Walter, Ross, and Tony that I would go riding with them this afternoon and am due there at two, so I ought to hurry."

"Would you like me to come with you to lend a hand?"

"You are too kind, Katie, but no, I will hire a boy to carry my trunk, which is really all I have."

"Of course," was all Katie said in answer, making Cassie wonder if she should have accepted her offer of help. She bit her lip but decided not to take back her words. There was really no way to undo what had already been said, and if she accepted Katie's help, she would have to carry the other side of the heavy trunk, and it would take them twice as long. With a silent sigh, Cassie swallowed her regret that she could never quite fit in and hurried back to the hotel.

After enduring another uncomfortable encounter at the saloon and then arranging for her trunk to be taken to Katie's house, Cassie stopped in at the general store, grateful to see that it was surprisingly well stocked. She picked up a few food items that she thought Katie and Melanie might appreciate. Cassie wasn't sure, on second thought, if she should offer them any money for staying with them, but she was sure they would be glad to have her contribute some food. Cassie knew neither of the other women would have a great deal of savings, and especially until Melanie found work, they would need to stretch their money as far as possible. It was the least she could do, since they were saving her from the indignity of the saloon.

"I am so grateful for you taking me in like this, Katie! A man who had been frequenting the saloon tried to follow me up to my room when I returned for my things. Thankfully the bartender noticed and stopped him, but it made me nervous and uncomfortable. I wouldn't have been able to sleep a wink if I was staying there tonight."

Katie made soothing noises as she bustled around getting things settled for Cassie. "You poor thing! We should have thought to ask you to stay with us from the beginning. I apologize, Cassie."

"Don't be silly. How were you to know?" Cassie was embarrassed to have made her friend uncomfortable. She briskly changed the subject. "Now, what can I do to help you be more settled? You mentioned earlier that there were still things to be done."

"Oh no, Cassie, we couldn't ask you to help with that," Katie protested. "All that is left is washing some walls. It can keep until later."

Cassie laughed. "You mean until after I've ceased imposing upon you? You absolutely must allow me to wash some walls. I made arrangements to have this afternoon to do whatever I could to help you and Melanie here, and I mean to do it to my best ability. I became quite a good wall washer on the train ride here, so you saved the perfect assignment for me."

Katie tried to protest a little more, but Cassie could tell it was half-hearted. She was glad there was something specific she could help the other women with. It didn't sit comfortably with her to accept their kindness without trying to return some of it.

"What do you mean you made arrangements?" Katie thought to ask.

"Ainsworth has said I may accompany them as he rides out through his property to show it to the boys. I asked that it be tomorrow, as I was hoping you would allow me to come stay here with you."

"Were the boys disappointed to hear you wouldn't be coming today?"

"Of course," Cassie replied on a laugh. "But it's better for them, I think, to have one more day of practicing their riding before we go out for a longer trek. According to the smithy, Mr. Ainsworth owns a great deal of property, so I'm anticipating that it will be quite a lengthy ride."

By this time, the efficient Katie had stowed Cassie's things in one of the bedrooms and had procured a bucket full of warm water and several cloths. She wrinkled her nose at Cassie. "Are you absolutely sure you want to do this? I promise you, I will not hold any ill feelings toward you if you decided you aren't up to it."

Cassie laughed then sighed. "I fear you have a similar opinion of me as does Mr. Ainsworth. I swear to you, I may have been a debutante back in New York City, but I have learned to be quite proficient with a damp cloth."

Katie trilled with laughter. "Very well. Let us have at it." She handed Cassie a cloth, and the two of them began scrubbing the walls in the main room. "But don't think you can get away without explaining yourself. What do you mean that you are proficient with a cloth? And it seems to me that you're protesting Mr. Ainsworth's opinion a little too much. He is a terribly handsome man…" She trailed off with a giggle, and Cassie could feel heat climbing in her cheeks.

Cassie tried to brazen through the other woman's words by focusing on her first question. "Didn't you find it horrifically filthy on the train with all the smoke everywhere? I couldn't bear to think of the boys breathing in all that soot through the night, so I took to washing the walls most days. I thought everyone was doing it." She could feel the heat in her cheeks intensifying at Katie's incredulous stare.

Katie laughed a little as she replied. "Unfortunately, most of us have gotten too used to grime. In many parts of the city back home, there was similar smoke at times. Maybe not as bad as on the train, but more than I suppose you would have been used to. So no, I can assure you, most of us did not wash the train walls daily."

Cassie couldn't help but laugh at Katie's words. "Well, I guess my sheltered life did a little bit of good for the children, then. And it was a good lesson for me." After their laughter died down, a comfortable silence settled between them, and they made rapid progress around the small room.

"You weren't joking when you said you were proficient with a damp cloth," Katie commented at one point, making Cassie beam with pride.

There were a few more moments of quiet before Katie giggled and stated," You never did tell me about Mr. Ainsworth. I'm getting more and more curious, you must realize."

Cassie sighed and protested, “There’s nothing to be curious about. I can assure you! The man always seems to be cross about something and thinks little of my presence. He has yelled at me, glared at me, and usually only offers me silence. I do not think he approves of the boys’ affection for me.” This flabbergasted Cassie, but Katie didn’t comment so Cassie continued. “Perhaps he is just jealous of how close I am with the boys and is being defensive without even realizing it. But I don’t really think it’s that. It seems to me as though he took one look at me on the very first day we were in Bucklin and found me wanting. He can probably tell from looking at me that I am nothing more than a socialite and has deemed me beneath his notice. But he hasn’t even given me a chance to prove there is more to me than that. He merely judged me from what he can see on the surface.”

She barely registered how furiously she was scrubbing the walls as she continued her complaints about the man. “I think he has been too good looking all his life and is used to everyone thinking him superior for it. It’s hardly an attractive quality, in my opinion. I try to keep my eyes averted when I’m there,” she confided with a small giggle. “Looking at him is far too distracting and can make one forget how grumpy he seems to be.”

“Is he grumpy toward the boys?” Katie worried.

“Not usually. He seems to save it for me. Except for the time I arrived on a half wild horse and the boys ran toward me. He let all of us have the rough side of his tongue over that, let me tell you.” She paused as she thought. “But it might have been prompted by fear that the children were going to get hurt.”

“If he’s saving his grumpy side for you, it could be because is trying to cover up warmer feelings he might have toward you.”

“Katie Carter! What are you getting on about? You have declared that you have no interest in marriage. Why are you suddenly playing matchmaker?”

Katie didn’t seem to take offense at Cassie’s scolding. She shrugged. “Just because *I* don’t want a husband doesn’t mean I don’t think anyone else should have one. I have never heard you make any declarations about wishing to remain a spinster.”

Cassie could feel herself begin to splutter. “Well, no, of course not. I have no intention of remaining a spinster. It is just that I cannot marry a man who would consider I have nothing to offer him.”

Katie frowned over her choice of words.

“In New York, if I marry someone from my own circles, I will bring value with me. My name, my father’s connections, my social experience will all be of value to a prospective husband.”

“Oh Cassie, surely you realize you are of far more value than your father’s name.”

Now it was Cassie’s turn to shrug. “Not really. I don’t have much in the way of useful skills. Being out here shows me that all the more clearly. I can’t make clothes like you and Melanie can. I don’t know how to cook very many things. I know nothing about animals.”

Katie interrupted Cassie's stream of self deprecation. "But you know how to make people smile. You can usually read people very well. And the children love you. Every single one of them. You are a bright young woman. Everything can be learned if you know how to use your mind. And I've seen you use your mind to accomplish whatever you set your mind to. Remember that time you came with me to the market for the orphanage? I couldn't believe how nice the produce was that we managed to buy. And the butcher gave us a far superior cut of beef than he would have given me, just because you asked the right questions and batted your eyelashes at the right time."

Cassie laughed. "That was such fun."

"See what I mean? You didn't even mind doing it. You are far braver than I am. Mr. Ainsworth would be lucky to have you."

Cassie laughed again. "While he would be lovely to look at, I am not convinced we would be the best match."

Katie merely hummed and cast her a knowing glance. There was nothing Cassie could do but laugh again. She didn't want to add fuel to Katie's exclamation that she was protesting too much. Cassie wondered if there was a chance Katie was right. She thought of the taciturn cowboy with a smile but quickly shook her head and returned to her task.

Within a couple hours they had washed every wall in the small house and returned it to a tidy state. Cassie felt as though her arms had turned to the consistency of oatmeal, but she also felt a deep sense of satisfaction from their labors.

"Cassie, thank you ever so much. I would not have had the motivation to get all this done at once without your help and company. It is such a relief to have it done. And it feels so clean and fresh in here. Our home will be a true pleasure to return to." Katie's gratitude warmed Cassie's heart but embarrassed her a little bit, too.

"No thanks necessary, I assure you. I am just relieved that I could be of real help since you have been so kind as to take me in. I feel a little like the orphans we have brought out here."

"Not at all," Melanie, who had since returned home, insisted. "You are our friend. We're glad to have you with us. But all the more so since you were so generous as to help with this onerous job. The treats you brought us from the mercantile would have been enough." When Cassie shook her head, Melanie continued. "Don't shake your head at us. Allow us to appreciate what you have done. I know you aren't used to doing this type of thing. So you probably also aren't used to genuine gratitude. Accept it."

With a shared laugh, the three young women sat down to rest from their day. Cassie couldn't keep the grin off her face. She was certain it was the most sore she had ever felt in her entire life, but she was also certain that it was the most content she had ever felt as well. She rather thought she would like to extend her time here in Missouri to enjoy these friendships a little longer.

The next morning, Cassie bustled around helping Katie a little bit before making her way to the smithy once more after promising to be back before dark. Katie had laughed with her when Cassie had assured her that Ainsworth's grumpy behavior would surely have her returning before too long.

"You ought to just buy yourself a horse, Miss. It don't make no sense for you to be renting every day," the smithy pointed out.

"I'm not going to be staying in town much longer. Besides, I haven't anywhere to keep a horse."

"You could board him here during your stay and sell him before you leave."

Cassie thought over his words as she rode toward the Ainsworth property. She knew he was only being reasonable from his own standpoint, but since she didn't know how long she would be staying, she didn't want to commit herself to owning a horse. Then she thought of another thing. She should have checked at the train station for the eastbound schedule over the next week or two so that she would have an idea of when she should be planning to head home. And she really needed to send a message to her family. They would be ready to skin her alive by the time she got home, she thought uneasily before she allowed the worries to get blown away as she urged her horse into a gallop.

She arrived at the ranch with time to spare. Again it appeared quiet when she rode up. After tying her reins to a fence, she walked up to the front door of Mr. Ainsworth's house. Before she even had a chance to knock, the door was flung open by an exuberant Walter, who threw himself into her arms.

"Miss Cassie, you made it!"

"Of course, I did," she answered with a grin as she set him back on his feet after a tight hug. "But I think I'm a little bit early. Are you boys in the middle of something?"

"We were just doing some school work. Mr. Charles wants to see what we know before he sends us to school."

"That's wonderful, Walter. But you don't sound too happy about it."

"I would ever so much rather be out in the barn."

"I know you would, but never mind about that. We are going to have a wonderful afternoon of riding." She smiled as the other boys came to join them. "I'm sorry that I have interrupted you. Hurry and finish up while I wait out on the porch. I wouldn't want Mr. Ainsworth to think I am interfering with your studies."

The boys laughed as though she had been joking, but Cassie was truly concerned that the austere man would curtail any future visits if he suspected she would interrupt their learning. She smiled at them, not wanting to interfere with their relationship with their new guardian and let herself back out of the house.

A few minutes later a gruff voice made her jump.

"What are you doing out here by yourself?"

She had been staring out into the sunny landscape, lost in thought, and hadn't noticed his approach. With a hand on her pounding heart, she turned her head toward Mr. Ainsworth.

"Good heavens, you nearly frightened a year off my life."

He scowled at her words. "You should be paying more attention. This isn't the city. You need to keep your wits about you."

Cassie tried to pull her dignity around her. "After the first couple of days at the hotel, I cannot say I completely disagree with you, but I would think the city would require more attention than out here. There is a pickpocket around every corner in New York. Out here you can ride for miles without encountering a single person."

"It's not necessarily people you need to be concerned about in these parts," was his cryptic answer before he continued. "But never mind that, why are you out here by yourself? You should have let me know you had arrived."

Cassie shrugged. "I got here earlier than we had arranged. When I arrived, the boys were still involved in the assignment you had left for them, and I didn't want to disrupt their work. I'm good enough company to keep myself occupied until our appointed time."

She had thought she was being genial, but he only grunted in reply. Cassie stifled her sigh but kept a smile on her lips.

"If I had realized you were here, we could have gotten on the way earlier." His surly attitude put Cassie's teeth on edge but she refused to rise to his bait. She was determined to enjoy the afternoon with her favorite boys.

Cassie shrugged again. “Well, now you know, so we can be on our way.” She forced herself to smile at him, not wanting the boys, who had just come out of the house at the sound of their voices, to see them arguing. Even though she didn’t like the grouchy Mr. Ainsworth, she could not undermine the boys’ respect for him or interfere with the relationship they were building together. Despite his unmistakable antipathy toward her, it was obvious that he was kind to the children and they were beginning to care for him. She started to frown as she thought about how confusing the man’s behaviour was but then caught Walter’s watchful gaze on her and smoothed out the crease that had formed on her forehead. She offered him a warm smile, and he came and took her hand.

Within a few moments, they were all saddled up and on their way.

The grass was so tall in some places that it was hitting her boots where they hung in the stirrups. It was probably an odd thing to notice, but it really struck Cassie as she took in her surroundings. She had been so preoccupied as she rode around visiting the boys and dealing with her mixture of emotions that she had barely registered the scenery around her. That all changed as they rode just for the sake of getting to know the land.

Back in the city, everything was so groomed and controlled. She couldn’t quite decide if she found the wilderness beautiful, but it was certainly exhilarating. It made her want to goad her horse into going faster. It made her want to scream and laugh and take the pins out of her hair so it could stream wildly down her back. Clearly it made her run mad.

She glanced back at Mr. Ainsworth. Cassie knew there was no way he could read her thoughts, but she felt the compulsion to check anyway. Of course, as usual, his face was inscrutable. It frustrated her that she couldn't tell what he was thinking. But at least he wasn't falling off his horse laughing at her. Not that she should care what he thought of her, she reminded herself. The handsome man was not for her, she insisted to her heart.

Maybe she just really needed to get back to the city. She would never have thought trees and grass and a wide, blue sky would be at all appealing to her, but she quite liked being able to see all around her. It gave her a sense of security that did not exist in the crowded avenues of the city. But the city was so much more genteel than this rugged wilderness. Her dithering thoughts were driving her mad.

Not that it really matters anyway, she mused and allowed her gaze to follow the meanderings of a bird as it flitted along beside them. It wasn't as though she were considering staying here. In Bucklin, Missouri, of all places. She would be disowned for sure. Even if she had an employable skill, she didn't think she could stay no matter how attached she was to the boys. She was a New York socialite, and she needed to return to the life she knew. So maybe she ought to simply enjoy the beautiful surroundings instead of questioning why she was enjoying it so much.

Charles struggled to keep his attention focused on watching for dangers as they rode near the boundary of his property. His eyes kept straying toward the blonde beauty talking animatedly with his new sons. He felt his chest puff up with pride over the thought that he was now a father. He would be the first to admit that he hadn't even considered being a parent until the nearby town had started to buzz with the news of the incoming orphans. But when he had heard about them, he couldn't rid himself of thoughts of the poor youngsters and what he could do for them.

Now that he had the three of them, he already couldn't imagine his life without them. But their attachment to Miss Morley was a problem he would have to deal with before long, since it would seem she wasn't in any hurry to leave town. He only wished he didn't find her quite so attractive. He reminded himself once more that it was merely surface-deep beauty. *A socialite from New York couldn't possibly have any noble qualities*, he insisted to himself. Perhaps if he talked to her, he could rid himself of this ridiculous attraction.

He guided his horse into position next to hers with practiced skill. She appeared startled by his sudden nearness. Charles ignored his instinctive pride over her obvious awareness of him. It shouldn't matter a jot whether or not she found him attractive; he certainly had every intention of overlooking any attraction he felt toward her. He was sure it would be made all the more easy if he talked to her.

“You must be finding it difficult being away from the city for so long. When will you be catching the train back to New York?”

She turned her head to look at him, a frown marring her forehead. “Are you trying to get rid of me, Mr. Ainsworth?” She laughed as she said it, but he could see the seriousness in her eyes. He wanted to ignore the obvious intelligence stamped on her face. It was easier to consider her nothing more than a silly socialite. What was even harder to ignore was the increased pace of his heartbeat when in her presence. He needed to focus on the matter at hand.

He remembered her question and shook his head. “Of course not, Miss Morley, I was merely wondering what your plans are.”

He could hear the sarcasm dripping from her reply. “It’s kind of you to be concerned for me, but you needn’t trouble yourself. I am not feeling the loss of the city overly. I shall survive the deprivation a little while longer. I haven’t decided when I will be returning.”

“Your parents won’t be too pleased about that.”

She offered a small shrug and kept her focus on the trail ahead. “That needn’t concern you.”

Charles clenched his teeth over her attitude. “As a new father, I can tell you that if one of my sons was far away, I would be very concerned about his whereabouts.”

She grinned at him, and he ground his teeth together. “I’m so happy to hear that you are becoming so protective of the boys.” She paused as she once again turned her focus ahead of her. “I am sure my parents are anxious to hear from me. They will be furious with me for leaving town. And I will probably be locked in my room as soon as I return so that I can never leave again."

He was incredulous. "Did your parents not know you were coming to Missouri?"

Again she shrugged. "They would have forbidden it if I had asked."

Charles was appalled at her callous attitude toward their feelings. "Do they know where you are now?"

"Yes, I sent them a message at the first stop the train made. They would never have understood my need to make sure the children were safe."

"Why are those three boys so important to you that you would do that to your own family?"

"It wasn't just Walter, Ross, and Anton that I was concerned about. I needed to see that they were all going to be well cared for. But I do have a particular fondness for your sons," she concluded with a soft smile.

Charles couldn't see past the fact that she had left her family to worry about her. "I don't think I want you around my boys anymore, Miss Morley. I would never want them to show such disregard for my feelings as you have for the feelings of your parents. You are not a good companion for them. You need to go back to New York and let them get on with their lives."

The look she turned on him was filled with reproach. "You don't know what you are talking about when it comes to my family, and I will leave when I'm good and ready to leave. I am most definitely not a bad associate for your sons, who, I will remind you, I know better than you do. You have already given your promise that I can spend as much time as possible with them before I return to New York. I am sure they will not take kindly to you trying to curtail that."

His already clenched jaw began to ache from his frustration. He felt as though she were extorting from him. And she was right. The boys would not thank him for removing her from them. They so obviously loved her. He wanted to ignore her but decided further conversation might help him get over his anger with her. His feelings were so divided. It was driving him mad. He didn't want to be attracted to her, but he couldn't seem to help himself. With a quiet sigh, he probed a little more.

"How did you get involved with the orphans in the first place? It doesn't really strike me as being in keeping with your position."

She looked puzzled over his word choices but offered him a polite smile. It was apparent she was happy to move on to some other topic rather than discussing her appalling treatment of her family.

"I don't think you really know my position, sir, but you are correct in saying that it wouldn't have been my first choice, and I have no intention of continuing at the orphanage when I return to the city. I cannot bear the losses. It is too easy to fall in love with the children, but being involved with the orphanage made me much too aware of the challenges that unfortunate people face, and there is far too little that I can do to help. It breaks my heart." He watched in fascination as she swallowed back the threat of tears. It was the most emotion she had ever displayed in front of him. "I am unsure what I will do with my time when I return to the city. My family will want me to marry, of course, and start a family of my own." Her gaze was trained on the boys ahead of them. "I am not opposed to the thought, but it is difficult to find a suitable mate, and I don't want to settle for merely acceptable."

He frowned with confusion over her words, but before he could ask her for clarification she continued on. "In answer to your question about how I got involved with the orphanage, I am ashamed to say it was not with noble intention. I had managed to get a reputation as being vain and spoiled, and it was suggested that I ought to do some volunteer work to improve my image."

"Why would a girl like you need to improve her image?"

"Apparently very few eligible men are looking for over indulged young women to be their wives." She shrugged again as though it really didn't bother her, but Charles couldn't decide how genuine her feelings were. "My parents wanted me to do something more genteel like sewing things for needy families, but I wanted to be more involved than that. They were not most pleased by my choice, but they were probably right in their assessment. I was too spoiled to care for their reaction. They were convinced I would catch some dread disease from the children. But nothing of the sort took place. And then I no longer cared about my reputation, I grew to love everyone at the orphanage and spent as much time there as possible, even though most of my friends turned their noses up at the thought of me being in that part of town." Cassie shrugged again, almost helplessly. "I really don't know what I'm going to do when I go back. I can probably join some committee raising funds for the needy. But it just doesn't feel the same as actually helping them with my own hands." She glanced down at her hands as they held the reins. "Of course, my mother would have apoplexy if she saw the state that my hands are in. I shall have to be sure to buy some salve before I leave town, and hopefully the ride back will give them time to be restored." She grinned and offered yet another shrug. "Or I will just have to make sure I wear gloves whenever I am in my mother's presence."

Now he was curious. "Why are your hands in a poor state?" He was growing fascinated with watching the girl talk. Myriads of emotions flitted across her face as she spoke. He couldn't identify most of them, but he was beginning to suspect she wasn't as depthless as he had thought. This wasn't helping him find her less attractive, but for the moment, he couldn't convince himself to mind.

Now she looked sheepish. "It started on the train. Thankfully there was no shortage of water, so I was able to keep things clean for the children. I cannot think the soot from the train is healthy for them to breathe. So I had to regularly wash the walls and their blankets. My hands were unused to such exposure. At least at the orphanage we have tools and equipment to assist. Then I helped my friends clean their new place here in town. They are going to allow me to stay with them until I return to New York, so helping them was really the least I could do."

Charles blinked, unsure how to reply or if a reply was even necessary. The young woman didn't look as though she were expecting him to say anything, but he felt as though he ought to. But to hear her say that she had been washing the children's walls and bedding with her bare hands left him a little speechless. He couldn't fathom a Morley of New York doing such a thing. He grinned.

"I don't think you need to worry about your mother. She would never believe that you would do something so menial as chores. She will no doubt blame the weather conditions in such a desolate place as Missouri."

His stomach clenched as she released a tinkle of laughter over his words. "You are probably right, Mr. Ainsworth. Thank you for that comforting thought. I may just face my parents' wrath for avoiding my latest suitor for so long."

Surprised by a surge of what could only be jealousy, Charles gazed at her, hoping his mouth wasn't hanging open. "Have you left a gentleman in the lurch while you are here?"

She frowned at him and searched his face, obviously trying to divine the intentions behind his question. "Of course not. Not that it is any of your business, Mr. Ainsworth, but I would never leave anyone in the lurch if I could help it."

"Not even your parents?" he pursued, although he questioned his own intentions at this point.

She immediately became defensive. “I swear to you, I sent them a telegraph at the very first stop the train made. I’m certain they were notified of my whereabouts before they would have even realized I was gone. I did not leave them to wonder about me.” She had the grace to blush. She paused before continuing a little more softly. “My parents’ expectations are impossible for me to live up to. They want me to replicate their lives with my own.”

“Would that be so terrible?”

She huffed a breath and appeared frustrated. “Not if I wanted the same life as they have. Then it would probably be quite lovely. But I don’t. Want their life, that is. The type of gentleman they wish for me to marry is no longer the type I can see myself spending my life with.”

He wanted to ask her more about that but suddenly remembered she had mentioned something about trouble at the hotel. “What did you mean when you said you could understand about trouble coming from people in these parts?”

She looked confused by his question so he prompted her, “Remember, earlier, when you had just arrived, and I was displeased that you were outside by yourself. I said you needed to keep your wits about you. You argued that New York was less safe, but you didn’t seem to completely disagree with me. Did something happen to you at the hotel?”

He was fascinated but troubled by the blush climbing her cheeks.

“I handled the situation and will no longer be staying there, so it needn’t concern you.”

Little did she know, he thought, her words made him all the more concerned, rather than alleviating any worry. He tried to resist the protective feelings building in his chest but feared he was not as successful as he would wish.

Much to his relief, she turned to him suddenly, changing the subject. “Have you ever been to New York, Mr. Ainsworth?”

“I have,” he answered reluctantly, wondering where she was going with this question. He wasn’t going to find out, though, because they were suddenly interrupted by Ross calling to them.

“You two need to hurry up. We’re never going to get there.”

With a laugh full of joy, the woman beside him spurred her horse into a faster gait and left him behind, watching after her with doubts filling his mind. She was not exactly how he had thought she was. In fact, if he allowed himself to dwell on it, he was probably going to start thinking she was pretty great. That just would not do, so he shoved such thoughts to the back of his head. There was no way he could be attracted to a Morley socialite from New York city! He too urged his mount to a faster pace and quickly caught up with the others — the boys were laughing and once again vying for Miss Morley’s attention.

Chapter Eight

The boys' chatter helped distract Cassie's mind from the conversation she had been having with Mr. Ainsworth. It rattled her to realize how hurt she was by his obvious judgment of her. She couldn't help who her family was, and she made every effort not to be like them. She was reasonably certain she was no longer anything like them, in fact. But Mr. Ainsworth had judged her nonetheless. Frustration simmered in her chest, but with a slight huff she pushed the restless thoughts from her mind and focused her attention on the boys' chatter.

"And then the kittens licked me and I laughed so hard I almost fell out of the haymow and Mr. Charles said I wasn't allowed up there anymore." Ross' mixture of joy and dismay was almost palpable and made Cassie's heart constrict with the desire to hold onto the young boy and never let him go.

"Well, the good news is, the kittens will probably soon be big enough to leave the haymow, so you won't be separated for long."

Ross shrugged, trying not to look upset. "Yeah, that's what Mr. Charles said." He looked at her with wide, eager eyes. "But what if he's wrong? What if they forget me in the meantime?"

Cassie almost choked on her own gasp. She had the exact same concern about the boys. *What if they forget me after I'm gone?* Pasting what she hoped was a reassuring smile to her face, Cassie wished she was on the ground so she could hug the small boy. Instead she said, "I'm sure if you love them enough they'll remember you no matter what." When he still didn't look convinced, she continued. "Even if she does, you can get reacquainted as soon as she leaves the hay, can't you?"

This, at least, the boy could accept. They were quickly interrupted by the other boys, and the conversation flowed away from the touchy subject. But Cassie's heart still felt achy after those thoughts. It took some effort to keep a smile on her face and to pay attention to the boys' banter. Despite her melancholy, they soon had her captivated once more.

She was a little surprised when Tony urged his horse as close as he could manage to hers. Glancing over at him, she could see he was eager to speak without being overheard. She had to stifle her grin. She so loved these boys, she thought; her heart felt as though it was swelling in her chest. Cassie was quite certain the boy's furtive glances were not going unnoticed by anyone, but she managed not to make eye contact with anyone else and thus succeeded in holding back her laughter.

"It's not very interesting around here, is it?" Tony whispered.

Cassie wasn't sure what she had thought the boy had wanted to discuss with her, but this certainly wasn't it. She could no longer hold onto her amusement and a quickly stifled laugh erupted from her. His disgruntled glower helped her get her amusement under control.

Looking around, she assumed the boy meant the scenery since the three youngsters had not ceased talking about all that had captivated them on Mr. Ainsworth's ranch. They were following a trail that had been worn into the landscape, although Cassie wouldn't be able to tell why they were following it. As far as the eye could see there wasn't a single building, just gently rolling, grass-covered hills, with a few trees dotting the landscape. The lushness of the greenery told Cassie that it was most likely very productive soil, and she was sure Mr. Ainsworth was successful in his agricultural endeavors. But she could imagine that would not interest the city-bred boy overmuch.

"Why are you whispering?" she needed to ask.

"I don't want to insult Mr. Charles," he answered as a dull blush crept into his cheeks.

Cassie had to bite her lip to prevent her laughter from returning. "I don't think he'll take it personally, Tony. I think it will just take a bit of time for you to get used to the scenery around here."

"But what if I don't get used to it? What if I'm completely bored?"

The poor boy seemed genuinely concerned. All trace of laughter left Cassie as her heart went out to him. “You are a smart boy, Tony. While it’s true that life out here is going to be very different from your life in New York, that doesn’t mean it will be boring. There are so many new things you will have to learn about your new home, especially if you’re going to help Mr. Ainsworth with his animals and land. I don’t think there will be a shortage of things to do. And while it will take longer to get to school or to visit your neighbors, at least you will get to ride a horse in order to get there.”

The boy grinned at that. “That’s true. That will be great.”

“And you can run and jump and play with your brothers so much better here than in the city, since there is so much more space. There won’t be anyone yelling at you or the chance that you’ll get run over by a passing carriage, either.”

He was nodding slowly, listening closely to her words. She continued, “I think you will come to love it out here. Most of the other children that arrived on the train with us are near enough that you might even go to the same school with many of them, so you will have plenty of opportunity to stay in contact with them.”

“I hadn’t even thought of that. That will be good. Walter and Ross will be particularly happy about that, I think.” He paused, thinking the matter over some more. “I guess you’re right, Miss Cassie. It probably won’t be boring once we get used to being country mice.” They exchanged grins before he sobered again and added, “But you won’t be here, so there will still be something missing.”

Tears welled in her eyes and she had to look away so the boy wouldn't see. At first she was staring sightlessly off into the middle distance, but then motion caught her attention. Blinking away her tears, her eyes focused on what she was seeing.

On a small rise, not that far away, three men on horseback were watching them. A shiver of apprehension shimmied up her spine. They did not strike her as fine, upstanding citizens. She would have thought that in such a sparsely populated area, if one encountered others, they would at least wave, but the three men seemed to be scowling at them. They put her in mind of some of the more unsavory characters that she had had to watch out for around the orphanage back in the city. She wondered if they had followed them here. She turned to Mr. Ainsworth and was just about to ask him about them when he spoke up before she could say anything.

"Let's turn off here and head down to the river. The horses could use a drink, and it will be a good place for us to have our lunch."

Charles had to concentrate so as not to squirm under her searching gaze. In that moment, he wished Miss Morley was the simple-minded socialite he had been convinced she was, but it was obvious to him that she was far from stupid, even if she was shallow. He watched as her gaze flicked between his face and the three ruffians watching their group. Then she glanced at the boys, and a smile bloomed on her face.

It seemed to him that it wasn't as natural as usual, but he was glad when she began talking.

"Oh, I do look forward to seeing the river. I am quite certain my poor horse is nearly parched."

"Why do you think that, Miss Cassie?" Walter asked predictably.

"Well, I'm very thirsty myself, and I haven't had to carry anyone around all morning."

Her droll tone drew laughter from the boys and even the ranch hands that were accompanying them. Charles felt his lips tip up in the corners in appreciation of her quick thinking, but he was too preoccupied with his own concerns to join in the conversation. He was surprised, though, to realize how reassuring he found her voice as she carried on conversation with the boys.

"Have you been to the river before, Ross?" She was always so careful to involve all three boys in most conversations.

"Not yet, Miss Cassie. Mr. Charles has been quite busy since we got here, and we haven't been on any long rides before today," Ross explained.

Tony interrupted. "It wasn't just 'cause he was busy, remember? He said we would be too sore if we went too far before we got used to riding."

"Well that was very thoughtful of Mr. Charles, wasn't it? I'm sure he's right. I've been quite used to riding, but after sitting on the train for so long I got out of practice and I felt it after my first day on a horse once we got here, let me tell you. Since you lads have never ridden before now, it is good that you work up to it."

The youngsters were listening to her as though she were an oracle, he thought sourly. He ought to be grateful that she wasn't contradicting him. He should even be glad that she was complimenting him. But it wasn't to his face, he acknowledged before returning his attention to watching for danger. He WAS glad that she was keeping the boys occupied, but her chatter was a distraction to him and he had to concentrate to maintain his focus, as part of his mind enjoyed listening to her conversation.

"Do you find that you like riding on horses, now that you are a little more used to it?"

This was met with resounding enthusiasm.

"Absolutely!"

"It's the best!"

"Yes!"

All three answers came simultaneously, resulting in her rich laughter ringing out. "Well I am certainly glad of that. You would be in a fine mess if you didn't like to ride."

There was a pause. The boys were still laughing, but Charles felt her assessing gaze flicker towards him again. He hoped his expression was as bland as he was trying to make it. He didn't meet her eye, so he wasn't sure how convincing he was. It didn't matter. She resumed her chatter with the boys.

"Did you name your horses or did they have names already?"

"They already had names, and Mr. Charles said they know their own names so it would confuse them if we tried to call them something else."

"That makes sense, doesn't it? You would probably think it was really strange if Mr. Charles started calling you something other than your names, right?"

"I guess so," Walter answered.

"You still sound disappointed," she pointed out. "What name did you want to give your horse?"

"Scout," came his quick reply.

"That sounds like a good name for a horse," she answered. "Maybe you can just save it until you get a chance to get a young horse that doesn't have a name yet."

"That's what Mr. Charles said. He said we can name all the animals that get born on his property from now on, but we have to take turns."

"That sounds very generous of him. I'm sure the three of you will have a great time naming all the animals as they come along." She paused for a moment before asking, "Do you think Mr. Charles knows how grateful you are that he is letting you use his horses and he is taking his time to teach you so many things?"

This earned her puzzled glances from all three boys before they all glanced back at Charles with sheepish faces. Charles was sure they were hoping he wasn't listening to the conversation. He tried to remain impassive but the urge to laugh was strong. He was glad when they quickly shifted their focus back to her.

Tony spoke up. "He might not realize it since I just realized it myself."

"That's alright, Tony. Now that you know, you'll remember to tell him next time he does something nice for you, I'm sure. It seems to me that he has done plenty for you. People usually appreciate hearing thank you once in a while."

Charles was curious how long she was going to drag that out but was surprised when she allowed the matter to drop. Of course, what the boys said next could have caught her attention.

"See, Miss Cassie, this is why you should stay here with us. How will we know about things like this without you here to teach us?" Tony was obviously trying to sound reasonable, but his tone shifted to wheedling.

Miss Morley laughed, although to Charles it sounded more forced than usual. "You boys will do just fine with or without me."

"But don't you want to stay with us, Miss Cassie?" Walter asked.

"Of course I do, Walter, but that's not how it works."

"You could have the extra bedroom, Miss Cassie," Ross offered. "Mr. Charles said it's for when we get comfortable and want our own rooms, but me and Walter can share and you could have it."

"That is kind of you to offer, Ross, but Mr. Charles hasn't invited me to stay." The boys looked as though they were about to protest, so she carried on. "Even if he did, it would not be appropriate for me to live with a bunch of boys and a man, don't you think?"

"Maybe you could marry Mr. Charles," Walter interjected eagerly. "Then you could be our mother."

Tony wrinkled his nose. “I don’t think Miss Cassie is old enough to be our mother.”

Walter was not to be dissuaded so easily. “Well, if she married Mr. Charles, she would be our family anyway. Mr. Charles said he’s our family now, even if he isn’t our father. So she would be our family, too, and could stay with us forever.”

Charles could hear every word of the conversation and was trying not to fidget in his saddle. He fervently hoped the woman came up with a suitable reply, although he couldn’t fathom what it would be. He was relieved to hear her tinkle of laughter.

“Oh, I do love you three so much! Thank you for wanting to keep me with you. I never want to leave you, either, but I don’t know if I can make a life for myself here in Missouri. Maybe I could in Kansas City, but not here in Bucklin. There isn’t much for a person like me to do in these parts.”

Tony spoke up. “You think we can learn to like it here, don’t you?”

The young woman blushed as she realized where the youngster was going with his question. “Yes, I do. And I suppose you’re going to say that I could learn to like it, too, aren’t you?”

The boy grinned and nodded eagerly.

“The thing is, whether or not I could learn to like it isn’t the issue. My life is back there in New York.”

“We had a life there, too,” Tony answered quietly.

She must have been feeling desperate because she finally looked at Charles as though searching for help. Charles wasn’t sure what was written on his face, but she must have realized he didn't have the answer because she turned back to the boys.

"For one thing, the three of you still have each other, and you are here all together so it isn't the same thing." When they were going to protest further, she quickly continued with a small laugh that sounded forced. "Never mind about it now. I promise that I will give it more thought later. But for now, I am famished, and if my ears are not deceiving me I am almost certain that we have reached the river Mr. Ainsworth promised us. Let us get down and give our horses a rest."

Charles watched as she deftly managed to turn the children's attention away from the uncomfortable conversation. A part of him was offended that she had not coquettishly tried to gain his approval of the boys' suggestion. But another part was grateful that she had handled it so deftly and he wasn't left to explain to the boys why he didn't want their beloved Miss Cassie in a bedroom down the hall from him. He ignored the part that thought the boys' suggestion had merit.

While they ate, Charles kept his attention divided between watching for the men who had been observing them and listening to the boys chatter with Miss Cassie. The hands who had accompanied them had taken their own lunch and spread out to stand guard further away. So far it would seem that they had not been followed.

He thought back to what the boys had asked her. She was perfectly correct, there was nothing for her here in the wilds of Missouri. The type of women needed here were tough, experienced women, trained in something more useful than how to entertain. A New York socialite wouldn't survive through the first winter on the plains, let alone the lonely realities of life on the frontier. Just because she was beautiful and the boys loved her didn't give him any right to even consider keeping her here.

The rest of the day passed without event, but he could feel Cassie's watchful gaze touching on him from time to time. He was rather sure that she had noticed the three men and wanted to ask him about them. Charles was surprised by her restraint.

Chapter Nine

Cassie woke up with a dull ache in her heart that spread to her stomach. She had barely been able to eat the delectable breakfast that Katie had prepared that morning. She had grown closer to Katie and Mel in the few weeks since they'd left New York than she had with any of the friends she had grown up with, and she was dreading saying good bye to them. It amazed her how attached she was growing to everyone she was coming into contact with in this remote part of the world. Perhaps it was the very remoteness that made each relationship so special, she pondered as she rode out of the town once more. She had just one more house to visit. The last of the orphans from the train had been placed and she needed to see for herself that they were well.

The solitary ride to the small farm where Liam and Henry now lived was peaceful, and Cassie was surprised by how much she enjoyed the fresh air and quiet. She had begun to see the beauty in what had previously seemed monotonous and dull to her city bred senses. Realizing she was on the verge of turning melancholy, Cassie entertained herself for the rest of her ride with thoughts of what she would do with her time once she returned home. Unfortunately, all of her previous pursuits now struck her as shallow except for her time spent at the orphanage, but she had vowed to herself that she could no longer volunteer with orphans. With a sigh, she realized she would have to discover new things to do with her time. Perhaps she could become a teacher, she thought. Getting a little more education for herself would keep her occupied when she first returned to the city, and then being in a classroom would allow her to spend time with children but keep her from growing overly attached. Thus resolved, she set her chin resolutely just as she arrived at the Smiths' farm.

"G'day, Miss Morely," the homely older woman greeted after Cassie knocked on the door. "Won't you come in and have a cup of tea? We don't often get visitors."

"Thank you, Mrs. Smith. I must apologize for stopping in unannounced, but when I heard that you had taken Liam and Henry, I just had to stop in and congratulate them on their new home."

Mrs. Smith blushed timidly over Cassie's words and fluttered nervously around her kitchen. "We were lucky to get them. We were late finding out about the trainload of children and were worried we were too late when we finally got into town to see about them. Mr. Smith and I haven't yet been blessed with children of our own, so being able to take two such healthy boys in is a godsend for us. They are so polite and eager to learn, I can hardly believe they hadn't been claimed yet."

While the older woman had been talking, Cassie had taken the seat she had indicated at the table and glanced around as surreptitiously as she could manage, pleased to see that while the home was humble, it was neat and clean. And she was delighted to see several books on a low shelf. While all of the families who took in the orphans were expected to ensure the children received an education, Cassie had no idea how that could be enforced. Seeing books in the home made her feel that learning might not be considered trivial to the farming family, which raised the Smiths higher in Cassie's estimation.

Mrs. Smith had just placed a steaming cup of tea in front of her and a small plate of cookies on the table when there was a commotion at the door.

"Miss Cassie!" chorused two young voices followed by a deeper, more restrained greeting of "Miss Morley" from Mr. Smith.

Cassie stood to greet the three male arrivals. Four arms quickly encircled her.

"You came to visit us, Miss Cassie," Liam declared with glee. "Did you know we have a new home?"

"Yes, I heard and just had to come in person to congratulate you."

Henry squeezed her tight before letting her go. "There are cows and chickens and I haven't been hungry once since we left New York, Miss Cassie."

Cassie had to blink hard and swallow the lump forming in her throat before she could answer him. "I'm delighted to hear it. And I brought a little something for each of you as a welcome home present."

"You did?" Liam asked as he exchanged a glance with Henry.

"What is it?" Henry demanded.

They were so excited to open the small packages. Cassie felt as though her cheeks were burning from the grin splitting her face. It was such a relief for her to see their happiness. The gifts were small and had cost her little, but the boys had probably never received gifts for themselves. Their eyes were glowing as they opened the bag of marbles and the box of quoits. They couldn't wait to try them out.

As the boys headed out to play and Cassie turned back to her cooling tea, Mrs. Smith smiled warmly at her. "That was mighty kind of you, Miss Morley, I thank you deeply. We don't have much, but we're going to try our best to give these boys a good life."

"I can see that, Mrs. Smith, and I am so happy for it. I have grown attached to all the children we came out here with and I haven't been able to rest easy until I knew that they have all found decent homes. Seeing you with them has taken a weight off my mind."

"It will be our pleasure to maintain that," the older woman answered with dignity. "If you would like, we can correspond occasionally so you can keep up with their development."

Tears once again welled in Cassie's eyes. "I would like that above all things, thank you."

After a little more conversation, Cassie stood to take her leave. "I shouldn't keep you from your day much longer. Thank you for taking the time to let me visit and see how lucky Liam and Henry are to have been found by you."

Mrs. Smith appeared gratified by Cassie's words but waved them away. "We are the lucky ones. They are bright, healthy, and eager boys. It will be our privilege and duty to guide them into fine young men."

Cassie rode away from the Smith farm with deeply conflicted feelings. She was relieved beyond belief that the last of the children had found a good home. She had been worried that Liam and Henry wouldn't find a good placement. They weren't related to each other, but had grown close and would be wonderful brothers to each other in their new home. She could tell that while the Smiths may not have a lot to offer materially, they were prepared to give them love and attention, which would benefit them more than gold.

But now there was nothing holding her in Bucklin. She had no more excuses to stick around. It was time to buy her ticket back to New York. And say her goodbyes to Walter, Ross, and Tony. She urged her horse to a faster gait as she turned towards the Ainsworth spread.

From a distance she could see an unusual amount of activity in the yard. As she drew even closer, she was shocked to see Ross sitting on the front porch stairs, crying. She jumped down from her horse before it had even come to a complete stop and ran toward him.

"What has happened? Are you hurt?" she felt frantic but tried to keep the panic from her voice.

Ross's tearstained face was tragic. "We can't find Walter. I think he ran away."

Putting her arms around the young boy, Cassie sat down on the step beside him and tried to stem his tears. "Tell me what happened," she said in a low, soothing voice.

Ross snuggled into her arms with a shuddering sob. "While we were eating breakfast, Walter was pestering Mr. Charles to ask you to stay with us. When Mr. Charles told him that you don't belong here and you need to go back to New York, Walter told him he hates him and that he would go find you himself and get you to take him with you. But since you're here without him, I guess he didn't find you."

"Oh no! No, I haven't seen him. What happened next? Is that the last you've seen of him?"

Ross nodded and sniffled. "Bob from the barn said Walter tried to saddle his horse but he wouldn't let him so he ran out behind the barn."

"Why didn't Bob stop him?" Cassie was horrified.

Ross shrugged. "He didn't think anything of it, I guess. And he was busy with his chores."

Cassie was rubbing circles on Ross's back and his crying had slowly subsided to shuddering breaths. She pulled a handkerchief from her pocket and wiped his face. "Don't worry, Ross, he couldn't have gone too far. I'm sure we'll be able to find him before long. He has probably just found a nice spot for a good sulk and he'll come out when he's good and ready."

"Do you really think so?" His small voice sounded so hopeful.

"Sure I do. Walter is a smart boy. He'll realize he won't be able to find me, even if he had a horse, let alone on foot." She stood up and held her hand out for Ross to grab. "Now, let's go find Mr. Charles and see what we should do."

As Ross took her hand, the loud clearing of a throat behind her made Cassie jump, and hot color flooded her face. Mr. Ainsworth was about ten paces away and watching her intently. He looked as though he had heard every word she said but doubted her sanity. He also looked furious with her.

"Have you seen him?" he demanded.

She blinked. "Walter, do you mean?"

"Yes, have you seen him? Are you going to take him back to New York with you?" he sounded actually afraid that she would.

"No, of course not. While I love him dearly, I would never take him away from his brothers like that."

"Well, then where is he?"

"How would I know? I just got here." Now Cassie's fury was growing to match his, but she was trying valiantly to keep Ross from being hurt by the adults' anger.

When she cast a significant glance down toward the boy, Mr. Ainsworth seemed to gather himself.

"I apologize, Miss Morley. We are a little anxious at the moment. Of course you couldn't know where the boy is. If you will excuse us, we cannot entertain at the moment."

Cassie gasped at his attempt to be rid of her. "I am not going anywhere. I will help you search. I could never leave with this uncertainty about his safety."

Mr. Ainsworth glared at her but then his gaze once again took in the vision of Ross clinging to her and his stance softened. "Very well, just make sure you don't get in our way," he accepted gruffly.

Chapter Ten

Charles couldn't keep from staring at her. She was curled up with her feet tucked under her flowing skirts and Ross held firmly in her arms. They were both fast asleep. He knew it was worry exhausting them both added to the long day of searching. She hadn't complained about the grueling pace, only taking breaks when he forced her to. As he pointed out to her, it wouldn't do anyone any good to have her collapse on the trail; she'd only be an added burden to them then. When he had said that, she had flushed a deep red but had silently eaten the sandwich he had been pressing on her. And she offered no more argument whenever he had stopped her to offer her a drink or to suggest she take a moment to get off her horse when they stopped to water the horses.

It was obvious that guilt was eating at Cassie. Charles knew it wasn't her fault, but he didn't know how to convince her of that. The fact was the boy had disappeared after declaring he wanted to go stay with her. It wasn't her fault, but she was obviously having difficulty dealing with her involvement. If they didn't find the boy soon, they would all be consumed with guilt.

He was well aware that Walter's disappearance wasn't Cassie's fault — the fault firmly belonged on his shoulders. If he had been more aware of the boy's needs or not quite as dismissive of his attachment to Miss Cassie, Walter might not have run off.

His sigh must not have been as silent as he had hoped. While he watched, Cassie's eyes blinked open and she suddenly looked alert and concerned as she quickly realized where she was. Without disturbing the youngster in her arms, she sat up, still holding his gaze.

"Is there any news?"

Charles shook his head. "I'm sorry for disturbing you. You should try to get a little more sleep. You're obviously exhausted, and the boys are feeling comforted by your presence. I can't have you collapsing on me."

He realized his tone and words were less than gracious when she grimaced and turned her face away from him. He felt like kicking himself.

"I apologize, Miss Morley. I didn't mean to sound churlish. I mean to say that I'm glad you're here. Your presence is of benefit, but I don't want to see you getting sick from the strain. Get some more sleep, tomorrow might be just as difficult as today was."

He watched with a little bit of amusement as she blinked in surprise over his words. She was obviously still half asleep and wasn't about to start arguing with him over whether or not she was being of help. Charles knew that whether he liked her being there or not, until Walter was found there would be no way he could pry her away from his property. And she really was of help with Ross and Tony. Charles didn't know what he would have done with those two boys if not for her presence that day.

Still looking a little wary, Cassie snuggled back up with Ross and drifted back to sleep. Watching the two of them, Charles wanted to wake her back up and send her down the hall to a bed, but he hadn't the heart to disturb her again. He just hoped she wasn't too sore to ride in the morning.

ꙮ

Cassie swam toward consciousness as the first rays of dawn filtered through the window. Being careful not to disturb the still deeply asleep little boy in her arms, she extricated herself from him with difficulty given how stiff she was. It took some effort, but she managed to regain her feet without waking Ross. She was amazed she had managed to get as much sleep as she had and gingerly stretched herself into alertness. She wished she had thought to pack a bag for herself when she had rode frantically into town the day before seeking any information on Walter. No one had seen him and she had left word with her two friends and at the hotel and smithy before racing back out to the Ainsworth property. It sure would be nice to have a fresh change of clothes, but that was a rather petty thought when the dear boy was still missing in the vast wilderness that stretched out as far as she could see from the wide window in the brightening light.

She was so lost in thought she nearly squealed when Mr. Ainsworth broke the stillness with his words.

"Did you manage to get much sleep?" His solicitous tone almost made him seem human. Yesterday as they had searched the buildings and he had bullied her into accepting his offers of food and water, she had doubted his humanity and marveled at his strength.

"More than I would have expected," she admitted with a grimace as she stretched a crick out of her neck.

"Were you terribly uncomfortable?" he asked before adding, "I should have sent you to a proper bed last night, but the two of you looked to be offering each other the comfort you needed so I didn't have the heart to disturb you."

Again Cassie was surprised by his words but didn't question them. "Don't worry about me. I'll be fine once I get a little blood flowing into some of my limbs. And maybe a little bit of that," she added with a grin as she watched him take a swig of what smelled like strong coffee.

He immediately handed her his cup before he noticed her hesitation. Cassie was surprised to see him blush.

"I'm so sorry! I will, of course, pour you a fresh cup," he exclaimed before bustling away.

Cassie burst into quiet giggles as she followed him from the room, not wanting to wake up Ross, who was still sleeping on the sofa she had shared with him.

When she arrived in the kitchen, Mr. Ainsworth was pouring her a fresh cup of coffee. From the smell she could tell that it was going to be very strong. She didn't usually drink the dark brew, but she knew she could use the help in clearing the cobwebs from her mind. She didn't bother commenting on his embarrassment, although she thought it would have been something to tease him about if they were friends. That thought made her sad but she tried to ignore it.

She bustled about the kitchen helping to make breakfast, conscious of Charles' gaze following her. She couldn't tell if it was censorious or not so she chose to ignore it. Before long they were ready to head out and search some more.

The day dragged on with no news. They had ridden out from the main area, searching wherever they could think to look. They also rode out to the neighbors to ask if he had been seen and to search their buildings.

As dusk was gathering on the second day of his disappearance, Cassie was beginning to despair. Once again Ross was in tears and she was losing her own fight against weeping. Sitting on the front stairs of Ainsworth's house, she had the youngster on her lap and was rubbing circles on his back trying to calm him. Tony was sitting beside them trying to be stoic, but Cassie could see his lower lip beginning to tremble.

Putting her arm around Tony, she gathered both boys as close to her heart as possible and tried to think what to say. As she herself was nearing despair, she couldn't make them any promises.

"We need to stay strong now, boys. We aren't giving up. Someone will surely have seen him."

"We never should have left New York, Miss Cassie," Tony declared. "It's too big and empty out here. In the city hundreds of people would have seen him by now."

Cassie sighed. "I know, Tony, but in the city many of those hundreds of people could have hurt him, too."

"You don't think there are bad men out here in Missouri?" he asked, scoffing.

She had no answer for him and felt her own tears finally give way. Ainsworth had been eavesdropping on their conversation as usual and chose that moment to sit down beside Tony and pull the three of them into his arms. His action stopped her tears, clogging her throat as she almost choked on her surprise.

"Come now, all of you. Do not despair. We'll find that rascal and bring him home safe and sound in a jiffy."

"He's not a rascal," Ross mumbled through his slowing tears.

"Sure he is," Ainsworth answered with a false note of joviality in his tone. "Leaving us all here to worry about him. Perhaps he's off having a good laugh at our expense right this minute."

Cassie was shocked. She tried to pull away from him, but he kept his grip firm. She turned to look at him, aware that her dismay over his words was probably written all over her face.

"You don't seriously believe that do you?" she demanded.

"No! I don't think he's hiding from us, but I do think we will find him. But we cannot give up or give in to despair. We need to rest up and keep searching again tomorrow."

His tone was warm but firm, and Cassie began to feel comforted by his grip. She laid her head on his shoulder over and around Tony. It felt as though they were a unit, sharing their fears and drawing strength from their mutual feelings. She tried to maintain a grip on her heart as it picked up its pace being this close to the handsome man. *He's just offering you comfort, you ninny,* she reminded herself. *Don't get carried away.*

Chapter Eleven

The next morning everything fell down around them. Cassie awoke with a start. Tony was standing at the end of her bed with his anxious gaze fixed upon her. It was immediately obvious to her that he didn't want to wake her up, but he had something to tell her. She sat up and beckoned him close.

"What has happened?"

He was trying to be tough, but she could see how upset he was.

"It's all right, Tony. We'll figure it out. You don't have to carry this burden by yourself. Tell me what has happened."

"Someone is asking Mr. Charles for lots of money if he wants to get Walter back."

"They are?" Cassie was stunned. "Why would they ask Mr. Charles for money?"

Tony's lip trembled and she was instantly contrite. She quickly overrode her own demands in order to deal with the boy's concerns. "Come here, Tony," she commanded softly, holding her arms open. With a soft sob he practically jumped into her arms.

“What if he doesn’t want to pay it?” he asked in a small voice.

“Why would you ask that? Of course he would want to pay it,” was her immediate answer.

“But we just got here and it’s turning out to be too much trouble.”

“Oh, my dear boy, Mr. Charles knows this isn’t Walter’s fault, or yours or Ross’s. You aren’t being too much trouble. I am absolutely certain he will want to pay it.” She placed gentle emphasis on the word want. She didn’t mean to, but she couldn’t imagine that the rancher would have any amount of extra money available to pay a ransom for the boy no matter how much he might want to pay it. She would have to contact her father. It would take considerable begging, but she would do anything for Walter. She just hoped she could be sufficiently convincing in a telegraph. And that he would be able to arrange the money for her quickly.

When the boy seemed calmer, Cassie got up and went in search of Mr. Ainsworth.

“Mr. Ainsworth?” she asked tentatively.

“Oh, surely you can call me Charles by now, can’t you, Cassandra?”

Her hot blush scorched her cheeks. His impatience combined with the use of her given name confused her. It wasn’t the time to argue so she pressed on, ignoring his words.

“Tony said there has been a ransom demand.”

He cast his searching gaze over her before handing her the sheet of paper.

She couldn't open it just yet. She had some questions first. "All this time I've been thinking he wandered off and is lost or a wild animal got him. But now that there's a note from someone, it makes me wonder. Do you think this could be one of the townsfolk?"

Charles' gaze sharpened on her in question. "Why would you ask that?"

"The first day I came out here to visit the boys, the man at the smithy said some strange things about you. About the size of your property. It struck me at the time that he was probably jealous of you. Jealousy can cause people to do some terrible things."

"I agree that jealousy can cause people to be cruel and awful, but I really don't think the smithy had anything to do with Walter's disappearance."

"How can you be sure?" Cassie wanted to trust his judgement, but all the possibilities terrified her.

"For one thing, despite how he might feel about my land, I actually consider the smithy to be a friend. For another, I'm not completely sure the man is literate."

Cassie looked back down at the paper in her hand and finally forced herself to open it. Her eyes quickly scanned the missive.

"One thousand silver dollars?" she exclaimed and then had to sit down. That was as far as her eyes had gotten. She gazed at him without comprehension. "How can this be happening?"

"Don't worry, Cassie, we'll get Walter back. Don't you see, this is good news?"

"How can you say this is good news?" Her eyes had returned to the paper she held. "They are demanding the money by tomorrow evening. I can't abide the thought of Walter being with these blackguards another moment, but I don't know how I will be able to get the money by tomorrow evening."

She could feel tears welling up in her eyes but couldn't turn away when she saw the arrested expression on his face. "What do you mean YOU can't get the money?" he asked in an odd voice. "You might have noticed that it was not you from whom they have demanded the ransom."

Cassie felt hot color staining her cheeks once more. "Well, no, perhaps it was not addressed to me, but surely I must have access to more money through my father..." She trailed off, quailing under his incredulous stare. She returned her eyes to the paper in her hands.

"Actually, it would appear that it isn't addressed to either of us. Who is Gibby? And why would they be speaking to him about Walter?" She could hear her voice becoming shrill but was powerless to stop it.

Charles knelt before her and grasped her hands. "Shhh, Cassie, it's going to be all right, don't worry."

"But how?" She wanted to trust him and found his warm grasp comforting but was overwhelmed by her fear for Walter. "Do they even say where he is or why they are doing this?" She still held the paper, but it was crumpled with Charles holding her hand. "And where are we going to get the money? And where are we supposed to leave it?"

Again Charles tried to quiet her fears. "Shhh, you have to calm down, Cassie. Take a deep breath."

Cassie did as he said. She joined in his laughter when he started to laugh and reminded her, "All right, now let it out or you'll faint on me."

She almost squirmed under his penetrating gaze while she continued taking deep, fortifying breaths. He must have decided she was calm enough because he got up from the crouch he was in before her and sat beside her while still holding on to one of her hands.

"Thank you, Mr. Ainsworth." Upon noting his censorious expression she colored slightly and corrected herself. "That is, Charles, I appreciate your patience with me. I'm sure you are just as anxious as the rest of us about Walter and have had just as little sleep. I shouldn't have lost my composure like that."

"I shan't hold it against you. It was perfectly understandable."

"But what ARE we going to do, Charles? I'm relieved to read that Walter hasn't been carried off by some wild animal as I had feared, but if someone is holding him for ransom, we need to get him back."

"I agree with you wholeheartedly, Cassandra, but I don't think paying the ransom is the answer."

Cassie could only stare blankly at him. "Whatever do you mean? Of course we have to pay it!"

Charles patted her hand, reminding her not to lose her presence of mind. Cassie kept her voice low, not wanting the boys to hear their discussion.

"Walter has been missing for almost three days. We cannot be sure this note is actually from a kidnapper. It could be someone taking advantage of our tragedy. We cannot just bring a large sum of money and hand it over without proof that Walter is alive."

Cassie could see the wisdom of his words. "But how are we going to arrange that?" While waiting for his answer, she disengaged her hand from his grasp and spread open the ransom note, scanning it for more information. "It's not signed. I wonder if that's a message in itself. Have you ever encountered a situation like this?" She searched his gaze. "I have to ask, Charles, why are you so calm? Is it just that you're trying to be manly and strong for me and the boys or are you somehow experienced in these types of matters?"

This prompted another laugh from Charles. "No, I cannot say that I have ever had anyone demand ransom money from me before."

Cassie felt like she was in a fog and kept staring at the paper in her hands. "Why would they write Dear Gibby?" she mused. "That is decidedly strange. Do you know anyone named Gibby?" She finally looked up at Charles and was surprised to see the discomfort on his face that he was trying to hide from her. "What is it, Charles? What aren't you telling me? Who is Gibby?"

When he didn't immediately answer her, she turned the paper over, hoping there would be more information on the other side. There was. In a messy scrawl, where it would have been visible when the page was folded in three, was a name – Gibson Charles Ainsworth Emerson – and she felt certain pieces of the puzzle shift into place and all the blood drain from her head.

"You're Gibson Emerson?" she asked, accusation evident in her tone. She wanted to laugh hysterically but tried not to get sidetracked from the point at hand. It was obvious by his continued silence that he didn't want to talk about his name issues. "Since this is apparently not the name you go by, whoever sent this letter knows more about you than you would like. Who in these parts might know this? And are you aware of anyone who might call you Gibby? Which is a horrible appellation, if you ask me."

Again Charles laughed. It had a hollow tone to it, but at least he was no longer keeping silent. "You aren't nearly as empty headed as you would like New York society to think, are you, Cassandra Morley?" he asked in a quiet, admiring voice.

Cassie could only stare at him disdainfully. Charles sighed. "I would have to agree with you. I've always hated it if anyone calls me Gibby. The only person who insists upon it is my cousin, Cedric."

"I know he is the black sheep of your family, but do you think he would stoop so low as to kidnap a child?" she asked. She could hear the chill in her tone but couldn't be bothered to disguise it.

"I wouldn't have thought so, but I wouldn't put it past him, either. On the other hand, since he has been highly resentful of my successes in life, he could just be taking advantage of this adversity and may not actually have Walter but is just hoping to relieve me of some of my funds, since he is always with his pockets to let."

Cassie was furious but was trying valiantly to keep it in check. It wasn't Charles or Gibson or whatever his name is, it wasn't his fault his cousin was a wretch. "Do you have any idea how we might get in touch with dear cousin Cedric?" she asked in a restrained voice. "Or if we could ascertain if he does, in fact, have Walter?"

"Do you remember the men who were watching us when we went for a ride the day before Walter went missing? I know you noticed them even though you didn't say anything."

Cassie frowned, unsure why he was answering her question with more questions. "Yes, I remember."

"I'm pretty sure those men are associates of my cousin."

Cassie felt the bottom drop out of her stomach. She had been hoping that somehow this situation could be cleared up easily. Those men had made her uncomfortable that day. She hated to think how terrified Walter must be if he were in their clutches. She went back to the slow, deep, measured breaths she had been taking in an effort to control her reaction.

When she felt that she had herself in hand she asked, "Why did you not say something sooner? Did you suspect them from the beginning?"

"One never wants to suspect their own family of stabbing them in the back, metaphorically speaking. I was suspicious of those rough looking men. It was too coincidental that he disappeared the day after they were watching us, but I wouldn't have imagined Cedric's involvement until I received that letter. I still cannot say for sure if he actually has Walter or if he's just wallowing in my pain. I would expect kidnappers to demand ransom immediately, not wait a few days."

"He was always into torture, if I recall correctly. You should have seen what he did to my doll on the one occasion that I had the misfortune of meeting him when I was a child." Cassie paused and watched Charles assimilate the fact that she knew who Cedric was. "So tell me, Gibby," she said with sarcastic emphasis, "what are you going to do now?"

She was surprised and slightly mollified to see color creep into his cheeks but would not allow herself to soften toward him. She had been so worried Walter's disappearance was her fault, but it had been his all along. He should have known his terrible cousin had a hand in this. But then she was horrified by the remembrance as he had pointed out that Cedric might not have Walter at all. She tried not to panic and waited to see what he had to say.

"I've already dispatched messengers to wherever I can think of to find Cedric. And I will send telegraphs to my aunt and parents to see if they have any information on his whereabouts if my messengers come up empty handed." He paused and searched her face. "I swear to you, we will get to the bottom of this *and* bring Walter home safely before much more time has passed."

“But what if, as you say, Cedric doesn’t actually have him and this is just an unnecessary diversion?” Cassie grimaced over the quaver she heard in her voice, but it could not be helped. She held Charles’ gaze and willed her lips not to quiver.

“I know I said that, and I cannot say why he would wait to send the ransom note, but we have looked everywhere. Surely someone has taken the boy and no one else has claimed responsibility, so it is only reasonable to think Cedric must have him.”

Cassie nodded but felt sick to her stomach. “So now there’s nothing to do but wait, it would seem.” She felt as though she had aged at least a decade in the last three days. “I had best go and see if I can distract Ross and Tony while we try to keep our hopes up. Thank you for your patience with all my questions.”

Charles watched as the young woman left the room, admiring as she tried valiantly to hide her mixed emotions. It was obvious she was furious with him for hiding his identity from her. And of course, she was sick over his involvement in Walter’s disappearance. But he was impressed that she had the sense to realize that now was not the time to raise a fuss about it. All their energies needed to be focused on rescuing the boy. Recriminations could wait until he was safe. He hoped she would be able to keep the brothers busy while he saw to dealing with Cedric. It turned Charles’ stomach to think that his own cousin would be so nefarious, but he couldn’t focus on that at the moment or he could lose his mental dexterity. He would have to keep his emotions at arm's length to see them all through the next days and bring Walter home. He thought again of Cassie and realized that it would take more effort than he would have thought to hold back his feelings. Who would have thought that he would care about a socialite's opinion?

Chapter Twelve

Charles stood in the hallway listening as Cassie read to the boys. It was a story of rollicking adventure, sure to keep the boys' minds occupied while the adults dealt with their missing brother. And her manner of reading would keep them captivated, he thought as he realized that he too was becoming preoccupied.

Shaking his head, he walked quietly away and left the house. He hated to leave them but he was hoping to keep the rest of the proceedings away from those three. He didn't want them marred by the ugliness that might follow. He knew Cassie would probably want to be involved, but he thought it was for the best if he could keep her from it. His heart constricted slightly at how natural it was to leave his boys in her care. *Perhaps Walter had been right, and we need to keep Cassie here with us*, he thought wistfully. He pushed the thought from his mind — he needed to keep his focus on the task at hand.

It was perfect timing. As soon as he stepped onto the porch he spotted one of the men he had sent out for information returning and looking purposeful. He was glad to intercept him before he could knock on the door.

"You look like you have some news, Brad."

"I do, sir. I found where Cedric and several others are holed up in a rundown shack on the outskirts of the next town over. I asked around as discretely as possible. Seems they were asking for milk at the mercantile. I doubt that sort has taken to drinking milk, so I'm thinking they do have the boy after all."

Charles almost sagged with relief but couldn't give in to the wave of emotion. Now the really tricky part was to begin. How could they rescue the boy without anyone getting hurt?

Sitting back firmly into his saddle, Charles looked around at the men. Those he could see were all in position. The ones he couldn't see, behind the small, rough building, he trusted implicitly so he knew they were where he asked them to be. All would go as well as could be hoped when dealing with a rough customer like Cedric and his associates. Charles couldn't figure out for the life of him why the bounder had chosen to follow him to Missouri. They had never gotten along. With the vastness of this land it was ridiculous for his cousin to seek him out. Of course, it could just be, as he had told Cassie, that his cousin just wanted to cause him trouble.

Glancing to his right, Charles was glad to have the sheriff by his side. His family back East wouldn't be happy about it, but he wasn't going to give Cedric a pass when he had attacked Charles right in his home – there was no forgiveness for taking one of his sons.

The plan was simple. They were counting on the element of surprise. And outnumbering their opponents. He just prayed Walter would have the sense to take cover and not get hurt in the process.

After a nod from the sheriff, Charles dropped his raised hand and all the men advanced at once upon the shack. Within minutes it was over. Seeing as it was late in the afternoon, Cedric's men had already drunk themselves into a stupor. They couldn't respond quickly enough when Charles and his men had broken in from all directions. The shack had completed its collapse when some of Charles' ranch hands had kicked a space for themselves to enter from the back. Thankfully, Walter had been huddled in a corner and didn't sustain any injuries. The sheriff's deputy had a grin on his face as he quickly tied up the three men who had been following Cedric. Of course, Cedric was nowhere to be found. Charles gritted his teeth at the thought that the brute might get away free. As long as he kept himself far from Charles' family, he supposed he didn't much care what became of his cousin. And for the sake of family relations it might be for the best if he wasn't responsible for his cousin's arrest. Charles shook his head. He wasn't responsible in any case. He had certainly not asked the ruffian to make off with his son.

Speaking of the boy, Charles quickly gathered the youngster into his arms and strode from the debris of the shack while his men helped the sheriff with the criminals. Settling himself against a tree, he took a deep breath before looking intently at the boy. He would've fallen over from the shock if he wasn't already sitting.

Having expected to see fear or panic on the boy's face, Charles wasn't prepared to see Walter's bright shining eyes and huge grin. He burst into laughter.

"Shouldn't you be panicking or something?"

"That was swell, Mr. Charles!!"

"That's not how I would describe it, but I'm glad to see that you weren't afraid." Charles examined the child for any signs of injury or harm. "Did they hurt you in any way?" Now that the boy was safe, he was feeling the reaction to all the fears he had kept hidden. He wanted to squeeze the boy to his heart and never let him go, but the youngster's lack of distress was mixing up his feelings.

The boy's grin began to fade, and he couldn't meet Charles' gaze. "I was scared some of the time, Mr. Charles. I didn't think you would come for me, especially when I heard them talking about asking someone for money for me. It didn't make much sense, but I thought maybe Miss Cassie would come if she knew I was taken."

"She has been trying to find you, along with me and your brothers. She is going to be furious when she finds out that we left her behind when we came for you."

This helped to restore Walter's grin. "She'll probably have some words for you, Mr. Charles."

Chapter Thirteen

Walter had been correct in his assessment. Cassie was furious when she realized Charles had left without her. When she couldn't find him anywhere in the house, she had gone outside to look for him. Hank, the farm hand who had been left behind to watch over the ranch while everyone else rode out to rescue Walter, had been a little bitter when he informed her of his whereabouts.

"Left me here to see to you all," Hank had said in such an aggrieved tone of voice that Cassie would have laughed if she didn't feel similarly.

"I'm terribly sorry that you were left behind, Hank. I cannot believe that Mr. Ainsworth would stoop so low as to trick me into staying behind."

"He wasn't being low toward you, miss. He's that concerned about keeping you safe. Seems to me, you ought to be grateful."

Cassie made every effort not to be offended by the man's words. He was just trying to be honest and defend his employer. He certainly wasn't trying to hurt her feelings. And he was even hurt himself for having been left behind. She offered him a tight smile.

“I’m sorry you are stuck with us. We will make every effort not to cause you any difficulty.”

A few hours later, when they heard the sound of many hoofbeats entering the yard, Cassie felt as though her nerves had frayed. She wanted to yell like a fishwife at Charles for leaving them behind with no explanation. Needing to keep Ross and Tony entertained, while not knowing if Walter and Charles were safe, had nearly done her in.

Cassie could tell he felt guilty by the way he wouldn’t make eye contact with her when she shot a glare his way. But she couldn’t hold onto her anger for long in the face of her joy at being reunited with Walter. The boy’s safety meant everything to her. *How am I ever going to leave them behind?* Despite how angry she was toward Charles, she knew he was included in the “them” she would mourn the loss of when she returned to New York.

Cassie could barely bring herself to let go of Walter but she realized in order to help him overcome his ordeal she would have to try to hide the depth of her own feelings. She forced herself to smile brightly as she released him from her tight hug. He looked at her seriously.

“It’s all right, Miss Cassie, you can squeeze me a little more, I don’t mind.”

This sent her off in a peal of giggles. Everyone joined her, and the tension that had accumulated quickly dissipated as they all laughed their relief.

“Are you hungry? We could make you whatever you would like to eat,” she offered, determined not to hover.

Her heart rolled over when he smiled sweetly at her. “I would be happy to eat some pancakes, please.”

She couldn’t resist; she bent down and placed a brief kiss gently on his brow. “There will be plenty of pancakes served momentarily. I think we could all use some sweetness right about now.”

Cassie had been hoping for a moment or two alone to collect her thoughts and pull herself together emotionally, but the whole gang followed her to the kitchen. Walter didn’t want to be away from Cassie while the other two boys weren’t letting Walter out of their sight, and it seemed as though Charles didn’t want to be left by himself. The four males made themselves comfortable while Cassie bustled around the kitchen.

There was a moment of uncomfortable silence behind her but then Cassie heard Tony asking Walter about his experience.

“Were you scared?”

“Of course not,” the youngster declared. Cassie rolled her eyes and had to resist turning to see the other boys’ reactions.

“Well, I was scared,” Tony admitted while Ross added, “I even cried.”

“Really?” Walter seemed shocked that his brothers would admit as much. There was a heartbeat of silence before he continued. “At first I didn’t even realize what was happening. I thought it was a joke or something. The men were talking about Mr. Charles, so I thought they were ranch hands that I just hadn't met yet. But they weren't very nice. By the time I realized what was happening, I was too mad to be scared or even to cry, even though I wanted to, especially at night."

"Why were you mad?" Tony wanted to know. "How could you be too mad to be scared?"

"I figured I would get in trouble for running away and it would be their fault."

Cassie snorted trying not to laugh and tried to cover it up by coughing. She almost jumped out of her skin when a soft voice at her shoulder admonished, "You need to be quieter if you want to take up eavesdropping as a pastime."

She whirled to confront Charles, furious that he would startle her when they had all barely begun to recover from their earlier frights. He must have realized his blunder because he was immediately contrite.

"I apologize profusely, Cassie, I didn't realize you were unaware that I was beside you. I didn't mean to surprise you." He gave her a significant glance. "Now, please point that knife somewhere else."

She glanced down and realized she still held a knife clenched in her hand. She laughed softly. "I had just started peeling some apples." She followed through and continued with her task before glancing at him with apprehension. "I hope you don't mind that I have made myself at home in your kitchen without even asking your leave. It was the first thing I thought of, the need to feed the boys, and didn't even think to ask if you would mind."

"Don't even give it a thought. I don't mind at all. I don't think any of us have eaten properly in at least three days. Besides you look far better in here than I do. And from what I've seen in the last day or two, you are far more skilled than my cook."

"For a socialite, you mean?" she couldn't help asking.

He laughed. "You are definitely far more skilled than any socialite I've ever met. And I suppose I owe you an apology for having judged you so harshly when I first met you after so many years. I realize you had no idea who I was, but I recognized you almost immediately. Even before I heard your name, I was pretty sure you were Mitch Morley's daughter. The set of your jaw when you stepped off the train was exactly how he would look when he was considering a new business arrangement."

Cassie laughed. "Oh dear. Did I look terribly arrogant?"

Charles joined her laughter. "Not arrogant, just determined. And I now realize you were trying to hide all your misgivings behind a layer of bravado. I wonder if that's your father's strategy," he trailed off.

"I doubt it. Father always knows what he's doing. Or thinks he's right even if he doesn't know." She grinned. "But you are correct. I had no idea who you were. I was only four or five when I saw you last, and I had no thought that there could possibly be a family acquaintance out here in Missouri. No one has mentioned it. I had quite forgotten about your existence in fact," she added with another grin. "Besides the fact that you are going by a different name out here. I haven't yet had the chance to ask you about that." She could feel his eyes watching her closely as she whisked together the apples, setting them to simmer with sugar to make a warm sauce for the pancakes. Cassie willed her hands not to shake while she measured the flour and other ingredients. Her nerves were already shot from worrying about Walter. She could barely tolerate Charles' scrutiny. She was relieved that her question caused him to shift his eyes away as he pondered how best to answer her.

"I was fairly disillusioned when I left New York. My parents' wealth had so many strings attached to it. I didn't want to be a puppet on the end of those strings, so I set out to make my own way in the world. I was determined that anything I accomplished was going to be on my own merit, so I needed a new name. I didn't want to be completely disloyal, though, so I chose two of the names my parents had given me, just not the ones anyone would recognize or associate with them."

"Well, your ploy worked. I even know your family, and I didn't realize you were you." She paused while she carefully broke a couple eggs into her bowl, ignoring his amused grin over her need to concentrate. "Don't make fun, Charles. I am sure you realize I haven't actually spent too very much time in a kitchen."

"I would never have guessed. You seem right at home."

"Never mind that, I need to ask you something. Did you end up having to telegraph your family to find out anything about Cedric? I forgot to ask you earlier."

"No, I didn't, but why do you ask?"

Cassie sighed. “I would ever so much rather my parents never discover that I met you out here. You will remain Charles Ainsworth in my recounting of any of my adventures in Missouri.”

“That still doesn’t answer my question.” When Cassie searched his face, he appeared genuinely puzzled.

“Are you being deliberately obtuse or have you been gone from New York too long?”

“That is doing nothing to clear up my confusion, Cassie, but it is certainly making me all the more intrigued to know what you mean.”

Cassie sighed again. “If it is ever found out that I encountered an Emerson bachelor and did not manage to ensnare you, I will be deemed utterly too stupid to live.” There was a pause where she contemplated this melancholy thought but then she brightened. “On the other hand, perhaps they will realize I am a completely lost cause and will give up on trying to force me into the mold they have designated for my life.”

Charles gazed at her in silence while she fidgeted with the pancake batter. He finally broke his silence. “Why bother going back to New York?”

“I can’t stay here. I don’t have skills like Katie and Melanie. They will be able to provide for themselves just fine. There’s not much of a place for a New York socialite outside of New York.”

“You’ve been pretty great here for the last three days, keeping our spirits up and insisting we sleep or eat, even when you yourself didn’t want to. I would have lost my mind trying to keep Ross and Tony occupied and comforted while also searching for Walter and trouncing my cousin. I have come to realize that even boys need both a father and a mother."

Cassie blinked rapidly, trying to clear from her mind the idea that was beginning to form. She feigned amusement. "If I didn't know any better, I would suspect you were thinking that I might fill that role."

"You can't tell me you don't want it or that you wouldn't be any good at it, even if you are a little too young to actually be their mother."

She felt hot color flood her face from her neck to the roots of her hair. "I would love to be the boys' mother, but the title of mother most often accompanies that of wife, and I know nothing about that." She couldn't look at him as she busied herself with the stove. "Of course, you probably didn't think through what you are saying, so let us just pretend this conversation never happened."

He watched her fidget with her sauce under his lowered lids. "I actually did give this a great deal of thought over the last couple of days. I think you would make an exceptionally good wife." He paused briefly before adding, "And mother to my three sons."

They hadn't noticed that the boys were listening. "Yes, yes, yes, yes, yes!" exclaimed the three youngsters as they jumped up and down and began running around the kitchen.

Walter clasped his hands together and earnestly said, "This was worth getting kidnapped for."

Cassie could feel that the hot color was once again covering her face, but she laughed over Walter's words. “Never mind boys, this is not a conversation for you to participate in. Mr. Charles and I will finish discussing it after we have all enjoyed our pancakes.”

It was perhaps her inexperience showing to suggest because it proved impossible to keep the topic from being discussed by the excited boys but thankfully they were too busy stuffing the delicious pancakes into their mouths to say too much. Their relief and joy lent them huge appetites, and Cassie was kept busy filling their plates. She only managed to force one small pancake down her own dry throat and it tasted like sawdust to her, but the males in the room seemed to be enjoying them so she didn’t worry too much about her cooking, despite her discomfort with Charles’ hot gaze following her constantly. She half expected that she would lose her mind and set the house on fire since she could barely pay attention to what she was doing.

Cassie was filled with half relief and half despair when the three boys were finally full and they asked to be excused. Charles granted permission and they hurried from the room. But not before Walter stopped beside her and whispered loudly, “Please say, yes, Miss Cassie,” and then quickly followed his brothers.

Cassie could feel tears gathering in the corners of her eyes and tried to blink them away as she gathered up the plates and fidgeted around the kitchen. Her fidgets came to an abrupt end when Charles’ warm hand closed over hers.

“Stop squirming around the topic. The boys have gone and left us to our private conversation. You are right to be irritated with me. I shouldn’t have forced your hand by asking you with the boys in the room, but I thought they were fully occupied."

"But you didn't ask me anything," she protested, blushing.

He stared at her in amazement. After a brief, stunned silence, he gathered both of her hands into one of his large ones and then with his free hand he held her chin and forced her to meet his gaze.

"Cassandra Morley, would you please do me the great honor of being my wife?"

She could feel her chin trembling despite his warm grip on it. "But why would you want to marry me? You keep saying how little regard you have for New York socialites. Surely you would be better off with someone like Katie or Mel. They have skills far more suited to life in Missouri."

"Cass, don't be obtuse now. I've barely met Katie or Mel. But I have watched you carefully through what I expect was the most gruelling experience of your life. You remained kind, unselfish, and caring. I realize now that while you are from a wealthy New York family, you are not a socialite no matter what your mother might say. And that makes you uniquely suited to be my wife."

Cassie blinked at him. Her puzzlement must have been clearly written on her face. He sighed before elaborating. "Just as I can see you are not cut from the same cloth as the rest of your family, I most certainly am not like the rest of the Emmersons. Don't get me wrong, I have no interest in living as a Spartan. I'm happy to work hard and provide well for my family. I just refuse to be sucked into the showy lifestyle that my, and your, family seem to love. I have finally realized that you feel the same way."

When Cassie made to protest, he hushed her. "I know, you didn't always feel that way. I've heard you protest your questionable motivation for starting your work at the orphanage. But it is how you feel now, isn't it? You yourself said you don't want to be pushed into the mold your parents want you in."

She wasn't sure what to say to him in response. She merely nodded, keeping her wide eyes focused on him watchfully. He nodded firmly and continued. "You will fully understand my background and my complicated relationship with my family, but I know you will be a lovely partner for my life here, and you would be equal to the task if we ever decided, as a family, to return to the city. You are, in fact, perfect for me."

Cassie wasn't sure what to say. The past several days had been a whirlwind for her emotions. She wasn't sure if she should trust what he was saying. She wanted to believe him, but needed to be certain.

"Charles," she began before pausing to gather her thoughts.

"I will beg if I have to, but please, Cassie, be my wife."

She offered a watery chuckle as she fought emotional tears. "I might like to see that."

Charles grinned at her. "Are you trying to torture me as revenge for my cold reception to you when you first arrived in Bucklin?"

"Not at all, but you cannot argue with the fact that it seems to be a rather sudden change of heart. Is this just an emotional reaction to the stresses we've all faced with Walter's disappearance?"

Cassie was surprised by the emotions that quickly chased themselves across the handsome man's features before he showed her an impassive face. It slipped a little around the edges, but she was fairly certain she had hurt his feelings.

"I apologize if I have made you uncomfortable with my words. I can assure you, I am quite sure of my feelings. They are sound and stable, not brought on by our recent stresses."

Cassie allowed the silence that followed his words to lengthen as she studied his face carefully. He wasn't giving much away but she felt he was being sincere. She sighed softly. "The only thing is, Charles, you haven't actually told me what your feelings are. You mentioned that our backgrounds are compatible and you no longer consider me to be superficial. I am not completely convinced that is sufficient for building a life together so far from what is familiar to me."

The silence stretched out after her words while Charles frowned and thought over what she had said. Suddenly his face split into a grin and he eased down onto one knee. "Very well then, begging it is," he said with a chuckle. Cassie began to giggle but quickly sobered as he tightened his grip on her hands and his grin drifted into seriousness.

"Cassandra Morley, you are as lovely on the inside as you are on the outside. I may not have always shown it, but I found you delightful every time you came to visit the boys. I loved watching you struggle to be polite whenever I was being surly. Your patience with the boys as you helped teach them to ride made me want to pull you into my arms, even as I tried to keep you at arm's length. I didn't want to have any feelings for you because I was convinced your place was back in New York."

Cassie tried to prevent it, but tears were welling in her eyes as he expressed his thoughts to her. One solitary tear broke its confines and slid down her cheek. She didn't speak. He surged back to his feet, reaching out gently to wipe the tear away. "As hard as I fought my feelings, they continued to grow. You might not have much experience at country living or even running a household, but I have watched you, especially while Walter was missing. You make up for whatever you might lack in knowledge or experience with your intelligence, willingness, and enthusiasm. I am completely convinced that you could make a success of whatever you might put your mind to. I hope you might put your mind to making a life here with me, and with those three boys you love so much. Even more, I am most certain that, while you will be a wonderful mother to the boys we've already got and any more children that we might be blessed with, I look forward to spending an adventurous life with you long after the children have left home. I love you Cassie, and I want to spend the rest of my days with you by my side. If you need more time to figure out if you could possibly feel the same way, I will try to understand, but I reserve the right to work very hard at convincing you. Please say you'll have me."

With a delighted whoop of joy, Cassie pulled her hands from his grasp and threw them around his neck. "That is the loveliest thing anyone has ever said to me. I've been fighting my feelings for you ever since I met you. I didn't think you could possibly love me. But I can see what you're saying. We *are* uniquely suited. I can see that you love the boys and will be a wonderful father. More importantly, though, you understand where I have come from and will be able to help me adjust to this new life. I love you, too, Mr. Gibson Charles Ainsworth Emmerson," she declared with a giggle while he growled at her.

"We needn't be so formal. Charles will do." He squeezed her tight.

In his tight hold, she didn't have much air, but she couldn't find it in herself to care. She didn't want to be anywhere else. With laughter filled with pure joy, she finally gave him the answer he was waiting for. "Yes, please, Charles, I would very much love to be your wife."

Charles had already been squeezing the breath out of her, but after one quick, tighter squeeze, he loosened his grasp and one of his hands came up to cradle the back of her head. Cassie was already feeling lightheaded from being in his arms, but now, as their breath mingled and his eyes stared hotly into hers, she felt as though her legs would have given out if not for the fact that his other arm was still wrapped around her. She was already up on her tiptoes, now it felt as though her feet weren't even touching the floor. He started at the corner of her eye, placing a soft kiss just where it was crinkled up from her wide smile. Then he trailed down to her cheekbone with a featherlight kiss there. She held her breath as he moved again.

His lips were a hairsbreadth away from hers when he whispered once more, “I love you, Cassie.” And then there were no more words as he sealed their bargain with the press of his lips. He tasted of coffee and sweet applesauce and something else that could only be uniquely him. A multitude of thoughts chased each other around her head in the split second before she could no longer think as they enjoyed the sweet moment.

They broke away to catch their breath, but he continued to hold her securely in his embrace. Cassie threw her head back and laughed. “My parents will have to forgive me after all. I managed to catch myself an Emmerson.”

Charles joined her in shared laughter before his lips descended onto hers once more.

The End

Katie

BOOK 3

Orphan Train Series

WENDY MAY ANDREWS

Sparrow Ink
www.sparrowdeck.com

www.wendymayandrews.com

Can she risk love without sacrificing her independence?

When Katie's husband and baby died, she vowed to never face such heartache again. Accompanying a trainload of orphans to their new lives in Missouri affords Katie the opportunity to start a new life of her own. She jumps at the chance, determined to grab life with both hands.

Doctor Wyatt Jeffries doesn't appreciate Katie's independence and determination. Having had his heart broken when his first wife's illness turned her into a hard-hearted hellion, Wyatt is looking for a wife who will be happy staying home and raising babies. So he doesn't understand why he can't stop thinking about the town's new seamstress.

When the deadly threat of a mysterious illness looms, Katie and Wyatt are forced to work together to save their town. Is there any chance they can save their own hearts too?

Dedication

Because I was heartbroken when my big brother started school, my mother spent time reading to me and my love affair with books began. Books have been my haven and escape ever since. So I dedicate this book to all those whose favorite place is in the pages of a book. And to Mum and Dad for reading to me way back when.

Acknowledgements

Thanks go to my beta readers: Marlene, Suzanne, Monique, and Alfred – your zeal for my stories and making them better makes my heart happy.

Thank you to my editor, Julie Sherwood, I love working with you. Any mistakes left are my fault, not hers.

Thank you too to my online communities full of wonderful readers and writers who help me with research or cheer me on.

And sincere thanks need to also go to my husband for being my everything – friend, partner, companion, web guru, formatter, idea sounding board, counterpart. You're the best, Mr. Andrews.

Chapter One

Katie walked along the dusty trail reveling in the sweet clutch of the small, warm hand holding tightly to her own, careful not to reveal how much it meant to her by holding on too tightly. One of the few little girls to have been included in the group of train orphans, little Annie still hadn't found a family to take her in. While Katie wanted her to find a good home, she was secretly glad that she could spend a little more time with her. If only she were in a position to take her herself. She swallowed the sigh that pushed to escape. She smiled instead.

"Good day, ladies," the gentleman lifted his hat slightly and bent a little, as though to bow to them.

Frowning, Katie wanted to ignore him, but Annie, usually so shy, stopped in her tracks to gaze at the man. Katie couldn't very well carry on without her.

"Hello," the little girl answered simply and continued staring at the stranger.

When he crouched down to be on her level, Katie's heart softened ever so slightly before she hardened her resolve once more. It didn't matter that he was approachable. Being handsome as the devil with his thick dark hair, clear gray eyes, and strong cheekbones and jaw line was a drawback if you asked her. Made her think he was in league with the Dark Knight to be that good looking. He probably had a black heart to go with it. She wanted to snatch Annie up into her arms and run away while babbling a mantra of "handsome men are devils you must avoid," over and over. But that would never do. She gritted her teeth and bore the silence that felt like it stretched for eons but was probably merely a couple heartbeats in length.

When it seemed like neither of the females were going to say anything further, the stranger broke the silence, directing his words toward Annie. "You must be new around here, young miss. I haven't yet had the pleasure of making your acquaintance."

"I just arrived," she answered, her small chest seeming to fill with importance at the adult attention. She wasn't used to men being around; it was usually only women who worked at the orphanage, except for the laborers, and they never paid her much mind anyway.

Katie swallowed the lump in her throat when she saw the depth of fascination in the little girl's gaze. Katie again suppressed the urge to snatch her away. She didn't want to develop the reputation as a madwoman in her new town. She couldn't flee from every stranger. She was new in town — everyone was a stranger.

"Welcome to Bucklin. My name is Dr. Wyatt Jeffries."

Annie's eyes grew wide at his words, and she stepped closer to Katie. "I don't like doctors," she declared firmly.

Katie pursed her lips together to prevent a grin from spreading across her face. She needn't scare the girl off about this man; he'd done it all by himself. She avoided his curious gaze as the doctor looked at her for some sort of explanation. She didn't oblige.

She realized she ought not to brush past him wordlessly. If he truly was the town doctor, she would probably have to encounter him from time to time about town. She would never seek out his services, of course, but she didn't want to appear to be a total boor.

"We really ought to be on our way, Dr. Jeffries. It was nice of you to welcome us. Good day."

With those words, she hurried away with Annie tucked firmly beside her. She ignored his words that followed her.

"But you didn't even tell me your names."

Her strides were purposeful and Annie had to almost run to keep up. Katie tried to talk herself into a state of calm once more. She needn't drag the child for the next mile while she worked off her fidgets.

"Well that was too bad, wasn't it, Sweet Pea? What are the chances of us running into a doctor here? I wasn't even sure if a town this size would have a doctor."

"He seemed nice until he told us that, didn't he?"

"It wasn't really long enough for me to decide," Katie answered carefully, not wanting to put her own issues onto the child. "But never mind about him, we're almost to the mercantile. I can't wait to see what they have."

"Do you think they might have some lemon drops?" The child's hopeful tone put a grin back onto Katie's face.

"There is a strong possibility. And an even stronger chance that I'll buy you a couple. But you mustn't spoil your appetite for dinner."

The little girl skipped along beside her, delighted at the prospect of such a treat. Katie's heart turned over. The poor child had faced so much trouble and loss in her six short years. It was a marvel that she could still delight in such simple things as the prospect of a treat. Katie resolved to do all in her power to ensure the little girl was soon settled into a happy, secure home. How she would do that was still to be determined, but she would worry about that later. Now she had the delightful prospect ahead of her of exploring the local general store. She knew it would be nothing like what they had in New York, but she was anxious to see what there was. It would help her know where to begin with this new life she had set for herself. She was determined to make it a success despite her rocky reaction to any men she encountered. With time, surely that would pass. Or she would at least be able to hide it better.

With a firm tread and her chin lifted to enforce her determination, Katie stepped briskly through the open door and felt her eyes widen as she looked around.

She suppressed a giggle. It was nearly everything you could find in New York but on a much smaller scale, all packed into one open room. She could barely take it all in there was such a variety of items on display.

“Lemon drops,” Annie whispered reverentially.

The little girl’s tone surprised a giggle out of Katie’s throat despite its tightness. She took a deep, fortifying breath. Determined to show the little girl a good time, Katie kept the smile pinned to her face, maintained her relaxed grip on the girl’s hand, and began to stroll around the room.

“We’ll get the candies when we’re ready to go,” she told the eager youngster. “We can’t eat them until we’ve paid for them, anyway.”

The store owner must have overheard because his kind smile encompassed them as he beckoned them closer. “Surely you can have one for now to tide you over,” he said with a wink as he pulled one of the coveted candies out of the case and dropped it into Annie’s eagerly outstretched hand.

Her eyes round as saucers, Annie looked from Katie to the kindly shopkeeper. “Thank you ever so much, mister.” There was no way she was going to refuse his largesse. She popped the candy into her mouth and graced both adults with a wide grin.

“That was kind of you, thank you,” Katie murmured, trying to ignore his questioning gaze, knowing he probably wanted to chat. She didn’t have very much experience with towns and villages, but she had no trouble interpreting the look of curiosity painted on his face. Despite the long train ride, she still hadn’t fully settled on what she would be willing to share about herself. She offered a polite smile, took Annie's hand once more, and proceeded to meander around the store.

There was an amazing array of articles. Not the variety of each type that you would find in New York, of course, but she was surprised to see that she couldn't think of anything she might want or need that wasn't present in the crowded emporium. No doubt the presence of train service made keeping the store stocked that much easier, despite how far they were from a real city. It reaffirmed for her that she had made a good decision when she thought to settle here. She felt the first hint of assurance settle into her mind, and with it, her shoulders relaxed incrementally.

Looking over the many bolts of fabric, Katie nodded to herself. She would be able to set herself up as a seamstress. Hopefully there wasn't already one in the town, or if there was, they wouldn't make too much fuss about her efforts to get some business. Surely the town was big enough that anyone who wanted to start a business could do so.

Katie glanced back at the shopkeeper. She would have to discuss with him whether or not he could offer her a discount on fabric since she would obviously be a frequent customer. Her stomach knotted itself up at the thought. Perhaps another day. It was enough that she had ventured out this far. With a sigh, she picked out the few items she absolutely required and made her way to the counter.

"And a small bag of the lemon candies, please, sir."

The shopkeeper, although seemingly pleasant, hadn't said anything as he added up her purchases. Katie appreciated that he was sufficiently perceptive to realize she didn't want to talk. *Maybe people here mind their own business*, she thought to herself with an inward smile.

"Have a good day," was all he said as the two girls left the store with a wave.

Annie cast her a sideways glance. "Did you like the store?"

"I did, did you?"

The little girl shrugged. "There were too many things for my eyes to see. I'll have to go again to decide for sure."

This prompted a chuckle from Katie. "Why is that?"

All Annie did at first was shrug again. She lapsed into silence for a moment, as though pondering the depth of the question. "I s'pose it's nice that there was so much stuff. But I think it's better if there aren't so many things. That store made me think of a New York street. All crowded and colourful. I like it better here."

"Do you really?"

The girl nodded vigorously.

"I'm so happy to hear that. I would have thought you would be a little bit homesick for the familiarity of the city."

"Everything I was used to was already gone," the girl answered, her wistful tone making Katie's heart ache.

"Of course," Katie replied and squeezed her hand. "This will soon become familiar, I hope."

The child's sunny smile appeared in response.

Katie marvelled at how resilient the child was. She had lost everything. No parents or siblings. Only strangers to care for her in the orphanage. And now a strange new place to call home. Hopefully a nice family would soon claim her as their own. The thought made Katie's heart clench once more, even though it would be the best thing for the child. Again, she wished she could claim her herself. But she shoved the useless thought away. The child needed a mother and a father. Not a broken widow like herself.

"Shall we go sit on the edge of the planks to eat our candies while we watch to see what there is to see?"

Annie's vigorous nod was accompanied by a grin.

Chapter Two

Wyatt Jeffries watched the woman and her daughter walk away. He stood stock still with his heart hammering. He ought to sit down. There was clearly something wrong with him. It didn't take his doctor's degree to know it wasn't healthy for a man's heart to hammer at such a speed.

His eyes followed the pair as they made their way into the mercantile. He ought to be continuing on his way. Mrs. Jenkins' boils wouldn't be getting better on their own. And she certainly wouldn't thank him for dawdling.

Shaking his head wouldn't rid it of the image of the lovely brunette with her crooked smile and wary eyes. The color in her cheeks had proclaimed her vigorous health despite her cold reception to his greeting. Even though she was a tiny little woman, she had seemed to be brimming with life as he watched her interacting with the child before he had interrupted them. Wyatt would guess she was in her early twenties. He wondered who her husband was.

"Surely you're committing several sins at once by thinking about how attractive another man's wife is," he muttered to himself as he set off in the direction of Mrs. Jenkins and her boils.

The afternoon pressed on as he made his rounds of the few patients he needed to visit. He tried to give his undivided attention to each person as they deserved, but he found his mind returning again and again to the mystery woman and the little girl.

"What's ailing you today?" Mr. Hunter asked, as he peered over his spectacles at the doctor, making Wyatt's face heat up.

He tried for innocence. "I am feeling perfectly fit today, thank you for asking."

Mr. Hunter chortled. "That ain't what I meant, and well you know it."

Wyatt's face felt even hotter as he tried to brazen it out. "I apologize, sir, if I have not given you sufficient focus today."

"Get on with you, boy, that ain't my concern. I jest thought you was troubling with something, and I was being neighborly. But if you don't feel like sharing, I s'pose I'll have to mind my own affairs."

Wyatt knew his face was aflame at this point and appreciated that the old codger before him didn't laugh at his expense, despite the twitch of his lips. He made an effort to apologize again, but the old man brushed it away.

"You were right, my thoughts are elsewhere today, but they seem to be muddled, and I wouldn't be able to put them into words, even if I wanted to."

The older man finally seemed satisfied with this explanation, nodding sagely. “That happens to the best of us at times, young man, you needn’t be so embarrassed by it.”

Wyatt flushed again, cursing his pale skin that gave away his every discomfort. But to his relief, the older man just chuckled. Closing his bag as he got to his feet and willing away his embarrassment, he cleared his throat and strived for a professional manner. “Your wound is healing nicely, Mr. Hunter. I should be able to remove the stitches the next time I stop in to see you.”

This reminded the old man of his initial complaint. “I don’t see why you can’t do it now. Cursed stitches. I can’t do nothing with them in there.”

“Well, it would be best if you don’t do much for at least a week or two even after their out, so with an attitude like you’ve got, I might have to leave them in a little longer than planned if you don’t plan to behave.”

The disbelieving look on the oldster’s face forced a chuckle out of Wyatt.

“You wouldn’t be so mean spirited, would you, Doc?”

“See that you behave for the next couple of days, and we’ll discuss it when I see you again.”

“Maybe I’ll hide the next time you call round,” Mr. Hunter muttered, forcing another chuckle from the doctor.

“You could do that, but then what would happen with your stitches? And what if you were to develop an infection?”

The older man paled at his words, making Wyatt regret them. "Never mind, Mr. Hunter. I will be back in a few days. You will be perfectly fine in the meantime. Just try to keep the bandage clean and dry, and everything will be fine, have no fear."

Wyatt tied his bag onto the back of his saddle and swung his leg over his sturdy horse, grateful for the animal's steady personality. With how distracted he had been that day, he was lucky the horse hadn't wandered away and gotten him lost. Thinking about his distraction led his thoughts back to the source of that distraction.

The small child had seemed to be the picture of health. And her mother as well. The lovely color on her cheekbones proclaimed how well her blood was circulating from the rigors of their walk through town. The mother had been a little on the thin side, he mused, but the child had been exactly the right size for what appeared to be a five-year-old girl. He frowned as he thought a little more about the two strangers, wondering who they belonged to. He thought he knew everyone in the small town. Of course, the little girl had said they were new to town, but he wondered briefly which of the men they belonged to.

The mother's reception had certainly contrasted with the child's until the girl realized he was a doctor. He wondered if he had guessed accurately about her age. Her face didn't have a single wrinkle or line to mar its perfection, although her eyes had seemed shadowed, as though she had seen too much in her short years. Wyatt sighed. He could relate too well to that.

Giving his head a shake, he tried to pull his thoughts away from woman and child. It wasn't seemly to be thinking so much about some other man's family. In his years as a doctor, it had never happened to him before, and he wouldn't allow it to last for long. He urged his horse into a gallop, hoping the wind rushing by his ears would whisk away his troubled thoughts.

He forced himself to consider the patients he had seen that day. He had made brief notes after each visit, but he really ought to write more details and plan what to do for each of them in the future. He was particularly concerned about Mrs. Jenkins' boils. If she didn't do a better job of keeping them clean, she was sure to get a terrible infection. He didn't feel equipped to look after her properly in her home if that was to happen, but she had already been adamant about not wanting to visit him in his office. The poor old woman barely ever left her home. He would have to prevail upon her family members to help her out a bit more. That probably wouldn't go over very well with Mrs. Jenkins, but it was entirely possible that her life was at stake, so there weren't many options. He would rather suffer her anger than have her death on his conscience. But these thoughts brought him back to Mr. Hunter and his teasing when Wyatt's mind had been occupied with the pretty young mother rather than where it ought to have been, with his patient.

Wyatt was relieved when his house came into view. His chest swelled with pride whenever he looked at it. It was everything he had ever wanted in a house. Now all he needed to do was fill it with a loving wife and a few children, and his life would be complete. A vibrant, healthy wife, he reminded himself. One that would be able and happy to bear and raise his children. He shook the thoughts from his mind once more as he reached his small stable.

After doing the necessary ministrations for his horse, he grabbed his bag and headed to the house. As he stepped into the front entrance, he paused when his eyes snagged on the small portrait of Patricia. His heart clenched at the familiar sight. He really shouldn't have put it there. He should have left it in Boston with the rest of her things. But somehow that felt cold and heartless. One more thing to push to the back of his mind. He continued to the kitchen, dropping his bag by the table before going to the stove to boil some water. A good cup of coffee would fortify him to get through the rest of his paperwork for the day.

ꙮ

"That sigh sure sounded heartfelt."

Katie smiled at her friend's words. "Sorry, Mel. I'm feeling a little melancholy this evening."

"That's nothing to be sorry for," Mel replied. "Would you care to discuss it?"

"There isn't really much to discuss," Katie began. "I spent the day with Annie today."

Mel's steady, understanding gaze made Katie falter in her speech. Her throat clogged with the threat of tears, much to her disgust. She had given up on tears long ago. Katie swallowed hard to rid herself of the unwelcome sensation. Melanie hadn't stopped watching her, so Katie felt obliged to continue.

"Do you think they would let me keep her?"

Melanie's gaze didn't falter even though her kind smile dimmed slightly. "They might, if the poor dear doesn't get spoken for soon. But do you really feel that you're in a position to care for her?"

Katie looked around their small home. "Would you be willing to have her here? I know that would probably be asking too much of you. We're a little cramped with Cassie here, too."

"I doubt Cass will be with us for too much longer," Mel began, "but space isn't really what I was concerned about. If it came to space, you could share your room with Annie, I would imagine. And she's a sweet child. She wouldn't be too much trouble, I'm sure. But you would have to be responsible for her expenses. I don't know if either of us is fully prepared to provide for ourselves, let alone taking on responsibility for another. I'm sorry to be cold about it, but I'm not prepared to take it on right now. I need to make sure I feel secure for myself first."

"No, no, Mel, I swear to you, I'm not asking for you to take on any responsibility, just as long as you would be willing to let me have her here. That, in itself, would be a big help." She paused in thought for a moment before continuing. "It's probably a foolish thought, but I just want it so much. I hope that isn't selfish of me. I cannot say for sure if it is in her best interests for me to take her on. A child really ought to have a mother and a father. But surely I would be better than letting her languish in the hands of a custodian that I cannot say I am fully convinced even cares about the wellbeing of the children." When it looked as though Mel was going to object, Katie hurried to continue. "Even Cassandra is concerned about the children."

Mel grinned. "Cass is a special case who has never witnessed the realities of life before, so she isn't the most reliable of supports for your argument. But I don't completely disagree with you. And I think Annie would be lucky to have someone as caring as you look after her. My only concern is that you haven't yet established yourself here. I don't think you could live with yourself if you took her on and then couldn't provide for her."

Melanie's kind tone threatened her emotional control again, and Katie frowned to push the feelings away. Perhaps she was foolish to even consider it. Mel's concerns were valid. But the remembered feeling of holding the little girl's hand and listening to her chatter made Katie feel distinctly that she needed to at least try.

"I will see about putting up some sort of advertisements around town for our sewing and alterations. I haven't seen too very many women around, but surely there must be a need for seamstresses in a town of this size."

"I actually have already found us one customer. I almost forgot to tell you. Mrs. Spencer. She helps her husband run the mercantile."

"Oh, I was in the mercantile this afternoon with Annie."

"Did you meet Mrs. Spencer?"

"No, but her husband seemed like a nice enough man."

Mel grinned over Katie's grudging tone, but chose not to comment. "Perhaps you were there at the exact time I was speaking to her," she surmised. "She's a lovely woman with the biggest, blonde, curly hair I have ever seen. She was telling me that with the growth of their business, she hasn't the time to even think about doing any sewing herself but that she is in desperate need of several new articles. So we should get a fair bit of business from her. And she could end up being walking advertisement for us, seeing how visible she would be at the store."

Katie offered her friend a shrewd glance. "So you offered her a significant discount, didn't you?"

"Well, under the circumstances, it seemed wise. I would think we'll be able to negotiate an arrangement with them for getting our supplies. And if she is happy with us, she will be eager to recommend us to her own patrons."

"You don't need to convince me, Mel, I can see the wisdom in it. I just hope lots of business rolls in quickly so that I can speak with Mrs. Parker about Annie."

Mel's smile returned to the understanding state that was grating on Katie's nerves. "It's a rather circular process, isn't it?"

Katie's smile was rueful. "It would seem so." She lapsed into silence for a moment before sighing again. "Well, we should have an idea soon how much business we are likely to get. I will have a word with Mrs. Parker tomorrow about whether or not they would even consider me. It would be better to know right off if it's not even possible before I get my heart completely set on it, anyway."

"That sounds like the course of wisdom."

Mel's sage tone brought a chuckle out of Katie.

Katie got lost in thought for a moment as she reminisced about how far they'd come. It seemed like only yesterday they had met while volunteering at the Foundling Hospital in New York City. It was hard to believe it had been two years already. In some ways, it felt like only days had passed. In other ways, it was a different lifetime. Their volunteer work with the orphans had seen them escorting groups on the train out to farm towns to be adopted. Mrs. Parker, the director of the orphanage, was a wonderful older woman, who seemed impervious to the emotional toll it was taking on some of the younger women. Katie and Melanie hadn't been able to do it any longer and had decided to stay in the town when they brought this latest batch of orphans to their new lives. It had been the best decision either of them had ever made.

Chapter Three

While Katie hadn't originally planned on joining Melanie in the sewing business, they had quickly decided it would be for the best when things had settled down soon after they had arrived in Bucklin. Katie had thought she was going to be the town's new teacher, but when that opportunity disappeared, Mel had offered a partnership. It was turning out to be for the best. Melanie did not enjoy dealing with the clients, and Katie found that she really enjoyed it. And they both enjoyed the work. Doing it together was just that much more fun.

Mrs. Spencer was a dream client. Not overly demanding but knew exactly what she wanted, generous in her praise, and generous in her placement of orders as well. They were kept busy with all the items she was requesting. At first, Katie wasn't happy about the discount they had offered her, but Mr. Spencer had been generous in the discount he offered them on their materials, so it was all working out well. Mrs. Spencer was so pleased with her new clothes that she took to wearing them immediately and was quick to tell everyone where they had come from. Before they knew it, the two women were almost overwhelmed with business. Katie had to work to keep the grin on her face within bounds as she set out to visit another potential client to discuss what she was looking for and to see if they could agree on service.

Katie visited with Annie regularly. She was torn between considering it a risk for the child to become attached to her rather than her potential future parents and the sadness of leaving the poor child to languish on her own without any special adult attention. Mrs. Parker hadn't expected it take so long to find someone to take the youngster, and was itching to return to New York.

"You can be sure I'll not encourage Mr. Brace to be sending girls out here in the future. She is a dear, but if she cannot be placed, there's no sense in sending any more out this way. We've never had this kind of trouble in other towns or cities before," Mrs. Parker had mused. "I wonder if it's just a strange coincidence or if it's how far west we are. Being a bit more primitive, maybe they just don't see how much of an asset a daughter can be."

"And the town will eventually need women for all the men these boys are going to grow up to be," Katie added with a smile as she watched Annie playing. They were keeping their voices low, not wanting the little girl to overhear their discussion. "I do hope you can find a nice family for her soon."

"Me, too," Mrs. Parker's agreement was heartfelt. "If she were a boy, I'd leave her for Mr. McDonald to care for and be on the next eastbound train, but I just cannot leave her with him on her own. I'm not even comfortable with the man, let alone leaving a little girl in his care."

Katie chewed her lip as she thought of the burly placement manager and how unsuitable it would be to leave the little girl with him. "You could always let me adopt her." It wasn't the first time she had brought this up.

She hated the pitying look Mrs. Parker cast her way. "You know Mr. Brace is particular about the children going to families, Katie. You're a dear for caring about her, but you must see that it would be better for her to join a family."

"I do see that, but if there isn't a family for her, I'm better than letting her languish alone or taking her back to the orphanage, aren't I?"

Mrs. Parker patted her hand. "Katie, dear, you are lovely, and it is certainly not anything personal. I would give her to you in a heartbeat if you had a husband."

Katie grimaced at the words, making Mrs. Parker smile in response. "I'll tell you what. I'll telegraph Mr. Brace and ask him for a decision. If we don't have a family for little Annie soon, I think you're right. It would be much better for her to be with you than for her not to have anyone."

Admonishing herself not to get her hopes up, Katie nodded and thanked the woman. "I'll be around again tomorrow, but I ought to get on with my appointments. Thank you for your diligence on behalf of the children, Mrs. Parker."

"Well, how sweet of you to say that, Katie. And thank you for your constant care of the little ones. Good day, Mrs. Carter."

Katie was surprised that the older woman had resorted to formalities but then realized that the manager, Mr. MacDonald, had entered the room. She couldn't grow comfortable with the man.

"Mr. MacDonald, good day," Katie acknowledged, as she left the room with a small nod. Brief but polite. Since she was trying to gain custody of the little girl, it wouldn't do to offend the placement manager, no matter how incompetent he seemed to be.

She wondered briefly if she should write to Mr. Brace herself. She didn't want to speak ill of the placement manager, but she wondered how hard Mr. MacDonald really was working to find homes for the orphans Mr. Brace's Children's Society was sending out west. Katie knew the warm-hearted philanthropist would be incensed to learn someone he trusted was failing in his duties to the children. But on the other hand, she wanted Annie for herself, and if Mr. MacDonald's incompetence made that possible, she wasn't about to complain.

Katie made her way through her day's activities in a bit of a daze. She was making every effort not to get her hopes too high that she would be allowed to keep Annie, but she couldn't seem to stop herself. She tried not to betray her rising excitement as she visited a potential client. It took effort to focus her attention on the matter at hand. She wasn't experienced enough as a seamstress not to have her mind on the subject and needed to concentrate to make sure she fully understood what the woman was looking for. Thankfully, the potential client was a kind, middle-aged woman who hadn't had a new frock in a few years and was delighted with whatever Katie had to suggest. And she had seen Mrs. Spencer's new clothes and wanted some for herself, so she was already prepared to pay whatever price Katie and Melanie named. They didn't want to take advantage of their new neighbors' desperation but they had agreed to reasonable prices that would support them comfortably without having to work all hours of every day.

There was an even bigger skip to her step as Katie walked away from the house. The woman had given her a deposit on two new frocks and a gown. Katie wasn't sure what use the woman had for it, but if she wanted a fancy gown, they would make it for her. It would actually be a pleasure to make it with Melanie.

The increase in their income made her feel that much more secure in her desire to take custody of Annie. *If Mr. Brace and Mrs. Parker allow it,* she reminded herself for maybe the twentieth time that day. It was so hard to restrain her excitement. But so little had gone her way in her adult life, she really ought to keep a firm grip on reality. It wouldn't do to hope too much or she would slip into a decline when they finally told her no.

Katie burst through her front door. "Mrs. Smith placed a larger order than I expected, and the mercantile is getting us a larger variety of fabrics so we don't have to worry about our clients running around town in identical clothing," she called out to Melanie as she shut the door.

"That's wonderful, Katie. Thank you for looking after both of those things. Are you very sure you don't mind being the one who always deals with the clients?" Melanie's tone revealed her anxieties, despite her effort to repress them.

"I'm more than certain. Your stitches are finer than mine. We're both playing to our strengths." She breezed through the small room, opening the window above the sink to allow more of the spring air into their tidy home. "Have you been outside yet? It's a gorgeous day."

Melanie admitted that she had not but then she chuckled. "You sure seem to be in a fine frame of mind. Whatever has happened to you?"

Katie grinned. "Mrs. Parker is going to ask Mr. Brace if I can adopt Annie."

Melanie's eyebrows rose, but so did the corners of her mouth. "And so you are thrilled," she stated with a laugh before sobering. "But how likely is he to say yes, do you suppose?"

Katie shrugged in an effort to demonstrate a lack of concern but couldn't help feeling uncertain and chewing her lip. "Even a widow is better than no one," she explained. "They wouldn't want to take her back to New York after dragging her out here, so Mrs. Parker said if they do not find a family for her soon, there is a good chance he will approve it. It helps that he knows me, of course." She paused, looking out the window for a moment, trying to regain control over her hopes, but then she whirled toward Melanie and exclaimed, "Oh, Mel, I know I oughtn't to hope too strongly, but I just want it to be true. I want to be a mother again. Surely they must say yes."

Melanie made a tsking sound and pulled Katie in for a quick hug. "Let us try to keep you too preoccupied to dwell on it until you can know for sure. I know you want the best for Annie, and I trust that Mrs. Parker does as well. If they can find a family to take her in, then that might be for the best, but if not, I know you will be a wonderful mother." She then briskly strode across the room. "Now let us get to work on Mrs. Smith's order. It will help you keep your mind away from your wishes and dreams."

Katie laughed. "I hope you're right, but sometimes sewing leaves little for the mind to do other than think."

Melanie grinned. "True, but not this time. You will be the one to figure out the pattern. That should keep your mind fully occupied."

Katie pulled a face but gamely set to work.

Several days passed with Katie nearly wearing herself to the bone trying hard not to dwell too much on the possibilities. They finished Mrs. Smith's order and she delivered it. "That was much quicker than I expected," the delighted client exclaimed. Katie had had to smother her smile over that. It probably wouldn't happen again.

She visited with Annie every other day. She didn't want the child to grow unreasonably attached to her if she was going to be living with a new family, but Katie couldn't bear to leave the poor child completely. It had to be difficult for the little girl, being the last one without a new family.

Finally, on Friday, when Katie arrived to see Annie, Mrs. Parker called her aside while the child was absorbed in a book Katie had brought for her.

In a low voice, the older woman asked, “Were you completely serious when you expressed an interest in adopting Annie?”

Katie had to fight not to yell. “Of course,” she exclaimed in a loud whisper.

“Very well, then. Mr. Brace has agreed to allow it.”

Tears welled in Katie’s eyes. Mrs. Parker must have mistaken the cause. “Katie, dear, you know our hesitation was not any personal judgement against you, don’t you?”

“Of course, I completely understood. I am just so thrilled that I am going to have her as my daughter. I have been trying not to hope too strongly, but it has been a challenge. Are you completely sure that I can have her?” she couldn’t help but ask.

Mrs. Parker smiled at her, warm understanding spreading across her face. “I am certain. If you’d like, you can tell her the good news now.”

Chapter Four

Katie made every effort not to skip as she walked beside Annie, leading her back to the little house she was sharing with Mel. She was a mom, she reminded herself. She needed to be responsible. But oh how she wanted to twirl in circles and jump for joy!

Thankfully, Cassie had already moved out, so space wouldn't be such an issue. And the little girl had only the one bag of belongings, so she wouldn't be cluttering up the place either. Katie glanced down and intercepted the apprehensive glance of the small girl.

"Are you nervous, Annie?" Katie was surprised at the possibility.

She got a slight nod in answer causing Katie to stop in her tracks and crouch down in front of her.

"Why are you nervous? We know each other quite well. Do you not want to come and live with me?" Katie hoped her disappointment didn't come through in her voice. She wanted the child to know she had a say in her future. "Would you rather stay with Mrs. Parker and keep waiting for someone else?"

Tears welled up in Annie's eyes, which made a lump form in Katie's, and she had to blink several times to keep the tears out of her own vision.

"What is it, honey? You can tell me. I promise not to get upset with whatever you have to say."

"I don't want anything bad to happen to you," Annie whispered.

Katie was shocked into silence by the little girl's concerns. "Oh, Annie, my dear, I promise you, I am in perfect health. Nothing is going to happen to me. Certainly not as a result of you coming to live with me."

Standing up, but keeping Annie's hand firmly in her grasp, Katie continued. "I had been thinking that I need to be dignified about this, but I realize now that I was mistaken. Today is a day we should be celebrating. We each have family now. We have each other. And that is something to rejoice about, don't you think?"

Annie just looked at her with wide, serious eyes. Katie felt her stomach drop with disappointment once more, but she didn't allow that to stop her. She put Annie's small bag of possessions carefully down on the ground and grabbed Annie's free hand with her own. Keeping her gaze focused on Annie's face, Katie forced herself to grin at the child, despite her insecure wish to curl up and cry. She was the adult here and she had to act like it.

"This is going to be just great, and I am so happy that we are going to stay together. Don't you think it's great?" Her gaiety, however forced, was beginning to get through to the youngster and the corners of her mouth were starting to lift. After another searching glance, the little girl finally nodded.

Katie wrinkled her nose at her and then grinned. "That wasn't very convincing."

Finally, Annie couldn't help it, a giggle escaped.

"There it is!" Katie declared, joy filling her heart. "I knew you would see reason. We are going to be the happiest pair in this town, just you wait and see." She eyed the girl with mock seriousness. "It is both our responsibility to make sure we are happy, wouldn't you agree?"

Annie again looked uncertain for a moment, and Katie regretted her words, but then the little girl giggled again and nodded. "I will do my very best, Mrs. Katie, I promise."

"As will I," Katie vowed in return. "Now, I do believe we ought to celebrate this pact by skipping all the way home."

Finally, Katie's heart nearly overflowed as full-throated laughter erupted from the youngster and she almost fell over with how vigorous her nodding was. Katie's laughter, while not quite as carefree, swelled forth to join Annie's. Tightening her grasp on one small hand, Katie picked up Annie's small bundle of possessions, and the two skipped along the road, their differing strides giving them more reason to laugh.

They were lost in their own enjoyment of the moment and didn't notice the horse and rider coming up behind them. They both jumped and spun around when the man spoke to them. Annie didn't even try to suppress her shriek, which caused the large horse to shy away. The rider quickly gained control of the animal then slid off his back.

Lifting his hat, he bowed politely. "I apologize for startling you. I should have realized the soft ground was muffling my steed's hoof beats when I saw how oblivious you seemed to my approach. I do hope you will forgive the intrusion."

Katie wanted to sweep by him and ignore him like she had the first time she and Annie had encountered the doctor, but she knew she ought not inflict her own issues upon her new charge. Annie had enough of her own emotional baggage toward doctors; Katie didn't want her distrust of men to rub off on the child. She forced a polite smile to her lips.

"We were having too much fun to pay attention to what was going on around us, sir, which wasn't all that wise, considering we are on a well-traveled road. It is surely not your fault that our inattention lead to our discomfort." She paused, seeing that he seemed to expect something more from her. "But thank you for so graciously offering an apology." She cringed when she heard the questioning tone at the end of her own sentence. Katie offered another smile in an effort to cover up her discomfort.

He lifted his hat and made another little bow while a deep chuckle came out of him and seemed to curl around Katie's stomach. "It does the heart good to see two such lovely ladies having a good time. No harm was done. But do try to be more careful in the future. I would hate for either of you to need my services."

Katie felt a momentary urge to relax and spend more time with the man. The thought made her stiffen and withdraw mentally. That would never do. She needed to end this meeting.

"Well, sir, thank you again for stopping and being so gracious about our occupation of the road. We ought to let you get on with your important work. We wouldn't want to prevent you from seeing to your patients." She congratulated herself on her handling of their exit. She hadn't even had to lie. No doubt, being the only doctor in town, he was a busy man. And it was true that she wouldn't want to keep him from visiting the sick.

The doctor looked reluctant but nodded his head before gathering up his reins and regaining his seat on the large horse. He tipped his hat to them once more. "Until we meet again," he said before riding away without another glance.

Katie felt a tremble down her spine. His words struck her as ominous. She didn't want to see the doctor ever again. Any doctor, really, but especially not a young, handsome one. Handsome men were trouble she had no interest in.

She forced aside her feelings and turned to Annie, whose large eyes were widened towards her with worry dulling their shine. Katie pinned a smile to her face.

"Wasn't that something? We were having so much fun we didn't even hear a horse coming. I suppose we ought to be a little more careful. Why don't we skip along through the grass here on the side?"

"Won't that be harder?"

Katie shrugged. "I think it will just make it more interesting. Come along now. We need to be getting home and making some dinner for ourselves. I don't know about you, but I think my tummy is going to be grumbling quite soon."

This finally brought the smile back to Annie's face, and the two hurried to Katie's house, returning to skipping as they had before. Katie's laughter was a little forced, but she was glad the child didn't appear to notice the difference.

Chapter Five

Wyatt rode away from the two females, castigating himself for once again not getting the woman's name. Which was beyond foolish since she was no doubt married, so her name was of little consequence. Except for it being neighborly, of course. He ought to know the names of everyone in the vicinity, since they could, at some point, be patients. His lips twisted with the irony. He truly hoped she would never be his patient. He doubted he would have the clinical detachment needed. And he fervently hoped she was never in a position to need a doctor anyway.

But she really was the loveliest woman he had ever seen. Oh, he'd seen more beautiful women, in cities, or when he was away for school. Women who were beautiful on the surface with fashionable clothes and their hair styled precisely. But those women rarely had anything going on behind their eyes. Their beauty was only surface deep. Whereas the woman, he still didn't even know her name, was very pretty on the surface, but also seemed to be thriving with life underneath. The rose color of her cheeks spoke of a rich vitality. He thought of Patricia, and the corners of his mouth turned down. She certainly hadn't been full of vitality. He quickly shoved the thought away.

And the little child, he thought again, changing the subject in his mind slightly. Annie. What a darling, timid, little thing she was. He wanted to scoop her up and hold her tight and reassure her that her future was sure to be bright. But she wasn't his to concern himself with.

Perhaps he could approach that fellow, Mr. MacDonald, who was arranging homes for the orphans who had arrived on the train. It would be wonderful to have a child in his life. Not that they would entrust a young, single man with a child, he surmised, even if he was the town's doctor. He really ought to look around the town and find himself a wife. He realized he didn't know of any available single women in the town, but surely some of the town folk must have sisters or cousins that could come and visit and give him the opportunity to meet a possible wife. Wyatt made a mental note to pay more attention when any patients spoke of their family. Surely they would be willing to set him up if he asked.

Making his way home, Wyatt tried not to feel lonely as he rode up the path. Perhaps he should get a pet. A dog or a cat might be nice. Surely a pet would be happy to see him when he returned. Of course, being called out at all hours of the day or night might make him a little less welcomed by a pet. *But dogs don't hold grudges,* he thought wistfully. *Cats might, though,* he reminded himself with a grin while wondering if his solitude was making him lose his mind.

At least he didn't have to worry that a pet was going hungry while he was gone for the day. His faithful horse had grazed throughout the day whenever he stopped to visit his patients. The horse had earned his hay and oats tonight, for all the work he had put in throughout the day.

Wyatt swung his leg over and climbed down. Fatigue seeped from his pores. He wondered what he could quickly cook up to eat before he climbed into bed. It would have to be another night of fried eggs on bread. Thank heaven for the chickens!

"You did a good job today, Boss." Despite his fatigue, Wyatt grinned when the large horse's ears swivelled, as though he were listening. He had to chuckle when the horse huffed and nodded his head, as though in agreement.

"Is it a tough job carrying me around all day?" When the horse shoved his head into Wyatt's chest, his laughter grew. "Seems to me that you're looking for a reward." He pushed the large head away but pulled a sweet lump out of his pocket. "It *is* your job to carry me around, but you probably deserve a treat anyway."

Wyatt pulled the saddle off and tried not to dump it with a thump. He was more tired than he ought to be, and he didn't have the usual strength in his arms. Despite his weariness, he needed to look after his horse. Picking up the brush, he set to work on the smooth coat, smiling as the horse twitched and stamped, demonstrating his enjoyment.

"Yeah, it's probably quite a relief to be done for the day, isn't it, big guy?" When the horse whickered,

Wyatt shook his head. "Maybe I'm losing my mind if I'm starting to think that the best conversation I've had all day is this one."

The horse seemed to be lulled nearly to sleep by Wyatt's rhythmic strokes and he allowed his mind to drift back over the day. His thought jumped from the day to the past, never a good thing for his state of mind.

"Patricia would have loved to see how big you've gotten," he commented to the large horse. "She was determined that we ought to keep you instead of selling you when your mama surprised us by being pregnant. What did I know about training horses? I tried to reason with her. I'm a doctor, not a cowboy, I told her. But she wouldn't take no for an answer. She could be like that sometimes. You probably would have liked her. And it turns out, she wasn't completely wrong. Not that I think I had much to do with it. I think your mama must have taught you right because you turned out fairly well, and I certainly didn't know what I was doing."

The only reaction Boss had to offer to indicate he was still listening was the periodic shifting of his ears. Wyatt grinned again. "Yeah, I should probably get a dog. Then I wouldn't have to bore you with all this talk."

After one last stroke of the brush, Wyatt patted the horse's rump as he tossed the brush onto its shelf. He tossed an armload of hay in front of Boss and then put a scoop of feed in his trough after checking that there was enough water available to the horse.

It hadn't taken very long to care for the animal, but the brief interlude had been surprisingly restful. There was something so calming about animals, Wyatt mused. Much more so than people, he thought before reminding himself that he would still like to have an actual person around. Family, while quite able to make you a little crazy at times, was really at the heart of all that is good in life. And he didn't have any. You could hardly count third cousins out East. Although, he would take even them at this point, since he was beginning to annoy himself with his lonely whining. Hopefully a good night's sleep would put an end to his whiney ramblings.

He finally made his way into the house, taking his boots off at the door, as though he could still hear Patricia's command to do so.

What was it about today that made her so tenaciously stuck in his thoughts? He passed her favorite watercolor on the way to the kitchen. Is it any wonder, since her marks were still everywhere in his life? The painting of the small child reminded him of the little girl he had seen that day. Patricia would have loved her. If only he had been able to convince her to adopt.

With a sigh, Wyatt pushed away thoughts of his wife and proceeded to conclude his long day with an egg sandwich then climbed into bed. Morning was sure to come quickly with another long day to follow.

The following afternoon, Wyatt was surprised to run into his mystery woman when he stopped in to check on old Mrs. Jenkins.

"I'm sorry if I've arrived at an inconvenient time, Mrs. Jenkins. I'm happy, though, to see that you have a visitor."

"Isn't it something, Dr. Jeffries? My daughter-in-law has hired this lovely young lady to make me a new dress. Sue thinks it will make me feel better. I don't know what goes through that woman's head sometimes," the cranky old lady chuckled. "As if new clothes can make me forget about these terrible sores. But having Katie here visiting me sure isn't a hardship."

Wyatt couldn't do anything but grin, which brought a wicked twinkle into the old woman's eyes. "Have you had the pleasure of meeting the town's new seamstress, doctor?"

"No, ma'am, I have not," he replied, taking the opportunity to shake the pretty brunette's hand. "Doctor Jeffries, at your service, ma'am."

He almost laughed over the comical look on the young woman's face. She had avoided introducing herself when they had first encountered one another. He wondered how she would handle Mrs. Jenkins' introduction. He wasn't left in suspense.

While offering him the briefest smile, she actually dipped into a slight curtsy, much to his surprise. "How do you do, doctor?"

Mrs. Jenkins took exception to her lack of elaboration. "Tell the man your name, girl. You couldn't do any better than snapping up the handsome single doctor." She cackled while the seamstress' face flamed.

"My name is Mrs. Kate Carter."

"Never mind with the Mrs., Kate, you know you're a widow. What you need is a fine, young husband to look after you," the older woman declared. "None better than our handsome doctor."

Wyatt wasn't sure how to put the poor woman at ease. Her face was so red, he worried for her health. But he knew from experience there was little one could do to stop Mrs. Jenkins when she was on a roll. He had thought Mrs. Carter timid, so he was surprised when she spoke up.

"Actually, Mrs. Jenkins, I do *not* need a husband to look after me. I am quite capable of taking care of myself and my new daughter on my own. I have had the experience of being married. I can assure you that I do not care to repeat it." Wyatt was affronted by her vehemence but had to smile when he observed her struggle to control the strength of her reaction. She must have realized it would not do to offend her client. She offered the old woman a sweet smile while she laid her hand gently on her arm. Wyatt wished he could feel that pleasant pressure himself, despite her declaration of having no wish to remarry.

"It is kind of you to be concerned about me and Annie, though, Mrs. Jenkins. Thank you for that." She cast a quick glance in Wyatt's direction. He would have never noticed if he hadn't been watching her so closely. He wished fervently that he didn't find her quite so charming. The lady continued talking.

“Now Mrs. Jenkins, since the doctor is here, would you prefer I come back some other time? I have no wish to invade your privacy.”

“Never mind about my privacy. If you’re going to be taking my measurements, you’ll be seeing everything the doctor needs to look at anyway. We can kill two birds with one stone. Works out pretty convenient for me, I’d say.”

Wyatt suppressed his grin at Mrs. Carter’s obvious discomfort. She tried to hide it with brisk speech while she stood.

“Very well, Mrs. Jenkins. Since we no doubt do not wish to preoccupy the busy doctor, shall I help you undress?”

“You’re a good girl, aren’t you, Kate? Even if you have strange notions.” The old woman cackled again as the color rose in the seamstress’ cheeks anew. “Pull me to my feet, and we’ll get this over with.”

Mrs. Carter made short work of getting Mrs. Jenkins on her feet and her dress removed, leaving the older woman in a loose shift. The younger woman then looked quite uncomfortable as to what to do with herself. Mrs. Jenkins solved that.

“Make yourself useful, girl, and put the kettle on to boil. We can offer the doctor a cup of tea before he leaves.”

Wyatt was torn between his desire to spend more time with the woman and wanting to put her at ease from her obvious reluctance to spend time with him. He stifled his grin and waited to see what she would do.

Her color remained high, but she did nothing besides offering the old woman a brief nod and hurrying to the stove. It was obvious she was relieved to be away from the doctor's examination. Wyatt wondered if she had an equal distaste for doctors as her daughter expressed. Or if it was just one particular doctor who made her uncomfortable.

He grinned when his eyes encountered Mrs. Jenkins' shrewd gaze. She surprised him by not saying anything, containing herself to a suggestive wiggle of her eyebrows. Wyatt winked at her but merely murmured his instructions regarding his examination. He was relieved to see that the salve he had left for her was obviously having an effect, since he was only able to apply, at best, half his attention to the matter at hand. The rest of his attention was listening for Mrs. Carter's activities in the kitchen area.

The doctor heartily wished he could watch the young woman. There was nothing more beautiful, in his opinion, than a woman bustling about the kitchen. That is where he longed for a woman of his own, in his lonely home, keeping his kitchen smelling delicious. Obviously the widowed seamstress would disagree with his viewpoint.

Wyatt finished his examination of Mrs. Jenkins just as the kettle whistled. He was surprised to see that the seamstress had placed some cookies on a plate and arranged all the fixings for tea on a tray, even though it had been obvious she didn't want to prolong her time with him. He admired her gumption, even though he disagreed with her philosophy.

Katie wholeheartedly wished the doctor had timed his visit differently. If only he were old. Or ugly. Or married. Or any number of things, really. It was strange that she had encountered him, already, a number of times. There were many townspeople she had yet to meet. Ones who could be potential clients. Not handsome, single doctors who were of no use to her. She had absolutely no interest in feeling any sort of attraction to the man.

She had learned early in life that wishing things certainly did not make them happen, so she had taken a deep breath and set to the task Mrs. Jenkins had assigned her. If she made quick work of it, hopefully the doctor would move along to his next patient and she could get her client sorted in time to collect Annie from school. The poor dear had been so apprehensive about her first day, Katie certainly didn't want to be late.

"Thank you, dear," Mrs. Jenkins smiled at her as she poured her a cup of tea. "You did a good job in my kitchen, despite your independent ideas of having a career."

Katie laughed. She wasn't offended by the old woman's words. She knew her refusal to remarry was a little unusual, but this was 1854 for heaven's sake. It was perfectly acceptable for a woman to be independent and rely on herself rather than a husband.

"I consider that high praise coming from you, Mrs. Jenkins, thank you." With no desire to talk about herself and even less to show any interest in the doctor, Katie turned the subject. “Have you always lived her in Bucklin?”

“No. My dearly departed Mr. Jenkins brought me out here from the East when we married.”

“Was it a big adjustment for you?”

“Probably not as much as an adjustment as you’ll be going through being from the big city. I grew up on a farm, so it wasn’t so different. But of course, Bucklin barely existed when I arrived, so we had to make do with no stores and no train. I came by stagecoach. It took days on end. Not like it is with the train now. We’ve become so modern.”

Katie had to laugh again. Mrs. Jenkins was quite right. Bucklin, Missouri was nothing like New York City. If she thought this was modern, Katie shuddered to think what it was like when Mrs. Jenkins first arrived. But she couldn’t say that.

“It must have been so exciting to see the changes.”

“I don’t know about exciting, but I guess it’s been interesting,” was all the cranky woman would allow.

Finally, politeness would not allow Katie to ignore the doctor any longer. She would have to talk to him.

“Have you always lived in Bucklin, Doctor Jenkins?”

“No, ma’am. I grew up not far from where Mrs. Jenkins is from, in fact. Pittsburgh, Pennsylvania. Have you ever been there?”

Katie just shook her head. “I’ve never been anywhere but New York until coming here.”

“This is quite a change for you, then, isn’t it?”

She couldn't tell if it was censure or admiration in his voice. She felt her chin rising.

"I am quite convinced that experiencing new things causes character growth." Katie didn't want to feel charmed when he grinned at her and nodded his agreement. She turned her face away, not wanting to admire how handsome he was. She ignored the flutter of attraction in her belly.

Her eyes encountered Mrs. Jenkins' shrewd gaze and she couldn't prevent her mouth from returning the old lady's crooked smile.

Chapter Six

Katie needed to extricate herself from the awkward encounter but wasn't sure how she would accomplish it. The doctor looked unfortunately comfortable in Mrs. Jenkins' lacy room with a cup of tea in his large hand and a plate of cookies balanced on his knee.

She had hoped to get Mrs. Jenkins' measurements done, but to do so, she would have to wait for the doctor to leave. While he obviously didn't mind the sight of the old woman in her shift, it just didn't strike Katie as seemly. She felt a sigh rising up from her toes and tried to stifle it.

She must not have been successful as Katie could feel the doctor's eyes upon her, speculating. He tossed back the rest of his tea, placed the cup on the nearest table, grabbed another cookie from the plate, and got to his feet.

"Thank you for the tea, ladies. It has been a pleasure, but I ought to be on my way. I have more patients to visit before the sun sets."

Katie felt her cheeks warm at the thought that he might be leaving to make her more comfortable. Why would the man do that? She had never experienced any man putting a woman's feelings before their own. She must be mistaken and he had caught sight of the clock and realized he ought to be going. Katie offered him a cool, polite smile as he came to shake her hand.

"It was a pleasure meeting you, Mrs. Carter. I'm certain our paths will cross again shortly."

Katie merely nodded. She couldn't say it was a pleasure, and he was probably correct. In such a small town, it was inevitable that they would meet on occasion.

He took his leave of Mrs. Jenkins and then left with only the slightest backward glance.

"You certainly know how to rid the room of an eligible gentleman," Mrs. Jenkins observed drily.

Katie hoped her face projected the innocence that she felt. "I didn't say a single word to send him on his way."

Mrs. Jenkins harrumphed. "Well you certainly didn't say a single word to make him stay, either, did you?"

Katie had to laugh but persisted in her claim of innocence. "The man is a doctor and ought to be seeing to his patients rather than dallying with us."

"He wasn't dallying. It's good for my health to be able to feast my eyes on such a fine specimen of a man."

Katie laughed again. "Why, Mrs. Jenkins, that sounded almost poetic. Are you sweet on the doctor?"

Now the older woman guffawed. “He could be my grandson.”

“Hardly that, Mrs. Jenkins.”

“Well I am certainly at least old enough to be the man’s mother. I am most certainly not sweet on him,” she protested, but then had to add, “But I cannot claim to mind the man’s company.” Her gaze again turned shrewd. “Which is why I cannot fathom why you wouldn’t want the man to stick around. You won’t do any better than him in these parts.”

Katie merely offered a smile in return. “Well, then it’s a good thing that I am not in any need of a man or a doctor.” She then turned the subject. “Now shall we get on with our plans? Your daughter-in-law mentioned that you could use a couple of new day dresses. I must tell you that the selection at the mercantile, while limited, is of good quality. I will have no problem making you what you’d like. Did you have any particular colors in mind?”

With relief, Katie was finally able to turn the older woman’s attention away from the doctor and onto the matter at hand. Without too much more difficulty she had her measurements, color selections, and style determined. Katie promised to have the dresses ready within a week.

“Are you certain you can work that fast, girl? That seems like a rather optimistic estimate.”

“Oh, no, Mrs. Jenkins, I am certain to be finished by then. As you can imagine, since I’m new in town, I don’t have too many contracts arranged as yet. So your order will take priority.”

The older woman harrumphed again but seemed quite pleased at the thought of being anyone's priority. "You make sure you allow enough time to chase after other clients though, too, young lady."

Katie grinned. "It is kind of you to concern yourself. I will have a care. Now I must be going. It has been a pleasure, Mrs. Jenkins, but now I am off to collect Annie from school. It was her first day today."

"Well why didn't you say so? Get on with you, and take good care of that little one of yours."

Katie smiled at the woman's changeable demeanor. "Good day, Mrs. Jenkins. I will see you again soon."

She then hurried to the school, hoping she'd make it on time. She had made quick work of gathering her things and taking her leave. With only one wrong turn, she arrived at the school breathless and only a minute or two late. But it was long enough to have worried the little girl.

Katie couldn't bear the stricken look in Annie's eyes. "I am so sorry, Annie. I got turned around on my way here and had to ask for help to find the school." The little girl looked confused, and Katie offered her a twisted smile. "That's the problem with us both being new to town. I wasn't completely certain how to find you. But here we are, safe and sound. No harm done, right?"

The little girl still looked concerned but she answered Katie with a nod. Katie's heart sank a little further. It was going to be difficult to entrap the child's heart with her own. She had faced so much loss in her short life; Katie couldn't really blame her for being skeptical about her adoptive mother's intentions. Katie tried not to allow it to hurt her feelings; she was the adult in the situation after all. But she had her own losses to deal with and she couldn't help wishing they both had an easier life to deal with. With a shake of her head, she gripped her satchel of supplies she had been showing Mrs. Jenkins a little tighter and determined to overcome this little setback with her new daughter.

"So how did your first day of school go, anyway? What do you think of the teacher? Are there many children your age?"

Annie was reluctant to volunteer much information, but she did answer Katie's questions. "It was all right. Mr Jones, the teacher, seems nice enough. There are three others my age, and another boy a year older but doing the same schoolwork as us. He was late starting school."

"Do you know why?"

Annie shrugged. "I don't think they lived here before."

"So, you aren't the only new one in the class. That's good, right?"

Annie shrugged again.

"Do you like school, Annie? Are you going to be able to bear going there every day?"

They were walking slowly home, and Katie thought Annie wasn't going to answer her last questions, so long was her silence. Finally the little girl looked up at her.

"I like to learn. But I worried about you all day."

Katie's heart dropped. "Oh, honey, it's not your job to worry about me. It's my job to worry about you." She pulled the child into her side with her free arm. "You needn't be worried about anything anymore. You've got me. And even Miss Melly. It's your job to be a little girl and have fun, not to worry about the adults."

"But what if something happened to you, and you didn't show up?"

Katie kept her arm tightly around the little girl. Dropping her satchel, she crouched down to be on eye level with her.

"Annie, my dear, I cannot promise that nothing bad will ever again happen in your life, but we aren't in New York anymore. The air is clean and healthy here. I'm strong and healthy. You're young and healthy. I'm quite certain we are going to be perfectly fine here together. But you're right, since I am on my own as the adult in our relationship, I ought to make some legal arrangements for someone to care for you if something did happen to me. But I can promise you this, I will do everything in my power to make sure nothing does happen to me, all right? And I promise not to be late again for picking you up from the school."

Annie regarded her with her serious gaze for another moment before a small, sweet smile peeped out on her face and she threw her arms around Katie's neck. "All right, Katie, I will try not to worry. But I cannot promise for sure."

Katie laughed with a mixture of amusement and relief. "That's all I can ask from you, sweetheart. Now let's hurry along. I left some cookie batter ready at home so we could have freshly baked cookies while you tell me a little more about your day."

Giggling, Annie stepped out of Katie's arms and started running toward home. "Come on, Katie, there are cookies waiting for us."

With a giggle of her own, Katie grabbed up her satchel with one hand, lifted the hem of her skirt with the other, and raced after the girl. With all their laughter, neither of them were very fast, and they were a giggling, exhausted heap by the time they made it to their small house on the edge of town. Melanie was just arriving home at the same time, but rather than scold them, she merely offered them a long-suffering roll of her eyes and went into her own room, leaving them to catch their breath and bake the cookies.

"Those were the best cookies I have ever tasted, Katie. Where did you learn to cook so good?"

Katie grinned at the girl. The back of her mind twitched with the desire to correct her grammar, but she caught herself before it left her mouth. She swallowed it down and decided to leave the girl's grammar to her teacher for now.

"My mother was a wonderful cook and baker. I'm not nearly as good as she was, but everything I know, I learned from her."

"Did your mama die, too?" the youngster asked quietly, her joy in the afternoon diminishing at the reminder of loss.

"She did. I'm an orphan, just like you."

Annie looked at her with wide eyes. "Did you get adopted from a train, too?"

"Well, maybe not JUST like you. I was a fair bit older than you when my parents died. But I was all alone in the world before I found you."

"Is that why you didn't have any children already?"

Katie's mind shifted to the impossibly small coffin as it was lowered into the ground. Her breath caught for a moment, and she nearly choked on her grief. She couldn't share that with the six-year-old. Not yet. She hoped her face didn't reveal her strain as she tried to smile at the girl.

"I've been waiting for you for quite a while."

It was the right thing to say. Annie grinned at her, allowing her sorrows to recede into the background once more. Katie wished she had the resilience of a child. She had to shove her feelings aside with force. She didn't want them to worry the child.

Blinking rapidly to ensure no tears were gathering in her eyes, Katie turned away for a moment but then quickly turned back to face Annie. "Did the teacher give you any assignments you need to work on at home or would you like to help me make our supper?"

"Only the big kids get home assignments," she said with a face Katie couldn't interpret.

"Are you jealous that you didn't get one or relieved? I can't really tell."

"I think it would be way more interesting to be a big kid," Annie explained slowly. "But I don't think I would like to do school work at home."

Katie smiled. "Don't worry — you'll be a big kid soon enough. You're already six. Before you know it, you'll be all grown up. You should enjoy each day as it comes."

Annie looked at her for a moment as though she thought she had lost her mind, but then she must have seen some reason in Katie's words. She nodded. "Well, any day that comes with warm cookies is a day to be enjoyed, I'd say."

The two shared a smile before Katie started bustling about preparing the supper. Annie set the table for three and chattered away telling Katie all about the friends she had made and what she thought of her new teacher.

"In New York, I didn't get to go to school until they made me go to the orphanage. I think this school is better than that one. So I think I'll go back tomorrow."

Katie smiled. She hadn't realized that was in question. "I'm glad it's not a drudgery for you."

"What's drudgery?"

"It's hard, dull work."

Annie scrunched up her nose. "Maybe it is drudgery," she decided. "But the people are interesting."

Katie stifled the desire to laugh at the child's observations. "Were any of the other students children we met on the train?"

"Walter and Ross are in my class. They were on the train with us. I think they are very smart. Do you think it's because they're boys?"

Katie almost choked. "Are you asking me if I think they are smart because they're boys?"

Annie nodded, her eyes wide and serious.

"Most definitely not." Katie could hear the indignation in her voice and tried to quell her instinctive reactions. "I think they are a bit older than you, aren't they? That would account for them seeming smart to you. They have had more opportunity to learn things. I have every expectation that you will be as smart as or even smarter than them."

Now Annie's eyes were as wide as saucers. "Now you're telling tales, Katie. I can't be smarter than them."

"Why ever not?"

"'Cuz I'm dense."

Katie blinked at the child. "I beg your pardon."

"I'm dense. That's what the ladies at the orphanage told me. It means I'm not very smart, right?"

"I am certain that you must have mistook their meaning," Katie said while gritting her teeth to prevent herself from telling the child what she thought of any adult who would even consider saying such a thing to a child. "Never mind about them anyway. You are making a fresh start here with me, and there is every reason to believe you are going to grow up to be as successful and intelligent as you could possibly wish." She took a deep breath and switched the subject. “Now, tell me a little bit more about the game you played at recess.”

The rest of the supper preparations continued without incident, and before long they were cleaning up from the meal and Katie was tucking the child into her bed.

Her heart swelled with the feeling of the small little arms around her neck as Annie told her good night.

“Sweet dreams, my dear,” Katie whispered around the lump in her throat before closing the door.

She turned around to encounter Melanie’s shrewd gaze upon her.

“All sorts of perils for you to navigate around as you get to know that child, aren’t there?”

Katie offered a wry grin and a shuddering breath. “So many,” she agreed wholeheartedly.

“Are you going to tell her about Lacey and Jason?”

“Eventually, I will. But I need her to feel secure first. If I tell her about my own losses, it will make her feel as though I do not have any power to keep her safe. She needs to see me as an authority and a source of strength for her. If she knows about my past, that will be harder for her.”

Melanie’s eyes filled with sympathy, but Katie tried to ignore it. Sympathy would only make her heartache swell. She needed it to be squashed down and ignored. She needed to be strong, fierce even. Nothing was going to stand in her way of making a success here, on her own, far from New York and the shadows she had left behind. She looked around her tidy little kitchen and the friend sitting at the table with her wise eyes trained upon her and grinned. She wasn't actually alone. And she was already succeeding.

"I got Mrs. Jenkins' measurements and fabric choices today. We can get started right away."

"That's wonderful. Thank you for doing that. Let's get started in the morning, though. I don't know what it is about all this clean air out here. One would think it would be invigorating, but I find that I am so sleepy."

Katie laughed. "Perhaps it is so invigorating that you wore yourself out."

"Or perhaps it was listening to your little one's prattle of her long day that wore me out," Mel countered. "I am delighted for her that she is adjusting so well to all the changes in her little life."

Katie nodded. "It's amazing how resilient a child can be." She surprised herself with a wide yawn, and they both had to smother their laughter so as not to disturb Annie.

"All right, you had the right of it. Tomorrow is soon enough to start on Mrs. Jenkins' order."

Chapter Seven

Katie and Mel made short work of Mrs. Jenkins' dresses and delivered them when Katie had predicted to the amazed delight of the older woman. She was so pleased with their work that she promised to tell everyone she encountered about their abilities. True to her word, they soon had almost as much work as they could handle. They were relieved and delighted. Their life soon settled into a comfortable routine.

Annie was chattering away as usual as Katie walked with her to school. It crossed Katie's mind that she seemed to be the only mother walking her child to school. But she so enjoyed those moments with her new daughter that she had no desire to curtail them. Besides, she hadn't been gone from New York long enough to be over the fear of all the things that could happen to a small girl on her own. Katie was certain it would be several years before she would allow the girl to go anywhere on her own. She was grateful for the circumstances that allowed her to make the short journey.

"Do you think I could?" Annie concluded.

Katie blinked. "I'm sorry, honey, I think my mind got clouded there for a moment. I didn't catch everything you said."

Annie turned her puzzled gaze up to Katie's. "But you always listen, don't you?"

"I thought so," Katie smiled. "But could you please repeat yourself?"

Annie frowned but did as she was bade. "I was telling you that Suzie wants me to play at her house on Saturday."

Katie smiled. "That sounds like it would be fun. Do you want to go?"

"I think I do."

Katie heard the uncertainty in the child's voice and wondered why this hadn't come up the evening before. "Is there a reason why you might not want to go?"

"Suzie's grandmother died. What if there's a sickness in their house?"

Katie's heart lurched for the poor child's fears. "Oh, my dear, it is sad that Suzie's grandmother died, but from what I understand, she was a really old woman. It's not unusual for people to die when they are very old. And that isn't something you can catch." She paused, allowing the child to absorb that logic. "Does Suzie seem sick to you?"

Annie shook her head. "No, I've never heard her cough, and her skin is quite pink, really."

It hurt Katie's heart that the child knew what signs to look for to sense someone's health. She offered the girl a soft smile and squeezed her hand. "You don't have to go if you don't feel comfortable, but if you would like to go, I'd be happy to take you there on Saturday. Since you don't have any brothers or sisters, it would be good for you to play with other children from time to time."

The little girl gazed at her with serious eyes. She nodded slightly. "I will think about it a little longer. But I think I'll go. It would probably be fun."

She still sounded uncertain. Katie just squeezed her hand again but decided to turn the subject. She had no intention of forcing the child.

"I have a new client to visit today. I do hope my sense of direction is improving." She laughed. "That is one of the few things I miss about New York. Since addresses were so clearly marked, it was easy to find where you were going."

The small child agreed with a sage nod before finding something new to worry about. "But you wouldn't want to move back there, would you?"

"I don't think so. I am fairly certain you and I will be quite happy here. But if I ever do find myself hankering to return, I will be sure to discuss it with you — have no fear. You and I are a team now. Where I go, you will go, so I wouldn't make a decision like that without you agreeing to it."

"Really?"

"Truly," Katie replied with a firm nod. "Now promise me that you will try to have a marvelous day."

Annie grinned. "I promise!"

Katie watched the little girl scamper off to join a cluster of children entering the school. Her heart felt like it turned over in her chest. Having a child to love was the deepest joy, and she was eternally grateful for Annie's presence in her life. She only wished she could bear the child's concerns on her behalf. It wasn't right for a six-year-old to have so many worries. Katie hoped she would be able to restore the child's sense of security with time.

As Katie walked to her new client's home, she encountered various townspeople. It was very different than in New York. There, you would barely acknowledge other people's existence on the sidewalk, merely attempting to stay out of other people's way. Here, one must return nods and greetings, stopping to meet and exchange a few words with anyone she hadn't met before. It was the expected thing to do here, and Katie was coming to learn it was also good for business. Whenever people found out she and Melanie were seamstresses for hire other women's eyes would light up and whichever gown she was wearing would be scrutinized. Katie had taken to wearing her best examples of their workmanship whenever she left her house.

It was not in her nature to be an extrovert. Not to say that she minded the sociability of the other townspeople, but she had to struggle with her instinctive reaction to distrust those she met. She wondered if the lessons learned from her husband's hand would ever leave her.

"Good day," she nodded to another new face.

"Ma'am," the rough looking man lifted his hat and offered her a smile that appeared genuine despite the lack of a few teeth. The middle-aged woman at his side appeared delighted to encounter Katie.

"Are you the new sewing lady I've heard tell of?"

Katie contained her amusement and nodded. "Most likely," she smiled kindly. "My name is Katie Carter. My friend, Miss Melanie, and I work together on most of the sewing projects we are hired to do."

The woman clasped her hands to her chest with barely contained rapture. "Mr. Smith, this is the lady I was telling you about. Do say I can hire her. My stitches aren't nearly so fine as hers. It would be beyond wonderful to have a new going-to-church dress."

The gentleman looked slightly less pleased to meet Katie than he had originally, most likely at the thought of having to part with some of his coins, but he patted his wife's hand anyway. "Sure, sure, we'll see what we can do."

Katie didn't press the matter. "It would be a pleasure, ma'am. I am certain we will meet again. Whenever you're ready, we can make arrangements."

Much to Katie's surprise, she encountered Cassandra just coming out of the mercantile. They had arrived together on the train accompanying the orphans but had each been swept up in their own activities since soon after arriving in Bucklin.

"Katie, what a pleasure to see you!" Cassie exclaimed as she swept her into a tight hug.

Katie was amazed at the display of affection from the previously reserved young woman. She was unused to such actions from anyone but returned the woman's squeeze.

"You must accompany me to the hotel dining room for a cup of tea and fill me in on what has become of you and Mel of late. I have been so tied up with my own affairs that I haven't been much of a friend to either of you."

"Well," Katie answered reasonably, "you have certainly had many things going on."

Cassie waved her hand. "That is insufficient excuse. Do say you'll come."

After glancing at the small time piece in her reticule, Katie grinned and nodded. "I have a few moments. You are right, it would be lovely to share some tea and catch up."

Cassandra made short work of ordering for them after they had been shown to a table by the window in the starkly furnished, but still inviting, dining room.

"It is surprising how nice this room is despite the décor," Cassie commented.

"I think it's all the windows. And the smell of baking bread," Katie added with a smile. "Any room that smells like freshly baked bread is one that makes you want to linger."

Cassie nodded and grinned. She quickly brought Katie up to date on her news in a few sentences before demanding, "Now you share. Mrs. Parker told me you have taken the last child. I was so caught up with my boys on the train that I didn't get to know little Annie very much at all. Tell me everything."

Katie smiled again at the younger woman's enthusiasm. As far as she knew, there weren't too many years between them in age, but life had beaten a little of the zest out of her. Being with Cassandra reminded her of how she used to be.

"I'm not sure if I can tell you EVERYTHING. I probably don't even know all there is to know about the little darling. But she is a dear. I find it difficult to believe she was the last child remaining."

Cassie nodded and shrugged. "Most of the families wanted boys or older girls so they'd be more able to work."

Katie wrinkled her nose. "Doesn't that feel a little bit more like exploitation than adoption?"

"Don't think too hard about it or you'll break your heart. Just know that I did visit every single one of the children from our shipment, and they are all being reasonably well cared for."

"Thank you for that. You're right. I went to work at the orphanage to try to heal from my own heartbreak, but all those abandoned children just made it ache a little bit more. But I'm grateful that you checked on them. I wouldn't have had the courage."

Cassie shrugged again. "I didn't trust that the agent was going to do much. But we got lucky. This town seems to be overflowing with decent people. I don't think every single one of the children has ended up in utopian circumstances, but none of them are being mistreated."

Katie sighed. "That's better than what they had on the streets of New York, so I will try to be satisfied with that." She paused and smiled at the waiter who brought their tea and biscuits. After he left, she continued, "As for my little Annie, she is just turned six. Her entire family died from the flu that took so many last year."

"Including your family — that's something that you share," Cassie added softly. "Does she find that a comfort?"

"I haven't told her yet," Katie answered, shifting her gaze to the window before girding her courage and facing her friend. "I'm trying to inspire confidence in the child. If she knows about my losses, it might add to her fears."

Cassie didn't push the matter, for which Katie was grateful, but the compassion in her face made Katie have to swallow the lump forming in her throat. She coughed lightly to clear it and carried on briskly. "Anyhow, she's a bright little girl, quick to learn, and responds well to any guidance from me. For the most part, she seems to be taking her change of circumstances in stride, but she has a heightened fear of death. She is afraid of the doctor, and worries about going to her friend's house because the girl's grandmother died recently." She paused to sip her tea. Katie then continued in an even softer voice. "I fear I'm not going to be enough for her as a single woman. I won't be able to provide siblings for her. And I worry that every child needs the influence of both a man and a woman in their lives."

Cassie reached across the table and patted her friend's hand. "I know there's enough love in your heart to fill all the spaces this child needs. You will be enough for her — I am certain of it." There was a pause before she continued. "Of course, in a town like this, there's no shortage of potential mates for a single woman like yourself."

Katie felt that color leach from her face. "I have less than no interest in remarrying, Cassie. I am happy for you that you seem to have found a good man that makes you happy, but I am unwilling to take that chance myself. Once was quite enough for me to learn my lesson."

"Most men are not like he was," Cassandra countered quietly.

"But you never really know someone until you live with them." Katie's voice trailed off before she rallied and carried on briskly. "Anyhow, as you said, my heart definitely has plenty of room for my dear sweet Annie, and I will do all in my power to make a good life for her. Mel and I have already found a comfortable number of customers to sew for, and it provides me enough flexibility to be there for Annie. I walk with her to school and collect her after class. I visit customers while she is at school, so thus far there haven't been any conflicts. Of course, it hasn't been too long yet. I am sure there will be challenges. But so far so good."

Cassie squeezed her hand again and refrained from arguing. "I'm sure you'll make a huge success of both your sewing and being a mother." Cassie paused again. When she carried on, her tone was apologetic, as though she regretted her question even as she asked it. "Are you disappointed the teaching position fell through? You would have been able to be with her all day if you were at the school."

Katie smiled at her friend to let her know she had taken no offense from the question. “Not at all. I think it has all worked out for the best. In hindsight, it might have been too much for me to take on a large classroom of children from varying ages and backgrounds. There are currently only two classes at the school, so each teacher has children from a span of five years. I am quite content with my one little girl. And this way, I can assist her learning without being responsible for all of it.” Now she turned an impish grin on her friend. “And what about you? How are you managing with your three boys on a permanent basis? Have your parents forgiven you yet?”

Cassie laughed. “Well, I never aspired to be a teacher, so I am delighted when the little darlings head off to school. It’s all I can manage to keep up with their questions at the end of the day.” She laughed again then sighed with contentment. “But I wouldn’t have it any other way. As for my parents, I’m not completely certain if they have forgiven me for not having a high society wedding, but according to my mother’s most recent letter, they are considering coming out for a visit. It does help that Charles is an Emmerson, of course.”

“Of course,” Katie agreed with a chuckle, shaking her head over the ridiculousness of the wealthy. She was determined that her daughter would learn to fend for herself. Katie would never expect the girl to need a husband to support her. Realizing that her heart had begun to race, she took a deep breath to calm her nerves, reminding herself once again that surely not all men were dangerous.

The clock in the hallway sounded the hour. With a start, Katie realized that time was slipping by. She quickly got to her feet.

"It was so nice to have a little visit, Cass. Do stop by the house the next time you're in town, please. I'm terribly sorry to cut it short, but I really must be on my way."

"No apologies needed, my friend. Get on with your business. You were straight with me from the beginning. I promise I will come by really soon."

With a quick, tight hug, Katie said goodbye and then hurried away. She needed to reach her destination, conduct her appointment, and then return for Annie before the child became anxious. Katie's new reason to live was to ensure Annie was comfortable. It crossed her mind that this sounded obsessive, but she shoved the thought from her mind. It was a mother's obligation to see to the well being of her child, she reassured herself. Once they were settled into a routine, she would strive for balance. But in the meantime, it wouldn't harm either of them if she obsessed a little over her new daughter's happiness. After the losses they both had endured, it was just what they both needed.

Katie was relieved that her new client knew exactly what she wanted and was ready for her when she arrived. The style the woman was asking for, while a little more complicated than what she and Melanie usually did, wasn't beyond their abilities.

"It might take a day or two extra, though, to make sure all the pleating and embroidery is just so," Katie cautioned the woman.

"That's all right," Mrs. Levitt assured her. "I've been waiting for years for someone to say they could make me my dream dress. I can easily wait a couple extra days."

Katie was relieved by the woman's easygoing reaction and reminded herself once more that her decision to settle in Bucklin had been a wise one.

She was nearly skipping with contentment as she made her way back toward the school. Her bouncing steps came to a swift, stuttering halt when she recognized who was striding toward her. She glanced around quickly for an avenue of escape. One more thing to miss from New York. There were always alleys one could scurry down in the big city. Here in this town, it would be far too embarrassingly obvious if she tried to avoid him.

"Good afternoon, Mrs. Carter. What a pleasure to run into you on this fine day." Dr. Jeffries lifted his hat to her. She tried not to find it gallant. She averted her eyes so that her gaze wouldn't be drawn by his handsome features. Katie would not allow them to dwell on his sharp cheekbones or warm green eyes. And she most certainly would not glance at the charming dimple that was sure to peep at her if he smiled. The cookie Mrs. Levitt had offered her began to revolve uncomfortably in her stomach.

Katie realized she hadn't responded but was merely standing still staring off into the distance like a simpleton. With a disgusted roll of her eyes, she offered the doctor a slight curtsy.

"Good afternoon, sir. I cannot tarry as I have to collect my daughter from the school."

“Of course, I would never wish to detain you.” He offered her a slight bow.

Katie could feel hot color splashing high on her cheeks, but she avoided meeting the doctor’s gaze as she hurried past him. She knew it was ridiculous. He was probably a decent man. She had never heard any of the townsfolk speak anything but well of him.

She felt like a fool. And well she should, she assured herself harshly. It was foolish to be afraid of a man just because he was handsome. Surely not all handsome men were cruel and dangerous. Most would consider his good looks an asset. Katie had even heard some of the women giggling about what good medicine it was to look at the doctor. But she couldn’t agree.

Chapter Eight

Katie strolled along, content to enjoy the music in the air. The leaves rustling, the birds chirping, the crunch of the gravel under her feet. It was nothing like the city. And she loved it. For the first time in years she felt contentment. It had taken her a while to figure out what the sensation was. Then she realized that for the first time in maybe her entire life, she wasn't consumed with worries or anxieties. Sure, she was concerned for her and Annie's future, but she was filled with confidence that she was up to the task of facing it. Despite the abuse she had faced at her husband's hands and words, she had fought hard to regain her sense of self. She now knew what it meant to be happy. And she would do whatever it took to maintain that for herself and her daughter.

She felt like skipping but thought it would be too undignified for a matron like herself. She grinned. Maybe once Annie was with her. She picked up her pace, eager to see Annie after the afternoon's absence. She laughed out loud before glancing around quickly. Even though she wasn't in a city anymore, there were still people around and she didn't want anyone thinking she was crazy. She grinned. What did it matter? No one's opinion mattered but her own. She laughed again. She felt as though she were glowing from the joy in her heart.

When she arrived at her destination, she couldn't find anyone at first. The house appeared to be empty. No one responded to her increasingly fervent knocking. Her worry escalated. She ran around to the back of the house. It felt as though her heart was lodged in her throat when she saw the group clustered behind the barn. She couldn't see clearly through the tangle of legs, but lying on the ground was a bright splash of color that exactly matched the frock Annie had worn that morning to go play with her friend.

Katie shoved her fist into her mouth to stifle the scream that was trying to escape her throat. Picking up her skirts, she ran over to the group. Suzie's mother grabbed her before she got all the way to her daughter. At the moment, in her mounting fear, Katie couldn't remember the family name and wasn't about to tax her brain with figuring it out.

"Mrs. Carter, dear, you can't be letting your wee one see you in a taking. We've called for the doctor, he should be here any moment. Take a deep breath now." The older woman had spoken in a low, soothing voice but right by her ear, so Katie heard her clearly. She knew she needed to calm down and the woman had meant well, but the thought of the doctor coming for her daughter had her in a worse state than seeing her on the ground had. She knew that no one called the doctor unless it was absolutely necessary. Most farmers had the basic skills needed to patch up the usual scrapes and bruises children accumulated.

Closing her eyes, Katie willed strength into her limbs. *You've been through worse, Katie girl, you can handle this. Nothing will happen to Annie. Breathe.* She listened to her inner voice and took a deep steadying breath before pulling her arm out of the other woman's grasp with a small smile to let her know she meant no offense. The crowd parted, and she was by her daughter's side, dropping to her knees and hovering to ascertain the damage.

"What happened?" she asked, proud to hear that her voice sounded reasonably steady.

"The girls thought they would try flying," Suzie's father answered wryly with a gesture toward the opening above their heads. Katie could see it was a well stocked haymow. Her eyes widened as she looked back down at her daughter.

"Is your daughter all right?"

"She lost her nerve and didn't jump. She climbed down and came for help when your little one got hurt. I'm right sorry, Mrs. Carter. I know your girl is from the city. Ours should've known better and stopped her."

Katie appreciated the man's words, but despite her devastation, she couldn't let the other little girl take the full blame. "I would have thought Annie would have the sense to know jumping from such a height is a bad idea. But never mind about that now. Has she been moved? Can I touch her? Is she bleeding anywhere?"

"I will ascertain that for you right now," came a deep voice from behind her. Katie stifled her involuntary reaction. For a moment, she wanted to throw herself into the doctor's arms. But that would be wrong on so many levels. Most of all because he was there to tend to her child, not soothe her rattled nerves. She offered him a tight smile by way of greeting.

"Thank you, doctor."

He didn't return her smile, keeping his full focus on Annie. Katie didn't mind; it was where it should be. She could barely breathe; her chest was so tight with anxiety. She reminded herself once more to keep the air flowing into her lungs. The last thing any of them needed was for her to collapse next to her daughter.

The doctor made short work of examining the child. He worked swiftly but before he could even finish, Annie coughed and slowly opened her eyes. When what she saw was the doctor, she screamed her alarm and burst into tears. Katie quickly pushed the doctor aside and gathered her daughter into her arms.

"Oh, my poor darling, everything is going to be fine. Tell me where it hurts." Katie tried to be soothing.

"Am I dying? I don't want the doctor. I told you I shouldn't have come here." Her words came out in jerking gasps around her sobs.

"Hush now, Annie. You most certainly are not dying. But you did a very foolish thing when you jumped out of that window, and this is the consequence. You need to let the doctor finish checking to make sure you didn't do any serious damage to yourself."

"No, please, no doctor," Annie whimpered.

Katie forced herself to meet Doctor Jeffries' gaze. "Were you finished with your examination?"

"I still need to examine her head," he answered quietly.

Annie burrowed closer into Katie's arms. "Shhh, darling, it will all be fine. How about if I hold onto you, and he just feels around to make sure you didn't crack it like an egg?"

Her pitiful attempts at levity actually had an effect. Annie's sobs were interrupted, and a watery chuckle emerged from the child. "I'm not an egg."

"No, and you're not a bird either, as you have learned the hard way, didn't you?" she reminded the child quietly. "Now just cuddle right into me, my dear, and I'm sure Mr. Jeffries will be as quick as he can." She offered the doctor a pointed look when she mentioned speed, hoping he wouldn't take offense over her lack of his medical title. Katie felt there was no need to remind the child she was being examined by the dreaded doctor.

He must have understood her meaning since he offered her a small wink before he continued with his gentle examination.

"I am quite sure she only knocked the wind out of herself with a rough landing, but this lump on her head does give me some concern. The fact that she hasn't vomited is reassuring, but you will have to watch her closely for the next day or two. Will that be a problem for you? If you cannot remain with her, perhaps Mrs. Marsden could keep her for you."

Katie was horrified at the suggestion. She didn't want to offend the other woman, but she could barely contain her gasp of shock. "I beg your pardon? Of course, I can manage to keep close watch over my daughter." She glared at the man, but her dirty look barely seemed to faze him. His cold stare chilled her to the bone as she clutched her now quiet daughter to her chest. She couldn't understand his sudden change of attitude. Just a moment ago, he had seemed almost comforting as he accepted her reluctance to call him doctor. She didn't think she had any composure left, but she gathered the last shreds of her dignity and, with Annie still clinging tightly, she managed to get herself to her feet. Glancing around at the gathered spectators, she offered them all a tight nod and a thinly polite smile.

"Thank you for your help," she offered vaguely to everyone and stepped away from the group, walking slowly so as not to jar her pale child.

"Are you mad at me, Mama?" Annie's quiet voice broke the silence that had surrounded them as they made their way home.

Katie's heart constricted at the sweet sound of being someone's mother. But she hurried to reassure the child. "Of course I'm not mad at you, sweetheart. You have many things you have to learn. It's unfortunate you had to learn this lesson the hard way, but I'm sure you'll never make the mistake of trying to fly ever again, will you?"

"Never, ever," the child said. Her voice was still low but her mouth was less droopy as at least one of her concerns was lessened. "The doctor seemed to be mad, though, didn't he?"

Katie sighed. "Yes, he did, but don't worry yourself too much over that. We don't need to concern ourselves with what anyone else thinks. If he didn't see fit to tell us why he was mad, then we needn't bother about it either."

"Are you very certain?"

Now Katie had to grin. "I am absolutely one hundred percent certain that I do not give a fig for that man's thoughts, as long as he has assured me that you are well, he can keep the rest of it to himself."

Despite her continued pallor, Annie grinned at Katie for a moment before more concerns came to her mind. "Am I too heavy for you to carry? Maybe you should put me down and I can walk."

Katie shook her head. "You gave me quite a fright when I saw you lying on the ground. I am finding comfort in having you in my arms. And you are not nearly heavy enough. I am starting to think that I haven't been feeding you as much as I ought."

This seemed to do the trick of turning the child's mind away from her worries as she was able to let out a small giggle and begin to imagine how she could fatten up.

"Maybe we could stop at the mercantile and buy some sweets," she suggested with a wiggle.

Katie laughed. "Or maybe we could bake a cake when we get home."

“Oh, that would be wonderful, then we can share with Miss Mel, too.”

“I think that is the best idea. No doubt Miss Mel could use some extra flesh on her bones as well.” Katie said that just as they were approaching their small house, her voice pitched just right so that Melanie, who was standing near the open window, could hear. She burst into laughter as she opened the door wide for them to enter.

“Might I ask why we are discussing plumping me up?” the laughter in her voice revealed that she had not taken offense.

Katie quickly explained what had happened in as light a tone as she could muster. She was relieved to see that while Melanie’s brows furrowed with concern, she saved her questions for later.

The afternoon and evening passed quickly while they kept the youngster occupied with quiet activities, enjoying the quickly assembled and cooled cake before they tucked her into bed.

“Now you really must tell me why you are as pale as death. It seems to me that the child has come to no serious injury.”

Katie flushed over her friend’s words. “If you had seen her lying there on the ground with everyone standing around her wringing their hands, you would not be quite so complacent.”

“I dare say I wouldn’t, but it still seems to me that you are concerned about more than just the girl’s injuries. Did something else happen today? Did something go wrong with the client you went to visit?”

Katie grinned. "No, I almost forgot about it, but the visit with Mrs. Bainbridge went very well. I think, if we please her with this first commission, we will get a good bit of business from her. The dear woman was almost beside herself with delight at the thought of someone else making her gowns and frocks. It seemed to me that while she had exceptional taste, her skills are merely middling. But since her husband seems to be doing quite well for himself, he shan't begrudge her the expense."

"Well that is excellent news. I am certain we will please her. So what else is troubling you?"

Katie chuckled, then sighed. "I do believe you have come to know me a little too well." She paused, rubbing her neck to try to release some of the tension that had accumulated there. "Annie's accident brought back a few too many unpleasant feelings. I'm sure you can relate. You never completely leave old grief behind, and new frights can bring them to the fore."

"That's certainly true." Mel's soft, accepting tone prompted Katie to continue.

She looked at Mel and felt heat creep into her cheeks. "The doctor was called before I got there."

"Oooo, the handsome, young doctor?" Mel teased.

"I do believe this town only has the one doctor."

Mel laughed. "Perhaps so, but why does his having been called cause a crease to your forehead? I know Annie has an unreasonable fear of doctors — has she infected you with her concerns?"

Katie laughed too but added a small shrug. "After seeing all the sickness and death we have seen, doctors don't usually bring warm feelings to the heart."

Mel nodded but then added reasonably, "They do occasionally bear good news, such as when they assist with a birth." Katie shot her a wry look, prompting a laugh from Mel. "Very well, I will agree that doctors are usually accompanying trouble. But since he's so very handsome, it must help assuage the problem a little bit, or at least distract you from your troubles."

"I will admit, the doctor is one of the best looking men I've ever laid eyes on, but he seems to have taken me in dislike. I don't think he approves of women who work."

Mel appeared to be taken aback by this statement. "All women work," she replied firmly.

"Well, of course, but I meant for pay, as in employment."

Mel sniffed. "Well, then you needn't wrinkle up your forehead over such a ridiculous man. If he is so backwards as that, you needn't bother considering his thoughts."

Katie chuckled. "That was exactly the conclusion I had reached myself, but I worry about how influential he might be in this size of a town."

"Never mind about him. Very few of the women, who we are hoping will be our clients, will pay him any heed if he starts spouting off about women working outside the home. Most women have the sense to realize that life is not so straightforward."

Katie agreed with her friend but still couldn't put away the worry that buzzed around the back of her mind as she settled into her bed that night. Thankfully, the fresh clean air of Bucklin and all the walking she had done that day were more powerful than her troubled thoughts, and she quickly drifted off into a deep sleep.

After waking Annie up a couple times during the night to ensure she was doing well, they all slept later than usual. But after a hearty breakfast and getting Annie settled with a small chalkboard, Katie hurried away from the small house to meet with one client nearby.

"Mrs. Carter?" Katie froze in her tracks when she heard the incredulous tone of the familiar, deep, masculine voice.

"Good morning, Dr. Jeffries," she replied, keeping her tone light, as she wondered whether or not she should just brush by him or if she ought to stay and converse with the man. The disapproval clearly displayed on his face made her feel much inclined to do the former. She was about to do just that when he interrupted her thoughts.

"I thought you said you were in a position to keep an eye on Annie for a couple of days. It hasn't even been twenty-four hours."

Katie bristled at his accusatory tone but tried to convince herself that she appreciated his concern for her daughter. "I woke her up every few hours through the night, just as you instructed, doctor. And I spent most of the morning with her. But I had to make one quick call on a neighbor today. I haven't been gone long. In the meantime, Melanie is with her."

"What was so important that it couldn't wait until you were absolutely certain your child is well?" the doctor scoffed.

"Keeping food on her table and a roof over her head, doctor." Katie bit out the words, trying, but failing, to remain polite. "Not that it's any of your business what I do with my time."

"I don't know how you convinced the ones organizing the adoptions to entrust you with a child, but it seems to me that you are unfit for the assignment."

Katie could feel the color drain from her face as she felt his insult all the way to her core. A part of her wanted to curl up in a ball in a secluded corner and wail her grief at all the injustices life had handed her. But another part of her refused to let another man speak to her in a hurtful way.

"Dr. Jeffries, you do not have any right to speak to me in such a manner. Surely a man who has sworn to care for the well being of others would be sufficiently informed to realize that a woman on her own with a child has to do whatever it takes to care for all the responsibilities. While it would, of course, be absolutely lovely if I were somehow independently wealthy and didn't have to be gainfully employed, that is not the reality I face. I need to be attentive to my clients in order to make sure that Melanie and I can have enough business to succeed. Thankfully, my business partner is a trustworthy woman who could sit with my child for the few minutes that I had to be away. I am not being derelict in my duties. And you are exceedingly foolish to have thought that I was, and unnecessarily cruel to have told me so, especially given the stress that I had to contend with yesterday and the less than restful night I dealt with last night. I pray I never require your services in the future." If she was of a calmer mind, she would be happy to see that he seemed to have been struck mute by her words, but all she wanted to do now was be somewhere else. He seemed rooted in his place so she had to prod, "Now, if you would be so kind as to get out of my way, I will no longer trouble you with my presence."

Wyatt stepped off the path in order to allow her plenty of room to pass. He watched, dumbfounded, as she swept away from him with her head held high but her lips trembling. If he could, he would rip out his own tongue for the pain he had obviously caused her.

It was this ridiculous attraction he felt toward her that had muddled his mind, he was certain of it. He was so torn up about his feelings for the lovely young widow. A part of him wanted to sweep her into his arms and care for all her worries. But another part of him balked at the thought of taking such a headstrong woman into his life. With all that he faced each day, he was certain he required a soothing presence in his home at the end of the day. While Mrs. Carter was more than pleasant to look at, he was quite certain she had too many thoughts of her own to ever be able to soothe away his cares.

But Patricia had been a soothing presence, at least for the most part, and that didn't work out so well, his subconscious reminded him. He chose to ignore that mocking voice and hurried on to his next appointment. But before he got too far away, he couldn't resist turning back to observe the pretty brunette's progress. It troubled him to see that her head was no longer held high, and her strides were not nearly so purposeful as when she had swept away from him. It looked to him as though she had drooped.

The doctor had to fight hard to stop himself from running toward her. He fought the impulse that made him want to draw her into his arms and croon to her like a small child. She always seemed so strong; he doubted she would welcome such a gesture anyway. But she didn't look quite so strong now. He really ought to have curbed his tongue. He resolved to speak more kindly to her the next time they encountered one another. Despite her desire to never require his services, he was most certain they would cross paths many times again in the small town.

Chapter Nine

Wyatt was quite correct in his assumptions. It was barely two days later when they were forced into one another's company once again.

He knew he was meandering, but he couldn't bring himself to hurry. Checking Mrs. Jenkins' boils was sure to be the low point of his day. He would much rather enjoy the beautiful sunshiny day and allow his mind to wander to its favorite hobby of late – daydreaming about remarrying and starting a family. It troubled him slightly that in recent days the imaginary wife had taken on the features of Mrs. Carter, but he tried to ignore her face and just enjoy the imaginary sensation of having someone to come home to at the end of the day. And the imaginary enjoyment of the delicious scent of freshly baked bread or cookies. Wyatt chuckled as he caught himself inhaling deeply, as though he really could smell the delectable aroma. Shaking his head over his own foolishness, the doctor goaded his horse into a faster pace. He really ought to get on with the dreaded task.

After tying his horse loosely in the shade of a large tree near the road, Wyatt made his way toward the house. He stopped for a moment to admire how tidy the yard was despite Mrs. Jenkins' health problems. It was one more benefit of having a wife. Even an invalid was more benefit than trouble, he thought, remembering the good times with his dearly departed.

Shaking his head again, he quickly approached the door and rapped decisively.

"Is that you, Doctor Jeffries? Please hurry and come in."

Wyatt blinked. Had his imaginings conjured the woman? That sounded like Mrs. Carter.

"Whoever it is, please come in. We need your help."

Wyatt pulled himself out of his sudden inertia and opened the door. He was unsurprised to see Mrs. Carter but was shocked to see her huddled over Mrs. Jenkins' prone form.

"What has happened?" he demanded. He had almost asked 'what have you done,' but caught himself before making such a foolish mistake. But his tone must have given away some of his thoughts because the lovely widow shot him another one of her fierce glares.

"I cannot say for certain, Doctor Jeffries, what has happened to her, but she is bleeding quite terribly, which is why I wasn't able to run for help. Thankfully, she had mentioned to me that you were to be stopping by today, so I was able to remain here without losing my mind completely. I can assure you, my daughter was in the pink of perfect health when I left her at school this morning. And Mrs. Jenkins' bleeding was not my doing. Even if I had poked the poor dear with needles while checking her hem, there shouldn't be this much blood."

She seemed to be rambling, no doubt caused by her fear, but his silence didn't seem to be reassuring her at all. Perhaps she realized she was giving too much away. Her face hardened, and she offered him another glare. "I should actually be demanding of you what has happened to her. Why did you take so long in getting here? While it feels like I have been sitting here with her for several lifetimes, it has in reality been at least half an hour. And why is she not healed already? She was suffering from her boils the first time I visited her. Surely you should have fixed her up by now, shouldn't you?"

Wyatt grinned. He hadn't been railed at by anyone in ages. He normally appreciated the respect afforded him by the townsfolk, but it was refreshing to be treated like a regular person. It was obvious to him that Mrs. Carter most certainly did not place him in any position of reverence.

The young woman was looking at him as though he had lost his mind. He realized he was just standing there grinning like a simpleton when he should really be doing something to help his patient.

"You are quite correct, Mrs. Carter, I should have gotten here sooner. I didn't realize she was in such a bad way. When I was here last time, I thought her boils were almost better. Something must have happened to make her take a turn for the worse." There was a moment of silence while Mrs. Carter absorbed his words and appeared somewhat mollified.

"She's most fortunate that you were here to lend her assistance. You did very well in staunching the bleeding."

"Imagine that! You are saying the poor soul is fortunate that I was visiting a client rather than sitting at home being a housewife." The widow's sarcastic tone made heat accumulate in Wyatt's face. He offered her a wry smile.

"Well, it was fortuitous that she was not alone," he commented as he continued his assessment of the situation. "You say you have been here for half an hour, and it is still bleeding? That is very odd."

"The bleeding has slowed significantly, but whenever I would remove the towel, hoping I could go for help, it was obvious that it hadn't stopped. I was concerned she would lose all her blood if I left her."

"You did the right thing in staying with her. Thank you for remaining calm," he remarked.

She offered him a crooked smile. "I did not say I remained calm, doctor. I remained present. Most of me wanted to scream with fear. It was the first time since I arrived in Bucklin that I wished we were still in New York. In the city, all I would have had to do is shout and someone would have heard me and come to our aid. All this beautiful space can be a problem when you run into trouble and are alone."

Wyatt frowned. "That is why it is best for women not to be alone, then."

The widow laughed lightly. "Well, you certainly don't change your tune, do you?" Without allowing time for him to explain himself, she continued, "Now tell me what I can do to assist you. While a part of me wants to run out of here as quickly as my feet can carry me now that you are here to take care of her, I cannot bear to see the poor dear so pale. Surely there is something to be done."

Wyatt blinked, brought back to the task at hand. He was being daft, staring at the lovely young widow and forgetting about the poor woman on the floor. He focused his mind and started issuing orders as clearly as possible.

"We will need lots of warm water and as many towels as you can find. If there is not enough water in the house, one of us will have to go out to the well. Poor Mrs. Jenkins doesn't have running water in the house. If you'd like to stay with her, I can go fetch a couple pails of water."

"No!" she declared before blushing charmingly. She lowered her voice. "I am ashamed to admit, I cannot bear the thought of being alone here with her again feeling so helpless. I can manage the water. You stay with your patient." Her flush deepened while she paused before adding, "But I thank you for the offer. I'm sure you meant to be chivalrous, but I am quite capable despite being squeamish."

Wyatt had to laugh despite the seriousness of their situation. The defensive woman was cute when she got flustered. He realized she resented his implication that she was less capable than he was, but she also resented her own weakness in admitting how afraid she had been while alone with the bleeding older woman. He ought to tell her how impressed he was with her presence of mind, but she was likely to consider his words to be condescension. Besides, she was already out the door. At least she wasn't standing around wringing her hands. As much as he might think women ought to be tending to the home and the children rather than trying to be employed, he had to admit that Mrs. Carter was being quite sensible in this difficult situation. If he had been here by himself with Mrs. Jenkins, he would be almost as stuck as Mrs. Carter had been, despite his tools and training. Sometimes more than one pair of hands was necessary. That thought could be quite distracting in the context of thinking of the lovely widow, so he shoved it from his mind.

The bucket made a loud splash as it hit the surface of the water. Katie gritted her teeth as she turned the winch that would pull the full bucket back up. She had been a little too full of bravado when she told the doctor that it would be no problem to fetch the water. But she would rather do it than stay with poor Mrs. Jenkins on her own. It was too bad, though, that no one had told her how to get the bucket to be only half full. Maybe if she had been faster. Katie sighed and tugged on the handle. There was no question that she would sleep like a log tonight after the fright she had and now the exertion. With a great deal of effort and more grunting than she would like to admit, she finally had two pails full of water. She carefully lifted them, desperately trying not to spill a single drop after all the effort it took to collect. Going as quickly as she could while balancing the buckets gingerly, Katie returned to the house in time to see Mrs. Jenkins regain consciousness.

"Oh, my dear girl, I am so sorry for the trouble I've caused you. Look at your face, all red from fetching the water. You should have let the doctor do it, dear."

Katie laughed. "I am so glad to see you awake, Mrs. Jenkins. I'm sorry to admit to you that I had no wish to remain with you by myself in this house for another minute. When Dr. Jeffries gave me the choice of fetching the water or staying with you, I chose the lesser of two evils. I was terrified when you fainted on me earlier."

The older woman chuckled and then winced when the doctor prodded her wound. "You are a good girl, Katie. I am grateful you were here."

Katie grinned back at her client. "Despite the fright you gave me, I'm glad I was here, too. But I'm even more glad that the doctor finally arrived." Katie set the buckets down carefully in the kitchen before ladling some of the water into a large kettle to boil. Once she was satisfied that it would soon be ready, she hurried to the closet where she had seen Mrs. Jenkins stored her towels. With an armful of towels, she turned back toward the other occupants of the room and almost dropped them all when she realized they were both watching her like a curious specimen.

"What is it? Do I have smut on my face?" She was embarrassed and didn't pause to wait for a reply. "You know, I'm not very used to using a well like that. It was more work than I expected because I didn't really know what I was doing. But I managed to get quite a bit of water, which should be almost boiled by now."

She could feel the heat as it climbed high onto her cheekbones, but she tried to ignore her embarrassment as the other two exchanged amused glances. Katie didn't want to be rude to her customer, but a part of her desperately wanted to stick her tongue out at the two of them. Ignoring them, she turned away to check on the water after carefully placing the bundle of towels near the doctor's left hand.

"She's such a good girl, wouldn't you agree, doctor?"

"I would, Mrs. Jenkins. You would be in a bad way if she hadn't been with you when you started to bleed."

Katie's embarrassment mounted as she listened to them discuss her.

"And she's such a pretty little thing, too," Mrs. Jenkins continued. Katie could just imagine the devilish twinkle in her eye as she said that, but she kept her hot face turned away and tried to focus on her task of getting the water to boil. She doubted if watching the pot would make it boil faster but maybe the heat from her face would help, she thought with a wry twist of her lips. Involuntarily, her ears strained to hear the doctor's response.

"She's so little, I would think that a good stiff breeze might blow her away, but she did manage to bring in two heavy buckets of water for us, so there's a fair bit of might packed into the little package." The doctor had kept his voice low, but Katie still heard him and was touched by his words. She prided herself on her independence. It had been such a fight for her to regain confidence in herself after the treatment she had endured under her husband's hands. She was a little disgusted with herself for the fact that hearing a man voice a positive comment about her felt so good to her heart.

Despite her watching it, the kettle finally began to boil, and she couldn't dither any longer. She poured some of the boiling water into a pot half full of the cooler water from outside and carried it back toward the patient.

"I think this is a good temperature. If you'll check it, I can add more boiled water or more cool, if you think it needs adjusting." She was trying not to babble, but it was a challenge with the handsome doctor's gaze on her.

He reached out and touched the pot. "It is perfect. Thank you, Mrs. Carter."

Katie kept her head down in an effort to hide her heightened color and to avoid Mrs. Jenkins' knowing gaze. But she couldn't get away from the older lady's delighted chuckle.

The next few minutes passed in near silence as she worked in remarkable harmony with the doctor. Despite her antipathy toward him, they were able to cooperate quite well, as though they had experience working together. No doubt her experience nursing her family as they were sick and dying gave her a skilled perspective to the task at hand.

They soon had Mrs. Jenkins patched up and settled onto a comfortable chair with her feet propped up and a cup of tea within reach.

"I'm sorry, Katie dear, that you had to take so much time with me today, and we still didn't get our business concluded. At this point, I'm just not up to it now."

"Of course not, Mrs. Jenkins, please don't trouble yourself over it at all. I am glad that I was here when you needed someone, and I'll be happy to come back in a few days to check on you. If you're up for it then we can proceed, otherwise, I will return again another time."

"You are a dear, thank you."

Katie grinned. Even though the older woman was a bit crotchety at times, Katie was becoming quite fond of her. And she was amused and delighted to find that the cranky woman had decided to approve of her. She was a firm believer in a woman's need for friends, and she would be proud to count Mrs. Jenkins among her own small circle.

The doctor was quickly packing up his things as Katie was taking her leave. "If you'll wait a moment, I'll walk you out," he said to her. Katie wanted to refuse but didn't want to do so in front of Mrs. Jenkins. She offered him a tight smile but didn't say anything. With her own small bag of supplies looped over her arm, she waited by the door with something slightly less than patience as he said his goodbyes.

"I will stop in on you tomorrow, Mrs. Jenkins. See that you move as little as possible so you don't reopen your wound. You should have one of your daughters-in-law or granddaughters come in to help you for a few days. You do too much. You really need to get these all healed properly, and it seems to me that only bed rest will do the trick."

Mrs. Jenkins grumbled a bit about this but finally agreed to ask for help. Katie couldn't help but smile about her cantankerous attitude, and so she wasn't frowning when the doctor finally joined her.

They walked out of the house and toward the doctor's horse in silence. She didn't have anything to say to him. She didn't appreciate his vacillating attitude toward her and her need to support herself and her daughter. But she didn't want to antagonize him any more than she already had. And she hadn't hated working with him this afternoon, either. She sighed.

"I must thank you again for your assistance today, Mrs. Carter." The doctor's voice sounded stiff, as though he were reluctant to utter the words.

Katie laughed. "You don't have to do that, doctor. It seems to be a chore for you. And I didn't mind at all. Mrs. Jenkins is a dear, and I was glad to help her."

"Well, I would have been hard pressed to look after her so well if I had been there on my own," Doctor Jeffries insisted.

Katie laughed again. "That is true, doctor. I cannot even tell you how terrified I was when I was there on my own. I doubt you would have been scared, as you have the knowledge and experience that I lack, but there is only so much that can be done with two hands."

She didn't know how to interpret the expression on his face. It was as though he didn't know what to do with her. She could relate. Her feelings toward him were such a jumble. She didn't want to be near him but tended to enjoy herself when she was with him, so long as he wasn't commenting on her need for employment. She felt like laughing again but didn't want him to think she was a lunatic.

"I ought to be going. Melanie will be worrying about me."

"And well she should. You really shouldn't be roaming around on your own like you do."

Katie laughed, with a little less amusement this time. "And there we go, back to where we started, despite how well we were doing this afternoon." Her tone was dry. He looked as though he was going to interject, but she didn't allow him to. "I'm glad I was there to help. Thank you for rescuing me and poor Mrs. Jenkins this afternoon. I will wish you a good day."

Without waiting for him to respond she hurried away.

Wyatt watched her go. He just stood there and watched her brisk strides as she got on with her own affairs. He didn't say anything to stop her. He didn't grab her arm. He did none of the things that were rushing through his mind to keep her by his side. A part of him was disappointed to see her go. The other part was wondering where he had left his mind because it seemed to be lost.

You want a mild-mannered, lady-like woman to stay at home, look after your babies, and have your house smelling like freshly baked cookies when you come home, he reminded himself. *Yes, Mrs. Carter is a pleasure to look at and was amazingly helpful today, but she is not the one for you, so keep your eyes to yourself.* Despite his lecture to himself, he remained standing there watching her retreating form until she disappeared into the copse of trees that separated the Jenkins' property from its neighbors.

When he could no longer see her, he glanced around sheepishly, hoping Mrs. Jenkins hadn't seen him mooning around like a love-struck teenager. She would be sure to let him know what she thought of him on the morrow. He felt his lips twist into a wry smile. He surely was losing his mind.

His wife had been a sweet, gentle soul when he had met her when they were children. Her illness had confined her to the house, and she had kept herself occupied with books. The more she learned, the more opinionated she had become. While Mrs. Carter's healthy vitality was beyond attractive, her fierce independence and strong opinions had a tendency to irritate him beyond reason.

ꕥ

"Why are you still single, Doctor Jeffries? Did you never want a wife? I saw you watching Mrs. Carter yesterday. You cannot tell me you are indifferent to her."

He tried not to flinch over the questions as he examined Mrs. Jenkins' wound.

"I was married. I am a widower."

His bald words won him a moment of silence, but she soon rallied. "Really, doctor?" the fascination in her tone informed him he wouldn't be getting away without telling her at least some of his story. "What happened to the poor dear soul? She must've been awfully young to die. Was it childbirth?"

Wyatt stifled his exasperated sigh. Her questions were rude, but her curiosity was probably justifiable. The poor old woman was bored and hating her confinement.

"No, it wasn't childbirth. My wife had a wasting disease. We never could get a final, proper diagnosis. It is why I became a doctor, actually."

"Has she been gone long, dear?"

The sympathy he could hear in her voice brought a lump to his throat that he had to clear before he could answer her. "It was before I moved to Bucklin, of course. She has been gone three and a half years."

"You must have loved her very much if you have remained single this long."

Wyatt forced a grin. "I came out here not long after we buried her. And if you haven't noticed, eligible young woman are rather rare in these parts."

"Not so much anymore," Mrs. Jenkins argued, her tone sly. "The train with all them orphans brought some women with it, from what I've heard. Isn't Mrs. Carter one of those ladies?"

Wyatt hoped his face didn't betray his embarrassment. "I do believe you're right, Mrs. Jenkins. Perhaps I will get a chance to meet some of them."

"Well, you've more than met one of them. You can't tell me you didn't enjoy Mrs. Carter's company yesterday. I saw you watching her walk away. You certainly didn't look indifferent to me."

Wyatt sighed. "It's complicated, Mrs. Jenkins."

She snorted. "What is that supposed to mean?"

He couldn't help laughing over her question. His examination was finished. He wanted to run away, but looking after the old lady's mental health was part of his care for her. Appeasing her curiosity would probably help her stay off her feet.

Pulling a chair closer to the older woman, Wyatt made himself comfortable. He had a feeling he would be here for a while. Before the silence could stretch into discomfort, he finally started to explain himself.

"Mrs. Carter seems to be a pleasant young woman, but I think I would prefer a wife with a little less fire in her."

Mrs. Jenkins raised her eyebrows at him. "Seems to me, her fire is half her appeal."

Wyatt chuckled. He couldn't really argue with her observation.

"And if you have a mind to remain in Bucklin, a mousey woman might not make it," she pointed out.

"I didn't say I want a mousey woman," he protested.

"You can't have it both ways, doctor." She eyed him speculatively. "What was your dearly departed like?"

"We grew up together. She was my best friend. When we were children, she could climb a tree almost as fast as me. And then she got sick. We got married before we realized quite how ill she really was. I did everything I could think of to get her well. But nothing worked."

"Did her sickness affect her personality?" Her shrewd question made him wish he had never allowed this conversation to continue. He couldn't answer her question. She took his silence as affirmation. "Don't judge a strong woman by the same standard as a cantankerous sick lady. They are not one and the same — I'm sure you realize that."

Wyatt could feel himself sputtering. "Well, of course I know that."

When she just gazed at him, he felt his face growing warm and he sighed. "My head knows that, Mrs. Jenkins. But my heart would never wish to take the chance on living like that ever again. My wife had been my best friend. But I lost her quite a while before her death. It was a painful time."

"I am sure it was, and I should not be pestering you about it. But I think Mrs. Carter is lovely, and I would hate for you to dismiss her out of an unfounded misunderstanding of her disposition."

Now Wyatt smiled. He knew the older woman was trying to be kind in a backward kind of way. The fact that it made him exceedingly uncomfortable was due to his own issues, and he ought not to take it out on her.

"I will think about what you've said, Mrs. Jenkins. I appreciate your kindness in wishing me well. But now I must be on my way, and you must continue on bed rest for at least one more day. I am happy with how the wound looks, but it has not healed sufficiently for you to be up and about."

Mrs. Jenkins made a face at him. "Maybe I don't wish you as much happiness as I said earlier."

The doctor laughed. "I understand. You take good care of yourself, Mrs. Jenkins, and I will see you tomorrow."

He gathered up his bag of supplies and made his way outside, preoccupied by his conversation with Mrs. Jenkins. It was extremely rare that he discussed his wife. No one here in Bucklin had known her, so it never came up in conversation. Most assumed he had never married, he was sure. And even back home, out East, no one who DID know would make conversation about her, thinking they were respecting his loss.

"But they don't even comprehend my loss, Boss." He knew it didn't speak well of his mindset for him to be talking to his horse, but the beast was an excellent listener, and Wyatt found himself in need of expressing his thoughts.

"The guilt I feel about her death is what's hard to manage. I should have been able to help her. I'm a doctor for goodness' sake. But not only could I not find her a cure, I couldn't even help her be happy. She was my best friend, and I failed her. Is it any wonder I don't think remarrying is the best idea?" The only response Boss provided was the rapid twitching of his ears, as though he really was listening.

"And I know you and Mrs. Jenkins think I'm attracted to Mrs. Carter, but I'm not." The horse's ears flicked back causing Wyatt to chuckle. "Alright, maybe I am, but it's just a normal physical reaction to how beautiful and healthy she is. I'm sure every man in town has noticed her. It doesn't change the fact that she's far too independent for my tastes." There was another flick of the horse's ears. Wyatt grinned. "I don't care how helpful she was yesterday with Mrs. Jenkins. The woman is trouble, and that's all I'm going to say on the subject." He laughed and shook his head at himself. Surely he was losing his mind.

Chapter Ten

How are you feeling today, Mrs. Jenkins? I'm glad you have someone here to help you. Your granddaughter seems lovely."

"Good morning, Mrs. Carter. I'm right glad to lay eyes on you — let me tell you. Yes, Grace is a dear, but she doesn't have very much to say for herself. Thank you for stopping by."

"Are you up for company? Has the doctor given you the all clear to be moving about?"

"Bah, the doctor acts like I'm on death's door. He says I'm to stay in bed until he gives me leave to move about."

"Well, then shouldn't you be in bed?" Katie was startled by the older woman's seeming energy. She couldn't bear to have a repeat of the other day's experience.

"Don't look so worried, dear. I'm not overdoing it — I promise you. I just cannot see or hear much of anything up in my bed. Doctor Jeffries said it would be all right for me to be down here as long as I sit still."

"It doesn't look to me that you're sitting still."

Mrs. Jeffries let out a bark of laughter. "I promise not to faint on you. And I will keep myself in this chair. I probably won't be much use if you're wanting to do any measuring of me, but if you have some material samples, I would be giddy with delight."

Katie giggled at the older woman's words. "I did bring some swatches with me, as a matter of fact. Should I get you a cup of tea while we look at them?"

"Mrs. Carter, you are an angel."

Katie trilled with laughter again. "Surely by now you ought to be calling me Katie. I am certain we are to be good friends."

Mrs. Jenkins flushed with delight over Katie's words. "It would be an honor. And you must call me Althea. Or Thea, as my dearly departed used to say."

"Very well, Thea, I'm pleased to make your acquaintance." Katie shook her hand solemnly before grinning like a simpleton and then hurrying from the room. It was hard to believe that the crusty old lady was quickly becoming her closest friend.

With steaming cups of tea settled before them, the two women began sorting through the fabric samples Katie had brought with her.

"You have quite the selection, Katie, dear. I'm impressed."

"We have been fortunate thus far. The few women of Bucklin have been generous in the use of our services. So we have many scraps to make the swatches from. And the mercantile has a remarkably good stock for the size of this town. The shopkeeper has promised me that he'll be getting even more in, to keep us supplied. And if we don't yet have exactly what you want, we could probably get it ordered in, as well."

"Oh no, my dear girl, it looks to me like I'll be able to find exactly what I want from these materials. I have been more than happy with the first dress you made for me. But my daughter has been after me for so long about my need for new clothes. Now she says one new dress isn't enough." Mrs. Jenkins shook her head over the folly of the younger generation. "It's not as though I go around very much. No one is going to be looking at me."

"But you want to look good for your own enjoyment, don't you? I can assure you, while I wouldn't want to affront anyone's eyes with a decrepit appearance, I dress well for myself. I don't really care what anyone else thinks. I like looking good for me."

"And it doesn't hurt if it catches the eyes of a few gentlemen, does it?" Mrs. Jenkins teased her.

Katie blushed. "To be honest, I would rather gentlemen didn't look at me."

"Why ever not? You are young and beautiful. You should be trying to snag a good man."

"No, I shouldn't. If I thought it would keep them away, I would dress in a sack," Katie insisted.

"That hardly seems reasonable, Katie."

Katie shrugged. "You do know I've already been married, right?"

Mrs. Jenkins blinked at the question. "Well, we do call you Mrs. Carter on occasion, so I guess I must have known. Are you a runaway?"

Katie laughed, but it was a little hollow. "Not at all. I am a widow. My husband caught the flu and brought it home with him. He and our baby died within a couple days of each other."

"Oh, my dear, that is tragic. I am so sorry for your loss." There was a quiet moment while they both brushed a tear away. Mrs. Jenkins cleared her throat before asking, "How long has it been, my dear?"

"Two years, four months, and sixteen days since my sweet baby was taken from me. He was only nine months old, but he was such a charming little boy."

"I can only imagine how lovely a son of yours would be. He would have grown up to be a fine man, I'm sure."

Katie's smile was wan. "I struggled with wondering if he would, to be perfectly honest with you, Thea. While he was a sweet and happy baby, his father was less than kind, and it had troubled me terribly to wonder what he would grow up to be. Now I'll never know. I almost died from my grief. It's how I ended up with the orphans. I thought it would fill the hole in my heart where my baby used to be."

"Did it work?"

With another empty laugh, Katie shook her head. "Not really. But it filled my life with purpose, which was at least something. It saved my life. But it also broke a bit of what little heart I had left, which is part of why I needed the fresh start here in Bucklin. I couldn't take it anymore, seeing all the tragedy that the poor children faced, so I jumped at the chance to come out with the train of orphans and try a new life away from New York."

"But what about the hole in your heart? Surely finding a new love and having more babies is just what you need."

Shaking her head vigorously, Katie denied her friend's words. "Not at all. While no one could ever replace my sweet baby, now that I have my dear daughter, Annie, I am at peace. I have no need for a husband. In fact, I am far better off without one."

"I would beg to differ with you," Althea argued.

Grinning, Katie asked, "Why?"

"While men can be messy and stinky and annoying at times, there's nothing like having a partner as you walk through whatever life throws at you. Mr. Jenkins was an excellent father to my children and a steady companion for me. He worked hard to provide food and shelter for me and the children, but he always took the time to attend to any one of us. I think it's a good part of why our children grew up to be such wonderful adults. A good man is worth picking up after," she concluded with a girlish giggle.

Katie's smile was a little sad as she said, "Maybe so, but he's mighty hard to find."

The shrewd look Althea cast at her brought a lump to her throat. "Not so terribly hard, I'd say. I don't know many who aren't."

"Well then you've been far luckier in life than I have, Althea. I don't know very many men who are."

"I take it your marriage wasn't a happy one, then," Thea commented, her usually strident tones softened. "What about your parents'?"

Katie shrugged again. "While not as bad as my husband, my father was cold and distant. He wasn't very pleased about having daughters, I think. There were four of us girls before my mother finally had two sons. From what I can tell, he had gotten pretty bitter by then, and my brothers didn't turn it around very much. They weren't very healthy. My father blamed my mother for that instead of the poor circumstances we were living in. Both of my brothers, my parents, and one of my sisters died in the past ten years. I'm glad I'm not living in the stews of the city anymore."

"You sure have faced more than your share of tragedy in your short life, Katie dear. But going it alone isn't the solution."

"There isn't a problem that needs a solution, here, though, Thea. I'm more than satisfied with the life I'm building here in Bucklin with Melanie and Annie."

"But what if Melanie finds a husband?"

"Well, then there will be more room in the house for me and Annie," she laughed.

"But what about when Annie grows up? Surely you don't want to grow old alone."

"Like you're doing?" Katie asked gently.

"I'm not alone," Althea declared with a chuckle. "I have a big, beautiful family. And while my poor Mr. Jenkins is no longer with me, I have so many wonderful memories to keep me company."

Katie knew her smile was wistful but couldn't help it. "That's lovely, Thea, but I think it's very rare."

"I don't," the older woman insisted again. "And I don't think you should be so cynical at your young age, despite the tragedy you've faced. You really ought to give love a chance. It's worth everything once you've found it."

Katie gazed out the window, debating whether or not to open herself up to her new friend. She never spoke of her past to anyone. Not even Melanie knew the extent of what she had suffered. She didn't have to tell Thea everything, but maybe if she told her some of her experiences it would get her to forget about trying to find a husband for her.

She took a deep breath and proceeded. "I had just turned seventeen the week before I got married. My husband was so very handsome. That's all I had the sense to think of when I was so young. And he was so attentive. Coming around to visit me every day, wanting to know who I had been with that day, who I had spoken with. He hated to hear if I had spoken with any other man. Even my brothers. I thought his jealousy meant he truly loved me. I found out later it just meant he was a jealous person."

Her next deep breath was a little shuddery, but Althea hadn't said anything, so she continued. "He was a few years older than me. I thought he was wonderful. So handsome and experienced. And I was so happy to get away from my dull existence at home. But he used all that supposed experience to squash my youthful exuberance. After the first couple of weeks, he began to tell me how stupid I was. That I wasn't doing anything right. The apartment wasn't how he wanted it kept. The meals weren't cooked to his preference. And when I didn't get pregnant immediately, well that had to be because something was wrong with me, too."

Katie again paused, staring out the window at the swaying trees. She absently thought about Annie, hoping she had on a warm enough sweater. Althea still hadn't commented on Katie's story, and Katie didn't look at her. Her voice was strong despite her desire to crawl into a hole and not come out for at least a week after reliving these memories. Now that she had started, it seemed she couldn't stem the flow of words.

"He didn't hit me right at first. He stole all my joy and enthusiasm first. I almost never saw anyone in my family after the first few months. I *never* saw any of my old friends after the first couple of weeks. It wasn't worth the fighting. But just when I thought things had settled down and I was keeping him satisfied, he started drinking. And that's when he started hitting me. It was always my fault, of course. Or so he told me. I believed him at the time. I thought I was going to die several times. I wished I would die many times.

"When we realized that I was pregnant, he didn't hit me as often, nor as severely, for which I was grateful. Until right near the end of my pregnancy. Because I was so ungainly, I was clumsy and awkward. He didn't like that at all. Then he didn't want me to see a doctor because he didn't want anyone to see me like that. But I convinced him we could say I fell down the stairs and that we had to get help because the baby was coming. When my water broke, he finally believed me and went for help. I was profoundly relieved when the baby was born quickly and perfect. He gave me a reason to live. Until my husband brought the flu home and took the baby from me. I wasn't in the least sorry when he died."

Her eyes flew up. "My husband, I mean. I wanted to die myself when the baby died. I can still hear the rattle of his breaths as he gasped for air. There was nothing I could do. The doctor wouldn't even come into our neighborhood since the sickness was such a pandemic. No one could help me because anyone who was still standing had too many patients of their own to care for. I don't know which cruel providence spared me from death, but I didn't even get a sniffle. I was weak as a kitten by the time it was all over, but that was from crying myself dry over the baby and not sleeping at all from caring for my husband and child, as well as my sister. My sister made it. The others didn't. She was left a little damaged after the illness, but she's still alive to this day."

Katie finally looked up to meet Althea's gaze. Her own eyes were dry, but Thea's were streaming with tears. "I didn't have any tears left after my baby died. Not even when my mother passed. Once it became obvious that I wasn't going to be getting sick, and after most of my family had been buried, I started volunteering at the orphanage. I thought being with the children would help me feel close to my own sweet Henry. It sort of did. It helped me heal. Children are a gift to the world, even when their circumstances are tragic, like the orphans. But as I regained my sense of self, my tolerance for the suffering I was witnessing all around me began to decrease. By the time I had lost most of my numbness, I could no longer remain in New York. When I was asked to accompany the children to Missouri, I jumped at the chance to start fresh."

Katie took another deep breath, this time feeling restored, as though telling her story had lanced the wound. "And now that I have been blessed with another child, I feel whole again. I would never want to take the risk of marriage again. Too much is at stake."

Wyatt felt his jaw clench over what he had heard. He knew he shouldn't be eavesdropping. He hadn't even meant to. But when he had been about to knock, he had heard Katie's clear voice coming through the open window. And he had hesitated. Just long enough to hear what they were talking about. And when he realized what it was, he couldn't interrupt. There's no way Katie would talk about any of this in front of him. From what he knew of her, he was amazed she was talking about it with Mrs. Jenkins. But hearing what she had been through made everything in him clench, not just his jaw. His stomach burned. His hands were inadvertently forming into fists. A part of him wanted to give her husband a taste of what he had been doling out. Not that Katie would welcome more violence. She probably wouldn't welcome him having this knowledge either. He really ought to alert the women to his presence. But he just wanted to hear a little bit more. It explained so much about the woman's prickly response to him. Why would she welcome any contact with a man after what she'd experienced?

"But don't you think Annie would benefit from having a man helping to raise her? Don't shake your head at me, young lady." Wyatt almost gave away his presence with a snort of laughter over Mrs. Jenkins' tone. "You might not think she needs a father, after the rough ride you've had, but surely you could use help. I've always thought God knew what he was doing when he arranged for a father and mother. No matter how capable you are, you are only one person. Raising a family is hard work."

"I'm sure it would be ideal for her to have a father, but I will do everything in my power to be enough for her. At least there's only one child, so I won't be outnumbered. And her teacher is a man, so she won't lack for a different perspective."

Katie paused, and Wyatt wished he could see her face to try to figure out what she was really thinking.

"I understand what you're trying to say, Thea, and I appreciate you sharing your thoughts with me, but I think we might just have to agree to disagree on this one. I cannot take the chance now, even more so than before. I would never forgive myself if I brought someone into Annie's life only to have him hurt her."

Mrs. Jenkins made a sound of protest, and Wyatt realized he had learned enough from the conversation he had overheard. He really needed to make his presence known before they caught him spying. With some exaggerated clomping of his feet, he made his way to the door and knocked.

When Mrs. Jenkins' granddaughter opened the door, he wasn't even surprised to see Katie hastily grabbing her bag and kissing Mrs. Jenkins' cheek goodbye.

"I'll stop in again in a couple days. Hopefully by then your tyrant of a doctor will have given you the all clear for moving around." Katie tried to make a light joke, but Wyatt could see that her smile didn't quite reach her eyes. His heart ached for the pain he could see reflected in their depths.

"Good day, Mrs. Carter." He greeted her with a slight bow, chuckling when pink stained her cheeks.

"Doctor Jeffries." She nodded at him before scurrying away.

He stood, staring at the door after it closed behind her retreating form. He turned back to face Mrs. Jenkins.

"Was it something I said?"

She grinned at him. "You know perfectly well that it's something she said."

Wyatt felt all the blood drain from his face before it quickly returned with full heat. "You knew I was there?" he demanded.

"Of course," she retorted. "I might be getting old, but nothing gets past me."

"Did she know?"

If he hadn't been so embarrassed, he would have laughed over the withering look she cast him. "Do you really think she would have said any of that if she knew?"

The answer was so obvious that Wyatt didn't even reply.

Mrs. Jenkins continued studying him like a specimen in a science lab. "Does it make you like her any more now that you know why she's so independent?"

Wyatt smiled. "It's not a matter of not liking her, Mrs. Jenkins. I think Mrs. Carter is a lovely woman, despite her modern ideals. I understand her a little better now that I know about her past. But that doesn't mean I could live with those ideals. Yes, the strength of character she has displayed in order to survive and even thrive after what she has been through might be attractive. But a man wants to feel needed by a woman he's going to take for his wife. And he doesn't want to have to fear having his ears blistered whenever he does something not quite to her liking."

"Has Katie ever blistered your ears?"

Wyatt gave a half shrug.

"You're thinking about your wife again and putting that on her, aren't you?" Mrs. Jenkins asked shrewdly.

Wyatt sidestepped the question with one of his own. "Have you met the woman Mrs. Carter is living with? I believe she arrived on the same train."

"Now don't be getting any ideas about her, Doctor Jeffries. I know you think you want a meek and mild wife sitting home keeping your supper warm for you, but you need a woman who isn't afraid to speak her mind or leave the house once in a while. No, I haven't met Miss Melanie yet. While she has a way with her needle, I don't think it's normal that she has barely set foot outside their door." Mrs. Jenkins shook her head and interrupted whatever Wyatt was about to say. "No, you might not agree with how Katie has dealt with her past experiences, but at least she's dealing with them. And as sociable as you are, you need someone who can accompany you, not someone who is going to shrink into your shadow."

Wyatt frowned over Mrs. Jenkins' words, wondering if there was wisdom in them. She surely had seen more of life than he had, despite living in this small town. He hesitated to accept them, though. He couldn't picture a peaceful future with the small but mighty Mrs. Carter.

"Well, never mind about my quest for a wife, Mrs. Jenkins, tell me how you're feeling today."

"I am feeling like a new woman with the entertainment I've been provided between you and the dear, sweet Mrs. Carter." She cackled over her words before growing serious. "But I'm pretty sure my nasty boils are healing up now. Surely you'll let me get up soon."

"Well, let me take a look, and I'll let you know."

Chapter Eleven

Hello? Mrs. Mitchell?" Katie called out from the doorway. She checked her watch. Eleven o'clock. She was right on time. "It's Katie, Mrs. Mitchell. We had an appointment for me to take your measurements?"

"Help me! Please!" Katie heard a young voice coming from the back of the house. She dropped her bag of supplies and ran in that direction, skidding to a stop when she came across the boy standing over Mr. and Mrs. Mitchell's prone bodies. He looked terrified. "It's the flu, isn't it?" he demanded.

Katie's stomach turned over, and she wanted to run back in the direction she had come from. If she never heard those words again for the rest of her life, it would be too soon. She took a deep breath and did what needed to be done.

"Hello. My name's Mrs. Carter, what's yours?"

"I'm Matt. Can you help them? Please don't let them die."

"I'll do my best, Matt. How old are you?"

"I'm ten."

"That's great. That means you're a big boy, right?"

He finally tore his eyes away from staring at Mr. and Mrs. Mitchell and looked at Katie. He stood a little straighter as he nodded agreement.

"Excellent. Now, I need you to go find the doctor. Don't get too close to anyone while you're going through town, just in case it *is* the flu. You're one of the boys we brought on the train, aren't you?"

Matt nodded before his eyes skittered back to looking at Mr. and Mrs. Mitchell. "I don't want to lose them. I just got here."

Katie's heart squeezed with the thought of what this boy had already endured in his young life. She needed him to be brave just a little bit more. She offered him an encouraging smile.

"I know, Matt, we're going to do our very best. Somehow, you and I got lucky and we don't get this particular sickness. So we'll be able to help them if that is what they have. Now, go find the doctor so he can help us."

She couldn't believe she was voluntarily sending for the doctor, but she knew she couldn't face this on her own. And Katie was fairly certain the doctor would want to be involved in preventing the spread of the dreadful disease in this town. Her stomach turned over as she wondered if the train passengers had brought this terrible thing with them. She shook herself out of her momentary inertia. While she wanted to run away, she had a neighborly obligation to do the best she could for the Mitchells. She didn't know if she would be able to deal with any more death from this dreadful disease on an emotional level, but there wasn't much she could do about that now. She was involved. It just had to be dealt with. At least she didn't have to fear that she would bring it home to Annie. It would seem the child was also immune, since she had survived what had wiped out her family.

Katie set herself in motion, hoping Matt was able to return quickly with the doctor or some other responsible adult in tow. Her fears were besetting her. She had to shake it off and do what she could for the Mitchells.

She was in the midst of spooning lukewarm broth into Mrs. Mitchell's mouth when she finally heard the arrival of Doctor Jeffries and Matt. Katie felt a sigh of relief leave her before her anxieties returned once more. On top of her concerns for the Mitchells, she now had to cope with the uncomfortable presence of the doctor. Even though she had requested his help, she dreaded being around him.

"Katie?" the doctor questioned informally before quickly asking, "Are you all right, Mrs. Carter?"

With a tight smile, she nodded at him. There was a beat of silence before she responded. "Thanks for coming. I'm sorry for needing to involve you in this, but I can't face it completely on my own. I would actually rather not deal with this at all, but I could not walk away when I realized Matt was here on his own. I'm afraid it is as he suspected, the flu. They both have the rash, and they're burning up with fever."

While the doctor absorbed this information, Katie turned to the boy, who had followed the doctor into the room. "Were you able to get the doctor without getting too close to anyone else?"

The boy nodded vigorously. "Very good, Matt. Thank you. If you would, I have another task for you to perform. Could you take a note for me to my house?"

Poor Matt looked thrilled at the thought of not needing to stay in the room with his ill adoptive parents. He quickly ran to find a piece of paper and a pencil for Katie to write her note.

"Tell me what you have done so far," the doctor demanded, getting down to business.

"I set a pot on the stove. While that was heating up I bathed their faces and chests and then changed their bedding." Katie forced herself to be as stoic as possible, but she could still feel heat climbing in her cheeks with embarrassment over performing the very personal task for two people she barely knew. "I have since been trying to get as much of the broth into them as I could. From my experience, that's all that can be done for the fever. I really hope you have some other ideas."

"You have done well. Unfortunately, if this is the flu, there isn't much else that can be done. We can just keep doing what you've started. Keeping fluids in them will be the most gruelling task," he pointed out as Mrs. Mitchell threw up all that Katie had managed to get into her so far. It hadn't been much, and Katie had had the foresight to put a towel around the woman's neck, so all her efforts of cleaning the woman hadn't come undone.

Mrs. Mitchell moaned softly, but Katie just murmured gently to her. The older woman quieted and drifted deeper into sleep.

"Sleep and fluids will be what will save them."

Katie quickly wrote a note to Melanie, letting her know where she was and asking that she look after Annie for the foreseeable future. *I have no idea how long I will have to remain here,* she wrote. *I would rather not be here, but someone has to do it. Don't come by, and don't let Annie visit. She survived it once — I don't want to take any chances, nor do I want her to be frightened. Try to satisfy her by telling her I'm helping out some friends. I dearly hope I won't be too long.*

"How well do you know the Mitchells, doctor?" Katie asked after she had sent Matt off with her note.

"Fairly well," he answered. "It's a small town. Most everyone knows everything about everyone. Why do you ask?"

"Do they have any family we should send for to care for them?"

"Would you want to risk others?" He was incredulous.

"No, of course not, but I cannot remain here for too long."

"Why not?"

Katie started to feel frustrated with him. "For one thing, I don't think being in your company is going to be pure pleasure, and for another, I have a child to take care of. A fact that you have been repeatedly reminding me of, if you'll recall. And I did my duty with my own family with this dreadful disease. I'm not sure if my mind and heart can bear up under doing it again."

The doctor was grinning over her words when she first started talking, as though her show of spirit amused him, but he sobered at her reminder of what she had lost to the dreadful disease.

"Of course, I understand. We'll have a good idea in the next few hours what the future will hold for these two, so we'll have more answers as to whether or not we'll need help. As it stands, I would rather not involve anyone else. I will be able to remain even if you cannot do so."

Katie didn't appreciate his condescending tone even as he professed to understand her reasons for not wanting to be there. But there was little she could do. Even though she wanted to be anywhere but there, she knew in her heart, she could never abandon the Mitchells. She would much rather pass their care off to a family member, but she understood the doctor not wanting to risk anyone else's health. She just hoped her surprising immunity to the dreadful disease held. Katie offered him a tight smile and without a word left the room to go boil more water.

ꟷ

Wyatt watched through the window as Katie struggled to get the heavy bedding over the line to dry. He shouldn't be referring to her so familiarly, even in his head, since she had not given him leave to do so, but he couldn't help himself. It had now been twenty-four hours that they had been here together, watching over poor Mr. and Mrs. Mitchell. And poor Matt. The boy was trying to hide his fears, but it was obvious that he was terrified. Wyatt couldn't blame him. He now realized that Matt's entire family had been wiped out as the plague of influenza had swept through New York. That was how he wound up an orphan on the train out to Missouri. The same was true of Mrs. Carter. It was interesting to watch the two bond over their shared losses.

His attention had been wandering, but his focus was brought back to Katie as she snapped another sheet in the breeze before tossing it over the line. Wyatt wouldn't have thought it possible, but the small woman was even more beautiful today, with tendrils of hair flying wildly about her head after having escaped her tight hair style.

The doctor was amazed that she had remained. He knew she didn't want to be there. But she hadn't wavered in her care of the Mitchells. Wyatt knew it was his job, as the doctor, to care for people. Katie was only doing it out of neighborly duty. She barely even knew the Mitchells. He was deeply impressed with her diligence.

Despite his previous declaration that women should stay home and tend the family fires, there was no arguing with the fact that he would have been seriously challenged to handle this medical case on his own. Two seriously ill patients and a terrified boy would have been beyond his abilities, he was man enough to admit. But he suspected that even if he wasn't there, the brave little widow would have managed on her own. He didn't want to respect her, and he most certainly didn't want to have feelings for her, but he could feel his heart rate picking up as he stood there, watching her doing something so pragmatic as hanging the laundry out to dry. For the briefest moment, he allowed himself to picture her doing such a task at his own house. He quickly shut the idea down. He doubted she would consider it and, he reminded himself, he didn't want such an independent soul as his mate.

But he had a welcoming smile on his lips when she returned to the house. It turned to amusement as she cast him a suspicious glare.

"Why are you looking at me like that?" she demanded, keeping her voice low so as not to disturb the others in the house, but conveying her discomfort quite clearly as she set aside the basket she had been carrying. "I know I'm not the prettiest picture, but you are quite aware of what I have been experiencing in the last day besides not sleeping, so you needn't look at me so."

He protested. "I swear to you, I was not looking at you in judgement of any sort. Quite the contrary, in fact. I was just thinking that I would not have been able to handle this situation without you."

The look of surprise that swept across her features made him want to laugh out loud, but he managed to restrain the impulse, realizing that it would cause her to leave the house in anger.

"Well, thank you," she answered grudgingly. "I wouldn't have been able to do it alone, either," she admitted. There was a pause while she couldn't meet his gaze before she continued. "To be honest, I think if I had been left alone here, while I wouldn't want to abandon them to their fate, I'm not sure if I would have been able to handle it. My fears would have overwhelmed me. I think of how it was when I was on my own with Mrs. Jenkins after she fainted. And that was just a few days ago. I don't think I could have borne it again so soon. Even having Matt here wouldn't have been enough to keep me grounded, since the poor boy is struggling so hard to control his own fears. Having a real doctor present is keeping him comforted. If he had only me, I don't think the two of us would fare well."

Wyatt chuckled, which brought a glare from her, and hot color flooded her cheeks. It only subsided as he soothed, "I, on the other hand, think you would have fared as well as was needed. You seem to be one of those remarkable people who manage to do whatever needs to be done. You managed just fine with Mrs. Jenkins, and you're doing wonderfully here."

He admired her beauty as her cheeks remained a light pink but this time out of embarrassment as she turned bashful. "Thank you, Doctor Jeffries, that's kind of you to say. But while I have an aversion to doctors out of principle, I have to say I'm in the same camp as Matt. Having someone present who has actually been formally educated in the art of medicine is a comfort in this situation. In New York, when the plague was running rampant, there were far too many patients and not nearly enough doctors. And when your pockets were to let, there was no hope for you. You had to muddle through as best you could with only prayer and hot water on your side. And clean water was even hard to come by. That is one beautiful luxury out here in Missouri. It doesn't seem that anyone is concerned about water."

She stopped talking for a moment, but Wyatt didn't comment. Despite having worked side by side now on two occasions, this was the most the independent woman had shared in one sitting. He hoped she would continue. He was finding it singularly fascinating. And he was bored silly from watching their two patients sleep. His patience was rewarded when she offered him a small, sheepish smile.

"Do you know, I awaken each morning in such a thankful frame of mind as I drink a large cup of the sweet water that comes from the well behind our little house. Melanie does the same thing. Neither of us can quite believe how much water is around. And it's so clean. And sweet. Of course, I still love my tea, but it feels almost decadent to be able to drink fresh, cool water and not fear that it might make you sick if you don't boil it first. Thankfully, Annie is too young to have been filled with the fears we had. I think her parents must have done a wonderful job of keeping most things from her. The poor little dear has enough fears as it is."

"Don't I know it," Wyatt interjected with a wry grin.

The color rose in her cheeks once again making his heart feel like it was turning over within his chest. "I'm sorry she hasn't been very friendly toward you.

She sees doctors only as a source of bad news or who attend you when you're sick or injured."

"Most would be happy to have someone attend you when you've been injured," he pointed out.

"But the bad news overpowers any help you might have to offer, I'm afraid. I personally haven't had many dealings with doctors, previously. But my impression has been that doctors consider themselves to be gods sent to help those with the deepest pockets."

"That's terrible. And inaccurate of most doctors," Wyatt insisted, growing disappointed with the direction of the conversation.

She shrugged. "By saying it's inaccurate of most, you are admitting that it's not inaccurate of all doctors."

He grudgingly nodded. "Maybe not."

She smiled, apparently pleased with his honesty. "Perhaps, if we manage to help the Mitchells pull through, I'll invite you for dinner and you can tell Annie all about our success here. It might help her if she can see you as a bearer of glad tidings."

"Since I've had the pleasure of a sample of your good cooking here for the Mitchells, I will gladly accept," he replied with a chuckle.

He looked at her carefully and didn't much like what he saw at that moment. She was, of course, still beautiful, but he could see that the only color on her face was from her bashfulness over his compliment. Her eyes looked strained, and her mouth turned down at the edges when she wasn't smiling.

"Mrs. Carter, you really must take a break and get some sleep. I am feeling more confident that Mr. and Mrs. Mitchell are going to pull through this illness. It won't do for you to collapse as they are improving. You must take some rest."

For a brief moment, she looked as though she were going to be mulish and refuse, but then she offered him a sheepish smile. "Are you certain you'll be able to remain awake if I lie down for a bit?"

"I'll keep Matt with me, and we'll watch over them while you sleep. Then you can take a turn after you've rested a bit."

Her face filled with relief as she accepted his offer. "You're probably right. I won't be any good for Annie when this is over either, if I go and get sick myself. Thank you, doctor."

Wyatt watched as she slipped from the room. She was so slender she almost floated, he thought whimsically. He shook his head and derided himself. *You're a fool,* he thought, *you don't want her, but you can't stop thinking about her. Make up your mind, man.* Then he had to push all thoughts of her from his mind as he became fully occupied with keeping Matt reassured while the two of them cared for his adoptive parents.

A couple hours later, Katie slipped quietly into the room and startled them when she spoke up from the doorway.

"How are you two holding up? I never meant to sleep for so long. You must be nearly falling over with exhaustion."

"I'm not tired at all, Mrs. Carter. I slept all night, remember?"

The smile Katie offered to Matt nearly took Wyatt's breath away, but he managed to answer her calmly. "I haven't fallen over quite yet, but if my checker skills are anything to go by, my mind is not functioning at its best."

"Have you eaten? Would you like me to make you something before you go to sleep, or would you rather wait until you get back up?"

"Thank you for your kindness, Mrs. Carter. Matt and I have managed to look after ourselves fairly well. I think sleep is my priority at the moment."

She nodded her acceptance but had one more question. "Have you fed them?" she nodded quietly toward their patients.

"We gave them some tea about an hour ago. If you could get them to take some broth, that would be great." He was already leaving the room when he answered her. He was barely conscious as he climbed the stairs and collapsed on Matt's bed in the attic of the small house.

Chapter Twelve

After the doctor left, Katie struggled against feeling disappointed. She didn't want to enjoy his company and *definitely* didn't want to find him attractive. But she did have eyes in her head, she thought with a small smile. It couldn't be avoided that the man was good looking. And watching him care for his patients held a certain appeal. His patience with Matt had seemed endless. She admired his calm in the face of the various emergencies she had witnessed with him.

But the fact was that since she had met him, she had encountered three medical emergencies. Katie tried to be reasonable and pointed out to herself that with or without the doctor Mrs. Jenkins would have fainted, Annie would have knocked herself out, and the Mitchells would have gotten sick. Having the doctor there had helped, she had to admit. *Well, maybe not with Annie*, she protested silently. He did very little to help there. In fact, his lectures had only served to anger her and did nothing to aid the patient. But with Althea and here with the Mitchells he was invaluable.

While she didn't really want to be the one playing nurse, she was in agreement with the doctor that since she had already been exposed, it wouldn't serve to risk anyone else. She was just grateful that she was still feeling fit. Tired, yes, but still healthy. But she had been deeply relieved when Melanie had stopped at the gate that morning. Katie thought back to their brief conversation, smiling that it had been conducted with an entire yard between them.

"I've brought you a beef pie. You and the doctor need to keep your strength up. I'll just leave it here."

"Thank you, Melanie. How are you and Annie faring? Did she have many questions?"

"It's Annie, she had plenty of questions, but don't fret, she's untroubled so far. If you're gone too long, though, I'm not sure how long that will last."

Katie chewed her lip in thought. "If you must, you can bring her by like this so she can see that I'm fine."

"I've done one better than that," Melanie had declared with a conspiratorial grin. "I girded my courage and approached the father of one of her classmates to arrange a sleepover. Since there's no school tomorrow, she will be going home with Mary after classes. I won't have to face her questions until Sunday."

"Melanie, thank you so much. I know that must have been a challenge for you, but it was brilliantly done of you."

Melanie shrugged. "Apparently, they just had a litter of puppies, so I thought they'd be the best draw. But I cannot promise she won't be asking for a pet after this."

The two friends shared a giggle before Melanie sobered. "Are you doing all right? You look a little wrung out."

"I didn't sleep through the night. So I'm plenty tired, but I think I'm faring fine. I can't say that I'm loving the experience, but I think poor little Matt would be beside himself if not for my familiar face."

"You're an angel of mercy, Katie."

"Don't go getting carried away, my friend." Katie was embarrassed by her words and quickly waved them away, changing the subject. "I'll see you soon. Thank you so much for the food. We've been so occupied with the sick that I haven't been able to concentrate on keeping us fed. This will help so much."

Now it was Mel's turn to look uncomfortable. "It was the least I could do. You're the one doing all the hard work and taking the risk."

They shared a laugh over their mutual discomfort. Melanie, still grinning, waved and walked away.

The meat pie had been delicious. And Melanie's generous portions meant that there was plenty left over for another meal.

Katie was relieved that Melanie had thought to speak with Mary's father. She hadn't wanted to ask it of her, knowing how she was still struggling with speaking to people, especially men. But with the litter of puppies, Mary was the friend most likely to keep Annie sufficiently occupied that she wouldn't be overly worried about her new mother's absence.

Living in a small town was proving to be a blessing for them. Everyone was so kind and willing to help out. The voice calling from the gate was a testament to that.

"Hello there," Katie heard a questioning note from the feminine voice.

"Grace? What are you doing here?" Katie asked when she opened the screen door.

"Grandmother heard that you've been caring for the Mitchells and asked me to bring over some soup for you."

"That is mighty kind of the both of you. Thank you. And please tell your grandmother thank you from us, as well. Soup will come in handy as the Mitchells start to recover."

"So they're on the mend, then, are they? The townspeople are wondering," the girl added.

"We're fairly confident that the worst has passed," Katie assured her. "But it's best if everyone stays away for a while longer."

The girl nodded vigorously, relief clearly written across her face. Katie's heart went out to her. "It was brave of you to do your grandmother's bidding," she said, keeping her tone low enough not to carry far, but loud enough for the girl to hear. Grace nodded shyly before scurrying away.

The large pot of soup was going to be such an aid to them. They were nearly out of the broth she had made the day before. After the next meal they gave to the Mitchells, they would be out. She had been thinking of rationing it until she was able to make more, but now she wouldn't have to. And it would do them good to have a little bit more substance with soup instead of just broth.

Katie wondered if they would even be feeding the Mitchells anymore. They seemed to be regaining consciousness and were even moving a little bit. Surely they would be waking up soon. She certainly hoped the doctor was awake as well when they did.

Matt interrupted her musings.

"Can I do anything, Mrs. Carter?"

Katie gave him a warm smile. "What would you be doing if your parents hadn't fallen sick?"

He shrugged. "I've already done most of the chores. I guess I would normally have homework to do. Or I would go play with some of the boys from school."

"I'm sorry that you have to stay away from your friends. This must be a boring ordeal for you."

The boy shrugged again. "I'm worried more than I'm bored."

"I know, Matt," she answered softly. "But why don't you go outside and play? Even by yourself, you should be able to find something to do. The fresh air and sunshine will do you good. And it'll make it easier for you to sleep tonight if you've had a bit of activity through the day."

"I don't think I'll have any trouble sleeping tonight," he replied with a grin. "I'm not used to doing all the chores by myself."

Now Katie was chagrinned. "Was it too much for you? I'm so sorry, Matt! I have been so preoccupied with caring for your parents that I haven't thought that much about the chores outside of the house. Should we get someone to come in and do some of them for us?"

Matt was quick to protest. “No, no, not at all, Mrs. Carter. I don’t mind doing it one bit. It’s harder work than I ever did back in New York, but I actually find it quite fun. And since I can’t go to school, it gave me something to do.”

“Of course. I sure hope this passes soon. I’m not making any sense at all, am I?” Katie waved a hand in front of her face, trying to distract herself from the tears wanting to form in her eyes.

Matt grinned at her. “I think I will go out and see if I can find any frogs.”

Katie laughed. She was so glad she had adopted a girl, she thought with a slight shudder as the boy hurried to put his shoes on and ran from the room.

She was puttering around, tidying the house, when the doctor re-entered the room. She was preoccupied with scrubbing the stove and didn’t hear him until he spoke.

“How have—” he began before she whirled around and stifled her squeal of fright.

With a hand upon her chest she panted. “Doctor Jeffries! You nearly scared the wits out of me.”

He chuckled but quickly apologized. “I’m so sorry! I did not mean to startle you. I didn’t realize cleaning the stove required quite that much concentration.”

Katie had to laugh at his attempt at a joke. “It shouldn’t require that much thought, you’re right. But I’m exhausted, and everything is a challenge at this point.”

He smiled in agreement, and her breath caught once more. The man was remarkably handsome in a studious kind of way. Being as tired as she was, her resistance was weak, and she found her heart rate was picking up from his proximity. She tried to hide her discomfort with activity, setting back to work scrubbing the stove.

“You don’t really need to be doing so much work here, Mrs. Carter,” the doctor admonished. “You are going to wear yourself out even more than necessary.”

“If they pull through, Mr. and Mrs. Mitchell are going to be weak for some time. Mrs. Mitchell won’t be able to do as much as she would no doubt usually do. I cannot think she would mind if I set the house to rights before I leave.”

When she caught his gaze on her, she raised her eyebrows. “What?” she asked. “Don’t you agree?”

“I do, and I am certain she will appreciate your thoughtfulness. I just didn’t expect it from you.”

Katie flushed. “Why not? Because I’m a single woman trying to make a home without a husband?” she demanded. “You’re rather repetitious, doctor.” She probably shouldn’t have said that, but she couldn’t bring herself to retract her words.

With a roll of his eyes, the doctor turned on his heel and left the room to check on his patients. Katie stared after his retreating back and bit her lip in indecision. She ought not to have been so defensive. Maybe that wasn’t what he had meant at all. She wanted to follow him and apologize, but this was not the time or place for her personal feelings. They weren’t there on a social visit. With a shake of her head, she returned to her task.

The rest of the day flew past as they continued to care for the Mitchells. They had both indeed regained consciousness and were awake and eating the soup Mrs. Jenkins had sent over.

"I cannot believe you have been here for two days caring for us," Mrs. Mitchell croaked past her raw throat.

"Don't try to talk too much — spare your energy," Katie protested, not wishing to be embarrassed by her thanks.

The woman looked as though she were going to protest, but then must have realized the wisdom in Katie's words as she slumped back onto her pillow with a weak smile and a nod.

By the time the ill couple had finished the soup and were sleeping again, Doctor Jeffries had decided they were well and truly on the mend. "You ought to go home and have a proper sleep, Mrs. Carter. You have gone above and beyond your neighborly duty and should feel free to leave them in my care now."

When Katie went to protest, the doctor overrode her. "I am sure the neighbors will bring more food. You bathed Mrs. Mitchell after her fever broke, changed the bedding, and have washed all the sheets. There is really nothing more for you to do here. And I want you to get a proper rest before you end up one of my patients."

Katie gave him a wry smile in reaction to his last words. "Are you very sure you will be able to manage without me?" She flushed with embarrassment and began to stammer. "That's not to say that I was so very useful, but an extra pair of hands and being a woman…" She trailed off as he began to chuckle at her expense. She wanted to resent his amusement but couldn't prevent her rueful smile.

"You were far more help than I could have hoped for, and I would have been in trouble if not for you. But yes, I am quite certain that the worst has passed and I can manage from here. If that changes, I promise to send Matt for you."

This finally mollified her, and she agreed to depart. With a start, though, she realized that it had already fallen dark. The doctor caught her apprehensive glance out the window as she gathered her few things and said farewell to Matt.

"Matt, will you be comfortable sitting with your parents while I escort Mrs. Carter home?" Doctor Jeffries asked the boy.

Before Matt could answer, Katie protested. "I am perfectly capable of walking home on my own."

"I am certain you are capable, my good woman — that is not a question. I would just be left to wonder if you had found your way successfully and would not be able to have a peaceful night for worrying. If you allow me to escort you home, with a lantern to light the way, we can all rest easy tonight."

When he put it like that, Katie feared it would be churlish to refuse. She offered him a helpless shrug and inclined her head in acceptance.

Matt had been nodding vigorously along with the doctor. "It's much better this way, Mrs. Carter. You never know what might be out there in the dark. I wouldn't want to be wandering about by myself. But

I'll be fine here in the house until you get back Dr. Jeffries."

Katie grinned at the boy, picked up her small bag, and preceded the doctor from the house.

They walked along in companionable silence for a few minutes before the doctor remarked, "You must be anxious to get home to your daughter and your usual life."

"Oh, I have missed Annie almost unbearably, it's true. But there is something so satisfying about helping someone who is in such desperate need of aid. I think I envy you your profession, doctor. You get to have this experience every day."

Wyatt chuckled. "Luckily for the folks of Bucklin, there aren't people in dire need every single day. But you are right, it is an immensely satisfying way of life."

He couldn't decide if it was a reflection from the lantern or her own inner joy, but the lovely little woman at his side seemed to glow as they walked along.

"I'm sorry that I was resistant to the thought of staying when you first asked it of me. I am delighted that I was able to help poor Mr. and Mrs. Mitchell. They likely would have died if not for the train load of orphans, wouldn't you think?"

Wyatt lifted a questioning eyebrow and was rewarded by her sweet laughter drifting out. She quickly defended her position. "Think about it, doctor.

If not for the train, I wouldn't have been knocking at their door. And they wouldn't have had Matt. Even if I hadn't come along when I did, I'm sure Matt would have realized he needed to go for help eventually. But if not for the train, he wouldn't have been there. No one might have noticed they were ill until it was too late."

"I guess you have a solid point there, Mrs. Carter. Besides the Mitchells, I'm sure there are many in this town who would consider the arrival of the train of orphans to be a godsend. You are certainly a positive addition to the company of our town."

Despite the dim light, Wyatt could see that her color was heightened. It was most becoming. He almost held his breath as he took in her beauty. He tried to be nonchalant. She bashfully kept her silence.

"What do you suppose you will do first when you get home?" he asked to change the subject.

"I've thought of burning my clothes, but I used to be fond of this gown, so I will try not to do anything so drastic."

Wyatt couldn't help but chuckle. "Why would you do something like that?"

"I have never gone so long without changing my clothes," she explained. "Almost three days, including sleeping in them," she said with a shudder. "I may not burn them, but the first thing I intend to do is have a thorough bath." She must have questioned the correctness of discussing this with him as she hurried to add, "And then I feel like I could sleep for a week. But probably being in my own room without keeping an ear open for anyone's moans, I'll be able to sleep like a rock and waken fresh as a daisy by morning."

"I certainly hope so." Wyatt almost moaned himself over the fervour in his tone. He didn't want her reading anything into his enthusiasm. He quickly tried to explain himself. "You were such a help — you deserve your rest."

"Thank you, doctor. I will take my sleep seriously, as doctor's orders."

He was surprised and heartened by her teasing tone. She always seemed so serious. He was glad to see her being playful. But it made his pulse quicken, which was not at all acceptable. Wyatt questioned the sanity of offering to escort her home, not that sending her off on her own would have been acceptable. He sighed heavily.

"That sigh sounded rather deeply genuine, doctor. Are you feeling all right?"

Her solicitous tone only served to make his pulse quicken further and his palms began to sweat. Maybe he was catching the fever the Mitchells had, he thought in desperation.

"I find I'm more tired than I had realized," he excused.

She made a sound of protest. "You ought not to be out here with me. I really could have managed on my own."

The doctor now offered an exaggeratedly heavy sigh. "I am well aware of just how capable you are, Mrs. Carter, but I can assure you, no gentleman of honor would allow you to traipse about the village on your own in the dark. While most members of our town are fine upstanding citizens, you can never be sure who might be passing through, besides the wild creatures you could encounter. Now quit your protests, and allow me to do my duty."

He could hear the disgruntled growl in his voice but wasn't prepared for the loud laugh that emitted from his companion. "Very well, doctor, I will cease resisting your assistance and will admit to you that I am relieved not to be out here in the dark alone. I am still not accustomed to the sounds of nature at night, and I would probably be beside myself with terror by now if not for you and your lantern."

There was a quiet pause while Wyatt quelled his surprise at her words and waited to see what else she would say. His patience was rewarded. "But I still feel badly that you are out here with me when you could be tucked up getting some rest."

"Don't pay it any mind, Mrs. Carter. A doctor's duty is often discharged in the wee hours of the night. It seems most illnesses wait for the night time to pounce. And babies love to arrive in the middle of the night as well."

Another gurgle of laughter followed his words, and Wyatt had to grin.

"So when do you ever sleep?" she questioned.

"It's a small town, Mrs. Carter, it certainly doesn't happen every night. But I've learned to take my sleep when I can get it. I have slept in the sunshine in an open field more times than I can count. In fact, the time I was late arriving when you were with Mrs. Jenkins was after the arrival of the Channing twins. It was a difficult labor, and I hadn't slept a wink, so on my way to Mrs. Jenkins' I came across an inviting patch of grass and meant to only take a couple of minutes, but it ended up being a couple of hours."

"Oh dear. That explains why your cheeks were so pink when you arrived. I hadn't really noticed at the time, since I was beside myself with worry over poor Althea, but I wondered about it later. Now I will cease holding a grudge for your absence."

He could hear the smile in her voice even though he avoided looking at her.

"I appreciate your forgiveness."

She gurgled with laughter over his dry tone.

"You can be remarkably entertaining, doctor. I would never have known."

"I think, perhaps, you might just be overcome with your exhaustion at this point. Everything seems to be setting you off into peals of laughter." His comment met with more laughter from her.

"You could be right, doctor. I am not usually subject to such fits and giggles. I do hope I am not causing you offense. I don't mean to be laughing at you, you do realize, don't you?"

"Of course. But I do wish you could be so well amused in my company when you are fully rested and in full possession of your wits."

ꙮ

His statement was met with silence while he wondered himself where his words had come from. *What was he thinking to make such a leading statement? Did he really want the woman's attention?*

"Why is that, doctor?"

"Surely by now you could call me Wyatt, couldn't you? We *have* spent the last three days saving two lives. Does that not qualify as the means for getting us past such formality?"

Katie had stopped in her tracks, so he was forced to turn around and face her. He raised the lantern to better make out her features and try to gauge her reaction. She blinked at the sudden brightness, but it also seemed as though she were trying to blink away her confusion, too.

"I suppose you are right, doctor, or Wyatt, I suppose. But do you think we are to be friends? Will it not cause gossip to spread about us if I were to suddenly start calling you by your first name?"

"What sort of gossip?" he asked, wondering where she would go with her line of reasoning. He was rewarded by a becoming blush staining her cheeks.

"The townspeople will think we're courting."

"Would that be so bad?" he asked her and himself at the same time.

She blinked again. "Doctor Jeffries," she began, trying to sound severe, showing that her familiarity was short lived. "I do believe I am much too tired for this conversation. If I had all my faculties, I am sure I would be horrified at the thought of people thinking we were courting. But right now, it doesn't feel nearly as bad as it should." She giggled again before adding, "I feel as though I have had a touch too much cordial despite not having had a single drop." She set off again. "Do hurry up, Wyatt. I am nearly falling over and am surely in need of my bed."

Wyatt grinned and trotted after her.

Chapter Thirteen

The next morning, Katie woke up suddenly from a sound sleep with a gasp. *Good heavens, did I proposition the doctor?* she asked herself. From the light streaming into her room, it was certain that many hours had passed. She was actually feeling remarkably rested despite all she had been through in the past several days. Throwing back the covers, Katie hopped out of bed, the need for action spurring her on.

After hastily donning clean clothes and scrubbing her face, Katie hurried from her room.

"Good morning, sleepy head. I was beginning to wonder if I needed to send for the doctor. It is so unlike you to sleep late."

Katie started at the mention of Doctor Jeffries. "Why would you send for him?" she demanded, worry and suspicion ringing in her voice.

Melanie laughed. "What's up with you? Did you wake up on the wrong side of the bed?"

A part of Katie wanted to stick her tongue out at Melanie, but she couldn't help but laugh along with her. "Maybe I did," she admitted. "I slept like a log, so there's no excuse for being grumpy. But I sure needed it. I have never felt so tired as I did last night when I crawled into bed."

"I'm glad you slept well. You weren't making total sense when you got home."

Katie could feel color creeping up her cheeks, but she managed to keep her response mild. "Oh, why do you say that?"

"You were giggling so much I couldn't get much out of you while I was helping you change into your nightgown. You were admonishing me not to burn your gown, as though you thought I actually might do so."

Katie had to giggle again over this. "I had actually told Doctor Jeffries that I felt I ought to burn it after having been in it nonstop for so long. I'm glad you saw I wasn't making sense."

"You were also babbling something about gossip and courting. I couldn't get you to explain yourself, you were too far gone in your giggles and being half asleep already. I do have this to say for you. You don't get mean when you're incoherent, at least."

Katie giggled again. "I suppose that's good to know. I'm sorry you had to deal with me in that state. I really was beside myself with exhaustion. That's the only explanation I have."

Melanie waved her words away. "No apologies necessary. It was kind of cute. And actually, a little reassuring. You are always so competent and together. Seeing you a little unhinged made you seem mortal."

"Melanie Jones, of course I'm mortal. And normal. And *far* from competent, I can assure you." Then with a cheeky grin she added, "But I'm glad to know I have everyone fooled most of the time."

The two friends shared more laughter before Melanie sobered enough to cast Katie a speculative glance. "But I'm still left wondering why you reacted so strongly to me saying I should send for the doctor. And when I add that in with remembering your mumblings last night, I have to ask, are you concerned there will be gossip about you and the doctor being cooped up with the Mitchells? Because I can assure you, from what I could glean from the townspeople I encountered while out with Annie, everyone only had good things to say about you being so kind to the Mitchells. And Matt was there the whole time, besides the Mitchells being an older, married couple. Surely there was nothing improper in the least."

Katie was shaking her head but couldn't keep her blush at bay. "No, no. I know no one will think it was improper. Well, no one in their right mind, at the very least."

"Then why are your cheeks suddenly so rosy then?"

Katie huffed and sat down at the table, accepting the cup of tea Melanie had prepared for her. "Doctor Jeffries told me to call him Wyatt. I thought that would give rise to gossip. I told him so. And apparently I was still going on about it when I got home."

"Well, with what you went through together, I guess it would seem silly and pretentious to remain formal with the man. I don't think it would give rise to gossip, Katie. Everyone would surely understand." She paused before turning widening eyes on her. "But being in such close quarters with a man would surely lead to warm feelings developing between him and a healthy young woman. Katie Carter, are you courting with the doctor?"

Katie felt as though her entire body was probably red. "No, I am not," she protested.

"Then why are you blushing from tip to toes?" Melanie asked with a laugh.

"I'm embarrassed by your question, if you must know. Surely you remember me telling you I have no intention of ever remarrying."

"I do remember you saying such a daft thing. Katie, you're young, healthy, and vibrant. And you have a child. I know you love children. I've seen you with the orphans. You can't tell me you wouldn't like to have more. Even a little baby. Doesn't every woman want a baby of her own?"

Katie wanted to protest, but her heart softened at her friend's words, wondering how much of them were directed toward her and how much she was speaking of her own desires. Katie squeezed the other woman's hand and they were silent for a moment.

Breaking the silence, Katie said, "Babies and children are not the only thing you get from a marriage. You get stuck with a husband. That is not always such a fun thing."

"That's when you need a good solid cast iron skillet," Melanie responded swiftly.

Katie's mouth hung open and only laughter could emerge. "You might have a point there, my dear friend," she finally gasped when she was able to control her laughter to a degree.

Melanie's eyes lit up. "So you'll consider the doctor?"

"I didn't say that, now did I? Can you imagine? We have already made so many changes in our lives in the past weeks and months. Starting our new lives out here in Missouri. I have a daughter. And are you really trying to get rid of me? What would you do in this little house all by yourself without Annie and me to keep you company?"

Melanie grinned back at her. "Of course I'm not trying to get rid of you, but don't ever let me stand in the way of your happiness, either. You and Annie deserve the very best in life."

"And you think the doctor is the best?"

Melanie shrugged. "I think it would be best for you to have a mate and for Annie to have a father," she said as lightly as she could before laughing again. "And imagine only having to do the dishes for one person."

Katie threw a dish towel at her while they laughed together in friendship.

They had the small house fresh and shining in short order. When there was a light knock at the door, Katie glanced at the clock. "I thought Mary's dad was bringing Annie home after lunch today," she commented as she hurried to the door, anxious to see her daughter.

She blinked in surprise when she saw it was Doctor Jeffries. Feeling color mounting in her cheeks, she offered him a shy smile. “Good day, Wyatt,” she said, barely above a whisper.

“You look none the worse for wear,” he answered her cheerfully.

Katie suddenly thought of something, and she felt the flush seeping from her cheeks. “Is everything all right with the Mitchells? Do you need my help again? You should have sent Matt.” Her voice was rising with each phrase, and Wyatt chuckled.

“Hush now, everything is fine. I just wanted to check on you.”

Now Katie frowned at him. “Should you have left them on their own like this?”

Wyatt’s grin didn’t falter. They were on the front porch of her small house. Katie’s frown deepened. “Are you all right, doctor? You probably didn’t have as restful a night as I did.”

“You are a worrier, aren’t you?” His tone was teasing but kind.

Katie shrugged. “Sometimes.”

“The Mitchells are on the mend, I swear to you. I managed not to burn the eggs I fried up for them this morning, and they ate with remarkably improved appetite, I am relieved to report to you. I will continue to nurse them a day or two longer as I don’t want to risk anyone else coming into contact with them when they might still be contagious. Fortunately for them, you left their house in such a good state, that I shouldn’t be able to run it completely aground before Mrs. Mitchell is back on her feet.”

Katie was able to smile at this. "And how is Matt faring? The poor boy was nearly beside himself with worry for a while there."

"He, too, is much improved. He was actually running around chasing cats this morning when I left, and Mr. and Mrs. Mitchell were sleeping deeply. I'll be hard pressed to keep them in bed much longer, I'm sure. Especially Mr. Mitchell. Matt has been doing well about looking after the animals, but I know Mr. Mitchell will want to see for himself, maybe even by the end of the day today. Which is why I took this opportunity to come and see you. I'll most likely have to stand guard over them for the rest of the day, so I'll be confined."

Katie chuckled. "They seemed to be a rather meek couple. I don't think you'll have much trouble."

"You've only seen them ill. Wait until you get to know them when they're well. You might have a change of opinion."

Katie laughed again. "I look forward to making their acquaintance then."

"Oh yes, Mrs. Mitchell was asking about you over breakfast. She was sorely disappointed about messing up her appointment with you."

Katie eyed him askance. "Are you making fun of me now, doctor?"

"Why would I do that?"

"Surely the poor woman isn't considering fashion at a time like this."

"Even sick women can be vain," he observed.

Katie went off in a peel of laughter. “And isn’t it good for me and Melanie that that is true? If it comes up again, assure Mrs. Mitchell that I will be happy to return when she is back on her feet.”

“She’ll be relieved to hear it.”

They shared a smile before Katie averted her eyes and briskly asked, “Was that what you came to tell me?”

Wyatt’s laugh was a little more awkward this time. “No, actually, I have managed to talk all around the bush and haven’t gotten anywhere near my point. Would you be so kind as to take a stroll with me? That might help.”

Katie’s frown returned, but then she caught her breath as he reached out to touch the small furrow between her brows. “Don’t frown, my dear, I promise it’s nothing dire.”

The butterflies in her stomach were starting to feel more like turkeys lumbering around her midsection. Katie tried to shake off the nerves, but there wasn’t much she could do about it. She licked her lips and smoothed her hands over her skirt.

“Well, I have a little bit of time before Annie is due to return, and I’m fairly sure my chores are looked after for now. Besides, you probably don’t have overly much time anyway. So, I will stroll with you. But mind you, we cannot go far. I have no wish to set the town’s tongues to wagging.”

By the time she had managed to stop herself from babbling all this out, they were already well on their way. Katie was feeling slightly mortified about all the words she had allowed to tumble from her lips and couldn't make herself make eye contact with her companion. They strode along in silence for a few minutes. It felt like hours to her, but she was fairly certain it might not have even been three minutes. Maybe not even two. Surely she was losing her mind. She tried not to fidget, but finally she couldn't take it anymore.

"Where are we going?"

"There's a lovely spot along this trail a ways," he said. "It's a little bit of a trek since it's up a small hill, but I think you'll agree that the view is worth it."

Katie finally glanced at him. "You are enjoying living out here, aren't you?"

"I really am. I cannot say for certain that I would never want to move back East, but I really don't think I will want to leave these parts. The beauty is astounding, not at all what I would have expected, and not what I would have thought would appeal to me, since Boston was what I always knew. But there's just something so appealing about the freedom and wildness of these parts."

"I know what you mean," Katie agreed. "While I was anxious for a fresh start, I didn't think I would come to love it out here like I do. I thought I was a city girl through and through. But it's quite amazing how exhilarating fresh air and trees can be."

They shared a friendly chuckle as they neared the top of the rise, and then Katie's breath caught as she took in the spectacle before her. It was green as far as she could see with very little to mar the landscape. A few small houses could be seen in the distance with some cows and sheep dotting the fields and a few trees lining the creek that meandered through the vista. The sunshine was warm on her shoulders, and the fresh smell was sweet and clean.

Katie finally broke the quiet. “I think it would take me decades to tire of this view.”

“I agree,” Wyatt said.

But he was looking at her, not at the scenery, and Katie could feel warmth creeping toward her scalp as the nerves that had dissipated while they walked returned in full force. She began to fidget once more.

“Thank you for sharing this with me. I’m a little surprised, though, that you would take the time to do so, since you must surely be fully occupied with your patients.”

Wyatt shrugged. “I didn’t want to visit any of my other patients just yet, in case I might be carrying the Mitchells’ illness. So far, I haven’t seemed to develop any symptoms, so hopefully I share your immunity.”

“Well that’s fortunate,” she replied.

“Yes,” he began, but she spoke at the same time and interrupted him.

“I ought to get back. Annie is supposed to be coming home after lunch, and I haven’t seen her for days. I wouldn’t want her to fret if I’m absent.”

Wyatt put his hand out and stilled her fidgeting fingers. “Just a moment, Katie, I’m trying to discuss something with you.”

Katie’s stomach turned over in a manner that she thought might be pleasant if she could get her mind to return to functioning. As it was, all she could do was stand still and blink at him and absorb the delicious sensation of having his warm hands engulfing her own.

"I know I have been rather obnoxious in the past in my opinions about independent women. I think I owe you an apology."

Disappointment swept through her, which she considered to be completely irrational. She wished she could wave her hand nonchalantly. But since it was still clasped in his, Katie tried for a breezy tone as she said, "Please, think nothing of it. I didn't allow it to weigh on me."

"That is certainly a relief," he said with a wide smile. "I wouldn't want you to be offended with me."

"Of course not, with us both being rather public people, our paths are sure to cross from time to time. It wouldn't do for us to be at loggerheads."

"No, it most certainly would not do." His voice was strained, and Katie wondered if he was laughing at her, but she again couldn't bring herself to meet his gaze. He continued, "You see, Katie, I was thinking that I would rather our paths more than crossed from time to time. I may not have been clear in my intentions, but I would quite like it if we shared the same path, if you know what I mean."

"I don't reckon that I do know what you mean, Wyatt," Katie answered, feeling as though her emotions were in a windstorm as they tossed about from one direction to another. "Won't it cause gossip if we take many walks together?"

Wyatt chuckled. "Not if you would agree to me courting you."

Katie gasped. “Courtship? Wyatt Jeffries, are you making fun of me again?”

Now Wyatt was left blinking at her. “Why would you think I’m making fun? I’m trying to engage your interest.”

Katie went off in a peel of laughter. “Melanie will have a great laugh over this.”

“This isn’t going exactly how I had envisioned,” Wyatt commented blandly.

“You envisioned this?” Katie asked, feeling a little breathless once more.

“I did.”

“How did it go in your vision?”

“Well, you didn’t consider it a joke. In fact, you thought it was a brilliant idea and flung your arms around my neck announcing your instant agreement.”

“Seems like your imagination might not know me so well.”

Wyatt chuckled. “A man is allowed to dream, Katie Carter.” His tone was dry, but there was still a twinkle in his eye. “I realize this might seem sudden to you. I didn’t want to declare myself as we were hovering over the Mitchells’ sick bed.”

“I can see that would be remarkably bad form,” Katie agreed with a grin.

“Quite right. But I find that while I have a remarkably good imagination, I cannot envision a future that does not contain you in it, by my side, sharing my life, even helping me with my patients, or pursuing your own interests,” he was quick to add, “whatever you think best, as long as you return home each night to share your thoughts and dreams with me and whatever family we manage to grow together."

Katie felt tears gather in her eyes. "That sounds wonderful, Wyatt." Suddenly though, she grew sober once more. "The only trouble is, this is all rather sudden, wouldn't you say? Just days ago we weren't sure if we could even bear each other."

"I knew I could bear you, Katie, I was just afraid."

Katie smiled over that admission, but continued, "The thing is, Wyatt, I'm a mother now, and I cannot only think of myself. Annie hasn't been along for the journey of us coming to this understanding. She has to be my first priority. And I need to make sure that she's all right with these changes. If I agree, you'll have to understand that you need to court the both of us."

Wyatt studied her seriously for a heartbeat before he broke into a grin. "I rather think that sounds like double the pleasure.

Katie then surprised him by throwing her arms around his neck. "Well then, I think I might have to quickly agree."

With a whoop of joy, Wyatt twirled her around while she laughed with delight. Finally, allowing her to sink down to her feet, he bent his head and sealed their bargain with a sweet kiss.

Epilogue

Katie was standing nervously in the spot where Wyatt had asked her to meet him. The exact place where he had declared himself two months prior. She was amazed how patiently he had courted her and Annie. She herself would have thought he needn't have taken quite so much time. Anyone could see that both she and Annie were head over heels about him. But he had been true to his word. He had taken his time with Annie, allowing her to get over her distrust of doctors. And he had lovingly allowed Katie time to get over her distrust of men. She had come to anticipate the sound of his knock each evening as he called by, even sometimes just for a moment or two, just to say hello and see how her and Annie's day had been. She knew it must have been exhausting for him after his long days of caring for others. But it had gone a long way to help both of his "girls" arrive at the conclusion that they couldn't imagine their lives without him in it.

But it had already been a couple of weeks since Katie had arrived at that realization. She was beginning to wonder if she was going to have to propose to him, she thought with a grin as she gazed out at the beautiful vista in front of her. She was beginning to grow impatient with the good doctor. Both in this moment of waiting for him — surely he was late for their appointment — and with this courtship. She was ready to get on with their new life together.

A sound behind her drew her attention. When she turned to look, tears almost clogged her throat. Wyatt was walking toward her, hand-in-hand with Annie. Annie was carrying a beautiful, enormous bouquet of flowers that surely must have taken ages to gather. That would account for the delay, she thought with a grin. Then she realized that Wyatt was carrying a shovel and she frowned in confusion.

"Well this is a pleasant surprise," she greeted them as Annie ran toward her. "Thank you, Annie, these are beautiful."

"They're from both of us. Because we love you," Annie said, making the tears swimming in Katie's eyes tumble down her cheeks. "That's s'posed to make you happy, not cry," Annie pointed out, becoming distressed.

Katie laughed. "Sometimes tears can be from happiness, not just for sadness." Annie looked slightly mollified but still somewhat skeptical. Her attention was quickly turned, though, when Wyatt gained their attention.

"Annie, please stand there with Katie. I have something important I want to discuss with the both of you."

Katie's heart thudded in her chest, and she felt momentarily light-headed as her mind filled with hope. But she couldn't help grinning over the wide-eyed confusion on Annie's face. The tears that had dried were soon joined by more as Wyatt crouched down onto one knee in order to be on the same level with Annie.

"Annie, my dear girl, I hope you realize how truly special you have become to me. I know you have faced many challenges already in your young life, and it has taken a great deal of courage to allow me into your life. I think you're the bravest little girl I have ever met. And I was wondering if you would be willing to make it a permanent arrangement."

The child blinked, staring at the doctor without fully understanding his meaning. Wyatt quickly elaborated.

"I know no one can ever replace the mother and father you lost, and I know you have made a new life with Katie, but would you be willing to allow me to join that life, so that we could all live together?"

"So we can be together every day, and you don't have to go home by yourself?"

"Exactly right. I don't want to go home by myself anymore."

The little girl stared at him solemnly. "I don't like being by myself either. If Katie says it's all right, I think it's a good idea."

Wyatt grinned; his gaze flicked up to Katie for a second, but he kept his focus on Annie while he pointed into the distance. "Would you mind going over there to play for a few minutes while I discuss it with Katie?"

"All right," she agreed and scampered off.

"Well, Katie, you can now see that my future loneliness or companionship comes down to your say so," he remarked as they both watched Annie skipping in the field. Turning to her, Wyatt gathered up her hands. "Katie, darling, I have tried to take my time and allow the two of you to grow accustomed to me, but I don't think I can wait any longer. I love the both of you more than life itself. Please, tell me you'll put me out of my misery and become my wife."

Katie burst into laughter. "I thought you'd never ask!"

"What? I've been nearly consumed with impatience for weeks."

"You hid it well, Dr. Jeffries." Katie's reply was arch.

He gathered her into his arms. "Are you really going to marry me?"

Katie smiled. "I really am."

He twirled her around, and their laughter mingled. "How soon can we manage it?"

Katie's laughter rang out louder. "From taking your time, now you're impatient?"

Wyatt was rueful. "Do you mind terribly? Do you want to wait for friends or family to come from New York?"

Katie quickly denied that. "Not at all. I have no need for a big wedding. In fact, I am as impatient as you. Maybe even more so. I love you, too, Wyatt, and will happily marry you as soon as it can be arranged."

They laughed together before Wyatt silenced them both as he stole her breath with a tender kiss.

The End

Melanie

BOOK 4

Orphan Train Series

WENDY MAY ANDREWS

Sparrow Ink
www.sparrowdeck.com

www.wendymayandrews.com

Two challenged hearts. One true love?

The death of her mother left ten-year-old Melanie Jones with too many responsibilities. Raising her younger siblings under the weight of her father's unkind words filled her with insecurities. Despite those early years, she's determined to make a new life for herself. Moving far away from home, she boards a train to escort the latest load of orphans to Missouri.

Abandoned by his wife then widowed, Cole Miller is forced to raise his daughter on his own. Though his sister is supposed to help, she's more liability than asset. When a beautiful newcomer arrives in town, her doubts and insecurities leave Cole uninterested. He's had his fill of women like his wife and sister.

When Melanie steps in to help Cole with his daughter, he's able to see beyond her timidity and discover her beautiful and gracious soul. Will his discovery be enough for him to let go of his own uncertainties? Is Melanie ready for a family of her own?

Dedication

To Mum & Dad who gave me the foundation upon which I stand.

This heroine holds a special place in my heart. Melanie struggles with her insecurities and would much rather stay home than face people. This book is for all those who feel alone as they face their challenges.

And for my own home hero who makes sure I'm not alone as I face mine.

Acknowledgements

As always, my awesome beta readers: Marlene, Suzanne, Monique, and Alfred, helped me immeasurably. Then, my lovely editor, Julie Spencer, took it all and made it shine. All remaining messiness is my own efforts.

Also, special thanks go to "GermanCreative" on Fiverr for all the gorgeous covers in this series.

Chapter One

Bucklin, Missouri - Early summer 1854

Melanie stared at the handsome man. She hadn't expected him to be so good looking. She quickly realized that was a ridiculous thought. Why wouldn't he be? She hadn't actually given the man's appearance any thought, so she shouldn't be quite this surprised by his flawless face and clear blue gaze. In fact, given how pretty little Mary was, it should have been expected. But nonetheless, she felt tongue tied and gauche and dearly wished she had not made arrangements for Annie to stay over at her friend's house.

"You must be Annie," the man said in a smooth baritone that did funny things to Melanie's stomach while Annie nodded and grinned. "And you must be Mrs. Carter," he continued, looking at Melanie.

Her nervous giggle embarrassed her as she shook her head. "No, I'm sorry for the confusion, I'm Melanie Jones, Mrs. Carter's housemate. Mrs. Carter being unavailable today is part of why I agreed to Annie coming to stay over when your wife asked this morning."

Mr. Miller's smile should be outlawed, Melanie thought as she blinked, hoping she didn't look like a dull-witted bovine as she did so. *But why is he grinning like that?* The thought flitted through her head just as he chuckled.

"Leandra's not my wife. She's my sister. She came out here to help me and Mary when my wife died."

"Oh no, I'm so sorry for your loss."

The handsome man lifted a shoulder in a half shrug. She could relate to the feeling. Really, what is there that can be said? Losing someone in death is the most permanent form of tragedy. And anyone saying sorry about it is kind but rather useless. There's nothing that can be done.

"It's good that you have had your sister to help you out," she added.

The look he gave her led her to believe that maybe his sister hadn't been such a help after all. *This is why I don't deal with people*, Melanie thought with a twinge of anguish. She hated the awkwardness she always felt when she was with other people. Her insecurities made interacting with strangers nearly debilitating. Once again, she was grateful for her business partner's willingness to deal with their customers.

Mary's father interrupted the flow of her disquieting thoughts. "Is there anything we need to know about Annie?"

Melanie's heart sank. She knew so little about the poor child. "She's a delight and doesn't make a fuss about much of anything, so you should be fine."

"Has she slept over at someone's house before?" Mr. Miller pressed.

"In a manner of speaking," Melanie answered, wondering if she ought to air Katie and Annie's business. With a mental shrug, she figured it wasn't all that private a matter. "Annie has just recently joined our household. Mrs. Carter adopted Annie. The sweet child has seemed to take it all in her stride so well that I suspect you won't have any problems with her."

Mr. Miller looked at her with curiosity clearly evident on his face, and Melanie fought the urge to squirm. "Would you like to come in for a cup of tea or coffee while we see if the girls settle in all right?"

Melanie quite strongly wanted to decline the invitation but when she glanced down at Annie, seeing the hesitation on the child's face, she realized she ought to do what she could to make sure Annie was comfortable. Melanie would have to set aside her own discomfort this time. Negative thoughts crowded around in her head as she struggled with regrets that she hadn't insisted Katie not adopt the little girl. But Melanie did her best to reject the negativity. Annie was a delightful child, and Melanie couldn't begrudge either her or Katie their newfound familial happiness.

Pasting what she hoped wasn't an overtly fake-looking smile onto her face, Melanie nodded and accepted the man's offer. "I suppose that might be wise."

When one side of the man's handsome face lifted into a lopsided grin, Melanie questioned her own words. No, it was not wise to spend any amount of time around him. She was sure to be tongue tied and awkward. She wished she could fall into a conveniently opened hole in the floor. But those things never happened, no matter how hard one wished for them. She swallowed her nerves as best she could and followed the two little girls and the large man into the house.

Glancing around, Melanie was surprised to see very little evidence of a woman's touch in the clean but sparse house. It would seem Leandra was not leaving her mark on her brother's home. To her chagrin, Mr. Miller must have read the curiosity on her face.

"My sister hasn't been enjoying her time her in Missouri. She is determined to return East as soon as possible, even though she has been here for almost two years now. I think now that Mary is in school, we'll be able to manage without her. I should really put Leandra on the next train headed east, but I find myself struggling with nerves."

Melanie was shocked to hear a man admitting to such a feeling. "What are you nervous about?" She colored slightly at the emphasis on "you" as it revealed her own issues, but she brazened it out and waited for his reply.

He shrugged and offered her another lopsided grin. "What do I know about little girls? Or big girls for that matter. I hate keeping Leandra here when I know she's hating it, but I hate even more the thought of Mary not having the best care."

Melanie glanced around to make sure the girls were out of earshot but also ensured to keep her voice low as she answered him. “Children are remarkably perceptive and are affected by how they think the adults around them are feeling. I have had a great deal of experience with children. In my opinion, Mary will thrive if she knows you care about her and are doing your best. I don’t know her well, but she seems like a bright, happy child. I don’t think you have to worry overly.” She paused for a moment before adding, “It speaks well of you that you have even given the matter some thought. Most men wouldn’t.”

Mr. Miller offered her a quizzical glance but didn’t comment, merely busying himself getting the water on to boil. Melanie tried to keep her focus away from him, but she couldn’t help being fascinated by the sight of a man moving around a kitchen as though he knew what he was doing there. His large hands managed to handle the kettle dexterously and scoop the roughly ground coffee without spilling. When it came time to set out the dainty cups, Melanie had to bite her lip to prevent a grin from spreading across her face. She wondered why he had such delicate things. She was embarrassed to realize her thoughts must have written themselves on her face when he looked at her with his eyebrows quirked quizzically. The color rose in his cheeks, but his gaze never wavered. He lifted his shoulder.

“My daughter loves to play tea parties, and a good tin cup just won’t do for her. She has convinced me that a well-equipped kitchen is fully stocked with teacups and nothing less should ever be offered to a proper lady.”

Melanie allowed her grin to spread. "Well, I'm honored that you think me a proper lady, in that case."

His answering grin made her nerves flutter, but she managed not to cower away, grateful beyond words when he didn't seem to notice, merely turning back to competently set out the coffee that was now ready. He placed a plate of cookies on the table between them as he sat down across from her.

Chapter Two

Cole watched in amazement as his guest nibbled on a cookie. It was better than when she had been nibbling on her lip. He had to work hard not to stare. She was obviously high strung. After the trouble he had been dealing with because of his sister, he should be completely unaffected by her nervous fidgets. But instead, he had to fight an overwhelming impulse to draw her into his arms and comfort her. It was the strangest sensation. The only other person he felt so protective towards was Mary. But the sensations he was feeling towards Miss Jones were most certainly not of the paternal type. It was definitely time for some conversation to divert the mood in the room.

"How are you enjoying life in Bucklin thus far, Miss Jones?"

He tried not to be charmed by the blush that colored her cheekbones as her eyes bounced around the room. Apparently, conversation wasn't going to help the situation. Cole stifled a sigh. He was glad he managed to retain a modicum of patience. It was soon rewarded.

With a deep breath that seemed to go all the way to her toes and an effort that appeared truly valiant, she brought her gaze to meet his and finally answered his question.

“I actually quite like it, Mr. Miller. Anyone I’ve met has been remarkably kind. Katie, I mean Mrs. Carter, and I cannot get over how clean everything is. We had rather expected it to be dry and dusty, but it’s not. It’s much more green than I thought it would be. And the air and water are so clean. We remark on it nearly every day.”

Cole watched in fascination as she became more and more animated as she talked, as though she were able to forget whatever caused her fears as she warmed to her subject.

“Did you not have clean air and water where you come from?” He knew she was from New York but didn’t think that great city was so very dirty.

“Have you ever been to New York, Mr. Miller?”

“I’m originally from Boston, myself. I had visited, of course, in the course of business, but I haven’t spent much time there. None at all in the past seven years, of course. Since we moved out here, I have had absolutely no desire to return East.”

“I can fully understand such a sentiment.” She nodded and smiled, seemingly a completely different person than the one who had arrived on his doorstep half an hour ago. Cole wanted to extend their time together.

“You aren’t feeling homesick?” He couldn’t help the surprise from sounding in his voice.

Her cheeks turned pink and Cole held his breath, hoping she didn't turn into the nervous wraith she had been earlier. Her shoulders lifted in a small shrug.

"There isn't much home to be sick for, I'm afraid. New York doesn't hold anything for me anymore. Everything here is so lovely. I can see this being my home forever."

Cole hesitated to ask, certain it would put her walls back up, but he couldn't just leave it.

"Are you one of the orphans, too?"

She offered him a half-hearted smile. "In a manner of speaking, I guess I am."

It was obvious to Cole that there was a world of information left unsaid, but he couldn't pry any deeper. It was unusual for him to be so intrigued by a woman. Especially one he had just met. No doubt it was the lack of single women in town that was causing this unprecedented reaction. He really ought to excuse himself from the situation. He had no wish to make the poor woman uncomfortable. But watching the little girls playing together, he could see that Annie was still keeping part of her attention on the two adults, so he needed to keep Miss Jones there a little longer to ensure the child was properly settled.

"I never did get your answer about why you are so taken with the cleanliness out here in Missouri."

The woman's lips quirked into a crooked smile, as though she were contemplating an amusing answer. "Well, as I mentioned, I was actually prepared for Missouri to be dry and dusty, so I was expecting dirt and am therefore quite pleasantly surprised. But, unfortunately, while there are beautiful, clean parts of New York, I did not grow up in those neighborhoods. Where I lived was rather cramped and a little filthy, so I am quite enjoying the space here. And some of the illnesses in my neighborhood were thought to be caused by the water, so I always boiled any water I drank. It is a lovely experience to be able to drink cool water straight from the well in our backyard. It is one that Mrs. Carter and I appreciate every morning. I think it will take me quite a while to get to the point of taking that for granted."

Cole watched in fascination as she seemed to grow flustered. He rather thought it was from sharing such personal thoughts. His supposition was confirmed when she tried to turn the subject.

"But never mind about me. I'm a boring old tale. Please, Mr. Miller, tell me what brought you and your family to Bucklin."

Turning his gaze back to his daughter and away from his visitor's pretty features, Cole allowed his mind to drift back to the past.

"Despite growing up in a well-to-do family in the heart of Boston, I always craved making my own way in the world, as well as wider spaces than the city allowed for. I didn't want to follow in my older brother's footsteps into our father's business. I knew I'd always play second fiddle to Jonathan if I stayed."

The way she was nodding made him feel as though she could understand his sentiments. Warmth spread in his chest. He continued his tale.

"I was young and headstrong. I convinced our neighbor's daughter to join me in my westward adventures. I don't think she truly thought we'd stay here. She never fully understood my need to be free of my brother's shadow. I'm pretty sure Sheila expected us to have our little adventure here for at most a year or two. She thought I'd get tired of working so hard physically and would want to return to the city. But I had been completely honest with her before we married. I have no interest in being my brother's underling."

"Of course not, who would?" Her understanding made his throat feel tight. *Why couldn't Sheila have ever understood?* He shoved the unwelcome thought away.

"Anyway, I won't bore you with all the details. As it turned out, Sheila eventually tired of life here and her inability to convince me to return East."

Miss Jones's jaw dropped in suitably appropriate shock. "She left you?"

"In a manner of speaking." He echoed her earlier words. "She claimed she was just taking Mary home to meet her grandparents, but I suspected she wouldn't be returning. I didn't have the heart to deny her. I planned to follow her after a few weeks and bring her back. I expected she wouldn't enjoy the city as much as she had thought she would after having lived out here for a few years. But she caught a dreadful disease that had swept through the city and died within three weeks of her arrival. For all she thought life was safer in Boston, being closer to doctors, she would still be alive if she had stayed here."

The sympathy swimming in his guest's eyes nearly undid him. He cleared his throat and tried to muster a small smile. "Well, you are a remarkably good listener, I must say, Miss Jones. I almost never share this story with anyone, most certainly not with anyone I've just met."

"Well, I am honored that you shared your history with me." She glanced toward the children before fixing her bright gaze back on his. "But I must ask that you not share it with Annie. She is very sensitive to any talk of illness, which is why she is now with you, after all, since Mrs. Carter is helping the doctor with the Mitchells. Dr. Jeffries has not decided what exactly has befallen the Mitchells, but we fear it could be the influenza that swept New York."

"Of course. I do hope Mrs. Carter and the Mitchells will be all right."

His guest cast her worried gaze toward the children once more. "As do I. Can you imagine if the poor girl was to be orphaned again? It isn't to be considered. Katie is convinced she's immune to whatever has infected the Mitchells and she will return home before long, and I have chosen to believe her." She rose to her feet. "Mrs. Carter and I both appreciate your kindness in helping us out by keeping Annie distracted."

"Not at all. I didn't even know about your situation when we asked if Annie could stay over. Mary is thrilled to have a new friend. I'm just glad that it's turning out to be mutually beneficial."

The pretty woman's nerves seemed to be returning in force. She nodded with a tight smile on her face but didn't say anything more. She didn't even say goodbye to the little girl, just turned on her heel and left the house with half a wave as she hurried on her way. Cole watched her retreat wondering if it had been something he said.

Thinking back over their conversation, Cole couldn't imagine what would have made her take her leave so suddenly. While she had seemed nervous at first, he had thought she had warmed up to him as they shared a cup of coffee. Perhaps it was the discussion of his wife's death. No one likes to think about such a thing. Maybe she thought it was his fault. He couldn't blame her for that. He beat himself up over it all the time. If he had insisted she stay with him, she would still be alive. *But how was I supposed to do that?* She had been slowly turning into a misery, and he didn't want that infecting his little Mary. He had thought a trip back to Boston would have helped her see the advantages of their life in Missouri. There hadn't been time for that. She was dead before he had even boarded the train to come after them. At least he had gotten to Boston in time for her funeral. And blessedly, no one blamed him for her death, other than him. And Leandra had been willing to accompany him back to Bucklin to help with Mary.

His eyes strayed to his daughter as she played with her new little friend. His heart swelled as he watched her. Cole had never anticipated the love he was capable of. He had never loved anyone the way he loved his daughter. Certainly, no members of his family. Not even his wife, he hated to admit to himself. They had rubbed along well enough together at first, but her grumbling about their life in Missouri had chipped away at their friendship. *Why couldn't she have looked to the future instead of dwelling on the past?* He thought again of Miss Jones. She was clearly haunted by something but was trying to make the most of it. He really appreciated her positive attitude toward Missouri. No doubt, she would be married quickly in this town where single men abounded. He found he didn't quite like that idea.

Chapter Three

Melanie tried to slow her steps but couldn't quite manage a sedate pace as she hurried back to the safety and comfort of the small white house she and Katie called home. She was torn between pride and despair over her encounter with Mr. Miller. It was the longest conversation she had shared with anyone other than Katie in months. And she had actually enjoyed it, for the most part. But then her fears had returned, and she had felt the need to flee his presence as though the hounds of hell were nipping at her heels. No doubt the man would think her an imbecile. Or just one more foolish female. Surely the poor man had had his fill of them. *He would probably like Katie*, she thought with a stab of irrational jealousy.

She tried to shake the negative thoughts from her mind by literally shaking her head and turning her attention outward. Castigating herself for her feelings had never helped in the past, so she wasn't going to continue. *Look at the vast, blue sky*, she reminded herself. *Breathe in that clean, fresh air. Feast your eyes on the vibrant green and yellow of the fields out behind the main street of the new little town. Ignore the dull gray of the little houses that line that main street. What does it matter if no one has planted any roses? Why don't you do it? Write to Mrs. Parker at the orphanage in New York and ask that she send you some cuttings with the next shipment of orphans.*

Her breathing and her footsteps slowed to a normal rhythm as she calmed her thoughts and neared her home. She dearly loved the little house she and Katie were renting. And she was so proud of the little business they were running. Thus calmed, she turned her thoughts to the sewing she would work on that afternoon. With Annie suitably settled and Katie otherwise occupied, Melanie thought she should be able to get quite a bit done as the hours stretched ahead of her with no one to demand anything of her. It was a heady feeling to be mistress of her own life.

For fifteen years she had felt the heavy burden of responsibility. She had been only ten years old when her mother had died within days of birthing Henry. Their father hadn't known what to do with the baby and his three-year-old daughter, so he had let his ten-year-old daughter take it all on. She had essentially become a mother at the age of ten. Now she was twenty-five. Her father had recently died and left everything to Henry. He was going through a rather obnoxious phase and no longer needed her. Sweet little Claudia was married and also no longer needed her. Melanie was relieved that Claudia had married a pleasant young man from a big, loving family. Claudia would be well taken care of if she needed anything. So, Melanie was free to get on with her new life. If only she could get over her issues from her old life, things would be perfect.

She stepped through her door with a sigh of relief then leaned against the door while surveying the tidy kitchen of their small home. She and Katie had done very well for themselves when they'd arranged for its rental. It was hard for her to fathom that someone had willingly moved out of the pretty little house. To Melanie's mind, there was nowhere better than the four walls holding up the sturdy roof. She loved living in a house. Never again would she willingly live in a tenement. While there were certain conveniences in living so crowded up with others, they were far outweighed by the drawbacks, in her opinion. If she never smelled another home's cooking, it would be too soon, she thought fiercely as she took an appreciative, deep inhale of the fresh scent lingering in the air. She had left the windows open when she left with Annie, and there were no lingering odors from the breakfast she had cooked that morning. It was wonderful. She couldn't remove the grin from her face. No one was about so she didn't even try.

Thinking back to the home she had grown up in, Melanie couldn't quite suppress the shudder that shivered down her spine. The tight quarters in the tenement building had seemed luxurious when they had first moved in. The landlord had made an effort to make the building attractive. But now, being out here in all the space that Missouri had to offer, Melanie couldn't bear to think of the three rooms that had made up the apartment she had shared with her younger siblings and their father. And they had been lucky. With only four of them, and none of them trying to run a business from home, they weren't nearly as crowded as some of their neighbors. Many of the other apartments housed five, six, even seven people in the same space that they were cramped with four. And then some of the ladies in the building were taking in sewing so they needed to keep one of the rooms presentable for any customers who might come around.

That was, of course, how Melanie had learned to sew. Mrs. Becker had been kind enough to teach her and then give her a job. She had been so proud of herself for helping her father support the family. Little did she know how little value he had placed upon her efforts. Melanie shoved the unwelcome thought hastily away. It wouldn't help her efforts at calmness if she thought about her childhood, even if thinking of Mrs. Becker was a highlight in her life.

Melanie took a few more deep breaths of the fresh, sweet-smelling air that flowed through her open windows and then set to the tasks before her. She began to hum a song that Mrs. Becker had always sung while they worked together. It kept the smile she had forced onto her lips in place. Within minutes it was no longer fake — she was happy doing her work.

Hours flew by and before she knew it, Melanie found herself in a darkened room with a finished garment. She grinned with satisfaction. There was nothing quite like the deep satisfaction she felt every time she remembered how far she'd come. She looked around in the gloom but felt not an ounce of fear. Everything here was hers, or hers and Katie's. There was no one to tell her what to do; no one would be able to take this away from her. She knew her smile was stretching her face, but she didn't care. There was no one about to try to tell her how she ought to be feeling and no one to censure her for looking silly as she grinned at nothing in particular.

Bustling about, Melanie put the sewing materials away after lighting the lamp. It wouldn't do to keep stitching. She had gotten to the point in the garment that finer work was needed. She would wait until the sun would illuminate her handiwork.

Bright and early the next morning Melanie was up and back at work, but the back of her mind niggled. She loved having the house to herself and all her newfound independence. But she had come to care about Katie, and she was worried about her being cooped up in the sick house under quarantine.

Guilt was uppermost on her mind, if Melanie was being truly honest. It was only because of her own insecurities that Katie was the one who had to visit their patrons. If Katie hadn't called to see Mrs. Mitchell to get her measurements, she wouldn't be stuck there trying to help them get well. Of course, if Katie hadn't been there, the Mitchells might be dead already. But it wasn't really fair that all the visits fell to Katie to make. In all actuality, it should have been at least a fifty percent chance of Melanie being stuck there with them. She shuddered at the thought. Katie was far more equipped for such a hideous situation, in Melanie's opinion.

Of course, the poor dear can't be enjoying being stuck with the good doctor, Melanie thought with a sly grin. *I think she protests about him a little too much.* Of course, given her background, Melanie couldn't blame the young woman overmuch. But anyone with eyes could see that the two were attracted to each other. *I wonder how many sparks are flying in that house?* Melanie hadn't seen the inside of the Mitchells' house, but from the outside it looked like it would be close quarters. Katie had looked exhausted when Melanie had seen her the day before. She really did wish there was something she could do to help the situation other than bring food. But Katie had been right when she said there was no use in them all being exposed.

With a sigh, Melanie set to baking. At least she could bring Katie and the Mitchells a meal. The patients might not be up to eating much, but the caregivers had to keep their strength up. *And then I'll finish that frock I was working on*, Melanie thought. *At the very least, I can make sure we meet our business obligations while Katie is stuck with the doctor.* With another, softer sigh Melanie thought of Annie and Mr. Miller. Melanie would have to make sure the little girl was kept occupied.

She determined to call round to Katie with the food and decide whether or not Annie needed to stay away a little longer. Mary's father seemed like a kind enough gentleman. If need be, he would probably keep the youngster another night.

Some time later, Melanie was surprised to feel a spring in her step as she walked away from the Mitchells' home. It made no sense for her to be feeling sprightly. She was worried about Katie and dreading speaking to the handsome Mr. Miller. Wasn't she? Of course, she was, Melanie reminded herself. She was just hurrying out of concern for Annie. She managed not to even roll her eyes at her own foolishness.

Chapter Four

By the time she approached the Cole residence, Melanie could see Mr. Miller working out in one of his paddocks. It seemed as though he was training a horse. She had never seen such an activity before, and the breath caught in her throat as the scene played out in front of her.

Melanie's city-bred sentiments had never thought much of horses. If she had thought of them, it would have only been to consider them slightly terrifying but useful, as they pulled the wagons and carriages that filled the streets of New York. But now, as she watched the powerful animal being trained by the handsome man, she found the scene moving, beautiful, even breath-taking. And it wasn't only because Mr. Miller had removed his shirt in the gathering heat of the day. As the horse tossed its head and pranced around at the end of its tether; it seemed to Melanie as though the beautiful animal was flirting with the man. She couldn't tear her gaze away and only realized she was holding her breath when Mr. Miller finally noticed her. When he raised his hand in a wave, the air whooshed out of her in a gasp.

Thankfully, he was far enough away that he couldn't possibly have heard, but Melanie felt the heat creeping up her cheeks anyway. She tried to keep her face neutral, but she was rather afraid that a sheepish smile was stretching her cheeks. With relief, she saw that he likely realised his state of undress and was quickly buttoning up his shirt as she walked toward him.

"Good morning, Miss Jones," Mr. Miller called as she approached.

Melanie was having serious second thoughts about coming out to his property. She wished she could undo the last half hour of her life. She should have returned home after seeing Katie. But instead she was standing still, looking at the handsome man. *Gaping really, if I'm going to be perfectly honest,* she thought with a cringe. Nothing could be done but to brave through the awkward moment.

"Morning, Mr. Miller."

"Are you here to collect Annie? I thought she would be staying through the day."

Even with a frown creasing his face, the man still managed to steal her breath. Melanie wondered if she were getting ill or losing her mind.

"Actually, sir, as it turns out, Katie is going to be staying with the Mitchells a little longer, so I was stopping in to see how Annie had fared and to see if we might prevail upon your hospitality a little longer."

"It has been a pleasure having the wee lass with us, I can assure you."

Melanie couldn't look him in the eye as he answered her for fear he would see just how compelling she found him. He misinterpreted her focus.

"Fond of the horses, are you, miss?"

Melanie felt the color rising in her cheeks anew. She started to stammer a reply. "Well, this one is certainly handsome."

"That she is," he agreed. "She might prefer you to say she's pretty, but she appreciates any compliment headed in her direction."

Melanie's eyes flew to meet his gaze. She was mortified to realize he was teasing her. The color staining her cheeks now spread to engulf her entire face and neck. She wanted to fan her face to try to cool down but didn't want to draw any more attention to her discomfort. So, she attempted to turn the subject.

"Does she have a name?"

"Not as yet." He was watching Melanie as though she were a fascinating specimen. "It's my turn to come up with a name, but I haven't been able to think of anything yet. For now, we've been referring to her as the new foal but since we've got pregnant mares, I really need to get on with it."

Despite how awkward Melanie felt, she couldn't help laughing over his words. "I guess that will get confusing soon."

He turned his interested gaze back from the horse and focused on her. "Do you have some suggestions? I swear, I'm clear out of ideas."

"Oh, well, no, I wouldn't have the first clue where to start." Melanie stumbled out her reply. Turning her focus back to the animal, she marvelled. “Is she really just a baby?”

“Well, I’m ashamed to say, she’s actually heading for two years old. We haven’t had any of our mares breeding for a while as we’ve been focusing our attention on other endeavors. I’ve clearly been putting off the task of naming her.” He scratched the foal’s head as the animal leaned into him. “I’m growing too fond of the young lady, and I’m trying to keep from getting too attached. I think I’ve been putting off the task of naming her in the hopes that it’ll prevent me from falling completely in love.”

Melanie giggled. “Would that be so terrible? I’ve never known anyone to complain about being in love.”

“When you plan to sell the object of your affections, it’s a terrible idea.”

Melanie’s face fell. “Oh dear. I can see how that would be uncomfortable. This must be a serious disadvantage to your line of work. What shall you do?”

“Do you want to name her? That might help. Then it wouldn’t be me that did it, so maybe my heart won’t become quite so engaged.”

Joy and dread intermingled in Melanie’s heart. She had never been able to name anything. She had always allowed the children to name any pets they had acquired through the years. And of course, her mother had named the children, even little Henry, just before she died. But what a huge responsibility. And she didn’t want to love the horse either. What good would that be to her poor abused heart?

"Oh, well, I don't know how I could possibly," she began to stumble out a response again.

"Well, at least think on it," the rancher replied, saving her from her discomfort. "Seeing as you're here, but you're planning to leave Annie with us, why don't you stay and spend some time? You can watch Baby Foal a bit and see if you have any ideas for names. And I'm certain Leandra would be glad for some company. She was mighty disappointed that she missed you when you called yesterday."

Melanie had been envisioning another quiet day alone, but she felt churlish to refuse.

"That's kind of you to say, sir."

"Not kind at all, it's the truth. Most of the reason Leandra wants to return East is because she's pining for the company of other adult females. You'd be doing us a mighty big favor if you would bide a while."

Now there was no way she could refuse. She could feel that her smile was a little weak, but she offered it anyway as she answered, "It would be a pleasure, in that case."

He nodded abruptly, and Melanie wondered if she ought to excuse herself from his presence. Why was she always so awkward? What was she supposed to do? She wasn't sure if her desperate questions were written on her face, but he answered them anyway.

"Would you like to help with her training while you think of a name? Leandra is probably just getting up so she won't be ready for a visit for a spell."

Melanie was surprised at the offer, yet her awkwardness eased slightly. Not that she had the first clue what she could possibly have to say to the man, she thought, even as she fought the urge to brush the lock of hair back from his brow as it fell down with his movements.

Again, he alleviated her discomfort. “You said you don’t have much experience with horses. Does that mean you’ve never ridden?”

She shook her head. “My father bought a pair of horses to pull his carriage a few years ago, but I didn’t have anything to do with the care of them. We couldn’t even keep them where we lived. He had to board them at the livery stables. And I didn’t even ride in the carriage all that often.”

He looked at her strangely but didn’t pry. She felt the flush creeping back into her face. “The carriage was for taking him to visit his customers, not for my use. I needed to stay home with the children, anyway.”

As though he could tell there was much she left out in her explanation, he again didn’t pry, for which she was deeply grateful. It was all she could do to bear up under the searching glance he cast her, as though he were assessing her thoughts.

“It doesn’t much matter if you’re experienced or not, but try not to be afraid. Horses can sense it, and it makes them skittish.”

“Telling me not to be afraid doesn’t really do much to alleviate my fears, sir.”

His chuckle set the butterflies fluttering in her belly. “I can see why you would say that, and I apologize.” He produced a carrot from his back pocket. “She’s been after this all morning. You can make fast friends with her by offering it to her.” He showed Melanie how to hold her hand in a safe way to offer the treat to the large animal.

Melanie was fascinated with the softness of the horse's nose. "Can I pet her?"

"Of course. She'll love you forever if you scratch her here between her ears. But gently. Horses' ears are very flexible and sensitive. It's a large part of why they can be so skittish. They have keen eyesight and hearing, so they can be easily frightened."

"Hello, lovely," Melanie crooned as the animal tried to cuddle with her, butting her head against her chest. She couldn't prevent her giggle despite the fact the large animal's affection nearly knocked her over. The rancher's answering grin sent shivers down Melanie's spine.

Part of her found the experience stimulating and delicious. But another part of her wished she had stayed home. Melanie could feel her face tightening as she tried to think of something to say, but her mind was a blank. Not to mention, the flutters in her stomach were not at all pleasant, and she fought for breath.

"Now that you've made friends, do you think you could hold onto her lead while I get the saddle?"

"What?" she squeaked. "How could you possibly think I could hold on to her if she has a mind to leave? In case you haven't noticed, there's a significant size difference between us."

The slow grin he offered as he cast an assessing gaze over her and the horse made her take another step back.

"As a matter of fact, I did happen to notice that you're no bigger than a tadpole." Melanie blinked at his comparison, but he carried on. "But it won't make a difference. Now that Baby Foal has decided that you're her friend, she'll stay with you. Besides, despite their sharp vision, or maybe because of it, she doesn't really realize how very little you are. Horses are remarkably obedient animals. Unless she gets spooked by something, she will listen to whatever you have to say. Of course, the saddle might spook her, so I'll stay close by."

Melanie didn't find his words overly reassuring, but she was of the opinion that she would die of embarrassment if she walked away before she died of injuries if she stayed, so she forced her feet to stay still and took the leather lead he handed her.

Before she realized it, time had passed without too much awkwardness. Melanie was ridiculously proud of herself as she continued to stand still, talking softly to the horse as Mr. Miller had slowly, gently placed the saddle on her back. The horse had shuffled her feet, flicked her ears and tail, and tossed her head a little, but she had tolerated the pressure. Mr. Miller had also crooned soft words of encouragement to the large animal to keep her aware of his presence and comfort her as well. Melanie had found it comforting too and had to work at keeping her eyes away from him.

Finally, Mr. Miller removed the saddle, took the lead off the horse's head, and turned her free with a gentle slap on her rump. Without the horse between them, Melanie was once again left feeling tongue tied.

"You were of great help, Miss Jones, thank you so much for your assistance." He paused as though waiting for her to reply, but all she could do was bob her head bashfully and look away. "Have you been able to think of any ideas for her name or were you too busy telling her stories?"

Melanie knew he was teasing her, but she was swamped with mortification. She had forgotten he was listening and had just been spouting foolish nonsense to the horse. Melanie wanted the ground to swallow her but struggled for coherent thought in case that didn't conveniently happen.

Clearing her throat helped her get words starting to flow. "All the ideas I've thought of are rather too obvious and trite. For example, I thought Star for the white marking on her forehead or Boots for the white on her legs. Or Brownie for the obvious reason of her color. But she seems to be too special for a mundane name. We could maybe come up with something from the Latin equus or caballus. Or even Aethon might be a good name. It's still for the marking on her forehead but far more interesting than Star. Of course, it might be a male name. If we're going to stick with Latin we could go with Gemmula and call her Gem for short since, she really is a jewel." Melanie was starting to feel like she was babbling and wished she could bite off her tongue. She managed to rein it in, and silence fell between them. "You probably shouldn't have asked me," she muttered. "All my ideas are ridiculous."

"Not a single one of them was ridiculous," he said in a firm tone. "Technically, the marking on her head is neither a star nor a blaze. In horse description, it's more like a stripe. But I still like all your name suggestions. I'm just surprised to find you are a scholar."

Melanie could feel the color ebbing and flowing in her face as she had paled in her mortification, but now hot embarrassment swept her. "I'm no scholar. Unfortunately, I didn't have much opportunity for schooling."

"Well then, how do you know Latin?" He sounded incredulous.

Melanie shrugged and offered an awkward chuckle. "I like to read. And learn. My brother went to school, and I had to help him with his studies."

When she finally glanced to his face for a brief moment, she was amazed to see that he appeared impressed, but she rejected her own observation and cast her gaze away. She must have been mistaken.

"Did your brother do well in school?"

"Fairly well," she answered, "when I could prevail upon him to sit still and do his studies. He couldn't see any sense in learning something like Latin, since he always knew he would be going into business with our father. Thankfully, he understood the need for mathematics, so that was far less of a struggle."

"You know your maths, too?"

Melanie shrugged again. "Somewhat." She was much too uncomfortable to discuss it further. "Do you think your sister might be ready to receive yet?"

"Oh, why yes, she probably is. I plumb forgot you were waiting to see her." He turned and began to lead her toward the house. "Come along, Annie will want to see you as well." He stopped in his tracks after a few strides and Melanie, hurrying to keep up with him, almost collided with him. As it was, she had to put out her hand to steady herself and encountered the tight muscles of his upper arm. She marveled at his strength even as she was pulling her hand back and trying to look anywhere else but him.

"Sorry to be so clumsy, Miss Jones," he apologized, even though it was her that hadn't been watching where she was going. "But I just thought of something in connection with Annie. If possible, it would be best if the girls think it's their idea for Annie to stay longer if you don't want her to realize there's something amiss with her mother."

Melanie, her mind still preoccupied with the man's physique, found her thoughts to be slow to catch up to his words. When she finally realized what he was getting at, she was impressed with his reasoning. "That's brilliant, sir, but how would we arrange that?"

"It shouldn't be too hard, my Mary doesn't have friends sleep over often, but when she does, she never wants their time together to end."

Chapter Five

Cole had never enjoyed a morning of horse training more. Even his late wife hadn't been quite so fascinating, he thought before chiding himself for such disloyal musings. But the young woman, he interrupted himself in his thoughts as he looked at her a bit closer. She wasn't exactly so young, he realized upon closer inspection. Her innocence and lack of experience made him think of her as young, but he could see that she must be in her mid-twenties. The perfect age, if you asked him. He had been in his mid-twenties as well when he had first come to Missouri and staked his claim on the land. He had returned to Boston to marry his wife, but his heart had belonged in the West for the last ten years.

He had loved his Sheila, of course. But it had been difficult living with someone who was so dissatisfied with the life they had chosen together. Cole stifled his sigh. The past was the past and needed to remain there. His attention returned to the conversation in front of him.

As he had suspected, Leandra was thrilled to have female company and was nearly talking Miss Jones' ear off. Cole grinned as he watched their visitor blinking at the onslaught of words headed her way. The pretty new arrival to town was clearly not dimwitted. She quickly realized that Leandra had plenty to say and didn't require a response, despite the questions she was asking. He was fascinated to see what he thought might be the first genuine smile to grace her face as Miss Jones seemed to relax subtly. The poor woman seemed to be a nervous little thing despite her professed delight to be in Missouri.

Cole wondered if he ought to leave the women to themselves, but he didn't get much company either, and he didn't have any pressing chores to care for, so he wanted to enjoy the visitor, too. Besides, he reminded himself, he had promised to help the little girls think it was their idea for Annie to stay. Thus reassured, he settled in to enjoy his tea.

Being well versed in his sister's stories and complaints, Cole didn't pay too close attention to her words, contenting himself with shifting his attention between the window that looked out over his land and their visitor's expressive face. If he had been questioned, he wouldn't have been able to say which view gave him more pleasure.

It was obvious Miss Jones wasn't completely comfortable. He wondered what had made her so awkward. It seemed to go in waves with the poor woman. When she forgot about herself, she was able to get beyond her issues, and conversation flowed freely, but when she grew self-conscious, she became tied for words. He was happy to see her relax into the flow of Leandra's words. Before his sister ran out of things to say, though, the two little girls spilled into the room, a jumble of small limbs, giggles, and exuberant energy. They tumbled to a stop when they spotted Miss Jones.

"Hello, Miss Jones." Cole was proud of his daughter for her polite greeting.

"Hello, Mary. Are you having a nice time with Annie?"

The little girl nodded vigorously while her gaze shifted between her father and their visitor. "You aren't here to take Annie away already are you?" she blurted out before biting her lip in indecision as she glanced at her father. "I'm sorry to be rude. But we're having lots of fun. And Annie really loves the puppies, don't you Annie?"

The other little girl looked nervously around the room, uncertainty written clearly on her petite features. Cole was surprised when Miss Jones quickly set the child at ease.

"Good morning, Annie, dear, how are you? I don't mean to interrupt your time with your friend. I just wanted to be certain that you were comfortable here, as you haven't slept over before."

It was the right thing to say for the little girl's face split into a wide smile and she nodded vigorously. "Oh, Miss Melanie, I'm having a grand time. We've been careful not to get hurt like the last time I played over at Suzie's place."

Miss Jones laughed. "Well, that's certainly a relief."

"Is that why you came to check on me?"

Miss Jones blinked. Cole was heartened by the observation that she clearly didn't want to lie to the little girl. "I just wanted to be sure that all was well." Cole had to rub his chin to disguise his amusement over her tactful answer. Despite not having her own offspring, she was clearly used to managing children.

The little girl took her answer in stride. She nodded acceptance. "You must come see the puppies."

"Are they absolutely darling?" Miss Jones asked, giving her attention completely to the little girls, including Mary in her question.

The two children were talking over each other, eager to share their tales with a receptive adult. Much to Cole's regret, Leandra didn't appreciate being cut out of the visitor's attention and soon interrupted.

"Girls, why don't you go back outside to play? We grownups are still finishing our tea."

Cole bit the edge of his tongue to prevent a smile from creasing his face as he watched Miss Jones absorb his sister's rudeness toward the children. She offered the little girls a kind smile.

"I'll join you outside shortly, and you can show me the puppies." Cole was impressed that she was so diplomatic. She didn't contradict the other adult, but she didn't exclude the children either.

Mary shifted from foot to foot as she looked expectantly at her father. "I'm not done playing with Annie, Papa. Can she stay over another night?"

Cole was pleased to see the other child's eyes light up. Obviously, Annie wasn't averse to the idea of staying another night. "Let Miss Jones and I talk about it, and I'll let you know, all right? When she comes out to see the puppies she'll tell you if Annie can stay longer."

He watched as his daughter's face fell, but he didn't want to give away that it had already been planned. He was fairly sure it was the right way of handling it and was pleased to watch as the visitor bent low and whispered to Annie. He could only guess that she was checking with the child to make sure she was agreeable to staying longer. Her vigorous nod to the affirmative set him at ease. He was surprised to feel anticipation toward the woman's next visit when she hadn't even left yet from this one.

Cole was feeling quite content until he glanced back toward his sister. Her face looked thunderous. Leandra was not pleased that the children hadn't yet left the room. Hoping to avoid an altercation, he quickly shooed the girls away. "Run along now, girls. Miss Jones will join you shortly."

With their giggles trailing behind them, the youngsters clattered from the room.

"Well now, where were we?" Leandra asked before resuming her monologue.

Cole contented himself with watching Miss Jones' face. He was relieved to see that while a myriad of feelings chased themselves across her features, uppermost appeared to be amusement. Rather than being offended by his sister's rudeness toward the children, it would appear she was accustomed to it and found it funny rather than off putting. Finally, his sister got to an interesting point.

"Well, Miss Jones, I must say, you are an exceptional conversationalist," his sister said, which caused their visitor to chuckle.

"That's terribly kind of you to say, Miss Miller." Miss Jones sounded sincere despite her amusement.

"But I don't think you have told me very much about yourself," Leandra observed. "How do you come to find yourself in this backward place? Surely you won't be staying for very long."

Cole watched as Miss Jones struggled to answer her question. She was too polite to contradict her hostess, but he was fairly certain she didn't consider Bucklin to be so very backward.

"Actually, Miss Miller," she began before being interrupted.

"Oh, you really must call me Leandra. We absolutely must be friends. I am so very glad to have another woman nearby."

Miss Jones' smile was warm. "Thank you, Leandra, I would be happy to be friends. And you must call me Melanie."

"Very well, Melanie. Tell me, what brought you to this dreadful place?"

Cole's gut clenched as he watched the pretty woman bite her lip before answering. Her smile was tentative as she began. "Actually, I haven't yet found anything to be dreadful since I arrived." Her tone was apologetic but firm. "My friend and I were volunteers at an orphanage in New York City and were assigned the task of accompanying a trainload of the orphans, who were coming out West to join new families here. We had already accompanied children on the trains a few times, but we felt that this time it was going to also be our turn to start new lives."

“Isn’t your family terribly disappointed to have you so far away?”

“I don’t have any family that needs me.” Her answer was simple but stark. “My mother has been gone for fifteen years. She died giving birth to my brother. My father died a year ago. In between my brother and me, I have a sister. She married six months ago. Life with my brother was no longer bearable, so I decided to get a fresh start here in Missouri.”

“Oh, my dear, I am right sorry.” Despite her selfish ways, Leandra still had a kind heart and hadn’t intended to dredge up painful thoughts for her new friend.

“Don’t be sorry, Leandra. It just is what it is. Mrs. Carter and I are having a fine time getting settled and starting up our seamstress business. She is delighted to have her new daughter, and I am happy to have a life of my own.”

Leandra nodded although she didn’t look as though she believed their guest. But she didn’t dwell on it for very long. She launched into her own thoughts, which Miss Jones politely listened to for a few more minutes before she rose to her feet.

“It has been such a pleasure to make your acquaintance, Leandra, and I thank you for your hospitality. But I really mustn’t keep you from your chores any longer, and I ought to be on my way.”

Again, Cole stifled his amusement as his sister looked confused. She didn’t do very much around his spread, so there weren’t many chores she would be doing once their guest left. He was surprised to see amusement twinkling in Miss Jones' eyes as though she knew what he was thinking.

"Thank you so much, again, for keeping Annie another night. Mrs. Carter is anxious to keep the child from worrying about her absence. Having her here is an excellent distraction. Hopefully, Annie needn't ever know that her mom hasn't been at home. I'm just so grateful that she wasn't suspicious why it was me checking on her rather than her mother."

"I'm just as glad to have Mary occupied as well, so we might as well say that it's a mutual favor," Leandra answered. "Do promise you'll stay for another tea when you come round to collect the child."

Miss Jones smiled but didn't completely accept. "Perhaps you'll have the pleasure of making the acquaintance of Annie's mother. I'll be sure to tell her to plan for tea if it's she who comes to collect Annie."

Leandra looked pleased at the prospect of another visitor as she followed her to the door. "Either way, don't be a stranger."

Cole accompanied Miss Jones as she stepped out onto the porch. Leandra appeared to be torn. She wanted to prolong her time with their visitor, but she didn't like to be around the animals. When she saw that Melanie was heading toward the barn, she stepped back into the house.

"I'm sorry about my sister," Cole began but was quickly cut off by a flash of what looked like anger in Miss Jones' face.

"You needn't apologize for her. Your sister is a dear."

Cole was taken aback and frowned. “I wouldn’t describe her in that way, myself.”

“Well you ought to. Didn’t you say she came out her to help you with your daughter when your wife passed?”

He sputtered a little bit but didn’t know how to reply. She carried on, all trace of awkwardness gone, at least for the moment. “Your gratitude should make you see that she has left all that is comfortable for her, and she is struggling just like everyone else. She is a dear,” Melanie repeated, her firm tone brooking no argument.

Cole grinned. “I see you’re the type who thinks all women should be loyal to each other.”

His words seemed to deflate her inexplicable anger, and she offered him a weak grin. “I am, yes. It might make me a little unreasonable at times.”

With a shrug and a nod Cole admitted, “Maybe so, but I think it’s admirable anyway. And since I love my sister despite her ways, I appreciate your loyalty on her behalf.” They walked in silence for a beat before he added, “And you needn’t thank us for keeping Annie. As you might have noticed, Leandra doesn’t have all that much patience for noisy play, so it’s good for Mary to have company to be able to play out of doors. I think she sometimes finds it boring to try to play by herself all the time despite what an imagination the girl has.”

Miss Jones nodded but looked uncomfortable once more. Cole was relieved they had reached the barn and could hear the girls playing in an empty stall.

Cole was impressed once more when she kept her voice low but called out to the girls. “Hello? I’m here to see the puppies.” She had the sense not to disturb the animals even if she hadn’t been on a farm before.

The two giggling girls called from the stall they were in. “Over here, Miss Melanie.”

When they reached the partition, Cole watched Melanie’s face rather than looking in. He was quite familiar with his daughter’s appearance and had already spent time with the puppies himself, so he wanted to enjoy the woman’s first experience with the young animals. He was so glad he did. The wonder and joy that spread across her face as she watched the little girls playing with the wriggling balls of fur was a pleasure to behold. It was obvious the woman had a deep sense of inner peace despite her occasional social awkwardness.

“Aren’t they the most darling things you’ve ever seen, Miss Melanie?”

“That they are, Annie,” the woman promptly replied. “But doesn’t their mother mind you playing with her babies?” She was obviously a worrier.

“No,” Mary answered simply.

This was obviously not enough of an answer for Miss Jones. She turned a face full of inquiry toward Cole, and he quickly soothed her concerns. “The puppies’ mother is a sweet, gentle dog that we’ve had since Mary was a baby. She’s quite used to Mary’s attentions. And this is her third litter of puppies, so she isn’t a nervous mother.”

“But they look so tiny. Are you certain the girls won’t hurt them?”

Cole grinned at her hushed tone. He wasn't sure if she was trying to avoid hurting the children's feelings or if she didn't want to disturb the puppies. He found it endearing.

"Puppies are tough despite how little they look. But they actually aren't so very young. It's not as though they were just born. They are already almost three weeks old. They can't stray far from their mother, but it won't hurt them to socialize with the girls."

Cole grinned when she turned her attention back to the puppies after she had searched his gaze for confirmation of his sincerity. It seemed to him as though her gaze on the little dogs was full of longing.

"Would you like to hold one yourself?"

"Oh, no, I couldn't possibly."

He chuckled softly. "Is that your response to everything?"

Her cheeks turned pink, and she looked mortified as she turned to him but then quickly cast her gaze to the ground in a bashful manner. Cole felt bad for teasing her. He quickly reminded her, "It's what you said about helping me with the foal, and about naming the horse."

Her cheeks remained brightly colored, but comprehension flooded her face. "I've never held a puppy before. Any animals we ever had were stray cats my brother or sister found. Cats, when they finally allow you to handle them, are either watchful and guarded or relaxed and prone. Those little balls of fur look like they would wiggle right out of your hands if you aren't very careful."

Cole could see that she had actually given the matter some thought, and he felt even worse about teasing her. “Why don’t you sit down on that overturned pail, then you’ll be able to hold the pup in your lap. I’ll grab one from the girls for you.”

He couldn’t help smiling as the woman looked nervous but eager while he grabbed what he hopped was the least squirmy of the litter. When their hands connected as he settled the warm bundle in her lap, Cole felt a jolt that he quickly fought to ignore. It suddenly dawned on him that he was attracted to the pretty woman, and that just wouldn’t do. She obviously had emotional issues to which he wasn’t privy. And he had enough emotional females on his hands with his bitter sister and motherless daughter. He didn’t need another one, no matter how soft and sweet she seemed or how kind she was as she crooned gently to the small animal cradled in her hands.

ꟿ

Melanie stared down at the brown ball of fluff in her lap. She was holding a puppy! The one thing her sister had always wished for, she thought wistfully before a grin split her face when the little animal started to lick and chew on her fingers. In that instant, Melanie’s heart melted. How would she live without the warm little bundle in her life? She quickly chastised herself for the ridiculous thought. *You’ve managed to reach the ripe old age of twenty-five without ever once having a puppy in your life. You can certainly live through the experience of playing with one for a moment and then giving him back.*

But oh, how she didn't want to return the little creature. Not that she had any need for such a complication, she reminded herself. *Just think of how you reacted when Katie said she wanted to adopt Annie. You thought the younger woman was foolish. And now, you wish you could have a dog? You scoop this little bundle up and return him right this minute, Melanie Jones!* The silent lecture didn't help her very much. She scooped up the little animal but instead of handing him back to the rancher, she cuddled it closer to her chest, a sense of peace permeating her as the puppy licked her once more and then settled down as though it were going to sleep. Melanie was so surprised she didn't know what to make of the development.

She blinked and met Mr. Miller's gaze as he watched attentively. Melanie wondered if he was worried she would hurt the animal. His smile did disconcerting things to her tummy while also assuring her he wasn't overly worried about the pup.

"I think the girls tuckered him out before we even got here. I hope you aren't disappointed that he isn't a little more playful."

Melanie was pretty sure her gaze was full of longing as she returned it to the sleeping animal. "Not at all. He's almost as restful as a purring cat."

"Do you prefer cats?" His tone led her to think he wasn't as impressed with her preferences.

She shrugged. "I wouldn't say I prefer them. I just have never held a dog before. We did have cats, though. In the city, it wasn't uncommon to have rodents invade. It was always a challenge to have a balanced animal – one that was able to hunt, but also would willingly accept the affections of my little sister and brother."

Again the man grinned, and the flutter it caused in her chest made Melanie surge to her feet while being careful not to disturb the sleeping puppy. "I really ought to be going," she stated firmly without meeting Mr. Miller's gaze. "Annie, if you're sure you want to stay another day, I will let your mother know that you are behaving nicely and having a good time."

"Thank you, Miss Melanie," the child answered politely despite being preoccupied.

Melanie was amused by the youngster but felt her smile fading as she turned to Mr. Miller to take her leave. "Thank you so much for your assistance, sir. Mrs. Carter and I are both very grateful."

"I told you, no thanks necessary. I appreciate Mary having a little friend to play with."

"Very well, then." Melanie needed to be brusque in order to excuse herself. "I will wish you a good day, then, Mr. Miller." She gently passed the puppy into his large hands, turned on her heel, and marched out of the barn without a backward glance.

Chapter Six

Melanie was berating herself every step of the way home. *How could you be so ridiculous as to go and get all aflutter about a handsome man? You are surely much too old for such nonsense. It's not as though you have any interest in pursuing a courtship with him. He's a father, for land's sakes! The father of a girl child besides, so you can be sure he'll be after having a son. No, Miss Melanie Jones, you are to get all thoughts of handsome ranchers with deep voices and cleft chins out of your head. You are a senseless woman who can barely leave the house. What you do not need is fluttery feelings about a man.*

Trying to cast her thoughts elsewhere, Melanie thought about the animals she had seen while visiting the Miller place. The horses had been magnificent. Having so rarely been that close to one, she hadn't realized just how majestic the beasts were. No wonder most people were mad about them, she thought with a wry twist of her lips. Perhaps she and Katie ought to think of getting a gig or carriage of some sort and a lovely horse to pull it. It would certainly make Katie's task of visiting their customers much easier. Of course, if you have a horse, you have to know how to care for it. Melanie shuddered slightly. She didn't think she could cope with the responsibility. It was best to think of something other than the lovely creatures she had spent time with, she decided with a little shake of her head.

She forced her mind to the tasks ahead of her. She still had several hours of good light, so she should be able to get ahead in their work. If Katie wasn't home soon, Melanie would be fully caught up, and her partner would have to go visiting right away to make the deliveries and take the measurements for more orders.

A stirring of guilt marred her thoughts as she settled in to her labors. Maybe it wasn't fair to Katie that she was the one who had to face all the customers. *But if I'm pulling my full share of the sewing, or even more than my share, then surely it balances out, doesn't it?* Katie had certainly never complained. She even said she enjoys the visits. Except for that time a couple days ago when she visited Mrs. Jenkins and the poor old woman fainted on Katie. That wasn't comfortable for either of them.

Thinking of that mishap caused Melanie to begin speculating about Katie and the doctor. They sure had ended up in one another's company many times recently. *I think Katie protests a trifle too much when I tease her about Doctor Jeffries. Perhaps I shouldn't be doing that though*, Melanie mused. *It's not as though I'm anxious to be rid of her. If she marries, that would leave me in an awkward position. I might have to face the customers for myself.* Melanie's stomach clenched, and it felt as though her heart skipped a beat or two. *More thoughts that cannot be borne*, she thought with frustration. *I really ought to figure out how to deal with people once more. But not today*, she argued with herself as she caught sight of her small house. She had dealt sufficiently with enough people for one day. *With how handsome Mr. Miller is, surely that encounter must count for more than one person. And now you're keeping score?* She mocked herself silently.

Shoving all the disquieting thoughts to the side, Melanie set to work. She was soon caught up in her project and relaxed into her tasks. The time flew by and before she knew it, it was too dark to see. As she put everything away and fastened her windows tight, the thought skittered through her mind that she didn't love being completely alone at night. *You really ought to try to dissuade Katie from a potential match with the doctor*, she reasoned before rejecting the disloyal thought. No matter how afraid she had become of people, she couldn't begrudge potential happiness for her friend. Either Katie would remain her business partner or Melanie would have to figure something out. She had been managing to figure things out for years, she could keep right on doing so, she assured herself. With a firm twist she pushed the bolt into place to lock the door. It didn't seem likely that people barred their doors in these parts, but it would keep Melanie's mind more at ease, so it would be foolhardy not to do it.

Cole had watched the pretty woman walk away with very mixed feelings. He was a little shocked that she had left without a backward glance. He had thought they were having an enjoyable time together that morning working with the horse and then visiting with Leandra. But the woman was easy to spook. Worse than the horses, he thought irritably. She might be good looking, but he didn't need any further complications in his life, he reminded himself. Sheila was complicated, and look where that got him.

Glancing down at the puppy he still held in his arms, he smiled. The silly woman had seemed terrified of the small animal. Or perhaps not truly terrified of the pup, maybe she was terrified of having feelings for it. He could relate to that after the conversation they'd had that morning about Baby Foal.

He really ought to pick a name for the poor little thing. *What had she said for potential names?* he asked himself. She had some really intelligent suggestions. Who would have thought that the pretty face hid such a brilliant mind? He had enjoyed hearing her mention some Latin words. It had been so long since he had felt intellectually stimulated. Perhaps that would explain his unprecedented reaction to Miss Jones. He just wasn't used to talking to pretty women, or well-read people.

Feeling satisfied that he had reached the proper conclusion, he set those thoughts aside and turned his attention back to his daughter and her little friend. Miss Jones' gratitude for his keeping Annie had made him terribly uncomfortable. He should have been the one to be thanking her. Or rather Annie's mother, Mrs. Carter, he thought. With all the ranting Leandra had been doing lately, he was glad to be able to send Mary outside with a friend to play. The less she had to hear of her aunt's vitriol, the better. Cole sincerely hoped the visit with Miss Jones had done his sister enough good that she would lay off her angry ramblings for a while.

As he walked into the house, his hopes were dashed.

"This god forsaken place." She was clearly deep into a rant and hadn't required an audience to get started. Cole was both disappointed and relieved over the development. If she didn't need an audience, and the visit with Miss Jones this morning hadn't set her onto a saner path, it was obvious the poor dear must be actually ill, rather than just distempered. It helped him have greater sympathy for her, but also made him realize it was time to send her away. He couldn't have her around Mary in such a state.

After checking to make sure Leandra wasn't in danger of harming herself, he set off for the train station, composing the telegram in his head as he marched to the office. His heart ached over the thought of sending his sister away and reducing his family to the count of two. He hoped Mary would be all right without another female in the house. But being with just him was better than living with someone not of sound mind, he assured himself.

With a nod and a small coin, his message was sent. Someone from Boston would be on their way to collect her shortly. He was glad he had written to his family earlier to tell them this was a possibility. Cole would just have to keep his sister calm and safe for two more weeks at the most. Now to decide if it was best to tell her or not. While she had been raving about her hatred of Missouri for ages, she had always been free to leave. There was obviously something still holding her here. Cole worried that she might go a little madder if he told her she was to leave. He would have to broach the subject gently. Or maybe he could enlist help.

The rest of the day passed in a blur as he split his time between tending to his chores and checking on the girls. After the evening meal, Leandra had taken herself to her room so he didn't think he had to concern himself with her for the time being. It was a joy for him to see the wide grin splitting his daughter's face as she tumbled into bed with her little visitor. The two girls were asleep before their heads had even hit the pillow, it seemed. Cole could feel that his smile was a little melancholy as he gazed at the two little sleeping forms. His heart ached for both of them not having their mothers. But it didn't seem to weigh on either of their minds today as they had played at full speed all day and were now sleeping the sleep of the innocent.

Cole didn't begrudge them their innocent sleep, but he did envy them for it. He knew, despite the bone deep fatigue he was feeling, he wouldn't be able to reach the land of nod quite so easily. There were too many thoughts swirling through his mind. One of them was an idea his sister-in-law had planted there in her last letter. She had offered to help arrange a wife for him. The idea held merit. He truly did want a mother for Mary. But bringing yet another woman out here? Just the thought of it made his stomach ache. So far he had tried it twice, and neither time had worked out so well. Sheila, despite making the choice to marry him and knowing it would entail moving to Missouri, had struggled with settling in the West. And Leandra had hated Bucklin from the moment she had stepped foot off the train. At first, her devotion to Mary had helped her overcome her feelings about the western town, but her negative feelings had steadily increased despite her love for her family. Since Mary had started school, Leandra's decline had picked up speed. There was no way he could risk sending for another woman from the East. But there were so few single women available.

Punching his pillow into a more comfortable shape, Cole tried to arrange himself in the best position for sleep, but it continued to elude him.

He had heard there were other women who had arrived on the train. Other than Miss Jones, that was. While she was beautiful and intelligent, her anxious state didn't appeal to him. He had enough from his sister; he couldn't risk it in a wife. Marriage was forever, after all. Or until death. And he didn't wish to be widowed a second time. But Miss Jones' business partner was a widow, from what he understood. She might be worth making the acquaintance of. And since she had adopted Annie, she was obviously not averse to children, even other people's children, which boded well for his little Mary. Besides the fact that Mary and Annie were already close friends. It could almost be deemed meant to be. Of course, if there had already been one train load of children brought out from New York, there was a chance there would be more. And if this batch was escorted by single women, then maybe more would be on their way.

Rolling over again, Cole turned his mind to another idea. Maybe he ought to forget the idea of a mother for Mary. While Miss Jones seemed anxious and fidgety, she had been kind to the little girls. Maybe Cole could prevail upon her to take an interest in his daughter. All she really needed was a little bit of attention from an adult female, especially in a few years when she gets into the awkward phases of which he knew nothing. Maybe he should just ask about adopting some older boys to help him with the land. He didn't want Mary to be an only child, and he wanted someone to be able to leave his land to when the time came. He didn't want Mary to feel obliged to stay here, but a son would probably take to the work just like he had, he reasoned to himself.

Thus settled with a bit of a plan formed in his mind, Cole was finally able to drift into sleep. If it wasn't as restful as he had hoped, he didn't let it trouble him overmuch. He hopped out of bed at his usual time as soon as the cock began to crow at first light.

ꙮ

Melanie was fidgeting. It was a telltale sign of her nerves, and she hated doing it, but it helped dispel the nervous energy. And there was no one around to take notice anyway. She had stopped by the Mitchells' house where Katie was stuck helping the doctor care for the deathly ill couple. Well, not so deathly ill after all, Melanie amended. Katie was fairly certain she would be able to return home that evening, and she hoped that Annie would be home when she got there. Melanie sighed. That meant she needed to be the one to go collect Annie. And explain to the child why her new mother wasn't at home waiting for her. Her stomach cramped just thinking about it. She started kneading a batch of bread in an attempt to dispel the anxiety.

Within a few hours, she had baked two dozen cookies, three loaves of bread, a pie, and was elbows deep in the preparations for a stew. Besides, all the sewing projects were completed. She had pretty much been in a frenzy. It was ridiculous. All because she didn't want to face the handsome rancher again, which was also ridiculous. Altogether, she, Melanie Jones, was ridiculous. If her dear mama were alive to see her now, she would surely be disappointed in her. Then again, if her dear mama were alive, she probably wouldn't have turned into a madwoman, she thought with a twist of her lips. Ah well, it must be borne. At least she had baked goods that she could take as a distraction for her sure-to-be-crazy behavior.

Katie would be pleased with how much of their work Melanie had managed to complete on her own. Maybe that would keep her from noticing that she had also depleted their flour supply, Melanie thought with a jolt of guilt. Good thing it wasn't overly expensive despite their isolated location. And with all the work she had done, surely they could afford some extra flour. Melanie began to fear that her circular thoughts really were a sign that she was losing her mind. She really ought to make a greater effort to not be so isolated. Perhaps she should have investigated whether the town offered religious services, since this was Sunday. But in the state of mind she had found herself after Katie asked her to collect Annie, it was doubtful she would have been welcomed in any congregation.

Melanie snorted at her own dark thoughts. *Now you really are being ridiculous, Miss Melanie,* she thought with a grin. *You might be a little off kilter, but surely no one could argue that anything you have said or done is completely beyond the pale. Now pull yourself together, go comb your hair, and head out to collect your friend's daughter. It shouldn't be so very challenging.*

Thus admonished, even if it was only by her own self, she set about righting her appearance and went on the prescribed errand. She dragged her feet a little as she neared the property, for which she again took herself to task. It really wouldn't do to be out after dark with Annie in tow. And it would be a long walk for the little girl, so she really ought to hurry. She brightened when she realized that could also be her excuse why she couldn't linger over collecting the youngster.

She had never walked so far during her days living in the city, but she was glad to observe that she was growing stronger each day. The long walk didn't even tire her anymore. And when she wasn't lagging with reluctance, her speeds were improving as well. While she had been thinking she and Katie should get a horse and wagon, she was glad to see that it wouldn't be a necessity, at least not for getting around the town. Of course, to visit anyone further afield, it would certainly come in handy. She certainly wouldn't want Katie to have to go much further afield than Mr. Miller's spread to visit any customers or to take Annie to play with friends.

Melanie could see the girls notice her from a distance. She had to bite her lip to hide her amusement as the two were clearly torn in their reactions to seeing her. The children were clearly pleased to see a familiar friendly face but also realized that Miss Jones' arrival spelled the end of their playtime together. Annie, still getting comfortable with her position within her household, didn't voice her disappointment, but her friend did enough complaining for the both of them.

"It's not even dark yet, Miss Jones, can't you stay a wee bit longer? Annie and I have been having too much fun for it to end yet."

"Mary, I'm sorry to disappoint you, but it would be best for us to get home before it gets dark. And surely you have things you'll need to get done in preparation for school tomorrow."

The little girl hung her head and scuffed her feet in disappointment. Melanie hated to sadden the children, so she quickly added, "I'm really happy to hear you had such a good time together. We'll be sure to arrange for you to play together again soon. Maybe you can even come to stay over at our house some time soon."

“Really, Miss Jones? That would be grand.” The little girls’ exuberance made all three of them giggle. A fourth, deeper laugh joined in, startling Melanie.

“Good evening, Miss Jones. I see you’ve come to collect your charge. Would you like to come in for a cup of tea before you leave?”

Melanie made a show of glancing at the position of the sun before shaking her head. “Thank you for the offer, but I wouldn’t want to get caught out in the dark, and I don’t want Annie to have to run all the way home.”

“We could hitch up the wagon and take you home,” Mr. Miller offered.

Melanie was surprised at the chivalrous offer. “Surely that would be too much of an imposition.”

“Not at all,” he assured her, much to her consternation.

Feeling the hot color splashing up her cheeks, Melanie tried again to decline. “I wouldn’t want you to have to put the horses to work on our behalf, and the walk will burn off the last of our energies so we’ll sleep like logs tonight, right Annie?”

“I’ve never ridden in a wagon before,” Annie answered, having no idea that Melanie was trying desperately to get away from the Millers.

Realizing it would be churlish to refuse further, Melanie accepted with as much good grace as she could manage. “Thank you for your continued kindness.”

She was grateful that the task of hitching two horses to a wagon didn’t take nearly as long as she would have expected. Before too many awkward minutes had passed, she was being handed up onto the seat, and the girls were clambering in behind. It was only when he was passing her Annie's small bag of belongings that Melanie realized she still held the parcel of cookies and bread she had brought for the Millers. Again her cheeks heated.

"How silly of me," she stammered. "I did some baking this afternoon and brought some for you."

Mr. Miller took an appreciative sniff. "I was hoping you were going to say that," he said with a grin, which only added to her discomfort as she realized he must have been able to smell the freshly baked items. His chuckle at her embarrassment inexplicably settled some of her nerves, and she joined him in laughing. He took the small sack from her hands but placed it under his seat instead of putting it in the house before they left. "I don't want it to disappear before we get back," he explained with a wink that only made Melanie giggle a little more.

His humor had managed to set her at ease. The fact that they were sitting side by side instead of having to face one another also helped her discomfort. And the children's constant chatter filled the silence between them. The ruts in the road, though, caused their legs to bump together at times, and Melanie worried whether she ought to try to move away. She was grateful when he finally spoke, easing her sense of disquiet.

"Is everything well with Mrs. Carter?" he asked, keeping his voice quiet so Annie wouldn't hear.

“She expects to be home tonight or tomorrow at the latest. Since she dearly wishes to see Annie, she asked that she be brought home. It seems the worst of the illness has passed, and she won’t be required any longer. And since Annie didn’t succumb to the illness before, the doctor expects she won’t this time either.”

“It’s a risk, though, bringing her home, isn’t it?”

Melanie shrugged, biting her lip. “I sure hope not.”

ꙮ

Cole watched the woman bite her lip and had to bite his own to choke back his reaction. He fought the urge to bring his hand up and rub his thumb along the abused skin. He knew she would not welcome such familiarity. He feared she would even jump from the wagon, he thought with amusement. She was a flighty little female. He really ought not be so powerfully attracted to her. Perhaps it was merely the lack of female companionship. Just imagine how forward he would become after his sister had left. He averted his eyes to control his impulses.

“Do you not fear for yourself?” he asked, still keeping his voice low, hoping the girls didn’t notice and think they were telling secrets.

“No.” Her answer was abrupt. “I have been exposed to the illness, but I wasn’t very sick when it swept through our building. I nursed many who died but for some reason, I was spared. I don’t fear death, though, except for the sadness it would bring to my sister.”

“That is rather macabre, isn’t it, Miss Jones?”

She shrugged. “I don’t search out death, Mr. Miller, but I’ve seen enough of it to think it more peaceful than life often is. But in this particular case, it would seem that Katie and I both have some level of immunity. As does Annie, for that matter. Her entire family died from the dread disease, and she didn’t even get a sniffle, poor little soul.”

He must have made a sympathetic noise of some sort because she finally turned her gaze his way and nodded as though in agreement with words unspoken.

“While family can be a trial, it is the source of all security when you are a child. I cannot bear to think on what the poor girl has gone through.”

“You have a soft heart, Miss Jones,” Cole commented begrudgingly.

His companion shrugged again. “I don’t really think so. Anyone would feel sympathy for the poor lass, I would think. And it takes nothing from me to feel empathy for her. I know what it is to lose my mother, and I was ten. I cannot imagine losing everyone at half that age.”

“My sweet girl lost her mother even earlier,” he commented.

Her glance seemed to be filled with approval as she replied, “At least your daughter has a doting father. That must surely make up for some of the difference. You do realize how very rare such a devoted father is, don’t you?”

Now it was Cole’s turn to shrug. “She is my life. I will do anything for her.”

There was a beat of silence while they both absorbed his words. He then continued, "Speaking of which, I have a favor to beg of you."

Her answering smile held a tinge of mischief despite the misgivings in her eyes. "It is only fair that favors be exchanged, I suppose."

"I do not mean it as a tit for tat, I assure you."

He was relieved to see her smile, but she still appeared wary.

"It is about Mary," he began, wishing he hadn't brought it up at this time but wondered when he would have another opportunity to speak with the timid woman. He could see that he had caught her attention and she was receptive to hear what he had to ask. "I have sent for someone to come for Leandra."

The expression on Miss Jones' face revealed that she recognized what a difficult decision that must have been, but she waited to comment until he had finished his explanation.

"I worry for Mary without a woman to answer certain questions for her," he explained as he felt heat rise in his cheeks again.

"Well, I think you're safe for a few years. The child is only five or six, after all."

"Yes, but for all my care of her, I still think girls need women in their lives. There is a shortage in Bucklin."

He felt her gaze searching his face and couldn't be sure what she saw there.

"Are you asking me to be a surrogate aunt to your daughter?" she asked, her voice gentle and understanding, which was remarkable considering her usual nervousness.

He was relieved. “Yes, that’s it exactly.”

She didn’t accept immediately, which made him uncomfortable.

“I will have to explain to you one day why I hesitate, Mr. Miller. I can assure you it is not out of a disregard for your sweet daughter. And while I hesitate, I will not decline. I suppose if I can find it in my heart to allow Annie in, I can find room for Mary as well. Perhaps it will even be easier for there to be two rather than just one.”

He didn’t fully understand what she was saying, but contented himself that she had accepted. He reasoned that her obvious emotions would make her even more empathetic for Mary, and that was all he could ask for.

As they neared her small house with its neat little yard, he had to end the conversation lest the girls take note. “Thank you, Miss Jones, I will be forever in your debt.” This brought a grin to her face.

“That sounds promising,” she replied, causing him to laugh. For all her strangeness, he found her fascinating.

“You keep a tidy home, Miss Jones,” he complimented as he helped her climb down from the wagon.

“Thank you,” she answered, pride evident in her voice. “I cannot take all the credit, but both Katie and I are so happy about having a house to ourselves that we cannot cease puttering around and grooming it. The only thing we lack are flowers. I shall have to figure out how to move some from the field into our front yard. It would surely brighten up the place."

"I could probably help you with that. I have a shovel and some sacks."

Cole was amused to see her trying to get away from his offer. "Oh, no, Mr. Miller, I wouldn't want to trouble you in such a way. I'm quite certain Katie and I will be able to figure it out quite nicely on our own."

"So you find it promising for me to be in your debt, but have no wish for me to try to pay that off?"

Her face turned red, but she actually giggled as he handed her down from the wagon. "I think it is much better to keep the favor owing, just in case I ever truly have need of something."

Cole laughed. She was such a strange woman, mercurial and yet pleasant. He enjoyed her company despite her awkward ways. "You have an interesting philosophy, Miss Jones."

"Well, thank you for bringing us home. We'll now have a more comfortable evening." She was clearly dismissing him, and he was more disappointed than he should be. She looked down at the little girl by her side. "Do you have anything to say to Mr. Miller?"

His daughter's friend looked nervous but managed to look him in the face as she politely thanked him. "I had lots of fun. Thank you for letting me visit Mary and the puppies."

Cole leaned over and took the child's hand in a light shake. "It was our pleasure to have you, Annie. You are welcome to come over any time."

It was endearing how she grinned and turned her body from side to side in a display of bashfulness. The two adults exchanged amused glances.

"Goodnight, Mary, goodnight, Mr. Miller," Miss Jones called out in a sweet voice as she shepherded her young charge into the house.

Cole stood and watched until they were behind the closed front door. When he glanced over at his daughter who had remained in the wagon, she was looking at him with a questioning expression on her face. He grinned again. He was making a cake of himself; even his daughter thought so.

Darkness was falling as they neared home. "Did you enjoy having Annie around?"

"Oh yes, Papa, it was great fun. It's funny that there are so many things she's never done before, like playing with puppies, but she's game for trying. I like having someone to show things to. I wish Mama had gotten me a brother or sister before she died."

Cole blinked, unsure how to handle this unanswerable comment. "You don't think it might be annoying to have a younger brother or sister always under your feet?"

She shrugged. "Maybe a little bit, but it's probably better than always being by myself."

Cole's stomach clenched, and he fought a tide of fury at his dead wife. It was ridiculous to be angry with a dead woman. It's not as though she *meant* to die.

"Did you know Annie's 'dopted?" He was surprised by her turn of the subject.

"I did. Do you know what adopted means?"

"She said she lost her mama and papa and then got a new mama." She paused, obviously pondering the situation. "It's too bad she didn't get a new papa, too, but I s'pose it's better than not having anyone."

There was another pause while he could almost see her mind processing her thoughts.

"Maybe we should 'dopt someone, Papa."

He should have seen that coming, as he had thought it himself, but he was surprised that his daughter had arrived at that conclusion. Obviously, it wasn't something to take on lightly, but he decided to probe a little bit further.

"Would you prefer we adopt a brother or a sister for you?"

She responded with a serious face. "Maybe one of each would be a good idea. Or two boys and a girl so that we're even."

Now he couldn't hold back his chuckle. "You want to really expand our family now, don't you?"

She shrugged and then offered very mature logic for such a small girl. "The boys could help you with chores, and if I had a girl to help me, Aunt Leandra might be happier."

"Adding three extra people to our family might be a lot to get used to, though, don't you think?"

"Prob'ly. But it prob'ly would be lots of fun, too."

The grin that accompanied her words was infectious, and they arrived home in good humor. Cole had already made the arrangements for his sister to leave. He could see sense in his daughter's words about having help on the ranch. But taking responsibility for three additional children all at once was a little much for him to consider. Maybe he would ask Miss Jones the next time they crossed paths. She would know if was even feasible to consider. And she might have some words of wisdom as to things to consider. Thus settled, he was in a fine mood when he entered his home. But, it didn't last.

"Where have you been? I've been worried sick about you. It's late. Already dark. How could you leave me here by myself? Anything could have happened to me." Each word was louder and shriller than the one before. By the time Cole managed to step in and take control, Mary was in tears, and Leandra was wild eyed and wailing.

"Leandra, calm down." He wasn't sure if it was the best way to handle her, but he spoke with authority, which managed to cut through her hysteria and stemmed the flow of her words. "Nothing bad was going to happen to you. We weren't gone for very long. You were sleeping already when we left, so we thought we oughtn't disturb you, so we didn't tell you we were leaving. I'm sorry, we probably shouldn't have left you unannounced. But when Miss Jones arrived to collect Annie, Mary and I decided to give them a ride home so they wouldn't be out on their own in the dark."

"So, you were more concerned about the pretty stranger than about your own sister?" Leandra was turning mean in her anxious state.

Cole took a deep breath, trying to stay calm and collected. "Of course not, Leandra. You're my sister, and I care deeply about you. But you were safe here in the house. Those two would have been alone in the dark if we had allowed them to walk home. And little Annie was already tired after a long day of playing with our Mary. I thought it would be too much for them, and the neighborly thing was to give them a ride. What would you have had me do?" He was hoping to appeal to her logic.

"You should've told me they were here. You know I always want to have a visit with any women we might chance upon."

"Didn't you know that Mrs. Carter or Miss Jones would be coming to collect Annie?"

Apparently, she was done with his attempts at logic. She burst into tears. "You just don't understand," she bellowed before running into her room and slamming the door.

There was an eerie silence that followed the loud thud while Cole and Mary stood frozen in their places. Cole could barely bring himself to look at his daughter. He should have contacted his family weeks ago. He would have never wanted his child to witness a scene such as this.

"I guess we shoulda told her," Mary said, a shrug in her voice, as though her aunt's explosion were a thing of little note.

Cole grinned. "I guess so." He paused for a moment, waiting to see if Mary would have any further reaction. When she just smiled at him, he blinked before changing the subject. "Off to bed with you, little miss. You have to be wide awake for school tomorrow."

"All right, Papa." She skipped away as though she hadn't a care in the world.

Cole was disconcerted. He was glad Mary didn't seem to be overly disturbed by the scene with Leandra, but he didn't like that his sister's outbursts were so commonplace to his daughter that she had little or no reaction. He certainly didn't want her thinking such outbursts were acceptable behavior. But how to discuss it? Perhaps he could ask Miss Jones. He didn't want to become dependent on that strange woman, either, though. He ought to be able to raise his daughter on his own. But he had already asked her for her assistance, and she had agreed, so maybe it wouldn't be so very strange to discuss this with her.

Chapter Seven

Katie was finally home and settling back into the fabric of their lives, except that her mind wasn't really there. It was obvious that at least half the time her thoughts were elsewhere while a silly smile stretched her face.

Melanie was happy for her friend, *truly she was*, she insisted to herself. She didn't want to think that she was such a curmudgeon that she would begrudge her friend some happiness. But she dreaded the change that was clearly on the horizon. They had barely gotten settled here in the small town of Bucklin. But they were doing well, had clients building up, and their little house was clean and well cared for. Melanie wanted to be happy, content with the way things were. But she doubted they were going to stay this way much longer, and for that she was a bundle of nerves.

Of course, with Katie all aflutter over the doctor, much of Annie's care was falling to Melanie. Not to say that Katie was neglecting her daughter. She was very much involved in her every day activities, but there were frequent occasions when Katie was off with the doctor, and Melanie was left to keep the child entertained.

Annie was a sweet, friendly little girl, so Melanie didn't mind it terribly, but she couldn't decide how to feel about Katie and Dr. Jeffries, which made it difficult to deal with the child's persistent questions about them.

"Do you like Dr. Jeffries, Melanie?" was today's awkward question as they were stirring cookie dough together in the small kitchen.

Melanie bit her lip. "He seems like a kind gentleman," she answered as diplomatically as she could. "How do you feel about him?"

The little girl didn't answer for some time. "Well, I don't like doctors."

"I can understand that. You haven't had much good experience with them, have you?"

Annie shook her head vigorously.

"But doctors are supposed to help people, aren't they?"

"I s'pose."

"So that's a good thing, wouldn't you say?"

Annie shrugged, not wanting to admit to such a thing.

With a smile she tried to suppress, Melanie persisted. "Have you ever had an uncomfortable experience with Doctor Jeffries?"

"What do you mean?"

"Has he ever made you angry or sad or upset?"

"Well, only because I don't like doctors."

Now Melanie couldn't hold back her laughter. "I understand that part, but what about Dr. Jeffries specifically? Has he ever been mean to you?"

"He was mean to Mama Kate. Remember when I jumped out of Suzie's barn?"

Melanie nodded. "That was a scary time, wasn't it?" The child nodded, too. "Why do you suppose the doctor was mean to Katie?"

"He thinks every little girl should have a mama and a papa and that my mama works too hard."

"There's nothing wrong with that, is there? It would be better to have both, if it can be managed, don't you think?"

Annie looked at her with wise eyes. "I like it how things are just fine."

Melanie smiled. "Well, it seems that Doctor Jeffries has gotten over his thoughts about your mama, so maybe you should try to get over your thoughts about him."

Annie scrunched her nose as she considered Melanie's words. "Well, he does bring me lemon drops from the mercantile whenever he calls round."

With a laugh, Melanie said, "There you go — he's clearly not all bad, is he?"

The little girl still looked skeptical, so Melanie thought she ought to try a little harder. "It seems to me that your mama is quite happy when she comes home from her walks with the doctor. Have you noticed that?"

"She sings or hums. Is that what you mean?"

"Yes, those are signs that she's happy."

"I want her to be happy." The child's tone was grudging and hesitant. Melanie decided it was enough for the time being.

"Of course, you do. And I want you to be happy. So, what would make you happy this afternoon?"

"Are you finished with your work for today?"

Melanie hated that the little girl was still so guarded. It was unfortunate that her mother was bringing change when the poor child was still so unsettled after the recent adoption. But these things couldn't be helped, she supposed.

"I am quite finished. Once our cookies are done, I have nothing left to do except spend time with you."

Annie clapped her hands and did a wiggling little dance. "Do you s'pose Mr. Miller would mind if we came to look at the puppies?"

Melanie's stomach dropped in dismay. She had managed to avoid the subject of Mr. Miller for more than a week. It had been causing her a little bit of discomfort, as she had promised the man to show an interest in his daughter. But the unsettled feelings he stirred in her were more than she wanted to face. With a sigh, Melanie answered.

"I doubt if he would begrudge us the fun. Have you been speaking with Mary at school? Has she told you anything about the pups?"

"She said they grow overnight and are getting to be even more squirmy."

"That sounds like fun, doesn't it?"

Annie's vigorous nodding convinced Melanie that she would just have to gird her loins mentally and face the man. He wasn't so terrible, she reminded herself as she bustled about, tidying the small house and herself before setting out on the long walk.

"Should we take a few cookies for the Millers?"

"For sure," came Annie's quick reply.

"What about something for us? Are we likely to get hungry on the way? Do you want me to bring an apple for you to munch on later?"

"Thank you, Melanie. And bring one for you, too."

Melanie smiled over the little girl's polite thoughtfulness. It was a shame she had faced such tragedy in her young life, but it had obviously forged her into a pleasant little person. Melanie chuckled as she arranged the cookies and a couple apples in a small sack to be comfortably carried on their trek.

She marveled over Annie's energy as the little girl bounded around her as they made their way to the Miller's ranch. Melanie thought she should admonish her not to expend so much energy before they even got there but thought better of it. The sweet child was so biddable, she would do as she was told, but Melanie hesitated to suppress her exuberance. Melanie just didn't want to have to carry her home if she exhausted herself completely. So, she let the child continue her chatter and energetic play.

The fence posts marking the turn onto the Miller property were well behind them by the time they finally caught sight of the house and barn. Melanie was surprised once more by how large the property was. Mr. Miller had mentioned on their first visit that it spread out behind for at least a mile. She hadn't thought to ask how far it went in the other directions. But it was large. And she was tired from the walk. She had thought she was getting accustomed to walking, but she probably ought to walk more on a regular basis. Perhaps it wouldn't seem so very far if she were more used to it. Not that she needed to get used to walking to the Miller place, she admonished herself.

Someone on the property must have spotted them because Mary came bounding out of the house, excited to see them before they even reached the porch.

"I'm so happy to see you! Can you stay for supper?"

Melanie blinked. "Oh no, we wouldn't want to impose. We were just wondering if we could see the puppies again."

"Of course!" Mary exclaimed. "But you should stay for supper, too."

Melanie laughed. "That's kind of you to offer, Mary, thank you. We could maybe have a cup of tea with you, but we should get along home before supper. Annie's mother doesn't know we've come, and we wouldn't want to make her worry."

Melanie couldn't interpret the look that crossed the child's face, but Mary quickly agreed. "No, you definitely wouldn't want her to worry. Let me just ring the bell so Papa knows you've come, and then we can go in the barn."

"Oh, we needn't disturb your father," Melanie quickly interjected. "He's surely busy with important things."

"I think he'd be happy to have a visitor," the child insisted as she banged on the loud bell and the sound rang out in an almost deafening manner.

"Well, no one could miss that," Melanie commented, her tone dry.

Mary grinned.

"Is your aunt up for visitors?" Melanie thought to ask.

"She's lying down," Mary answered with a guilty face. "I prob'ly shouldn't have rang the bell quite so good."

Melanie laughed. "Well, she was happy to have a visitor the last time I was here, so she probably won't mind if you woke her up."

The child looked doubtful but wasn't allowed to dwell on it overly. Annie's impatience to see the pups couldn't be quelled.

"Can we go to see them now, please? I promise I cannot wait another minute." She was hopping from foot to foot in a manner that made all three of them break into giggles. Mary led the way to the barn.

They were so engrossed in the small animals that Melanie barely registered his presence until Mr. Miller spoke at her shoulder.

"Good afternoon. It's a pleasant surprise to see you two."

Stifling her gasp of surprise, Melanie turned to him with a smile. "Good afternoon. I hope we haven't disturbed you too much. Mary insisted you would want to know we're here. Annie wanted to see the puppies again."

"And so you walked all the way here?" He was incredulous.

"It's not so very far." Melanie was embarrassed, but Annie hadn't even noticed Mr. Miller's arrival.

He must have realized he was making her uncomfortable, as he quickly tried to change the subject.

"Mary was quite correct. I would be very disappointed to find out we had visitors and I hadn't been called to say hello. Do say you'll stay for tea."

Despite her discomfort, Melanie agreed. "Mary actually invited us to stay for supper, but we had to explain that Mrs. Carter didn't know we were here so we couldn't do that. But tea would be lovely, thank you."

He too got a strange look on his face when she said Katie didn't know where they were. "Did Mary say anything when you said that?"

"No, but her face looked sort of like yours does now. What have I said that's so wrong?"

He quickly shook his head. "It isn't you. It's what you said." Her face must have given away that he wasn't making it better because he quickly recovered with, "That is to say, what you said reminded us of something that happened with Leandra a week ago."

"Oh dear, something not good, from the looks of your faces."

"When we got home from driving you and Annie home, she was a little put out that we hadn't told her we were going."

"Oh no, I thought she was sleeping when we left."

"She was. But she woke up."

"Is she afraid of being by herself?"

"It would seem so. It had never been a problem before, that I knew of, but then it might not have ever happened before."

"Poor thing. I'm sorry that we were inadvertently the cause of trouble."

"Don't be. It is absolutely not your fault. And how were any of us to know she would wake up and be nervous?"

ꙮ

The humming sound she made low in her throat let him know Melanie didn't exactly accept his absolution. She looked worried, as though she were wishing she hadn't come to visit. Even though she was always so strange and awkward, he liked having her there. He needed to set her back at ease.

"By the way, thanks for your help in naming the horse. A new foal just arrived yesterday, so Gem got her name just in time."

"You went with Gem!" A wide smile split her face. "That's great. She must be happy to have a real name now."

Cole tried not to look so skeptical as he said, "I'm not sure if she really noticed. She certainly didn't take it personally."

Miss Jones' warm chuckle tickled his ears. "You never know. I think animals might be more intuitive than you think. But in either case, it would have been far too confusing to have two Baby Foals on the property."

"That is certainly true."

He watched as she bent down and picked up one of the puppies, who was making a beeline to the end of the stall. "You're a little adventurer, aren't you, my furry friend." When she turned to face him, her eyes were full of warmth. "This one is going to be trouble, I'm afraid. He doesn't seem inclined to remain with his siblings."

"A sense of adventure might serve him well when he's big enough to train. It means he won't be timid or easily intimidated by the animals he's supposed to be shepherding."

Her warm gaze was full of curiosity. "Do you train them yourself? Have you done it often?"

He wanted to tug his collar. "Well, I trained his mother. I've trained a couple others and traded them for services."

Her cocked head indicated she wanted to learn more. "It didn't seem right to charge someone for a dog, even if he was well trained. So, I gave a couple of the trained pups away in exchange for help building my fence, for one, and I got a new ram for another."

"That seems to be a smart way of doing things," she observed. Her admiring tone made his chest feel like it was puffing up with pride. "Do you have similar plans for these puppies?"

His glance found his daughter and her friend with puppies in each of their laps. He had to laugh softly. "I have a feeling it will be a little bit harder this time. We haven't had puppies with her old enough to remember."

Melanie again made that rumbling sound in her throat, but this time it seemed to him to be sympathetic. "Maybe keeping one might help with various transitions you all will be facing soon."

Cole's throat tightened. Having an empathetic, intelligent adult to share life's burdens with was something he had been sorely missing. Maybe he should take his sister-in-law up on her offer of sending him a wife. But he just couldn't take the risk. He had already been down this road twice to pain and suffering all around. He surely wished some of his family would come for a visit, but they had wired to say that an official from a hospital would be coming to collect Leandra. He suspected it was going to be trouble. He cleared his throat.

"Could I please ask your advice on something, Miss Jones?"

She chuckled softly. "You can certainly ask, but I cannot guarantee that I'll have anything useful to offer."

He grinned in response. "That's fair enough. My family has wired to say that rather than come themselves to collect Leandra, they are sending someone from a hospital they want her to go to."

"Oh dear, that's unfortunate, isn't it?"

"Yes, I don't actually think she's so far gone that she needs to go into a place like that. But sending a stranger for her might make her worse, and then she'll need it. I feel so guilty."

"I can understand why you might feel that way, but in my opinion, you ought not to do so. You made the decision to contact your family, both for your daughter's and your sister's welfare. It is a little less than ideal that they decided to handle it in this way, but they're her family, too. Maybe there are factors you don't know anything about. And maybe it'll be for the best this way."

"I hope you're right." He hated sounding so fearful to his own ears and couldn't quite meet her gaze due to his embarrassment.

When she reached out and put her hand on his arm, he almost jumped with surprise, but the warm pressure of her small hand felt so good he wondered how he could prolong the sensation. It seemed to be exactly what he needed in that moment. But then it appeared as though she thought better of the impulse and pulled her hand back, quickly gripping it with her other hand. Her face took on that scrunched up, nervous appearance that he hated to see, as though she were afraid of whatever was coming next.

She cleared her throat, a delicate but nervous sound. "We really ought to be going. We just wanted to venture over for a few minutes of playing with the puppies. Annie and I don't want to intrude on you and your family."

It looked as though she were going to run out on them. "Have you changed your mind about staying for a cup of tea?"

Her face flamed with color, and she started to stammer. "Well, no, I, uh, just don't want to intrude on your family situation."

"It's no intrusion. I promise you. If Leandra is awake, I'm sure she'll be happy to see you. If she's not, Mary and I will enjoy your company."

Her high color didn't recede noticeably, but she didn't decline either, busying herself with collecting the puppy who was again trying to escape the confines of the stall. When she briefly cuddled the little animal tenderly to her chest, Cole felt his own chest constrict. It was such an unconscious action, as though she couldn't help herself. He was shocked to realize that he was jealous of the pup.

He too cleared his throat of discomfort. "I'll just go put the kettle on the stove to boil. Come in when you're ready."

Miss Jones cast him a half smile as she kept her face partially averted. He thought the little girls hadn't even noticed his words, but then his daughter called out.

"Thank you, Papa, we'll be right there." There was a muffled protest from what must have been Annie before Cole heard his daughter explaining, "But Annie, I can barely wait to eat some of those cookies you brought." This was followed by at least two females giggling, so Cole was left to surmise that Annie wasn't begrudging his daughter her tea. He hurried away to do as he had said.

Chapter Eight

Melanie was nervous. She rubbed her hands briskly against her skirt as she walked with the girls back to the house. She wished she had worn gloves, but she realized that would have been ridiculous in this heat and location. The Millers would have thought her pretentious, she was sure, putting on airs like some debutante from the Upper Side of New York. Her friend, Cassandra, who *was* a debutante, could have certainly pulled it off with aplomb, but Melanie was certain she would have just looked ridiculous. Of course, most all women wore gloves on formal occasions, even out here in Bucklin. She had noticed some of the women in the mercantile had worn gloves. But she would have looked absurd walking out to visit puppies with her gloves on. And her only owning one good pair anymore. The adorable little animals would have greatly enjoyed ripping them to shreds.

Sighing, Melanie tried to bring her thoughts into order. *Mr. Miller is merely being neighborly by offering us tea. Anyone would do the same thing*, she reminded herself. *I would make the same offer if the roles were reversed*, she insisted. Besides, *he wants help calming his sister, to be sure, the poor dear.*

Who's going to look after me so kindly when I go stark, raving mad? Melanie asked herself, her stomach clenching as she tried to shove the unwelcome thought away. *Who says you haven't already?* she mocked herself. This last thought caused her lips to tip up in genuine amusement. It was at that moment that her gaze was ensnared by that of Mr. Miller, and the pit of her stomach dropped down for a moment.

I wonder if this is what Katie is always talking about when she speaks of the doctor. She says she gets butterflies in her tummy. That sounds pleasant enough. Not like this queasy feeling I have when my heart is racing and I think I might be ill. Gulping for air, Melanie tried to still her racing thoughts. *It's just tea! Everyone drinks tea. The little girls are present. And oh look, there's Leandra. Oh dear, she doesn't look well.*

"Miss Jones," Leandra said, her voice hoarse.

"Please, you must call me Melanie as we agreed last time."

"Oh yes, pray excuse me. I had quite forgotten." Melanie didn't think she had, as her tone wasn't in the least genuine, but she allowed the statement to pass without argument.

"Your voice sounds a bit strained, Leandra. Have you been unwell?"

"In a manner of speaking," Leandra replied while her gaze darted around as though she couldn't settle on anything.

Melanie was confused until it dawned on her that perhaps the poor woman had been yelling herself hoarse. Her eyes sought out Mr. Miller's gaze. He looked resigned, and Melanie felt stricken. What tragedy.

Melanie thought a change of topic was in order. "Annie and I made some extra cookies this afternoon and thought we would bring them by and get a peek at the puppies." Leandra didn't make any comment in return so Melanie kept on. "It's hard not to lose your heart to the dear little animals, isn't it?"

When Leandra still didn't say anything, Melanie gave up and turned to Mary to ask, "Are dogs your favorite animal, Mary?"

The little girl scrunched up her face while she thought about her answer. "I love the puppies and really all dogs, but I think my favorite animal is a bobcat."

"A bobcat? Well, that's not at all the answer I was expecting. Is there a reason why a bobcat is your favorite?"

"They eat rats," the little girl answered simply. "I really don't like rats. I don't mind mice, but rats are too big for my liking."

"I can't say that I blame you for that." Melanie tried not to shudder as she thought of her next question. "Are there many rats around?"

"They like to eat the horse feed."

"Oh dear. Do the horses mind?" Melanie lamented her limited knowledge of animals and wildlife.

Mary shrugged. “I don’t know if they mind sharing their food, but they don’t like rats either. Some of the horses are afraid of them.”

“I can understand that,” Melanie answered with a nervous giggle. “I think I agree with you that bobcats are pretty great if they keep the rats under control. But aren’t bobcats a little scary?”

“No, they’re more scaredy than scary,” Mary answered with a wide smile. “I wish they weren’t so scaredy. They look pretty soft. I would like to pet one someday.”

Melanie bit her lip and glanced at the child’s father. He met her gaze and rolled his eyes. Seeing the humor lurking in their depths made Melanie need to fight not to burst into more giggles. Melanie turned back to the children.

“What about you Annie? Do you have a favorite animal?”

“I love the puppies. I wish we could have one. Or maybe a kitten. But I think I love most the birds that sing outside my window every morning. It’s the happiest sound I ever heard. It’s so much better than what we heard before.”

Melanie glanced at her small companion and was forced back to her last morning in New York. Once again, she had been awakened by the shrewish yelling of the woman who lived across the hall as her husband left for work.

“You better not be late coming home for supper again tonight, Murray. I won’t be cooking your meals any longer if you leave them to congeal on the stove.”

Who would want to come home to that welcoming screech? she thought as she rolled over and punched her pillow, trying to find a soft spot for her head.

But sleep would not be returning to her. Murray's departure had set the building in motion, and everyone was stirring. She had left the window open the night before in an effort to air out their rooms. The air was fresher, but through the opening could be heard the sound of horse shoes on cobblestones as the deliveries were being made up and down the street.

Then there was the heavy clomp of someone going back up the stairs carrying their family's water. Melanie needed to bestir herself and do the same. It was the last time she would have to do it, she reminded herself with a grin. While she was certain there would be effort required in fetching water in Missouri, she was determined that she would never again live on the fourth floor of a five-storey building. The heat and the odors always rose unpleasantly, especially in the summer. And having to go all the way down to the courtyard to relieve nature or fetch water was not something she wanted to continue doing for the rest of her life.

Blinking the vivid memory away, Melanie smiled at Annie. "I think I will agree with you, my dear. I love that cheerful sound in the morning, too. We should find out if that particular bird has a name so we can be certain of what our favorite is called."

Annie grinned back at her, pleased with the adult's reaction.

"I have a favorite," Mr. Miller interjected, gaining him all the females' attention.

Melanie smiled when she noticed his cheeks coloring. She prompted him. “What is it?”

“The red fox, even though he will eat the chicks if I’m not careful.”

Melanie was surprised. “Why would he be your favorite if he might eat some of your animals?”

“I think I’m like my daughter — I just want to pet him.” He chuckled softly. “Have you ever seen a fox up close?” When both Melanie and Annie shook their heads vigorously, he elaborated. “Their red coat looks so thick and soft, I would love to sink my fingers into it and then scratch him behind the ears. And then there’s the fact of how smart they seem to be. Wiley, you might say. The length I’ve had to go to keep the chicks safe, gives me a certain level of respect for the sneaky little creatures.”

All the girls laughed along with him, except Leandra who was glowering by herself, silently observing them as they conversed. Finally, Melanie had reached the end of her tolerance and stood to take their leave.

“It was pleasant visiting with the three of you for a few minutes. Thank you for the tea and for allowing us a bit of time with the puppies. Annie and I ought to be on our way. We shall see you again soon, to be sure.”

Melanie could see the understanding shining in Mr. Miller’s eyes, and she almost faltered in her determination to leave. She felt terrible about leaving him to deal with his situation on his own, but she reminded herself that it *was* his situation to deal with. Perhaps he wasn’t even looking for her help or sympathy, she reminded herself. He was just a kind man who had a terrible circumstance to deal with, and he understood that she didn't want to deal with it. There was nothing so terrible in that, was there? She kept her face as neutral as possible as she herded Annie from the room while saying their goodbyes.

On the walk home, she was glad that Annie was so energetically occupying herself because Melanie wasn't going to be of much company. Her mind had remained behind at the Millers' place. She thought back to the terrible situation she had lived through herself. Becoming the woman of the house at the age of ten had been more than she could handle, but she had managed. Her sister and brother were healthy and reasonably happy. For that she was grateful. The blame for the fact that she had become so fearful of everything rested solely on her own shoulders. She shouldn't have allowed it to come to this, but she was proud of herself for braving the huge change of leaving New York and moving to Missouri.

She had never told Katie the details of her situation and that sweet woman, having issues of her own to cope with, had never pressed her, merely picking up the slack of what she could or could not handle. Melanie would walk through fire for her friend. And at times, taking her friend's daughter out in public felt like walking through fire, but she was managing, and she was quite sure she wasn't projecting her issues onto Annie, which was her deepest fear. That poor child would have her own emotional baggage to live with given her background; she didn't need Melanie's issues besides.

“Miss Melanie?”

“Yes, my dearest Annie?”

“Do you think Mama Kate will have a baby if she marries the doctor?”

Melanie’s heart sank. She didn’t want to be the one to talk to Annie about her mother’s potential marriage or the consequences of what that marriage might mean for Annie. But there was no one else about, and the child needed to be answered.

“It’s quite possible. Do you think you would like a little brother or sister?”

Annie wrinkled her nose as she pondered the question. “I think it would be lovely to have brothers and sisters again. But maybe Mama Kate would love a baby more than me.”

Melanie had wondered if that’s where this conversation was leading. But she couldn’t let the moment pass. She stopped in her tracks and knelt down in front of Annie, not heeding the dirt and what it might do to her skirts. Taking the little girl’s hands firmly into her grasp, she looked Annie in the eye and reassured her.

“Your mama loves you from the very bottom of her heart. Nothing will ever change that. Not even if she has ten babies. I promise you, truly. Your mother is loyal and true. And she has enough love in her heart and soul for many children.”

The little girl looked somewhat mollified by Melanie’s words but not completely reassured, so Melanie continued questioning the child’s reasons for asking.

"Are you worried about the fact that you're adopted?"

Annie nodded vigorously. "She hasn't known me all my life."

"Do you really think that matters?" Melanie wanted to understand where the child was coming from.

"I don't know." Annie's answer was glum.

"Has anyone said something to you to make you think like this?"

The guilt on the child's face made Melanie's heart sink.

"Was it at school?" She kept her voice gentle even though she wanted to smack someone. How could children be so cruel?

Annie's nod was almost imperceptible. Melanie struggled to reassure the child.

"Do you truly believe your mama loves you?"

Annie shrugged but gave a small nod. Melanie couldn't really fault the poor girl; she had been through a lot in her young life.

"I truly believe she does," Melanie assured her. "I think you should try to talk to her about this. I know for sure she wouldn't want you to be afraid to talk to her about anything. And you know what? It's not even for sure that she'll marry the doctor, anyway."

The hopeful look on the little girl's face made Melanie's stomach hurt. She didn't want to encourage Annie to think the couple might not last, so she changed the subject slightly.

"When a mama has a new baby, the baby needs a lot of attention at first. You probably realize that, right?" Annie's puzzled face made her explain further. "Remember the first time we saw the puppies?" This brought a grin to Annie's solemn face. "What did you notice about them?"

"They were really little."

"Right. What else? Could they move very fast or look after themselves?"

Vigorous head shaking followed this. "No, they could only crawl over each other, and they were all trying to get to their mama so they could eat."

"Exactly. And human babies can't even crawl when they're born. It takes them months before they can. So, the human mother has to do everything for the baby. Just like puppies, human babies are really cute, and the mother loves them, so she does everything for the baby. But they aren't really all that interesting. Even though mamas sing to their babies and even talk to them, they can't have a conversation like you and I are having. So, if your mama has more babies in the future, she'll still love you and want you around. You could be a really big help for her if there are babies, you know."

Not that Melanie really wished that on the little girl, but she knew it was the natural way of things. And she was sure the poor child wouldn't be put in the same position Melanie had been when her mother died after giving birth to her little brother. Melanie was completely sure that Katie would be able to balance a baby with showing attention to her growing daughter.

“That might be fun.” The child sounded uncertain, but at least she was willing to see a better side to the possibilities.

“Since there’s no use worrying about it at this point, since your mama has only just started courting with the doctor so any babies are still a long way off, let us turn our minds to something much more interesting,” Melanie declared in as droll a voice as she could manage.

It did the trick. The little girl burst into giggles.

“Like what?” Annie asked between her laughter.

“Well, I don’t know about you, but I’m starving! Are you even a teensy bit hungry?”

Vigorous nodding was the only answer she got as the little girl was still dissolving in laughter.

“I think we should have mashed potatoes and fried eggs for supper. What do you think?”

“Sounds delicious.”

“And maybe some of the bread and cookies we made earlier would go well with it.”

“M’hmm.”

They continued the rest of the way home, skipping and laughing. But Melanie was troubled and determined to speak to her friend about her child’s concerns.

Chapter Nine

"Oh Melanie, I'm sorry that you had to deal with that." Katie was stricken.

"I'm not telling you to make you feel badly, Kate, I promise you."

"No, of course not, but I do none the less."

Melanie couldn't help smiling over her words, not over the situation. "I guess I can understand why. But while I do think you need to have a conversation with Annie about your possible future, I don't think she's as troubled now as she was before she and I talked." They were silent for a moment before Melanie continued. "My biggest concern is what the other children seem to be saying to her. I was too busy reassuring her of her place in your heart that I forgot to get more details about what some little monster might have said to her."

Katie chuckled over her friend's words. "I don't think the children are monsters."

"Well I do, if they're going to make our Annie feel unsettled," Melanie interrupted, causing Katie to laugh some more.

"While I'm delighted that you are taking your role as honorary aunt to my daughter so seriously. You have to watch that you don't become too ferocious in your protective stance. Perhaps she misunderstood or jumped to conclusions based on some other child's fears. You never know, maybe one of the other children has a new baby brother or sister and is feeling misplaced. One thing could lead to another. You know how children's minds jump to the most convoluted places sometimes."

Melanie had to force herself to see what Katie was saying. "I guess you're right. But I can empathize with Annie's fears, and it might've made me a little overprotective."

"Maybe a little," Katie agreed with a dry tone, making Melanie finally join in the laughter.

"Oh very well, I am a she-bear when it comes to the children in my care. That is as it should be. But never mind about that for now. I've told you, now it's your responsibility. But nothing can be done about it now, so you absolutely must tell me all about your excursion with the good doctor. I still cannot believe how quickly you have made an about face from loathing the man to being all starry eyed about him."

Melanie felt a stab of envy as her friend's smile turned secretive, even though Katie laughed at her words. "I wouldn't say I loathed the man."

At Melanie's raised eyebrow Katie giggled. "Well, all right, the relationship was pretty cold at first. But as you can see, these things can change pretty quickly, so you better watch out for yourself. With how outnumbered women are to men in this town, it could happen to you, even if you don't think you're susceptible. Look at me! I swore up and down I would never even consider remarriage, and now here I am courting with the doctor!" She seemed momentarily shocked by the thought before drifting off into dreamy reminiscence. "We did have a lovely afternoon yesterday. We walked up to the point again where he asked me to court. It is the most lovely view. And we talked and talked. As you know, the time got away on us."

Melanie laughed. "Yes, I know. You got in just in time to say goodnight to Annie."

"Am I abusing your friendship completely? I know you didn't sign up for mothering duties."

"No, no, I'm not filling mothering duties. I am strictly the favorite aunt. And I make no promises about not spoiling your child. It'll be left to you to unravel whatever messes I might make with the girl."

Katie laughed. "I trust you implicitly."

There was a pause while Melanie pondered her words. Always perceptive, Katie prodded. "Something else is on your mind. You made a weird face when I said that I trust you. Do you not think I should?"

Melanie's laugh sounded forced as she responded. "No, it's not that. Of course, I think you should trust me. I will guard Annie with my life. And I was only joking when I said that I'll spoil her. In your absence, I will do the best I possibly can."

"I know, thus the implicit trust. So, spit it out. Something is bothering you."

Melanie sighed and decided to confide in her friend. "Mr. Miller has asked me to take an interest in Mary."

Katie frowned. "Annie's friend? Why would he do that? Doesn't he have a wife?"

"No, that's what I thought, too, but it's his sister. And she's not well. Please don't share this with any of our clients, but he has contacted his family back East and asked them to come for her. Apparently, she hates it here in Bucklin and has only been staying from a sense of duty toward her brother and niece. Now that Mary is going to school, Mr. Miller feels that he can manage without her, and perhaps they will be better off without her negative presence."

Katie's eyebrows had been steadily rising throughout Melanie's explanation. "He has certainly confided a fair bit of information to you."

Melanie could feel heat rising in her face, and she began to feel defensive. "I think he felt he had nowhere to turn and was hoping for a female perspective."

Katie's eyebrows remained elevated. "So, he confided in a woman he just met rather than one of his neighbors that he's known for years? Ones who perhaps have even known his sister?"

Melanie frowned. "Do you think it's worrisome that he has discussed this with me? I think he just thought that since I am spending time with Annie, I might be in a position to take an interest in Mary and spend some time with her, too."

Katie's face split into a grin. "I don't think it's worrisome at all. But I think it is exactly what I was talking about. I've seen Mr. Miller. He is a handsome man. And from the gossip I've picked up around town while visiting our clients, it would seem he is quite well-to-do."

"His lands certainly seem to be extensive. But why does that make you look so strangely all of a sudden?"

"You are a good looking, intelligent, single woman. If a good looking, intelligent, single gentleman starts confiding in you, it could only mean one thing. I won't be the only one courting before long."

"No. Absolutely not. He is not interested in me in that way. He is merely concerned for his daughter. And he did us a favor, if you will recall, when you were stuck at the Mitchells' house with their illness. He kept Annie for us and prevented her from even realizing that you were gone until it was all over. We owe him our kindness for what he did."

"Why are you protesting so much? Are you really that opposed to a man showing a romantic interest in you?"

"He hasn't shown a romantic interest in me, Katie. I'm not like you. You're pretty and witty and energetic and outgoing. And you're such a tiny little woman. I think men like that. I'm awkward and nervous and shy and clumsy. I don't know what to say to people, and I would far rather stay at home than go out into the world. Surely, someone like Mr. Miller would prefer anyone else over me."

Loyal Katie swept to her defense. "For one thing, you are the loveliest friend I've ever had. I think you're beautiful. In the sunlight, your brown hair is every shade of nutmeg and walnut and amber."

Melanie laughed. "You make me sound like a tree."

Not to be deterred, Katie persisted. “And you’re so smart. When you aren’t nervous, you have the most fascinating things to talk about.”

“But I’m always nervous,” Melanie complained. “But never mind. I don’t even want him to be interested in me, so it doesn’t matter. I mean, really, what would I do with a man? He will want more children, and I don’t know if I could bear it. I’ve already raised my family.”

Katie’s laughing face softened into concern. “But a family of your very own is different than your siblings. And having a husband would be a completely different scenario than an absent father who only makes demands of you.”

“I’m sure it is, but I have no interest in learning it for myself, so never mind about it. I’m just glad to see you so happy.”

“Now you’re just trying to change the subject,” Katie laughed. “But what are you going to do about Mary?”

Melanie sighed. “I don’t know. The poor dear thing. I was thinking of offering to have her come stay with us for a few days when her aunt is being taken away. It’s sure to be an ugly scene that no little girl should witness. Would you be accepting of having her with us?”

“Of course,” was Katie’s immediate reply. “Do you think we should go see if we can help the poor woman?”

“Maybe you should go. You’re so much better with people than I am,” Melanie protested.

"But I have barely met her, just in passing at the school. I think it would be much more comfortable for everyone if you came with me." Now Katie had begun wheedling.

"Not more comfortable for me," Melanie pointed out with a weak laugh.

"Come on, it's time for you to get out of the house."

"I was just out of the house yesterday. Remember the uncomfortable conversation I had with your daughter on the way to that very house?"

"Bringing up my guilt over Annie isn't going to help you get out of coming with me," Katie answered tartly, but her laugh gave away that she held no hard feelings. "Come along, you can make your offer to Mr. Miller while the children aren't there to overhear and pressure him into it if he doesn't think it's the right choice."

With a sigh, Melanie capitulated. "Very well, just let me wash my face and tidy my hair. It wouldn't do for any potential clients seeing me a mess," she explained when she caught sight of Katie's arched brows.

"M'hmm," Katie hummed. "It wouldn't have anything to do with a certain handsome rancher, I don't suppose."

Melanie willed her pale cheeks not to reveal her discomfort at Katie's teasing, but she could feel the heat rising despite her best efforts. Katie's giggles followed her into her bedroom. As she changed her gown, she told herself it was just in case they were to run into a client. It would not do to be dressed in a dowdy fashion if they wish to promote their abilities. And no, it did not have anything to do with a certain handsome rancher, she insisted to herself with a wry twist to her lips.

Within moments they were on their way, discussing various upcoming commissions, deciding when Katie would visit the customers to discuss the unknown details.

“Now that we have the new fabric swatches that Mr. Spencer arranged for us, you need to visit Mrs. Spencer once more. It seemed as though she would have commissioned many more frocks if we had a more varied selection. Now that we do, she’s sure to place another order.”

“You’re right. And you’ve been so speedy on completing the latest orders, even without my help, that we have plenty of room in our schedule.” Katie smiled at her kindly. “You do realize how much I appreciate you doing so much for me while my head is in the clouds, don’t you?”

“Katie, please, there is no need for your flummery. I cannot even begin to express to you how much your companionship and partnership in this business means to me. I don’t know where I would be if not for you. Can you imagine? I don’t know what I was thinking when I planned to run this business on my own. I know you had planned to take the teaching position, but it was such a stroke of luck for me that you needed to find other employment.”

Katie grimaced. “Well it has certainly worked out for the best for me in the long run as well. While I love children in general and most of the specific children whom I’ve met from the school, I cannot imagine needing to be with them all day every day. And they are so varying! I'm not sure how the teacher managed to keep all their lessons straight. But he must be doing so since Annie is obviously learning and enjoying her schooling."

"Well there you have it, we are mutually benefited and therefore no thanks are necessary from either of us. We are friends and partners, and we each pick up the other's slack. You might have your head in the clouds, but you are still managing to keep up with the clients quite beautifully. And I'm glad you brought Annie into our home. I didn't think I would be happy about it and had every intention of steering clear of her, but she is a dear, and I'm enjoying having her to myself at times."

Katie's gaze turned teasing once more. "See, that is why you need to snare yourself a suitor. You ought to have some children of your own. They would most definitely grow on you."

Melanie laughed. "Your tune sure has changed since we arrived in Missouri. I was the one telling you that you'd find a mate straight off, and you swore you'd never remarry. Now you think everyone should be paired up."

Katie shrugged and grinned. "I want to share my joy."

"On the other hand, misery does love company," Melanie answered dourly, causing Katie to laugh and stick out her tongue.

They were in high spirits when they arrived at their destination. Once again, by some mysterious manner, their approach had been noticed, and Mr. Miller was striding toward them as they drew near to his front porch. Melanie shaded her eyes and stopped in her tracks.

"I absolutely must know before I perish from curiosity. How do you always know when someone is approaching? Every time I come here, you always seem to be on your way to the house."

Mr. Miller grinned. "I have my ways," he answered vaguely. The rolling of her eyes must have prompted because he elaborated. "Remember, I told you how sensitive the horses' hearing is? When I'm mounted, my horse's reaction tells me something is different. Too, there are often dogs around to alert me to arrivals."

"I had no idea a horse could be used as a watch dog."

"All the more reason to love them." With a pleasant smile, he turned to Katie. "You must be Mrs. Carter. I'm Cole Miller, it's a pleasure to finally meet you."

"It's my pleasure, Mr. Miller. I apologize that it has taken me this long to come by and thank you for helping us out with Annie."

"No thanks necessary, as I've already told Miss Jones. We have agreed that we can help each other out with the children."

Katie's eyes were dancing with mischief as she nodded in agreement. "It's wonderful that you should say so, Mr. Miller. Melanie and I were just discussing that very thing. She told me a little bit about your situation, and we thought it might be a good idea for Mary to come and stay with us for a few days."

Mr. Miller's bright blue eyes focused on Melanie for a moment, and her mouth dried as she tried to interpret his thoughts. It seemed to her as though his gaze had cooled significantly. Consumed with guilt, she lowered her gaze from his. Perhaps he truly had confided in her and had expected to keep it as a confidence. Her face flooded with heat.

Katie must have realized her blunder, and she suavely made a recovery. "Do excuse us if we are speaking out of turn, Mr. Miller. I can assure you that Melanie has not been gossiping around town about your personal affairs, but she did, of course, have to discuss it with me in order to be able to make you such an offer, since we share a home."

"Of course," Mr. Miller replied, his face brightening slightly but still not his usual warm geniality. "Won't you come in and have a cup of tea with my sister? I believe you've met her before, haven't you, Mrs. Carter?"

"Yes, in the schoolyard. Thank you, a cup of tea would be welcomed." Katie's answer was polite, and both women followed him into the house while exchanging confused glances.

Chapter Ten

Cole was quite well aware that his anger was misplaced and disproportionate, but he couldn't seem to simmer it down much. He had poured out his heart to Miss Jones, and it seemed as though she had shared it at her first opportunity. What Mrs. Carter said made complete sense — if she had a solution, she needed to ask her housemate if it was all right with her — but he would have preferred if she had asked him first. He had to ask himself why he was taking it quite so personally. He had assured himself that he didn't have warmer feelings for the woman, but he was starting to think he was lying to himself. Maybe he ought to leave town for a time. He could escort Leandra back to Boston himself and see what sort of women his sister-in-law had picked out for him. If he met them for himself, it might not be such a stretch to consider one as a potential wife.

But then he felt a warm hand on his arm, and he looked down into the brown depths of Miss Jones' concerned gaze. "I'm so sorry if we've offended you. I swear I'm not a gossip. But Katie's a mother. I'm not. I thought she would have some insights."

His heart clenched along with his stomach. He wanted to reassure her that he wasn't angry with her, but he wasn't sure if it was true. He gave her a tight smile instead. No further conversation was possible as Leandra entered the scene.

"Mrs. Carter and Miss Jones. What a pleasure to see you."

Leandra was having a reasonably good day, but she was brittle around the edges, and Cole needed to keep an eye on her. He was glad for Mrs. Carter's outgoing cheerfulness despite her apparent ability to get into other people's business.

"Miss Miller, a pleasure to see you, as well. I must tell you the droll mistake that Miss Jones and I both made. We thought you were your brother's wife when you originally extended the invitation for Annie to come and stay over with Mary."

Leandra's harsh laughter followed. "His wife is dead."

"So we've since found out," Mrs. Carter replied gently.

"But Melanie and I have decided to be friends, so I guess you must be, too. We are Leandra and Melanie."

"How lovely. Then you must call me Katie as all my friends do."

"Very well. I s'pose you ought to call my brother Cole, too."

Cole froze in the act of setting the kettle on the stove. He was grateful for Mrs. Carter's quick, warm chuckle.

"That might be a little too forward for us just yet, Leandra. We've just met him. And since it turns out that he's an eligible bachelor around town, we wouldn't want to set the tongues to wagging."

Cole noticed that Miss Jones had still not uttered a word. He cast a glance from the side of his eye at her. She was pale and taut. He wondered what she was thinking. Leandra quickly filled any silence.

"I've heard the tongues are already wagging about you, Katie. Word is you're courting with the doctor."

"Word does spread quickly in a small town, doesn't it?"

"So, it's true then? I thought he was a confirmed bachelor, wallowing in his grief for his dead wife. He didn't have much more than the time of day for me."

Cole could hear the bitterness in his sister's voice. It was rather a shame and quite unusual that she had remained unmarried out here where single women were so scarce. Perhaps many had made the same mistake that Mrs. Carter had spoken of. And then, once the mistake was cleared up, Leandra's negativity wasn't terribly endearing.

"It does take time to get over one's grief and prepare for a new relationship," Mrs. Carter answered in a soothing tone. "I, myself, had been determined that I would never remarry. But Dr. Jeffries and I found ourselves in the right place at the right time, and the sparks flew. There doesn't seem to be much rhyme or reason to it, does there?"

Cole was glad that his back was still turned towards the women because he couldn't help grinning when he heard his sister's disdainful sniff. She obviously wasn't convinced by Mrs. Carter's cheerful chatter. But she also wasn't overtly rude, despite her precarious sanity.

"I must compliment you on your daughter. We quite enjoyed her when she was here visiting. A very polite little girl." Leandra's tone implied she was surprised by the facts she was stating. Cole again had to choke back his amusement. He didn't want to interrupt or draw attention to himself. He waited to see how their visitors would react.

"Why thank you so much, Leandra, although, as you are no doubt aware, Annie hasn't been with me for very long, so I cannot take credit for what a dear she is. I am so blessed to have her." There was a slight pause before she continued. "I probably shouldn't say that, actually, should I? Since the poor child lost her entire family, I ought not say it's my blessing."

Cole wasn't surprised to hear soft-hearted Miss Jones jump into the conversation finally. "Oh no, Katie, don't say that. You and Annie are a blessing for each other after all the tragedies you both have endured. You are not benefitting from her tragedy just as she is not benefitting from yours. But in your current circumstances, you are making the best of it together."

Cole braced himself as he heard sniffling. Women and their waterworks, he thought with a shudder.

"That was beautifully said, Melanie," Leandra complimented.

Cole finally turned to face the women. Mrs. Carter was clasping Miss Jones' hand while dabbing at her eyes. Miss Jones looked decidedly uncomfortable, and Cole's amusement mounted. He had to clear his throat. This brought three sets of eyes to his. Two sets looked surprised to be reminded of his presence, but Miss Jones looked relieved at the interruption.

"How do you take your tea, Mrs. Carter?" he asked, his tone mundane as though he had no idea what had just transpired. He was pleased to see a spark of amusement brighten Miss Jones' gaze.

"Oh, just strong and black, thank you, Mr. Miller. I think I could use the fortification this afternoon."

"Very well," he turned back to the counter and finished his task. "I'm afraid I don't have anything quite so delicious as the cookies Miss Jones has brought us in the past." He could've bitten off his tongue when he noticed the chagrin filling that lady's face. He quickly continued. "But this raisin bread we baked yesterday isn't too bad."

"Thank you, Mr. Miller, this will be quite lovely." Mrs. Carter seemed to be quite the diplomat. She then began to gently probe his sister. "Melanie told me that you have been caring for Mary since she lost her mama. That was generous of you, Leandra. You must be deeply attached to her."

Leandra shrugged. "She's a very energetic child. She would much rather be with her father than cooped up in the house with me."

"Of course, I think that might come with the age," Mrs. Carter agreed with a smile. "Annie is so full of energy. I don't know how their teacher manages to get any learning into them."

Leandra sniffed again. "I don't really see much getting into Mary."

Cole, used to his sister's cutting remarks, barely registered her words, but both of their visitors looked troubled. It seemed too much for even the gregarious Mrs. Carter, who grew quiet. Cole rather thought it was too much for Miss Jones, which is why it prompted her into speech.

"Mary actually struck me as a very bright girl. I think she will take to her classes very well. I'm just so happy for both Annie and Mary that girls are encouraged to attend the school here in Bucklin and that the teacher seems well inclined to teach his entire class."

"I don't see how much good can come from teaching the boys with the girls. Seems to me that none of them will be able to learn anything that way."

Mrs. Carter had finally recovered her wits. "Since both Annie and Mary are only children, I think it will be good for them to have the experience, don't you?"

"Not really. But it's none of my business anymore, anyway. I suppose my brother has told you I'm finally getting out of here?"

"What do you mean?" Mrs. Carter neither agreed nor denied her knowledge.

"I'm going back to Boston." Finally, his sister seemed happy about something.

The two visitors exchanged a glance that made Cole think they had hoped the subject would come up, but he didn't think they were getting straight to their point when they probed with more questions. "Are you happy to be returning to Boston?" Mrs. Carter's question sounded cautious.

"Delighted," Leandra almost grunted, making it difficult for Cole to maintain a straight face.

"We shall miss you, Leandra," Miss Jones stated in a soft but firm voice. "You must have very mixed feelings on your departure."

"Why would my feelings be mixed? I'm finally getting out of this godforsaken place."

Miss Jones blinked but carried on. "No doubt, you'll miss your brother and Mary. Having been here for a few years, it has surely become home, at least to an extent. Are you not a bit nervous that things have changed in your absence and it won't feel like home anymore?"

"I don't think that's likely."

"I'm glad, then." Her answer was kind and gentle. For all her apparent awkwardness, Miss Jones obviously had a sweet heart. Cole closed his eyes in resistance to the thought.

"Is there anything we can do to help you with your preparations, Leandra? I know you and I have just met, but Melanie and I are both of the mind that women must stick together. We would like to do whatever we can to make it easier for you." Mrs. Carter was brisk and matter of fact.

Leandra's forehead wrinkled as though she didn't understand the question. Mrs. Carter elaborated. "Do you have much to pack? Or would it be beneficial for us to have Mary stay with us for a few days? Would you rather she be here or not when you take your leave?"

Leandra's confusion cleared, and so did Cole's. He deeply appreciated the consideration the women were showing. He agreed with their assessment; it would likely be better if Mary wasn't there when his brother's agents came for Leandra. But it would be best if Leandra didn't realize he was for the idea.

"That's mighty kind of you, Katie. I don't have much to pack, that's for certain. I will need to get all my washing done before I pack, and I would like to leave all the housework done up here for Cole so he won't even notice I'm gone for a while. It might actually be best if the girl isn't underfoot. If it wouldn't be too much trouble for you, of course," she added as an afterthought.

"It would be a pleasure for us to have her. And Annie will love it." Mrs. Carter's answer was immediate and sounded sincere. Again, the two women exchanged brief but significant glances. "How soon do you think you'll be leaving? Should we take Mary home with us now or come back for her in a few days?"

Leandra suddenly must have realized how close her return to Boston really was. For a moment, Cole saw his sister's true self displayed on her face, and his heart lurched. She looked for a moment as though she regretted her departure. But then she blinked and the moment passed. While it had seemed to him that she was at a momentary loss, she now gained in determination.

"Of course, the girl isn't ready to just up and leave. But maybe you could come for her things tomorrow and then collect her after school. That might be the easiest thing. Much like how we took Annie when you were unavailable."

Mrs. Carter blinked in surprise over Leandra's return to vicious manner of speech, but she took it in her stride. "Very well, that seems to be a sound plan. One of us will stop by mid-day to collect Mary's things for an expected stay of a few days." Standing up, Mrs. Carter began to bring their visit to a close; obviously, their purpose in coming had been concluded. "Mr. Miller, if you would like to come and collect her when you're ready, that would be appropriate."

Cole nodded his agreement, unsure how he felt about the managing woman. He was surprised to see Miss Jones' eyes twinkling in amusement once more.

"Thank you for the tea," Miss Jones murmured as she shook his hand briefly before taking her leave.

Cole stood at the window and watched the two women as they walked away. He was envious of the easy camaraderie between them. It was apparent that both women were well grounded intellectually and emotionally. Even Miss Jones, despite her awkwardness. It was in sharp contrast with his sister. He really appreciated what a good listener Miss Jones seemed to be. It would be good for Mary to spend time with the two women as well as Mrs. Carter's daughter. He looked forward to telling Mary when she got home from school.

Chapter Eleven

After glancing at the watch she kept in her small handbag, Melanie suggested they stop to collect Annie on their way past the school. "It's only fifteen minutes until class ends. There's no sense in going home."

Katie agreed but then added, "That was far more fascinating than I expected."

"What was? The fact that I keep my watch in my handbag?"

"Don't play coy, Mel, you know what I mean."

"No, as a matter of fact, I don't. What could you have found fascinating about that poor woman's terrible situation? And poor little Mary, being surrounded by so much negativity! It can't be good for her either."

Katie looked shocked by Melanie's words. "I was certainly not making light of Leandra's illness, nor the impact it's sure to have on Mary. I was just commenting on Mr. Miller's apparent fascination with you. Did you not notice that he could barely keep his eyes off you?"

Melanie felt heat filling her cheeks. “No, I noticed no such thing!” Her declaration seemed to fall on deaf ears as Katie laughed.

“Was that because you were making your own best effort to keep your eyes away from him?”

Now it felt as though her face were on fire, but Melanie tried to brazen it out. “I have no idea what you mean. I maintained my focus on Leandra and our conversation with her.”

“Of course, you did, because you are a lovely, loyal friend,” Katie replied promptly and sincerely, but then she turned teasing. “But you also have eyes in your head, and they seem to find great appreciation in turning toward the handsome rancher.”

Melanie debated with herself for a heartbeat but then she turned to her friend. “Was I so very obvious? I would hate for him to think I was setting my cap at him.”

Katie’s amusement burst into deep chuckles. “Now you’re sounding downright historical! Where did you get that expression from?”

Melanie didn’t think her embarrassment could grow any deeper. “I read it somewhere,” she replied in a stiff voice.

“Oh, don’t take offense, my dear friend, I just couldn’t help it. Surely you realize that a good laugh will release all the tension from that dreadful interlude. You are so sweet, you might not have noticed how very dreadful Leandra was toward me.”

Melanie couldn’t stay offended long and couldn’t help but release a few giggles of her own. “How could anyone not take note? She was such a dear the first time I met her, and even today, she didn't seem irked with me, but she certainly seemed to have taken you in dislike. I think it's because of the doctor."

"Well, that much was apparent. I feel badly for her and her situation, but that's no reason to tear down another woman's happiness."

"Oh, please tell me you didn't take her words to heart." Melanie was instantly struck by the unfairness of it all.

"Of course not, I could see through it at once. But it was decidedly uncomfortable. Except for the funny way Mr. Miller kept trying to ignore the conversation completely while still staying around to sneak peeks at you."

"Was he really?" Melanie was torn between denial and wanting to hear more. "I'm dreadful at conversing with him, or anyone for that matter, and of course, I have no wish to marry. But he is so very handsome. It's probably all that hard work and fresh air that must come from being a rancher. And he's so sweet with his daughter. And his kindness toward Annie was heartwarming, too."

Katie laughed again. "Oh my dear friend, I do think you have a bad case."

Melanie laughed as well but still asked, "A bad case of what?"

"The love bug." The way she declared it all drawn out and squeaky made them both fall into a fit of giggles. Melanie was the first to sober.

"I won't be able to see him again. You'll have to be the one to go tomorrow and collect Mary's things.

Maybe you can drop in there after you've visited one of our clients."

Katie blinked at her in surprise. "Why ever would you say that? Seems to me you should be all the more anxious to spend more time with the good rancher in his time of need."

Melanie didn't even crack a smile over Katie's words. "It is because of his time of need that he doesn't need me. He needs someone who can socialize and be normal in order to help Mary as she grows. Even someone who would happily bear children with him. That someone isn't me. Mary is a dear girl, and I plan to help her as much as I can, but I'm not normal. I can't help her with social things. And I have absolutely no interest in bringing any babies into this world."

Katie's eyes were kind but damp; she seemed at a loss for words. "Give it time, my dear Mel. You might change your mind. And I think you're completely normal. Just because you would prefer to stay at home doesn't mean there's something wrong with you."

"That's not what my father has said."

"Well your father is a nincompoop, and that's all I plan to say on the subject. Now, come along. We need to fetch Annie from school. And my stomach is starting to growl. Poor Mr. Miller's raisin bread was a touch dry. It was all I could do to get it swallowed, even with his delicious tea."

Melanie didn't bother replying, just picking up her skirts and hurrying beside her friend to fetch their small companion.

Early the next morning, there was a knock on the door. It was Dr. Jeffries stopping in on his way to an emergency, asking Katie to accompany him. As she gathered her things, Katie couldn't quite hide her smile.

"I swear to you, I didn't arrange this. You know I couldn't have, we were together all evening. And I would never implicate the good doctor in any of my schemes, besides. But now you're going to have to go collect Mary's things yourself."

Melanie stood still and blinked, knowing she must appear a simpleton, but there was nothing that could be done, so she tried to figure out the best course of action. "What about the clients you were supposed to visit?"

Katie bit her lip in uncertainty. "I don't have time to send someone with a message. I'm so sorry, Melanie. Do you think you could just stop in to see them and explain that I'll be by tomorrow? Or even later on today if this situation with Dr. Jeffries resolves itself quickly."

Melanie tried to stay calm. She knew Katie would be concerned for her as well as the patient. Biting her lip and trying to be brave, she shooed Katie out the door. "Just remind me the names, and I'll do my best."

"Thank you, Melanie, I'm so sorry to leave you with so many things to take care of. It's Mrs. Jenkins and Mrs. Spencer. I have notes on them on my desk in my room. You're the very best," she called out as she ran out the door after the doctor.

“Yeah, I’m the best idiot in town,” Melanie murmured as her stomach churned and a sheen of sweat broke out on her forehead. She tried to decide what to do first. There were no sewing tasks left; she had plowed through all that needed to be done earlier. That was why it was all the more urgent that the clients be visited. They needed more work. The house was spotless, so she couldn’t procrastinate under the guise of needing to do chores. With a deep sigh, she realized she needed to tidy herself and get on with the necessary visits.

As she combed her hair, she could see how very pale she was. *You can do this,* she reassured her reflection. After rummaging through Katie’s desk, she had all the information she needed. It was time to set off and find someone who could direct her in the way she ought to go.

Standing on her front porch, Melanie took deep fortifying breaths, willing her heart rate to slow down and her feet to hurry up. If she wasn’t careful, she would need Dr. Jeffries to pay a call on her before long. Or she’d be dead, she thought with a macabre sense of satisfaction. That would eliminate her responsibility to make these visits, at the very least.

While she was dithering, she almost didn’t notice the approaching wagon until it was drawing up on the other side of their little fence.

“Oh Mr. Miller, I’m surprised to see you here.” It was a dull-witted thing to say, but it popped out of her mouth without her permission.

"Good-day, Miss Jones. It seems I've just caught you in time. Were you headed our way, by any chance?"

She felt color finally touch her cheeks; hopefully she looked a little less like a corpse. "In a manner of speaking," she replied with amusement filling her tone. "I was trying to decide who to visit first. But I'm pretty sure that you would have had to be my last stop, since I would have things to carry afterward."

"Well, then I'm all the more glad that I've caught you."

His friendly smile and warm voice did a strange combination of settling her nerves and setting them to jangling all at once. Melanie wasn't quite sure how to manage the sensory overload. She merely smiled in return and hoped he would continue talking.

"I didn't want you to have to carry Mary's things, so I've brought them to you."

"Oh, that's so thoughtful of you, thank you so much." Melanie wasn't sure if she should approach him, or wait until he brought the things to her. When he began climbing down from the wagon, she decided to allow her feet to remain planted where they were.

"It's the least I could do since you've been so kind as to get my daughter away from the mess at home. Leandra held her composure fairly well this morning as she said her goodbyes to Mary. Mary seemed confused by the whole thing, though, I'm afraid. You might have some strange questions to handle this afternoon."

Melanie's stomach sank, but she had agreed to the arrangement, so there was nothing to do but assure the man. "I'm sure we'll manage to muddle through."

"Are you sure you're up to it, Miss Jones? You're looking a little more pale than usual. Are you feeling poorly?"

Melanie could feel color flooding her cheeks, putting the lie to his observation. But the sudden change made her feel suddenly lightheaded. She must have wobbled where she stood because Mr. Miller put his hand out to grasp her arm.

"Perhaps you should be sitting in the shade. The heat must be getting to you." He guided her gently toward one of the chairs she and Katie had placed in the shade of the covered porch.

Despite allowing him to direct her to a seat, Melanie protested. "No, no, I'm fine. It isn't even really all that hot."

"Well then what's wrong? Can I assist you in some way?"

His kindness made her want to weep. She hoped her chin didn't tremble.

"You are being exceedingly kind, Mr. Miller, I thank you. But I don't think there's anything you can do. I need to face my demons on my own." She avoided his gaze by putting the small sack he handed her inside the front door before closing it again behind her.

His compassionate gaze made her wish she could unburden herself, but she resisted. She had made that mistake in the past. She had no interest in repeating it.

"That sounds mighty serious. What sort of demons might a sweet woman like yourself be running from?"

Finally, she couldn't fight the temptation to share her burdens any longer, and tears welled up over her lids. She wanted to drop through the floor of the porch for turning into a weeping ninny in front of the sturdy man, but the expression on his face looked so much like understanding that she just couldn't resist.

"I have to go visit our clients," she finally answered him. She could hear the despair in her voice and would have found it amusing if it weren't truly how she felt. She felt despair over having to go speak to strangers. But it was obvious the steadfast man before her didn't understand what she was saying. He stared at her in anticipation of further explanation.

"I'm terrified, and I was trying to talk myself into stepping off the porch when you arrived."

His smile curdled the edges of her stomach. "And I went ahead and interrupted you. I sincerely do apologize, Miss Jones. I hope I haven't set you back too much."

Melanie couldn't help returning his smile. "Well, I hadn't made much progress. I had been standing on the porch for at least ten minutes when you arrived."

"Is there a particular reason why you are so mighty frightened of visiting your clients? Have they been particularly unpleasant? I wouldn't expect you need to keep a client that abuses you." His eyes were kind as he tried to understand her predicament.

Melanie hesitated but finally blurted the truth. "I haven't even met them, so no, they haven't been abusive. In fact, Katie, I mean Mrs. Carter, has already met both of the women I am supposed to be visiting and enjoyed them very much. In fact, she considers Mrs. Jenkins to be a personal friend by now."

"Well, I've met Mrs. Jenkins, and I could understand why a body might be a little nervous of encountering her. She has a certain personality that might not sit right with just anyone."

Melanie began to relax, just as he had obviously intended. She even mustered up a chuckle over his description of Mrs. Jenkins. "Yes, Katie told me of her first encounters with Mrs. Jenkins. But she truly sounds like a dear old soul. I just really don't like meeting new people."

Mr. Miller's forehead crinkled in concern. "Do you truly have to go, then? If Mrs. Carter usually makes these visits, why don't you leave it until she can follow up? You don't need to work yourself up into a taking over it."

Cole watched as the pretty woman stared out into the vista. He was fairly certain she was pondering his words. His heart wrenched for her. He couldn't quite relate to her fears, but it was obvious she was nervous of people. He couldn't help but notice it the very first day they had met. But she always seemed to handle herself well despite those nerves. Clearly, he didn't fully understand her situation.

She finally broke her silence. With a low voice she said, "I'm afraid if I don't do it now, I'll be stuck in this house forever, and then of what use will I be to anyone, including myself?"

He shocked himself by realizing that he was filled with pride for her brave effort, even though he still didn't understand.

"Besides, I'll be letting down Katie and Annie. We need the work to be able to support ourselves. I don't really care for myself, but we need to keep our clients happy in order to keep business coming. Something came up for Katie this morning, an emergency that the doctor needed her help with. She had promised these two women she would visit them. I need to at least let them know that she'll stop by another day. We've already done work for each of them, you see. I can't let any of them down."

Cole admired her diligence, but he wondered if perhaps it was part of her problem. "Seems to me like you might be putting too much pressure on the situation. Is it really so very vital that these clients get visited today? What would happen if you don't?"

He watched as she chewed her lip, deep in thought. The desire to run his thumb across the abused lip, to sooth it and her, overwhelmed him. He resisted the urge, unsure if he liked the fluttering in his midsection as he watched her but knew his feelings were becoming engaged whether he wanted them to or not.

"Since there wasn't a seamstress in town before we arrived, no, you're probably right, nothing dire would happen. It's not as though they can take their business elsewhere. But it's important to both Katie and me to keep our word. And we also believe that if we are reliable, it'll make the ladies more inclined to place orders, you know? I mean, if it's a truly positive experience for them, they'll want to repeat it."

Cole nodded, understanding her insistence on making her visits. "If it means that much to you, then why are you so nervous about it? Doesn't your motivation overpower your hesitance?"

"I was hoping it would," she answered, her glum tone making him want to smile, but he resisted, sparing her feelings. He was rewarded by her further words as she gazed out into the yonder once more. "I don't really even remember how it started. Probably some snide remark as I walked Henry to school. But I became more and more nervous about going outside. I forced myself for Henry's sake, but I was never so relieved as when he finally insisted that he was too big to be walked to school anymore. I didn't completely agree that he was big enough, but our father sided with him, and then I didn't have to make myself do it anymore."

"Was your father just trying to spare your feelings?"

The laughter that answered his question was bitter. "Certainly not. If he knew how much I dreaded the morning visits, he would have insisted Henry still needed to be escorted to this day, even though the boy is sixteen."

Cole blinked, wondering how anyone could mistreat this sweet woman. "But you're such a strong, determined female. I'm surprised the murmurings of a few nasty women would tie you up into such a knot."

Her smile was gentle as she finally met his gaze. “That’s kind of you to say, Mr. Miller, but I don’t really think I’m that strong. And the mothers at school were only the start of my problem. It grew exponentially when I was beaten and robbed while going for the shopping one day just after I had dropped Henry at school. I was fifteen. I should’ve known how rough the neighborhood was that I was walking through. And I shouldn’t have walked through it. But I was rushing to get things done because I had promised one of the upstairs neighbors to help her with something, and my father expected all my chores to be finished before I thought of doing anything else.”

Cole was shocked speechless when she said she had been beaten and robbed. It was all he could do not to pull her into his arms and try to soothe away the memories. “Were you very badly injured?”

Her answering shrug didn’t really tell him much. “It could’ve been much worse, I’ve been assured. At least they didn’t assault me in other ways, besides taking my money and punching and kicking me.” She was quiet for a moment before adding, “But my father’s anger was almost as bad.”

“Did he hit you, too?” Cole became enraged.

“No. But sometimes I wished he would and get it over with. I’ve learned from experience that words can hurt as much as physical blows.” Her soft, sweet voice belied the harsh words.

Cole had never felt so inclined to violence in his life. If her father were before him in that moment, he wasn’t sure if he would be able to resist giving the man a taste of his own actions.

Reaching out, Cole took one of her hands gently into his large one. Looking at it, it wasn't much bigger than Mary's, but the feelings inspired in him were most certainly not paternal. "I can certainly understand now why you were nervous about going outside in New York after the experiences you've had, but surely you know those bullies aren't here."

She met his eyes, and hers were full of pain. "The mind doesn't always make the most sense, though, does it? Just look at your sister."

"Your situation doesn't seem anything like Leandra's."

"Maybe not, but it's still all in both of our heads. I know those boys who beat me are not here in Bucklin. And my father is dead. But leaving our apartment had become such an ordeal that the feelings have spilled over to here."

"I'm rather amazed that you actually got up the gumption to get on the train and come to Missouri."

She grinned. "So am I." She laughed a little before adding, "But staying was worse, so I was able to just do it. Some days I don't know how I managed. But I'm grateful that I did." She paused again, avoiding his gaze. "Now all I have to do is make sure I don't turn into a house-bound crazy woman out here in Missouri."

"Well, I for one, am convinced you are not crazy. You have been dealt some dreadful circumstances and have managed quite well, from what I can see."

Her surprise was written all over her face as she turned her puzzlement toward him. "How can you say that? I've just explained to you how terrified I am to visit two women, who are reportedly either quite nice or at least quite unlikely to do me any harm."

"You might be terrified, but here you are dressed and ready to go make those very same visits."

His admiration must have finally gotten through to her. She grinned. "True. But I am still here on my own porch."

"That's only because you were interrupted. Now, I probably shouldn't take any more of your time. Would you like me to drop you off at your first destination?"

She was again back to chewing on her lip. Cole was surprised to realize he was still holding her hand. He wasn't sure why it surprised him. He still hadn't grown used to the warm press of it against his own. And the flutters in his stomach hadn't abated, perhaps they had grown worse. She didn't seem at all affected by his presence as he was by hers. That was disheartening.

"Won't that cause gossip? I think the townspeople are already buzzing about Katie. I wouldn't want them thinking New York women were loose."

Cole grinned and squeezed her hand. "I don't think you know very much about loose women if you think accepting a ride on my very open wagon would make you so."

He was gratified to see that her color had returned to normal from the dreadful paleness she had been displaying when he had arrived. Now her cheeks flushed a becoming pink in understanding of his meaning.

"Well, no, of course not," she stammered. "But I don't want you put into an uncomfortable position.

My father hated when tales were brought back to him."

"I can assure you, I am nothing like your father. And you will recall that I'm the one who extended the invitation."

Now she looked truly embarrassed, which had definitely not been his intention. But she looked so adorable as her eyes bounced around, looking for anywhere else to gaze rather than at him. "It's kind of you to offer, thank you, Mr. Miller. It might give me just that last little bit of gumption I was looking for."

Cole laughed. "Or at the very least, get you started on the way rather than with your feet glued to your porch."

Her eyes once again came to rest on his face. He was surprised to see another smile on her face. "Whatever works, right?" she asked. "I am determined to grow a spine while living here in Bucklin."

"I think your spine is already made of steel, Miss Jones. You are truly brave to come out here to a new life and face your fears."

"Do you really think so?" she asked, her voice sounding breathless, as though she couldn't quite believe her ears.

"I truly do."

"But I've been wondering if coming out here is just another way of hiding from my fears."

Now he was puzzled. "What are you hiding from here? It seems to me you faced your fear of strangers by getting on a train and moving to a new place."

She was frowning in concentration as she nodded in response to his words. "I also couldn't bear to see my baby brother, whom I raised by my own hand from when I was ten years old, turning into an exact replica of our father."

Cole turned so that he was fully facing her, grasping both of her hands in his own. She couldn't avoid his gaze any longer but was instead searching his face with concern etched upon her own.

"Miss Jones, or rather, I am going to be so bold as to use your given name, Melanie, listen to me carefully. Having the dignity to leave a bad situation is not giving in to fear. It is true bravery when considered along with your fears. I am in awe of you right at this moment."

She continued to search his face as though to determine the sincerity of his words. Cole wasn't sure what she read in his features but suddenly, tears spilled over her lashes and trickled down her cheeks. "That is the loveliest thing anyone has said to me in my entire life. Thank you, Mr. Miller."

"Please, you must call me Cole."

Now she was back to blushing as she tried to pull her hands out of his grasp. "Oh no, I wouldn't think that's appropriate."

He ignored her words, merely transferring one of her hands into the grasp of the other, using his free hand to wipe the tears from her cheeks. "I most certainly think it's appropriate, at least when it's just the two of us. We are friends after all, aren't we?"

Cole decided to take a step back for a moment from the lovely woman. While he knew his heart was becoming quite entwined with her, he was well aware that she wasn't anywhere near ready for a declaration from him. She probably wasn't even aware of his feelings or of the fact that he had been holding her hand for the last ten minutes, at least. With a gentle smile, he squeezed her hands and then let them go.

"Come along, Miss Mel, I'll drop you off with either Mrs. Jenkins or Mrs. Spencer. Which would you like to visit first?"

His tone brooked no argument and did the trick. She got to her feet and accepted that he was going to help her. She still appeared undecided as to her destination, but then she surprised him by answering firmly. "Since Mrs. Jenkins might be the toughest visit, I'll start there, I think. Thank you, again, Cole. It seems all I'm doing of late is thanking you for something."

He grinned over her use of his name but waved off her thanks. "You are doing me a massive favor in keeping Mary for a few days. Dropping you off somewhere on my way home is the very least I can do. It would be churlish not to, really."

Her giggle met his words, for which he was grateful.

They chatted about inconsequential things as they drove out to Mrs. Jenkins' neat property. She and her husband had a good amount of land, but it was currently being worked by her son-in-law. What she had kept for herself was well maintained, despite her age and declining health.

In his effort not to overwhelm Melanie with his attentions, he didn't get out of the wagon, just leaned down to hold her steady as she climbed down on her own.

Her eyes twinkled at him, despite the fact that he could see the nerves returning to her face. "Since you said no thanks are allowed, I will merely wish you a good day. Please, call around when you're ready to have Mary returned to you. Don't feel obliged to rush. We will enjoy having her for however long you deem fit."

Cole was surprised by her offer, especially when he knew she had been hesitant in agreeing to his original request for her help with Mary. He squeezed her hand and then let it go.

"Take care," was all he said as he stirred up his horses to carry on.

ꕥ

The tiny little woman who opened the door at Melanie's knock was a surprise. From all Katie's talk of Mrs. Jenkins' personality, Melanie had expected a larger woman.

"Good day, ma'am, are you Mrs. Jenkins?"

"That I am, and who might you be?"

"I'm Melanie Jones. You are more acquainted with my business partner, Mrs. Katie Carter."

"I know who you are. It's about time you stopped in to visit me. I was starting to think you were a figment of Katie's imagination, just a convenient excuse when she needs to make a decision. She's forever saying, 'oh I have to check with my partner on that.' I wasn't convinced there was any such partner."

The older woman's cackling laugh made Melanie's nerves tighten further, but she obediently followed when Mrs. Jenkins waved her into the sitting room. "You'll bide a while for a cup of tea, won't you? I suppose you're here to tell me Katie won't be stopping by, am I right?"

She barely allowed Melanie an opportunity to nod before she was off and talking again. "Katie always sits and has a visit with me whenever she stops by, so I baked up some biscuits, since she told me she'd be by today and that she enjoys my biscuits. Since she couldn't be bothered to come herself, we shan't have to save her any."

Another cackle accompanied these words, but Melanie was finally able to relax a little bit when she realized that the woman's bark was most definitely worse than her bite.

"Katie felt dreadful that she wasn't able to keep her appointment with you, but she was called out on an emergency with the doctor."

Mrs. Jenkins sniffed. "Far be it from me to begrudge the good doctor from someone in need, but I hardly see how he was in such dire need of Katie's assistance. He managed just fine on his own before she arrived in town. Seems to me that it's just a convenient excuse for the two of them to spend time together making calf's eyes at each other."

Melanie couldn't help a snort of laughter that escaped, making her feel highly disloyal toward her friend. She didn't want to agree with the other woman, but really, she was right. Dr. Jeffries seemed to have managed just fine before they arrived. But they did appear to be deeply in love, and Melanie couldn't begrudge it to them. Thankfully, aside from a delightful grin in response to Melanie's snort, Mrs. Jenkins didn't seem to require any response and just carried on talking.

"It's just as well that Katie wasn't able to come and you felt an obligation to take her place. I've been wanting to meet you, if you did turn out to be a real person. And here you are. And was that Cole Miller dropping you off? You girls certainly haven't been wasting any time in the gentleman department, have you? You just pull up in the train, and you capture all our best bachelors."

By now Melanie felt as though her face were on fire. She tried to stammer out a reply. "Oh, no, Mrs. Jenkins, it just so happened that Mr. Miller was heading this way, and he offered to give me a ride. There is nothing more to it than that."

"Where was he going that he was heading in this direction?" Mrs. Jenkins sounded suspicious.

"I believe he was going home." Melanie could hear how weak her explanation sounded and tried not to cringe.

"Well I'm most certainly not on his way home," Mrs. Jenkins responded, a note of glee in her voice. "Sounds to me like you and Mr. Miller are smelling of April showers."

Melanie blinked. She'd never heard the expression before but from the context, it was rather apparent what the older woman was implying. But Melanie refused to accept such an implication. She decided to brazen it out. "Whatever do you mean by saying this? It's nearly June, isn't it Mrs. Jenkins?"

Another cackle came in response. “I like you, Miss Jones. You’ve got a backbone for all your apparent timidity. Now, tell me about yourself.”

Thus admonished, and relieved that the old woman was willing to leave off teasing her about Cole, Melanie launched into an abbreviated explanation of her life and how she wound up here in Bucklin, Missouri. As she was telling the older woman a much less detailed version than she had shared with Cole, Melanie couldn’t believe that she had revealed so much to the handsome man. What must he think of her? She asked herself at the back of her mind, hoping her inner turmoil wasn’t revealing itself to Mrs. Jenkins. Some of it must have because Mrs. Jenkins was much more sympathetic than Melanie would have expected.

“You’ve definitely had your share of loss in your life, haven’t you, dear?”

Melanie blinked, trying not to show how deep was her surprise. “Well, many have had more loss than I have, just look at Katie and Annie.”

“It speaks well of you that you would say that, dearie, but it doesn’t change the fact that you’ve experienced heartache. More than many, I dare say. It’s no wonder you don’t want to go out amongst folks. You’re still in mourning, aren’t you?”

Melanie blinked again. “I hadn’t thought of it quite that way, but I dare say you’re right. Thank you, Mrs. Jenkins. That was actually quite a helpful observation.”

Mrs. Jenkins cackled again. “Well, I don’t see as how, but I’m glad you thought so. Now, tell me whatever message my friend Kate had for me. Are you here to show me more samples and badger me into ordering more gowns?"

"We would never badger a client, Mrs. Jenkins," Melanie replied with dignity before laughing a little. "But I do have some samples with me that Katie thought might interest you."

"She knows I can't resist now that I've gotten used to these nice things you've made. Make yourself useful and make us some tea while I'll look them over."

Melanie, feeling lighter than she had in ages, bustled about the tidy kitchen, admiring its size and the convenient location of things. It was obviously a well-used room in the house that had raised a large family.

Her visit with Mrs. Jenkins came to a conclusion well before Melanie felt the need to watch the clock. As she walked away, hopefully in the right direction, Melanie couldn't believe how comfortable she had been with the seemingly cranky old woman. She hoped her next visit went as smooth.

She had to ask for directions on the way to the Spencer house, but the couple had been kind and direct, and Melanie arrived on Mrs. Spencer's front porch without too much difficulty. Taking a deep breath, she knocked firmly, not allowing herself time to second guess the decision.

A tall woman with unruly curls and a wide smile opened the door almost immediately. Her face fell slightly when she saw Melanie. "Oh, I was expecting someone else. Hello."

Melanie couldn't help a chuckle. "Good day, Mrs. Spencer, I'm sorry for the disappointment. I'm Melanie Jones, Mrs. Carter's business partner. Katie has been called away to an important assignment, so I have stopped by in her stead. If you would prefer to speak with her, that is perfectly all right. But neither of us wanted you to be waiting for her and her not turn up."

"No, no, that's quite all right," the woman answered as she opened the door wide, waving Melanie to come in. "I'm just as glad to get to meet you. There are never enough women in town, so the chance to meet a new one is a treat I won't pass up, to be sure. Do come in and have a cup of tea."

Melanie grinned. She hadn't realized how much tea Katie must have to drink in the course of her day when she was visiting the clients. No wonder she sometimes declined the offer when it was just the two of them at home. She didn't tell any of that to Mrs. Spencer, of course. "Thank you, that's kind of you to offer," was the only possible answer.

With Mrs. Spencer being a bit of a chatterbox, Melanie didn't have to make any effort as she listened to the gregarious blonde woman tell her all about her life and how she came to be in Bucklin.

"And what a wonderful surprise to find the two newest women to town are fine seamstresses! You would never believe just how happy that has made me," the pretty blonde declared.

"Well, I am glad to be able to fill a need."

"Oh dear me, a need is an understatement. I can barely sew on a button, so I was of no use to myself.

All my pretty things that I have had since moving here were beginning to wear, and what was I to do? I didn't feel I could go to the tailor, although I know a few of the other ladies in town have done so, merely out of desperation, of course. But you two arrived before I had to sink to that level, praise be."

The woman rubbed her hands together, much like a child in anticipation of a treat. "Now tell me, do you have some new samples for me? Katie assured me more cloth would be arriving from Boston on the train, but I was trying not to get my hopes up too high. I'm sure anything silk would be just too much to ask for out here in the back of beyond."

Melanie's heart sank. Katie hadn't told her the woman was expecting silks. She would have to use whatever skills of diplomacy she could muster. Pasting a smile onto her face, Melanie was quick to pull out her swatches.

"No silks yet, I'm afraid, but I'm sure this blue would look wonderful on you. Let me show you what we have."

With a squeal, the woman happily plunked down on the settee beside Melanie and grabbed the bundle from her hands.

"You are quite right, this is the exact color I was looking for. It will be my new special occasions dress. Thank you. Katie has told me that the fancier stitches are your work. What do you think you can do with this for me?"

With that, they launched into a surprisingly enjoyable discussion of the merits of various stitches and tucks and what the woman expected. For someone who claimed to have no skill, she was certainly very knowledgeable about sewing. Melanie was shocked to see that an hour had already passed by the time they had ironed out all the details of what Mrs. Spencer was looking for in her new gown.

Coming to her feet, Melanie said, "I don't wish to occupy too much of your day, Mrs. Spencer. I apologize if I have overstayed."

"Not at all, Miss Jones, I assure you. It has been my pleasure to make your acquaintance. I don't wish to see an end to Mrs. Carter's visits, but I do hope you'll stop in from time to time as well, even if we don't have swatches to coo over."

Melanie chuckled over the woman's word choice. She didn't make any promises, but she thought she might be able to manage becoming friends with the outgoing woman. It certainly wouldn't require too much effort on her part, Melanie thought with satisfaction, as long as she could get off her own front porch.

Her feet felt lighter and her steps jauntier as she made her way briskly home. She had enjoyed a glorious day. Melanie realized she owed a great deal of it to Cole. She really ought to be still referring to him as Mr. Miller, even in her own mind. It wouldn't do to become overly familiar. But, oh, it had felt so comforting to have his large, warm hand clasping hers that morning as she poured out her woes. And he had been remarkably understanding.

No man she had ever come across had ever been so accepting of a woman's thoughts and feelings. Not even dear Mr. Brace at the orphanage she had volunteered at in New York City. While he was the dearest, kindest man she had ever met, Melanie had never felt inclined to tell Mr. Brace all her concerns. She had always felt he was already carrying the weight of too many with all the poor children to care for, she had felt no inclination to add her own burdens to his broad shoulders.

But with Cole that morning, it had been so different. Even though she was well aware that he had cares of his own with his poor motherless daughter and his sister with the precarious mental health, he had seemed so very receptive to her cares and concerns, not making her feel belittled even when he didn't understand what she was trying to say. It had been glorious really. Even better than talking with Katie, which Melanie found surprising and would have thought impossible if she hadn't experienced it for herself. But his perspective was welcome and she had appreciated his matter of fact help. She just hoped she hadn't made him sick of her when he thought on it later. Melanie refused to dwell on that possibility. She hurried home, determined to get a start on the various commissions from her two visits before she went to collect the little girls from school.

Chapter Twelve

The days flew by in a blur. The four females fell into a comfortable morning routine as they grew accustomed to Mary's presence in the small house. She was a cooperative little girl and seemed thrilled with her adjusted temporary circumstances. It didn't even seem to bother her that her father hadn't returned to collect her. There had only been one awkward conversation wherein she had expressed concerns for her aunt.

"She never really liked me much, but I feel bad that she's sick," Mary had said to Melanie on the first day as they walked home from school.

"Oh, my dear, I think her sickness is why she might have seemed not to like you at times. I'm certain your aunt loved you very much. That's why she stayed here with you and your father even though she was pining for Boston."

Mary's forehead and nose crinkled. "Why would she want to live in a stinky old city? Isn't it so much better here?"

Melanie laughed. "I agree with you, wholeheartedly, Mary, but not everyone sees it quite the same way as we do. There are certain conveniences that people enjoy in the city that we can't get here in Missouri."

"Like what?"

Melanie thought of Mrs. Spencer's silks but didn't think that would be the right explanation. "Well, in the city you can buy anything you might imagine. Here in Missouri, you will most likely have to make it for yourself or go without."

The little girl pondered that for a moment but didn't seem satisfied with it. "I think we have absolutely everything we could possibly need right here in Bucklin."

"Well, I must admit that I agree with you completely, Mary, but there are some people that might find it more work living here than in the city. I remember in New York, you could buy just about anything. You didn't have to have a cow if you wanted milk, and you didn't have to even have an oven if you wanted bread. All you needed was money."

"But how could you get money if you didn't have milk to sell?" The little girl's puzzled frown made Melanie want to smile, but she managed to contain her amusement.

"Back East there are large buildings were many people work all day making things. They get paid by the owner of the building."

Mary still didn't look convinced. "That sounds terr'ble."

Now Melanie did laugh. "I have to say that I feel the same way. But it works for some people. Some don't want to work with animals and are afraid of being outside the city, I think. I'm not really sure what your aunt's thoughts were on the subject, but she truly is pining for the city. That's why she has gotten so sick. So maybe she'll get better now that she's going back."

"Won't she miss us, though?" Mary asked in a small voice.

"Once she gets settled, I'm sure she will. She might even regret her choice to return. But for now, she truly believes it will make her happy, and we need to be glad for her that she's getting her wish. And we also should be grateful that she stayed as long as she did."

"How come?"

"Can you imagine what your papa would have done with a tiny baby by himself and with all the chores to do? Would you have wanted to be in the barn with him in your baby pajamas?"

The droll tone she used as she asked the questions helped the little girl find her humor, and she giggled along with Annie, who had joined the conversation.

"Well, I do love being in the barn with my papa now, but maybe it's not the right place for a baby."

"See, exactly, that's why we need to be thankful that Aunt Leandra came and looked after you and the house when your father needed the help. Now you're a big girl and in school for a good part of the day, so she can return to her own affairs."

They walked along in silence for a few minutes. Melanie noticed that the little girl still looked troubled.

"Are you thinking that you're going to miss your aunt?"

"I'm not sure," the child admitted. "Sometimes I wish she would go away, but now that it's here I feel sad."

"That's natural. Now that you're in school, you'll learn to write so you can stay in touch with her through letters. Maybe when your aunt is well and you're a little older, the two of you will be able to visit each other in person."

This seemed to lighten the girl's burdened heart, and she was able to play and giggle along with Annie as they skipped the rest of the way home.

Melanie, watching them play, couldn't help but be relieved that she had crossed the emotional hurdle with the youngster. She knew the child's father was relying on her to help in such a way, and she had worried she would be inadequate to the task. Thankfully, Mary was a sweet, biddable child with a kind heart. She wouldn't be a burden to spend time with.

A week had passed by the time Cole called round to collect his daughter. Melanie had half expected him on the weekend so was surprised when he didn't turn up until Tuesday to collect Mary's things while the girls were in school.

Melanie was glad that Katie was home, so it wasn't inappropriate to invite him in for a cup of tea while Mary's things were gathered.

"We were getting quite used to having her with us. It will take some adjusting to having her gone," Melanie remarked as she set the kettle to boil and then quickly folded Mary's spare clothes and placed them in a bag.

“And Annie will be disappointed not to have her playmate at home with her,” Katie added from her place by the window where she was hemming a client’s gown.

“Thank you for your kindness, Mrs. Carter and Miss Jones. I never meant to prevail upon your hospitality for quite this long.”

“Did things proceed in a more complicated manner than you had expected?” Melanie asked softly.

“Leandra didn’t take too well to being collected by strangers. She felt it made her seem like a disobedient child, she said. She refused to go at first. She missed the train they had planned to take. Leandra wore herself out with her protests but then in a lucid moment, she realized it was ridiculous to object to the manner of departure. She really had no desire to remain here, so why was she putting up such a fuss? She got on the train this morning, and I pretty much came straight here.”

“I’m so sorry that it was such an ordeal for both of you.” Melanie’s heart ached.

“Well, I’m beyond grateful that you two had the sense to realize it might be difficult and keeping Mary well away from it.”

“She was a pleasure to have. We’ll be sad to see her go.”

“I appreciate you saying that, but I’ll be glad to have her back.”

Melanie laughed. “We weren’t thinking to steal her from you, have no fear.”

They shared a chuckle and a cup of tea before the rancher set off for his own place after assuring them he'd be early to the school after classes so Mary would realize she was to go home with him.

Melanie was watching him drive away through the front window that overlooked the porch when she heard a girlish giggle from behind her. She whirled around, knowing a frown was pulling on her forehead.

"What's so funny?" Melanie was confused.

"You are, silly." Katie's answer was impossible to misunderstand.

"Why would you say that?"

"For all your protestations that you have no interest in the handsome Mr. Miller, you sure couldn't tear your eyes away from his back as he drove away."

Melanie knew her face was bright red with her embarrassment. What was there to say? She had stood there fawning over the man like a teenager rather than the sensible woman she thought she was. Katie must've realized she had no answer, and she broke the silence.

"There is nothing to be ashamed of, Mel, surely you realize that. You are a single woman with no obligations to hold you back from pursuing a relationship. Mr. Miller is a fine man from what I can tell. He, too, is single and only has responsibility for a sweet child that you seem to already care about. What seems to be the trouble?"

Melanie huffed and sat limply at the table. She felt helpless and didn't know how to answer her friend.

"I gave all I had to give to my little sister and brother. I did my very best for them and my father. But I ended up lonely and shunned for my efforts. My father couldn't even be bothered to name me in his will, leaving everything he possessed to Henry. And Henry has no use for me now that he feels he's a grown man at the ripe age of sixteen." Melanie paused as she wiped a tear from her cheek. "I don't know if I have anything left in my heart to give anyone, Kate."

Soft-hearted Katie gripped Melanie's hand tight and allowed her own tears to flow in sympathy. "You are a dear, and I know you have a heart full of love to share. Just look how you've taken to Annie even though you said you didn't want any responsibility."

"Well, I don't have any responsibility, she's your daughter."

"But with how side-tracked I am by the doctor, you're the one carrying the load most of the time." Katie's grin showed she had no resentment for her friend's care of her daughter.

Melanie shrugged. "It's different to help when it's not my own responsibility. I don't know if I can take on being a mother for real."

Katie nodded, clearly in thought. "There's one thing I think you should give thought to, before you dismiss the idea entirely. You were too young for the responsibilities you had to take on when your mother died. You did the very best you could, and it seems to me if your sister is married and your brother on his own, you must have done a fine job with them, even if you aren't too happy with your brother's personality. You did the best you could while dealing with the bad influence of a mean-spirited father. As a grown woman, if you have a loving partner to share the responsibility, I do think you would find the experience to be far different and much more rewarding than raising your brother and sister in a cramped apartment in the city."

Melanie didn't feel convinced, but she knew there was wisdom in her friend's words. "I think I'll go for a walk. I will mull over your words."

Katie nodded and returned to her hemming. "Don't feel you need to hurry back. I'll be able to collect Annie today. I'm sure she'll be disappointed that Mary won't be coming home with us, so I'll need to spend some time with her."

Melanie absently nodded her agreement and slipped through the front door, already lost in thought.

Chapter Thirteen

A few weeks slowly slipped past. Melanie made every effort to convince herself that she was satisfied with the routine that had settled over her life. Her first venture toward visiting clients had not been her last, even though Katie looked after most of that side of the business. Melanie was happy that she was slowly regaining confidence in her ability to speak with people, even strangers. She still got nervous, but it was not debilitating.

Katie was so often wandering away for walks with Doctor Jeffries that Melanie spent a great deal of time with Annie. Melanie had to make herself keep a rein on her love for the little girl. With the way Katie's relationship was progressing with the doctor, Melanie was sure it wouldn't be too very much longer before Katie and Annie were no longer her housemates. Melanie's heart ached at the thought of being alone. She had always thought it would be her greatest joy to be on her own, but she now saw that it would be sad and lonely.

Perhaps I ought to send to Mr. Brace for an orphan of my own, she thought one day as she watched Annie and Mary carefully cutting out cookies as she had instructed them. Mary had come home with Annie to spend the weekend with them once more. It had become another routine for them. Mary came every second weekend, coming home from school with Annie and staying until they went back to school on Monday. *As she supervised, her thoughts wandered to the last time she had seen Mary's father, a few days prior.*

Melanie was so surprised by the knock on her door that she almost put the needle through her finger. Shaking her head at herself, she hurried toward the door. She was surprised again to see that it was Mr. Miller on the porch when she opened the door.

"Hello," she said, cringing when she heard how breathy she sounded.

"Good day," he answered, touching the brim of his hat politely before lifting his other hand and showing her the sacks he held. "I've come to help you move the flowers you were talking about."

Melanie blinked at him. "I can't believe you remembered my saying that."

To her surprise, the man actually blushed.

"You've been doing so much for my Mary, I was trying to think of something I could do for you, and then I remembered that conversation we had." He ducked his head, clearly embarrassed. "If you'll just point me in the right direction of which ones you wanted moved, I could have it done in a flash."

Melanie was skeptical. "I don't see how it could be a quick task, Mr. Miller. The plants I like have thorns on them. Surely that will complicate matters considerably."

He just shrugged. "I have gloves."

Now she was getting excited and allowed a grin to spread over her face. "If you're very sure, I would love to have two of those prickly bushes with the bright red flowers brought here on either side of the stairs."

"Only two? That will be easy as pie."

"Maybe meringue pie," Melanie replied with a laugh. "Making meringue is hard."

"You needn't do anything but point me in the direction of the plants you want. I promise, I don't think it'll be difficult."

Melanie offered no further protests, delighted at the thought of having the bright splash of color in front of her small house. Her heart beat raced far out of proportion to the slow pace they set as they walked toward the wild flower patch behind her house. She was grateful he adjusted his long stride so she didn't have to run to keep up with him.

She tried not to stare at his handsome physique. His generous act of kindness toward her was not helping her keep her feelings in check toward him, Melanie realized and tried to distract her thoughts with light chatter as she watched him work. The play of his muscles easily viewed, even under his shirt as he dexterously dug, made her heart flutter and her palms sweat. Melanie again tried to keep herself from looking.

True to his word, before too long both small bushes were nicely positioned at the bottom of the stairs. She didn't think she had laughed so much before in her life. She was feeling absolutely giddy in the handsome man's presence. Melanie tried to keep a rein on her bubbling emotions, but her lessened anxieties in connection with people seemed to be spilling over into increased attraction. She would absolutely die of mortification if he thought she was throwing herself at him, so she tried to keep the volume of her giggles as low as possible.

As she was shaking his hand in thanks once more while he was taking his leave, she noticed he had sustained a couple scratches despite his thick gloves.

"Oh, no, Mr. Miller, I just knew it was going to be a detrimental exercise."

"Don't you pay those marks any mind. I've had far worse from the barn cats, I can assure you. I'm just glad you're pleased with my little contribution."

Melanie clasped her hands in front of her and beamed at him. "I am most definitely pleased. I thank you from the bottom of my heart."

Again, she was surprised to see a blush staining his cheeks. He looked bashful but didn't say anything more, only touching the brim of his hat again and waving as he drove off.

The girls' giggles brought her back to the present with a slight sigh.

Melanie enjoyed the chatter of the two little girls as she taught them how to cook and bake. She was also trying to teach them how to sew, but Mary especially found the task tedious at best. She would far rather be out working with her father on his ranch, but it would seem Mr. Miller was determined that his daughter get at least some education in the female arts, as he liked to put it. Melanie had to guard her heart from growing too attached to both girls. *I'll write to Mr. Brace and the Children's Aid Society first thing tomorrow,* Melanie thought as she watched them try not to spill too much flour around the tidy kitchen.

ജ്ജ

"I can't believe she was once the one insisting that we needed to play tea parties. Now she wishes she was a boy." The rancher shook his head in confusion as he sat with Melanie when he had finally come round to call several weeks later. No one else was home so Melanie hadn't invited him in. They were sitting on the porch, enjoying the slight breeze as it brought the scent of the flowers Melanie could never get tired of admiring. She was torn between excitement being in his presence and dread that someone would happen along and interrupt them. Or worse still, that Mr. Miller would realize she had nothing of interest to say and would take his leave.

"I think she likes to be contrary." Melanie explained, "It's just a phase. While I can't say she'll ever be a seamstress, she does love being in the kitchen. And every woman ought to know her way around the animals. I wish I wasn't so squeamish myself. It would be lovely to have some chickens and a cow for fresh eggs and milk."

Cole's face was serious as he looked at her closely. "You could have those without needing to do it on your own, you know."

Melanie blinked, surprised by the sudden turn in the conversation. "Whatever do you mean? I'm afraid I barely know which end of the cow the milk comes from," she excused with a nervous giggle.

"Now I know you're teasing me, but don't you realize by now that I would love to have you out on my ranch?"

Melanie frowned at him in true confusion. "What do you mean?"

Cole sighed. "I'm not going about this at all in the right way, am I? Melanie, I know I've only known you for a few months, but in that time, I've watched you blossom from a pretty but nervous little lady to a beautiful, strong woman who would be the finest wife a rancher could hope to have. I'm proud of the progress you've made. I've grown fond of you and would deeply appreciate it if you would agree to marry me."

Melanie stared at him in shock. "That is the most lukewarm declaration I have ever heard of. I've barely seen you in the past six weeks despite the fact that your daughter has been here on three different occasions, and you expect me to believe you have suddenly developed tender feelings for me? I'm sorry to be rude, but I think you should take yourself back from wherever you came. I don't need to take on that sort of attention. I have enough of my own concerns to occupy me."

She would have giggled over the expression on his face if she weren't so very hurt by his words. Melanie had found herself pining for a visit from the handsome, rugged rancher, but knew that the depths of her own feelings required more emotion from him than what he had expressed. While it had taken her a long time to accept that she had fallen for the man, she had finally come to terms with her desire for a family of her own. And watching Katie with her doctor, Melanie knew she wouldn't settle for a weak attachment. It would need to be all or nothing for her.

Cole was still gaping at her when she turned on her heel and stormed into the house, slamming the door behind her. Melanie wished there were someone else home so she could ask them to make sure the rancher had left. She contented herself with slamming her bedroom door for good measure before throwing herself on her bed as an unexpected bout of tears claimed her.

Cole sat in his wagon, pulled over to the side of the road, so as to not impede any traffic that might come along, heedless to the fact that he most likely looked like a simpleton staring off into the yonder like he was. That conversation had most certainly not gone how he had intended. Miss Jones was perfectly correct; he had stumbled through what should have been a proposal of marriage like a clumsy bull trying to drink from a teacup. All he'd done was make a mess.

But what was he going to do now? He had been so sure she returned his feelings. Maybe he had read the situation all wrong. He forced himself to pause and think back over her words. She hadn't said she didn't care for him. She just hadn't appreciated his lack of attention and the suddenness of his declaration. He couldn't really blame her for that, he supposed. It had taken him so long to figure out his own thoughts. Spending time with her had just muddled him further.

He thought of the time he had visited to help her move the flowers. She had seemed so full of light. He had the impression that he had helped her overcome some of her fears that previous day when she went to visit her customers. It had made him feel so proud of himself and of her. And then he had discussed his idea of adoption with her.

Cole loved the way she listened so attentively whenever anyone spoke to her. She had listened without interruption as he explained why he was thinking of adopting. A son to help him on his land and then to take over when he was old, seemed like a good idea.

Of course, the more time he spent with Melanie, the more he thought of a future with her. And maybe they might have more children together. Perhaps a little girl or a little boy with Melanie's bright, inquisitive eyes would fill any empty spaces still left in his heart.

The only trouble was, Cole hadn't had the best experience with women. That was why he had taken so long to come around to accepting his feelings for her. He just hoped his hesitation and blundering hadn't ruined all his chances. He would just have to convince her!

Setting his chin with determination, Cole guided his wagon to turn around slowly on the road and made short work of heading back to Melanie's tidy little house.

ꟾ

"Melanie? Melanie!" Her name was being called, accompanied by loud banging on the door. Melanie awoke in confusion. She got to her feet and hurried to the door, sure that an emergency needed her attention.

Cole was standing there with his hat in his hand and a bemused expression on his face. It wasn't apparent what he was feeling.

"What has happened? Is Mary all right?" Melanie hadn't shaken her sleepy confusion.

Cole's eyes seemed to devour her face, and Melanie suddenly became conscious of the fact that she had fallen asleep crying. No doubt she looked a fright. She gasped as he pulled her into his arms.

"Darlin'," he drawled, "I never meant to make you cry. I'm so sorry that I saddened you with my weak expressions. I'll never make that mistake again."

Melanie's stomach began to flutter, but for the first time in her life it was a pleasurable sensation. She searched his gaze to try to read his thoughts, but he didn't leave her in suspense for long.

"While I think you will be an excellent help with Mary and a wonderful mother to any other children we might be blessed with, children don't stick around forever. I want you for me as my partner, companion, helper, and mate. I thought I could be logical about the subject. I thought I didn't need you. I'm sorry I stayed away for so long, but I was trying to get it all straight in my head."

He paused briefly, his eyes searching her gaze and examining her face, trying to gauge her reaction to his words. He ran his thumb along her cheekbone, catching the tears that had once again begun to leak from the corners of her eyes. His own eyes crinkled. "As you know, I haven't had the best of luck in the female department. My wife left me, then died, and my sister lost her mind while in my company."

Melanie made as if to protest, but he stopped her by pressing his thumb gently on her lips. "Let me finish, darlin', or I might never get this said. The thing is, I had to figure if I could deal with the responsibility of another adult in my life. I feel at enough of a loss with little Mary, but I've known her all her life, and she's mine no matter what. I've been racking my mind and heart, trying to determine if I had what it takes to make you happy. But staying away was making me miserable. I have to think that together we could manage reasonably well. We're both fine, intelligent people."

He paused again, taking a deep breath before plunging on with his speech. "I love that you are willing to face your fears. I love that your kind heart makes you speak up even when you don't want to. I love that you have taken to my daughter and helped make her feel whole, even though you didn't really want to open your heart. And I really love that you want to make Missouri home, that you won't be pining for somewhere else."

Melanie was blinking back her tears, examining his face as Cole declared himself. She felt as though her heart were going to burst, but she didn't know if she was going to be able to force words out of her mouth. It felt as though her heart were taking up all the space and preventing her thoughts from spilling out of her mouth. Finally, he grew nervous or impatient with her silence, despite what must have been obvious love shining in her eyes.

"Please, I'm begging of you, Melanie, I quite desperately love you. Please say you'll consent to be my wife, my friend, and my companion until we're both old and grey and then one of us is pushing up daisies."

Finally, Melanie gasped. "After all those beautiful words, you have to bring up our deaths?" She couldn't help but giggle a little.

"Well, that's for how long I intend to stick by your side, if you'll have me."

Melanie wound her arms around his neck and answered him simply. "I didn't think I wanted to ever marry, but I have been fighting off misery these last weeks when I haven't seen you. I thought I had given you disgust of me when I told you all about what's behind my fears and anxieties. But I appreciate that you were taking the time to be sure, I suppose. It just might've been better if you had told me what you were thinking."

"I swear to you, I will do much better in the future. Maybe if you marry me, you could teach me." His eyes were twinkling, and he wiggled his eyebrows at her.

Melanie never would have thought, if she had taken the time to imagine such a moment as this, that she would be filled with laughter at the same time as overflowing with love. But she supposed it stood to reason that happiness couldn't help but bring laughter.

"Thank you so much for your kind offer, Mr. Miller, I think I would very much like to accept."

With a shout of joy, Cole lifted her off her feet and twirled her in a circle. As he allowed her to slip back to the ground, he lowered his head and finally sealed their match with a tender kiss. As first kisses tend to do, it went slightly awry, but he quickly made up for it by wrapping his hand around the back of her head, angling her jaw slightly to the side and settling his lips more firmly over hers.

It was only when they heard a couple of loudly cleared throats that they broke apart, but not very far. Cole kept his arm wrapped tightly around Melanie's shoulder as they turned toward the gate to see who had interrupted their moment of joy and commitment.

"I knew it!" Katie declared with glee as she dashed up the stairs to hug her housemate. "I told you that you were in love with him."

Melanie couldn't help giggling in response. There was no argument to be found because it was true – she was deeply in love with the handsome rancher and couldn't wait to begin her new life by his side. All the past sorrows were forgotten as she looked deeply into her promised husband's eyes. She could see her tomorrows all laid out brightly, and a happy future beckoned her to step into it.

Epilogue

It was a bright, warm day in September. As Melanie looked around at the gathered friends mingling about, she felt her heart swelling with gratitude and love.

Katie and Doctor Jeffries were waiting with her. Katie was standing up with her as her matron of honor as she and the doctor had just wed a couple weeks prior. Doctor Jeffries had agreed to the responsibility of walking Melanie down the aisle.

Cassandra Morley, or rather Cassie Ainsworth, and her new husband were in attendance, as well. Melanie would have never thought a socialite from New York would be attending her wedding. Not that she had ever thought she would be having a wedding, she reminded herself with a grin. But Cassie was not at all stuffy or snobby and was adjusting just as well as Melanie and Katie to her new life in Missouri.

Melanie had wondered if Cass's parents would ever accept her marriage and subsequent lack of return to New York, but the fact that they too were in attendance would seem to prove they had gotten over their anger with her for getting on the train with the orphans. It would seem there was something about Mr. Ainsworth that made them accept the situation with delight rather than the anger Melanie would have expected. She reminded herself that she needed to get the full scoop from Cassie the next time they met. Melanie had been a little too wrapped up in her own happiness to inquire as closely as she ought to into the details of Cassie's new family.

Katie and Melanie had received a letter from Sophie Brooks earlier in the week when the train stopped in town with the post. She and Renton would have loved to come for a visit, but they hadn't been able to convince Mrs. Rexford that they wanted a small wedding. It had taken Mrs. Rexford rather a long while to accept the fact that her darling son was intending to marry Sophie, but once she had, she was determined to throw the most spectacular event the city had witnessed. Melanie suppressed a shudder at the thought but was happy for her friend, who didn't seem to mind and was too caught up in her own happiness to begrudge her future mother-in-law her enjoyment.

Sophie, of course, was kind enough to want Melanie and Katie to attend her wedding along with their new husbands, but she also said she understood if they wouldn't want to return to the city so soon. Sophie promised that she and her husband would take the train out to visit them as soon as the trip could be done in less than five days. Melanie mused that with the way the train companies were pushing things, it wouldn't be long before that would be a reality.

Melanie had even received letters from both her sister and her brother. Her sister had baby number two on the way, so she wasn't up to the trip West but sent her love and best wishes, which meant so much to the big sister. Even Henry had something kind to say, much to Melanie's surprise, and sent a little money as a wedding gift, which she never would have expected, since he had been the most miserly boy she had ever seen as soon as he received his inheritance. Perhaps they would be able to maintain a relationship through the post.

Finally, it was time. Katie finished fussing with Melanie's hem; there was nothing more that could be done to the beautiful gown. It was the most wonderful garment the two women had made, in Melanie's doting opinion. It had been crafted with love and joy so nothing more could be expected of it. Melanie couldn't help but feel beautiful as she took one last glance at herself to make sure her hair was staying in place.

Mary and Annie danced into the room in a whirl of energy and swinging pink taffeta.

"You look beautiful," Mary breathed in awe.

Melanie laughed. "That is sweet of you to say. The two of you look to be glowing. Are you ready?"

Both girls nodded vigorously, thrilled to be a part of the special day. Melanie thought back on the moment when she and Cole had told Mary that they were to wed. The little girl had been beside herself with joy. Her only disappointment was that Annie wasn't going to be joining their household as well. They assured her they were still considering sending to Mrs. Parker for at least one orphan of their own.

"Then let's go," Melanie declared, sharing a grin with Katie as the two girls made to dash from the room.

"Try for some decorum," Katie called after them, and their strides shortened minutely. "I better try to keep up with them, but don't you rush — you need to savor the moment." Katie looked stern before her expression turned sly. "And you need to make your groom savor the moment, too."

Melanie's face heated in a blush, which was probably Katie's intention. She had always been such a teasing friend. Melanie couldn't believe that both of them were getting a happily ever after.

By then, she and Doctor Jeffries were joining the rest, and Melanie's gaze had been ensnared by Cole's. All other thoughts slipped away on the breeze. All she could think about was her love for this man and the joy with which she was facing her future. She knew the minister was saying some beautiful words that she ought to be pondering, but she couldn't bring herself to pay attention. Before she knew it, she was stammering after him, making her vows, and then it was official. She was Mrs. Cole Miller. The gathered townsfolk cheered and clapped as Cole bent his head and captured her breath and her lips with his warm embrace.

The End

About the Author

I've been writing pretty much since I learned to read when I was five years old. Of course, those early efforts were basically only something a mother could love. I put writing aside after I left school and stuck with reading. I am an avid reader. I love words. I will read anything, even the cereal box, signs, posters, etc. But my true love is novels.

Eight or nine years ago my husband dared me to write a book instead of always reading them. I didn't think I'd be able to do it, but to my surprise I love writing. Those early efforts eventually became my first published book – *Tempting the Earl* (published by Avalon books in 2010). There were some ups and downs in my publishing efforts. My first publisher was sold and I became an "orphan" author, back to the drawing board of trying to find a publishing house. It has been a thrilling adventure as I learned to navigate the world of publishing.

I believe firmly that everyone deserves a happily ever after. I want my readers to be able to escape from the everyday for a little while and feel upbeat and refreshed when they get to the end of my books.

Stay in touch:

Website Facebook Instagram Twitter

INHERITING
TROUBLE
WENDY MAY ANDREWS

Printed in Great Britain
by Amazon

23619496R00320